He Would Sacrifice
ANYTHING
For His Movie . . .
Even His Wife

Nick watched the evening rushes with a rising sense of excitement that was almost like a sexual rush. By God, he was meant to be a director after all! The riveting performance of the two actors up there on the screen was all due to his direction. He found he could almost ignore the small rustling sound in the darkness that meant Lewis had reached over to take Juliet's hand.

After all, that was what he wanted, wasn't it? To have his two stars fall madly in love?

Even if one of them was his wife.

RIVALRIES

Dona Vaughn

HarperPaperbacks
A Division of HarperCollins*Publishers*

HarperPaperbacks *A Division of* HarperCollins*Publishers*
10 East 53rd Street, New York, N.Y. 10022

First printing: May 1991

Printed in the United States of America

HarperPaperbacks and colophon are trademarks of
HarperCollins*Publishers*

10 9 8 7 6 5 4 3 2 1

For my parents,
Harvie W. and Nola Lee

Contents

There are two tragedies in life. One is not to get your heart's desire. The other is to get it.

—George Bernard Shaw

PROLOGUE

1989

THE WOMAN WOKE WITH A START AT 4 A.M., HER heart racing with panic. Nothing to worry about, she soothed herself as she lay staring at the ceiling. Nothing at all. Even if the gun were not safely back where it belonged, it would not be connected to her.

Not so the gloves.

Only a few women in Los Angeles owned gloves like those, custom-made of supple Italian leather. Only hers were stained with blood and soiled by minute traces of burned gunpowder, which was why she had tossed them inside a culvert on a canyon road so remote she doubted it had a name.

Even so, when she raised her right hand to brush her hair back from her flushed face, she thought she caught the faint odor of death, lingering on her skin beneath the heavier perfume of her hand lotion. Imagination, she thought, while she waited for the phone to ring. The mingled scent of gunpowder and blood could not have penetrated the gloves.

At 5 A.M., unable to lie there any longer, she rose and showered.

At 6 A.M., dressed, she sat beside the phone, waiting.

At 7 A.M., she walked to the top of the stairs and shouted down for a breakfast tray.

When the food arrived, she found she couldn't eat. The scrambled eggs dried to hard yellow marbles on her plate while she drank the coffee and stared at the phone.

The call came at 9:22 A.M.

Who had they telephoned first? she wondered as she lifted the receiver. Who would be notified last? Was there a protocol for death?

As the cool official voice on the other end of the line delivered the news, she gasped and began to cry.

The official voice softened, consoled her, begged her pardon for being so harsh, and became, in that magic moment, a fan.

When she hung up, she felt a furtive thrill of triumph at achieving that unlikely miracle one more time.

She knew that sometime later today, while she waited at the hospital, a piece of paper and a pen would be thrust into her hands. She would see in someone's face what she had just heard in the voice on the phone, and she would scrawl her signature across the paper with the same secret thrill she felt now.

She gasped again—involuntarily this time—as though she had just been struck a harsh and brutal blow.

Helplessly, she began to cry in truth, with huge, painful sobs she would never have used in front of the camera, because they made her look too hideous.

"Oh, Nick," she said aloud. "I'm sorry. I'm so sorry."

She really was.

But whether she felt remorse because she had tried to kill him or simply regretted that she had been unsuccessful and he still clung, however feebly, to life, she wasn't sure.

She only knew she was sorry.

Like so many other times in her life, it was Kate Mallory's

fault. She smiled through her tears. This time the bitch would pay.

Nicholas Picard was a lucky devil!

That was Jackson Cole's first thought when he walked into the small conference room Cedars-Sinai had set aside in the intensive care unit for Picard's former wives.

The balding LAPD sergeant knew everything about these four women. He knew everything about everyone in Hollywood from the stacks of supermarket tabloids he kept beside his bachelor bed. Only he never saw any of his idols in person. That was why he jumped at the chance to carry out the lieutenant's instructions. "Don't let them leave the hospital until I get a chance to talk to them myself," Lieutenant Sattler had ordered. "And—Cole? Be diplomatic."

Diplomatic? Hell, he was as tongue-tied as a kid in the presence of so much gorgeous female flesh. Lucky devil! he thought again.

Then Cole remembered the lucky devil was fighting for his life right now and would probably lose the battle, according to his sour-faced doctor. Still, Cole wasn't so sure he wouldn't have traded places with the poor son of a bitch. To go out with the memories Picard must have! A bullet in the chest almost seemed a small price to pay.

Juliet Brittany. Kathleen Mallory. Allison Hilliard. Toby Flynn. All blond. All still beautiful. That one man in one ordinary lifetime should have discovered—and married— all four of these superstars only proved to Cole how unfair life could be. It was uncanny how much the four of them resembled one another despite almost a twenty-year difference in age between the oldest and the youngest. They might all be sisters instead of ex-wives.

Over the years lavish photo layouts of each of the four

had appeared in *Playboy*, every picture snapped by Nicholas Picard himself while married to the woman bared on the glossy pages. Cole had masturbated to those photographs. He rubbed his sweaty palms together nervously, afraid the women might guess.

Yet even as a dull red flush heated his face, he realized the irony in the situation. Why should *he* be uncomfortable? After all, he was an officer of the law. The odds were that one of these four women would become a murderess in the next few hours.

Sometime last night Nicholas Picard had been shot and left for dead in the study of his home. Clinging to life until morning, he was found by his lawyer. When asked, as he was being loaded into the ambulance, who shot him, Nicholas Picard gasped two faint words: "My wife."

Of which there were four, all ex.

Cole gazed at them sadly. Although he had never met any of them before, he knew about them. And nothing he knew about them would have led him to suspect something like this might happen. He felt betrayed, just as betrayed as Nicholas Picard must have felt last night when the bullet tore into his chest.

Witnesses reported that all four women had arrived on the fifth floor of Cedars-Sinai within ten minutes of one another. Kathleen Mallory, Picard's second wife, had been the first to show; Toby Flynn, the fourth Mrs. Picard, had been the last. According to the hospital staff, each of the four, as she arrived, pushed the buzzer outside the double doors of the intensive care unit and announced herself as Nicholas Picard's wife.

All the women had been weeping earlier. Cole knew that meant nothing. They were actresses.

None of them wept now. The damage left by their tears had been repaired. No mascara tracks marred their perfect faces. Their lips gleamed like chrome. Blusher blazed along their cheekbones like defiant banners. Their shuttered eyes gave nothing away.

Inquiring minds want to know. Jackson Cole had forgotten the lieutenant's instructions. He licked his lips and blurted out the question that had been churning in his gut all morning. "Which one of you hated Nicholas Picard enough to kill him?"

A momentary silence filled the room. Cole could hear the rasp of his own breath.

Then Juliet Brittany, Picard's first wife, said, "You've phrased it wrong, Mr. Policeman. The question should be, Which one of us loved him enough to kill him?"

The rest of them nodded their agreement.

All except Kathleen Mallory.

Cole studied her face. He had been wrong about Picard's second wife, he saw. The glossy perfection of that face was a lie. Behind it lurked a very frightened woman. He nodded, satisfied, as the door opened behind him.

"Ladies," said Lieutenant Sattler. "Sorry to keep you waiting."

"We haven't called our lawyers yet." That was Mrs. Picard Number Three, Allison Hilliard. "Or at least I haven't. Is it time?"

"Not for you, Ms. Hilliard," the lieutenant said.

Hot damn! Cole thought. I was right!

In the next breath, Sattler confirmed it, as he turned to Kathleen Mallory. "Ms. Mallory? We would like to ask you a few questions."

Kate Mallory stared past the new policeman. Even while her mind fumbled numbly with his words, she couldn't keep her eyes off the door behind him. They would come through that door to tell her Nick was dead. Each time it opened, her heart jerked so painfully she thought it would stop beating altogether.

"Questions?" she repeated after a moment. "Certainly. I'll be glad to. . . ." Her voice ran down as the other three women turned to stare at her. It was like walking through a fun house. Each face was a near mirror reflection of her own and yet at the same time dismayingly different. The sensation had never bothered her as much as it did at this moment. She had the queasy feeling she stood in a fault zone and the earth was about to shift beneath her feet.

"Ms. Mallory?" the new policeman said, and the meaning behind his words finally penetrated. He thought she was the one.

Kate stared back at the fun-house faces. She had never really thought of these three women as friends; they were more like relatives.

Sisters. In some crazy way we were like sisters, bound together by our relationship to Nick.

"We all loved him," she said aloud. "Didn't we? Juliet? Allison? Toby?"

No one answered.

Kate was babbling now, but she couldn't stop. "I'm sure we did. Just—in different ways."

Then the worst of it hit Kate like a body blow, staggering her. *Oh, Nick! If the police think it's me, then they won't protect you from her!*

From the transcript of the taped interview with Sloan Whitney, the victim's lawyer:

Q: *How long have you been Nicholas Picard's lawyer?*
A: *Since his first divorce. But we were friends before that.*
Q: *Why were you at his house this morning?*
A: *At Nick's request. He left a message on my answering machine last night asking me to come out early this morning.*
Q: *What was the purpose of the meeting?*
A: *I have no idea.*

Q: *But you went anyway? Is that your normal procedure when a client calls?*

A: *I told you, Nick is my friend as well as my client.*

Q: *Do you still have the tape of his message?*

A: *Yes. I haven't erased it yet. There were other messages I hadn't answered.*

Q: *Did he sound disturbed or upset in the message?*

A: *Not at all. In fact, he was laughing when he left it.*

Q: *You're sure the manuscript was the only thing missing from his home?*

A: *As far as I could tell.*

Q: *What kind of book was it?*

A: *His memoirs. He'd been working on them for almost a year. He had a huge pile of manuscript pages on his desk beside his typewriter.*

Q: *Any chance he might have just put the manuscript away?*

A: *That's doubtful. He had a fit if the housekeeper moved the papers so much as a quarter of an inch.*

Q: *So what do you think happened to the manuscript, Mr. Whitney?*

A: *Isn't it obvious? One of those bitches took it! Pause. I'm sorry. I've known all four of them for years. But Nick is my friend, my good friend. Probably my best friend in the whole world. And he said one of them tried to kill him. Until I know which one, how can I trust any of them?*

Q: *Did you read the manuscript, Mr. Whitney?*

A: *A few scattered pages. Nick wouldn't let me read the whole thing. He said if I started carping about libel I'd spoil his creative flow.*

Q: *Would you have carped about libel?*

A: *Probably. That's what lawyers are supposed to do.*

Q: *You said he showed you a few pages. Can you remember anything about them?*

A: *I can remember everything about them.*

Q: I don't—

A: I have a photographic memory.

Q: *Then perhaps you'll be good enough to see if you can reproduce those pages for us?*

A: *Certainly.*

BOOK ONE

PYGMALION

Juliet

1954–1960

Juliet Brittany was completely naked the first time I saw her. Neither she nor I realized we would soon share that delicious sight with the entire world.

*—From the unpublished memoirs
of Nicholas Picard*

ONE

❧

1954

THE DANCING FLAME OF THE PINK AND GOLD CHINA lighter glowed brilliant yellow against the twilight shadows of the strange bedroom. Juliet Brittany focused all her attention on the bright tongue of flame, trying to ignore the angry pounding on the other side of the bedroom door. Holding the lighter before her, she took one step toward the curtained window—and then she faltered.

Little girls shouldn't play with fire.

That was what Papa always said. Juliet wished her papa were here right now.

"Open this goddamned door," Phil yelled at her from the hall.

Juliet didn't know Phil's last name. If he had told her, she had been too dazzled by his red Eldorado convertible to remember. Her hand trembled and the lighter snapped shut, killing the yellow flame.

She put the pink and gold china lighter back on the nightstand, beside the pink and gold china ashtray. She was puzzled to realize that the lighter and ashtray matched the pink and gold ruffled bedspread, which matched the curtains on the window. Somehow she hadn't expected a man who drove a brand-new red convertible to live in a pink and gold bedroom where everything matched. She

13

wondered if his mother had decorated it for him.

Phil kept pounding on the door with his fists. "Nobody in Los Angeles is a virgin at twenty-two!"

Maybe he was right. Only she wasn't twenty-two; she had just told him that to get a ride in the Eldorado. She was only fifteen and still in high school. Juliet thought about shouting that through the bedroom door. Phil would probably consider being a virgin at fifteen as ridiculous as being a virgin at twenty-two.

Sometimes Juliet thought so too.

She was tall, nearly five feet ten, with intense blue eyes and fair, almost translucent skin. Beneath her angora sweater, her breasts were almost too full for her frame. Tonight, her long ash-blond hair fell loosely around her face. At school, she tied it back in a ponytail and wore a cinch belt to define her waist above the three crinoline petticoats that swelled her skirts. Even the principal turned to stare when she passed him in the halls.

She liked that. She wasn't sure why.

The other girls called her a showoff. Juliet didn't care. When she turned twelve and her figure started to develop, the boys crowded so closely around her that she didn't have time for friends who were girls. She still didn't.

In October of her junior year, Juliet gave up necking on Mulholland Drive with high school boys. Instead, she began accepting dates with older men in their twenties and thirties, who wore suits and ties instead of Levi's, who took her to nice restaurants instead of coffee shops, or to the movies instead of school dances. She told all of them she was twenty-two, a student at UCLA.

Instead of grabbing and mauling her, the older men wooed her. Juliet cooperated enthusiastically, as each date took increasingly pleasurable liberties with her body. It was simply a game. She could never go all the way.

No matter how much her dates begged and pleaded, or

sulked and pouted, she wouldn't give in. One thing kept her from that final fateful step: Papa. For her whole life, Juliet had been the apple of Papa's eye, the favorite of all his children. Papa was determined that Juliet was going to be an actress. She had the looks, everyone said so, and Papa made sure she had the training too. Acting lessons, singing lessons, dancing lessons: Papa saw she had them all. At first she had gone along with the lessons because she wanted to please Papa. After a while she began to dream her own dreams of seeing her name on theater marquees. Other girls wrote *Mrs.* in front of their boyfriends' names. She filled her notebooks with endless scrawls reading "Juliet Brittany starring in *Sabrina*," or *The High and the Mighty*, or whatever the latest movie was. Getting pregnant would ruin everything.

And every girl knew that the first time you had sex you got pregnant. Look what happened to Mama.

"Prick tease!" Phil shouted from the hall.

Juliet trembled. It wasn't the first time she had been called that, but it was the first time anyone ever yelled it with so much rage in his voice.

Her glance went frantically around the room. Besides the door with an angry Phil behind it, the single window was the only other way out. Juliet shoved aside the curtains and tried to raise the window. Nothing happened. With a sinking feeling, she realized it had been painted shut.

If only she hadn't let Phil go as far as he had! Then she wouldn't be in this mess right now.

When he talked her into stopping off at his house on the way to dinner, she saw no reason to say no. He had done such wonderful things to her body, murmuring compliments all the while, that she forgot to be wary. Instead, she drifted off into her own little world of pleasure, a world abruptly shattered when Phil raised himself and unzipped his trousers.

All Juliet's alarm signals went off.

Phil rolled off her just long enough to push his pants down around his knees. Juliet used that moment to scramble out of his reach. He was between her and the front door, so she bolted up the stairs. She would lock herself in a bedroom. Surely she would be able to talk some sense into him from behind the safety of a locked door.

Maybe she could have—if she hadn't made the unfortunate mistake of turning to see if he was following her.

He was, hopping up the stairs with his pants down around his ankles and his stiff thing poking out of his underwear. He had looked so ridiculous Juliet couldn't help giggling.

The memory made her laugh out loud all over again.

Phil reacted to the sound of her laughter like an enraged bull, pounding harder on the door. "You spoiled little bitch!"

Frightened now, really frightened for the first time that night, Juliet fought with the window. It still refused to yield. Through the glass, she caught sight of a shadowy figure moving around outside the house next door. She smacked the windowpane with the flat of her palm. "Help!" she cried. "Help!"

The figure didn't look up.

The bedroom door creaked alarmingly.

Juliet grabbed the spindly little chair beside her and lifted it over her head. When she smashed it against the window, the crash splintered its legs from its seat. Glass showered everywhere. The pink and gold cushion went flying out the window and landed on the lawn.

That caught the attention of the figure next door, an elderly man in bathrobe and slippers. He stared up at the window for a moment and then started across the lawn toward Phil's house.

Unfortunately, it also caught Phil's attention. "What are you doing in there?"

Juliet dropped the broken chair and leaned out the window. "Help me!" she screamed.

The door groaned as Phil struck it. He was putting his shoulder into it now.

The elderly man on the ground stared up at Juliet. His glance moved from her mouth, puffy from kissing, to her breasts, full beneath the angora sweater.

"Help me," Juliet pleaded.

He shook his head and started to turn away. I don't want to get involved, his posture said, as plainly as if he had spoken.

Juliet's next words were without premeditation. "The house is on fire!" she screamed at the man below. "Call the fire department! Hurry! I don't want to be trapped up here!"

"Don't worry, miss," the elderly man called up to her, "I'll get a ladder! I'll be right back."

"Please hurry!" she screamed. "Hurry!"

Behind her, the bedroom door gave way.

Juliet turned as Phil's momentum carried him halfway across the room. Only the bed separated them.

How could she ever have thought Phil was good-looking? she wondered. She must have been blinded by the glare off his convertible.

"Don't come any closer," she warned. "Your neighbor will be right back."

"You . . . you bitch!" He was so mad he was shaking, but he stayed where he was.

Some instinct told Juliet she was no longer in any danger. Now it was a game again. She had won. Phil had lost. She tossed her hair back from her face and looked at him with bold eyes.

Phil met her glance for a brief moment. Then he dropped down on the bed and buried his face in his hands.

A package of cigarettes lay on the nightstand. Juliet took

one and lit it with the pink and gold china lighter. She
inhaled deeply and then exhaled the smoke in the sexy,
sophisticated way she'd spent hours practicing in front of
the mirror. In the distance she heard the first faint sirens.

Phil's head jerked up.

Juliet and Phil stared at each other across the bed. Phil
made an animal sound deep in his throat, a cross between
a growl and a moan.

From outside, Phil's neighbor shouted, "Miss! Miss! Are
you all right, miss? I've got the ladder. The fire department
is on its way."

Juliet inhaled deeply once more and then snubbed out
the cigarette in the pristine ashtray. "Here," she said, and
tossed the lighter to Phil. Startled, he caught it.

The sirens were closer now.

Juliet picked up the broken chair and scraped it against
the empty window frame to clear away the rest of the glass.
Then she grabbed one of the pillows from the bed and laid
it across the sill.

Phil stood up. He looked helplessly at the smashed chair,
the broken window, the bedroom door hanging by one
hinge. "What am I going to do?"

Juliet straddled the windowsill. "If I were you, I'd go
downstairs and start a fire before they get here."

The look on his face made her giggle.

"You must be crazy," he said. The angry light began to
rekindle in his eyes. She could see he was measuring the
distance between them. He could still grab her before she
got out the window.

"Don't try anything," Juliet warned him. "My papa will
make you sorry if you do."

Phil stared at her face as if he were really seeing her for
the first time. "How old *are* you?" he asked hoarsely.

Something in his voice checked her automatic lie. Her
best defense now was the truth. "Fifteen."

"Christ!" His face went dead white. He sat down on the bed again.

"Good-bye, Phil." Juliet put her other leg over the windowsill and lowered herself onto the waiting ladder. All she could think of as Phil's elderly neighbor helped her down was what fun it would be to tell Papa about Phil's expression.

She didn't dare.

Papa might do something awful to him.

Thank goodness Papa didn't know she had gone on a date tonight. He thought she was with a girlfriend. When she stopped dating the immature boys from her high school, he had been thrilled. He thought she had decided to concentrate on her studies. He had no idea she was dating more than ever. If he had, he would have locked her in her room.

Sometimes Juliet thought her mother might have guessed the truth, might even be going out of her way to help Juliet fool Papa. If that was true, Mama wasn't doing it for Juliet. She just wanted to drive a wedge between Juliet and Papa.

Only it wouldn't work.

Papa loved her the best of anybody, Juliet thought, a smug little grin on her face. Maybe even better than Mama.

"My wife, Mrs. Simpson," said Phil's elderly neighbor, as he ushered Juliet into his house. "Uh—she was at the Harrisons' house when it caught fire, dear."

The stout woman waiting just inside the door eyed Juliet in a way that reminded her of Mama. "Who are you, girl?"

"Juliet Brittany. A friend of Phil's."

Mr. and Mrs. Simpson exchanged glances. Mr. Simpson reddened.

"Could I have something to drink?" Belatedly, Juliet remembered her manners. "Please?"

"Get yourself a glass of water in the kitchen," the woman

ordered. "Down the hall. Last door."

"I'll get it," Mr. Simpson offered.

"She can get it herself. I want to talk to you, Ned."

Juliet stood on her tiptoes to look out the Simpsons' kitchen window. Smoke curled up into the night from Phil's open back door. Through his kitchen window, she could see firemen moving around inside. The thick fire hose snaking around the corner of Phil's house had crushed a whole bed of geraniums. Phil's mother would not be happy.

"Come along, girl."

Juliet started. She hadn't realized the woman was right behind her. "I haven't gotten my—"

"Now," said Mrs. Simpson.

She marched Juliet outside and across the yard. Mr. Simpson followed them. "Who's in charge?" Mrs. Simpson asked one of the firemen.

The fireman looked at Juliet. "He's busy right now. Can I help you?"

"This girl was in the Harrisons' house when it caught fire."

"Yes, ma'am?" the fireman said.

Mrs. Simpson turned away without another word. Mr. Simpson trailed along behind her. When he gave Juliet a last look over his shoulder, his wife grabbed the sleeve of his robe. She pulled him with her into the house and slammed the door.

"So what am I supposed to do with you?" the fireman asked Juliet.

"I don't know."

"Are you related to the Harrisons?"

She shook her head.

"Just visiting?"

She nodded.

"Have any idea how the fire started in Mr. Harrison's kitchen?"

"Nope."

The fireman grinned at her. "Neither does Mr. Harrison's wife."

"His *wife*!"

She *never* dated married men. She wasn't that kind of girl at all. Juliet had begun to feel just a little sorry for Phil. Not anymore. Let him suffer. He shouldn't have lied to her in the first place.

His grin widened. "I'm Mike."

"I'm Juliet."

"Want to call someone to pick you up, Juliet?"

She glanced back at the Simpsons' house. Mrs. Simpson was silhouetted in the kitchen window. "I guess not," she said. Two firemen, in the process of rolling up the hose, paused to give her admiring looks.

"I'll guard you from the dragon lady," Mike said. "Promise."

"Why don't *you* take me home?" Juliet smiled up at him.

"Yeah, Mike," said one of the firemen rolling the hose. "Why don't we take her home?"

"Beat it, Kline," Mike said.

"Yeah, Mike," the other fireman agreed. "Why don't we take her home?"

Mike turned red. "The captain wouldn't—"

"Sure he would." Kline winked at Juliet. "I'll ask him. Hey, Cap! Want to give a pretty girl a ride home?"

He did.

Juliet thought the captain looked like a walrus with his curly gray hair and gray handlebar mustache. He sent Mike off to finish retrieving the hose while he wrapped Juliet in his own coat. He helped her pile her hair on top of her head and then popped his fireman's hat on her. "Can't let anyone know a civilian's on board," he explained.

Mike glared and Kline smirked while the captain showed

her how to cling to the side of the fire truck. Then, finally, he told everyone else to scramble on board.

All the captain's efforts with her hair were wasted when the fire truck turned the corner at the end of the block. Juliet's hair fell free and streamed out from beneath the hat. She laughed in delight.

"Hang on!" Mike shouted. Not that she could have fallen off if she had wanted to. Not with that many friendly hands clutching her.

"You were slumming," Mike said as they turned onto her street. The fire engine rumbled past magnificent Tudors, stately Colonials, and sprawling Mediterranean villas. Each house sat in solitary splendor on its own acre of parklike grounds. "What does your father do?"

Juliet brushed her hair back from her eyes. She could see flashing lights ahead. She wondered what was going on. "He's a banker."

"She's out of your league," one of the other firemen muttered.

Mike shot back a reply, but Juliet was no longer paying attention. The octagonal turret of her French country-style house rising above the trees had always reminded her of a romantic French castle. She never tired of looking at it.

Tonight she saw nothing but the ambulance, crouched like a malevolent beast in the circular drive, its flashing lights reflecting off the multipaned windows. The whole house seemed to glow an unearthly red.

As the fire engine pulled up, the ambulance left, its siren screaming into the night.

"Papa? Papa!"

Juliet flung herself off the still-rolling fire truck, skinning her knees and the palms of her hands on the cement of the drive. She never felt the pain.

"Papa!" she cried as she ran to the house. The front door stood open.

In the living room she found her sister and her two little brothers. They looked at her with the same jealous contempt they always turned her way. For once, Juliet didn't care. "What's wrong with Papa?" she demanded.

They stared back at her blankly. No one spoke.

"Tell me!" Juliet grabbed her sister by the shoulders and shook her. "Tell me what happened to Papa!"

Marcy was thirteen, a baby compared to Juliet. But tonight she had the same quizzical expression on her face as Mama had, any time Juliet tried to talk to her.

"Tell me!" Juliet screamed.

When Marcy still didn't answer, something snapped inside of Juliet. She slapped Marcy across the face.

Her little brothers caught Juliet's hands and pulled her away from Marcy. Except for the red print of Juliet's palm, Marcy's face was dead white. She still wore Mama's quizzical expression.

Juliet dropped to the floor, sobbing uncontrollably. "Papa!" she wailed. "Papa!"

"It wasn't Papa," Marcy said. "It was Mama."

"If you make us late today, I'll kill you!" Marcy screamed through the bathroom door. She rattled the knob. "Hurry up in there, Juliet!"

Her father grabbed Marcy by the arm and jerked her away from the door. "Go to your room and wait. Your sister needs time to get ready."

Marcy brushed past Todd and Tony into her room and slammed the door behind her. Let Papa yell about that, too! Marcy had been up all night crying. Now she dropped down on the bed and burst into tears all over again. Juliet hated Mama, Marcy thought. She always had. It wasn't fair she should make them all late to Mama's funeral.

Of course, Papa would defend her. He always acted like Juliet was someone special, a princess, not like Marcy and her brothers. They might as well not even exist as far as Papa was concerned. Or as far as Juliet was concerned, either.

Mama had loved them, but now Mama was dead, and Juliet was still alive. "I hope God punishes you, you bitch," Marcy whispered through her tears. "I hope you fall down the stairs and break your neck, too. Only you'll go straight to hell!"

Marcy's bedroom door opened. She sat up as nine-year-old Todd slipped in, followed by six-year-old Tony. The boys sat on either side of her, and Marcy put her arms around their shoulders. The three of them hugged one another and cried for Mama while they waited for the princess to put on her makeup.

In the bathroom, Juliet raised the lipstick to her lips.

Too bright. That was Mama's voice. *Too bright. Too thick. Wash off that goo. You want to look like a whore?*

Juliet stared at her pale face in the mirror. "I miss you, Mama," she whispered. The lipstick slipped from her fingers and fell into the lavatory. The strength went out of her legs. She sat down abruptly on the edge of the bathtub and tried to hold back the tears.

Juliet couldn't believe Mama was gone. Something as essential as the air she breathed, something she had taken for granted all her life, had vanished without warning.

Always, there had been Papa: hovering around her, asking her questions, begging her to dance or show off her new clothes. All Juliet remembered of Mama was the eternal frown, the disapproving shake of her head, the huff of disappointment. Ruth Brittany approved of nothing about her daughter: not her makeup, not her clothes, not her hair, not her habits. Ruth Brittany's mission in life seemed to be to extinguish the one bright flame in her otherwise ordinary family.

It was Papa who encouraged Juliet to shine. "As God intended her to," Papa would yell at Mama when they argued.

Just last week, if someone had asked her whether she would miss her mother if she died, Juliet would have lied and said yes. Secretly, she knew the truth. It was Papa she would miss, not Mama.

So why did she feel so miserable now?

Because one of her shorings had been knocked away, a shoring she never realized existed until it disappeared. Maybe all the frowns meant Mama never loved her. But for the first time in her life, Juliet realized she had really loved Mama.

The soft knock on the door startled her.

"Juliet? Are you all right?" Papa's voice was soft and solicitous on the other side of the door.

No, she wasn't all right. Everything was different, even the way her father talked to her. Juliet didn't want things to be different. She wanted Mama back!

Papa knocked again.

"I'm okay, Papa," Juliet said listlessly. "I'll be ready in a minute." Her legs felt weak and trembly as she stood up.

The lipstick had left a crimson streak across the white porcelain of the lavatory bowl as it fell. Juliet picked it up and slashed the color across her lips.

Aunt Barb had come to the funeral straight from the airport. She was waiting for them on the steps of the church. "I was beginning to wonder if you were coming, Oliver," she said by way of greeting.

Papa just grunted at his sister-in-law's sarcasm as he herded them all inside. Except for the two pews at the front reserved for the family, no empty seats were left. Papa's business associates and his employees from the bank packed the church.

Juliet felt her cheeks grow warm as the six of them filed

into the first family pew, leaving the second one vacant. It didn't seem right that there was so much empty space where Mama's family should have been.

Aunt Barb was Mama's younger sister, all that was left of Mama's family. She lived in Oregon. Juliet had seen her twice in her entire life, when Grandma died and when Aunt Barb married the sailor. When the sailor died, only Mama had gone to the funeral.

Tony and Todd acted like they didn't know who Aunt Barb was. "It was Juliet's fault," Marcy whispered to Aunt Barb, just loud enough for Juliet to hear. But not Papa. "She was putting on her makeup."

Aunt Barb glanced at her in a way that reminded Juliet of Mama's measuring looks. She didn't say anything. Not then. But her eyes said, Just wait till after the funeral, Miss Juliet!

Aunt Barb was short, like Mama, and her hair was the same mousy brown Mama's had been. In her drab black dress and sensible heels, Aunt Barb looked so much like Mama Juliet couldn't bear to look at her. Seeing Marcy and the boys sitting beside Aunt Barb on the hard pew, Juliet realized how much her sister and brothers resembled Mama, too.

Juliet's height came from Papa, along with the blue of her eyes, although Papa's eyes were cloudier, more muted. His hair was graying at the temples now, but it had been blond like hers, not brown like Mama's.

She glanced sideways at her aunt and sister and brothers. Sitting with their hands clasped in their laps, staring at the front altar, the four of them looked like a family.

It was she and Papa who looked as though they didn't belong in the pew, strangers who had wandered into the church by mistake.

When the service started, Juliet tried to feel that Mama was looking down at her from heaven like the preacher said. All she really felt was alone. Instead of looking at the open casket, she focused on Papa, trim and elegant in his dark blue suit. Somehow she had to make the lonely, lost feeling inside her go away or she would die too.

I've still got Papa, she told herself. That's what's important.

"I have no objection to taking the children," Aunt Barb said in a low voice. She was walking side by side with Papa as they left the cemetery. "But they should finish the school year first. Otherwise it will be too much for them, losing their mother and all their friends at the same time."

The lonely, lost feeling hit Juliet again like a punch in the stomach. Why would Papa send them away?

"I don't have time to take care of them," Oliver Brittany protested. "You do. They can pack today and leave with you tomorrow."

"What about Juliet? She's almost sixteen. She could take care of the younger ones till the end of school."

"No," Oliver Brittany said loudly. "She has her career to think about. She stays with me. The others go with you— tomorrow."

Papa was sending them away but keeping her with him? Juliet's heart leaped so violently she immediately felt guilty. She looked at her sister and brothers.

Marcy stared back, stony-faced. Tony stumbled along behind Marcy, clutching her hand. Todd, walking by himself, began to sob.

"What career?" Aunt Barb said, twisting the word in a way that made it sound like something nasty. "Ruth wrote me about you, Oliver. That you were spending money hand over fist on Juliet. That you were neglecting the other children."

Todd sobbed louder.

Aunt Barb gave her brother-in-law a hard look. "We'll

discuss this later." She went back and took the boys' hands
and hustled them to the limousine.

Marcy hurried after them.

Juliet followed more slowly, while her father brought
up the rear. She felt so strange. She didn't feel like she
belonged in Oregon with Aunt Barb. She didn't feel like
she belonged here with Papa either.

Maybe she didn't belong anywhere.

Aunt Barb dropped two heavy suitcases at Juliet's feet.
"At least you can help carry out the luggage. That won't
take too much time from your 'career,' will it?"

"No, Aunt Barb," Juliet said quietly, her eyes downcast.
Last night had been the hardest she ever spent in her life.
Worse than the night Mama died. Aunt Barb and Papa
had argued long past midnight. Finally Papa shouted that
if Aunt Barb didn't take the brats right now, he would put
them in an orphanage. He refused to let them ruin Juliet's
chance at a career.

Juliet's room was the farthest from the stairwell. If she
could hear their angry voices, she knew Marcy and the
boys could too. That was why she'd stayed in her room
this morning instead of coming down to breakfast. She
didn't want to see the accusation in their eyes.

"Oh, Juliet!" Aunt Barb sighed. "I can't see why you want
this so much. Don't you even care about your sister and your
brothers?"

She turned away before Juliet could explain that Papa was
the one who wanted an acting career for her. If it hadn't
been for him, she would never have thought of it. Aunt
Barb was a stranger. How could she know what Juliet was
really like?

Look at Marcy. She and Juliet saw each other every day.
Yet Juliet might as well be a Martian for all she and Marcy
had in common.

Strangers, Juliet thought. I'm different from them. They're more like Mama. I'm more like Papa.

Papa came out while Juliet was trying to lift one of the suitcases into the luggage rack on top of Aunt Barb's Buick. "You shouldn't be trying to lift that," he told her, and swung it up on top of the car himself.

Aunt Barb huffed.

"Good-bye, Barbara," Papa said. "I'll send you a check every month."

"See that you do, Oliver," Aunt Barb said tartly. "Tell your brothers and sister good-bye, Juliet."

Juliet felt awkward. She had been about to hug the boys, but Aunt Barb made it sound as though she wouldn't have done it without being ordered to.

Todd and Tony let her hug each of them, but they kept their bodies stiff and unbending. Marcy looked right in her face. "I'll hate you all my life, you bitch," she whispered.

Juliet was so stunned she couldn't say anything.

Marcy gave her a quick hug so neither Aunt Barb nor their father realized anything had happened. Then she climbed into the front seat beside Aunt Barb, and the Buick roared out of the circular drive as though Aunt Barb couldn't stand to spend another second there.

Papa went inside the house. Juliet stayed where she was, watching Aunt Barb's car grow smaller and smaller in the distance. When the Buick finally disappeared, it was all she could do not to burst into tears.

Afterward, the house was so empty Juliet didn't know what to do with herself. She wandered through the rooms picking up the books and toys scattered everywhere. Aunt Barb had taken a few of Mama's favorite things to Eugene with her. Marcy and the boys had been snatched away so quickly they hadn't had time to gather up their treasures.

Juliet carried their things to their rooms. She wondered if she should box up their favorite toys and ship them to

Oregon. Then she realized that she had no idea what their favorite toys were. She sat down on the edge of Tony's bed and thought about crying some more, but all the tears had been used up.

"Three Coins in the Fountain" drifted up the stairs from the radio in the kitchen. Her father hummed along with The Four Aces. Juliet went in the bathroom and washed her face. Then she went downstairs to help him fix lunch.

"Fashion-show time," Oliver Brittany said as he mixed himself a drink. Afternoon sunlight spilled into the family room from the two pairs of floor-to-ceiling French doors. Papa had just had the walls repainted a delicate spring green to echo the garden beyond the French doors.

Juliet had collapsed on the low banquette in front of the fireplace. A morning spent shopping at Bullock's Wilshire and lunch in the Tea Room could take a lot out of a girl. Now she bounced up. "Which one do you want to see first, Papa?"

"How about that aqua thing?"

"Oh, Papa! It's a princess dress." Juliet pawed through the boxes beside her. "Here it is." She shook out the crisp taffeta.

"You can change down here," Papa told her as she started for the stairs. "I won't peek."

"It won't look right without the shoes we bought yesterday." It was hard to remember how things had been before Mama died, Juliet thought, as she took the stairs two at a time. When Mama was alive, Papa was away a lot, taking care of his bank and his other investments. Now he spent more time with Juliet. Oliver Brittany took his daughter everywhere: to her dancing lessons and her modeling lessons, to restaurants, to concerts. He took her shopping almost every day to the best clothing stores in Los Angeles. Each evening Juliet twirled and pranced before him, modeling the day's purchases. "My own private fashion show," he called it.

In the first weeks, when she remembered Marcy and Tony and Todd, up in Eugene with Aunt Barb, Juliet felt guilty. She even wrote them a couple of letters. None of them ever wrote back except Aunt Barb, asking Papa for more money. Gradually, Juliet stopped thinking about them.

It was harder to forget Mama. Juliet always had such a lonely feeling when she thought of Mama. After a while, though, she forgot that too, because everything was the same as it had been. She was still Papa's favorite, the apple of his eye, and she was going to be an actress. As long as Papa adored her, she didn't need anyone else.

In her room, Juliet peeled out of her skirt and sweater and slipped the princess dress over her head, struggling awkwardly with the zipper. Then she searched through her closet for the newest of her dozens of pairs of shoes. One last swipe at her hair with her hairbrush, and a fresh coat of lipstick, and she was ready.

She twirled before the mirror, enjoying the way the taffeta nipped in at her waist and swirled around her legs.

"What's holding up the show?" Papa called from downstairs.

"Coming," Juliet called back. When she started down the stairs and saw Papa beaming up at her, she felt like she was already a movie star.

Life couldn't get any better than this!

"Come on, Juliet!" said the voice on the phone. "Give me a break. I haven't been able to get you out of my mind." Mike was the fireman she met the night her mother went to the hospital. Hard to believe that had been six months ago. It seemed like another lifetime. In all those months Juliet hadn't dated anyone. Now she wondered why not.

Papa, of course. He was so sweet, so attentive, she hadn't

had time to think about dates.

"How about dinner?" Mike begged, and a little thrill of anticipation went racing up Juliet's spine. She had forgotten exactly what he looked like, but his phone voice was nice, a sexy baritone.

"I don't know," she stalled.

"Don't tell me you have homework. Pretty girls like you shouldn't have to do homework."

"School's out, dummy." Had she told Mike she was going to UCLA? She wasn't sure, so she decided not to mention that she had dropped out of high school in April when she turned sixteen. She was barely passing, anyway. Papa took her so many places and kept her out of school so much, she had only been able to come up with a D in most of her classes. Papa assured her it didn't matter. In the real world, there were more important things. She was going to be a movie star, and movie stars didn't need a high school diploma.

"Come on," Mike pleaded. "I know a great hamburger place."

Hamburgers! She might as well still be dating high school boys. But she couldn't resist that sexy baritone. "Okay."

Now came the hard part. Telling Papa.

"Absolutely not," Oliver Brittany said. "He's probably one of those duck-tailed, leather-jacketed hoodlums I see everywhere."

"He's not, Papa. He's nice."

Papa didn't say anything. He just went and fixed himself another drink.

Juliet frowned at his back. Papa was drinking so much lately. She had never seen him drink like that before. She wondered if he was missing Mama. It made her feel guilty about leaving him alone tonight, even if it was the first time she had gone out since Mama's death.

"I'll hurry back, Papa," she promised impulsively. "You won't even know I'm gone."

"Shush," Juliet whispered and then dissolved into giggles.

"You're the one who's making all the noise," Mike protested, as he helped her into the dark entrance hall.

"Then make me be quiet." Juliet's voice echoed in the double-height room. She looked up at him and parted her lips expectantly.

Mike groaned. "You're drunk, you little nut. Why didn't you tell me you couldn't hold your liquor?"

"I didn't know," Juliet said, which was the truth. "Kiss me again, Mike."

"I'm going to do more than that if you don't—"

The lights came on.

"Take your hands off my daughter." Oliver Brittany stood on the upstairs landing. He would have looked more imposing if his shirttail had not been hanging out.

Juliet spotted the whiskey glass in his hand. "You're drunk, Papa," she accused. Then she giggled.

"Sir, I'm sorry. I had no idea—"

"She's only sixteen, you little bastard." Papa staggered down the stairs, clutching the fretwork balustrade for support, and Juliet giggled again. "Do you have any idea how much trouble you—"

"Please, sir, I had no idea she was underage, but we didn't—"

"Get out!"

"I know how this looks, and I'm sorry, but I want to see Juliet again. If you'll let me explain—"

"Get out, I said!"

"Papa's mad." Juliet tried to frown. Another giggle spoiled her solemn face. "You better go, Mike."

He went. Reluctantly.

"Papa," she scolded. "How could you!"

"Go to bed, Juliet," her father said. He sighed wearily. She went.

She was almost asleep when her bedroom door opened and closed.

"Juliet?"

"Yes, Papa?" She couldn't see him in the dark room, but she could hear him breathing.

"I don't want you to date that young man again. He's not a suitable person for someone like you. You have your career to consider."

She snuggled down into the sheets. "A career's not everything, Papa. Sometimes a girl wants more."

Juliet felt the mattress shift as he sat down on the side of the bed. Papa used to come and talk to her in the dark like this before Mama died. Juliet could never relax and enjoy their conversations, though, because she knew sooner or later Mama would pop through the door and shoo him out. "She needs her sleep, Oliver. And so do you," Mama would scold. Now Mama wasn't here. Juliet let herself drift in the darkness.

After a minute, Papa reached for her hand and held it in his. "Tell me what else a girl wants, Juliet."

Juliet's cheeks grew warm; she was glad it was too dark for Papa to see. But the beer Mike had given her made her bold. "Well . . . kisses." She loved kisses, soft dreamy kisses. "I could kiss forever," she blurted. "Only—"

"Only boys want to do other things?" Her father's voice was hoarse in the darkness.

The room was so quiet she could hear Papa breathing. So quiet she could almost hear the thud of her own heart. "But I don't, Papa. I wouldn't. I know you don't want me to, so I don't."

He leaned over her, scooping her into his arms, holding

her so close she couldn't breathe. "Everyone likes kisses, baby. There's nothing wrong with that. Even ancient old papas like kisses."

"You're not old, Papa!"

"You make me feel old, baby. You're so fresh, and young, and beautiful. . . ."

His cheek was damp against hers. Juliet kissed the tear tracks.

"Oh, baby," he groaned.

He took her head between his hands and turned her lips to his. His mouth came down on hers. He gave her a long, lingering kiss. "That's the kind of kisses you like, isn't it?" he said when his lips released hers. "You see, I know everything about my Juliet."

This time when his lips came back, she opened her mouth to his. It was all right. It was Papa.

Even when the heat built up inside her, she didn't worry. What was there to worry about? The kissing could go on forever. For the first time, she didn't have to fear what would happen if things got out of hand.

Juliet let herself relax completely and enjoy all the wonderful sensations. When he raised her nightgown and put his lips to the firm globes of her breasts, she almost screamed with the agonized delight of the reactions he aroused within her. But she didn't worry.

It was Papa and she was safe. Even when he pulled away from her in the darkness and came back beneath the sheets, his body nude and cool against hers. Even when she felt the firm rod jabbing against her thigh.

It reminded her of Phil and the red Eldorado convertible. Phil, pursuing her up the stairs, with his pants around his ankles and his stiff thing poking out of his shorts. She could feel the giggle building up inside of her—and then Papa levered himself up over her.

He plowed a knee between her legs.

Juliet howled as his kneecap struck her soft inner thigh, bruising the tender flesh. She wore no panties beneath her gown. His hand searched until it found her sparse little triangle of pubic hair.

She gasped, twisting away from him.

His hand followed, clutching her there. Then his fingers were inside her.

She tried to close her knees, to push him away, but she couldn't. "Papa! Please, Papa!" she sobbed. "Please! Don't!"

His fingers kept moving inside her, searching for the barrier of flesh. When he found it, he grunted with satisfaction.

Still, she didn't understand. "See, Papa! I'm a virgin! I told you I was!"

He raised himself off her.

Juliet gasped with relief.

Then he shoved himself inside her with one violent push. His penis ripped through the barrier his fingers had found, tearing the flesh.

Juliet screamed, but in the huge empty house there was no one to hear.

She knew, finally, why Mama had always been there, eternally between her husband and her daughter. Never leaving them alone for a minute.

But now it was too late.

She woke, alone, in her bed. The dried blood on her thighs told her it wasn't a dream. When she moved, she felt the soreness between her legs. His kneecap had left a huge bruise on her right thigh.

Juliet rose in one swift motion and yanked the top sheet from the bed. Wrapping it around her, she stalked down the hall to her father's room.

It was empty, the bed untouched.

She found him downstairs, sprawled on the sofa, his

mouth open, snoring noisily. A whiskey bottle sat on the floor beside the sofa.

"Oliver!"

He woke slowly.

"Ruth?"

"Mama's dead, Oliver."

"Juliet?"

"I'm moving out, Oliver. I'm getting an apartment."

He rubbed his bleary eyes, trying to focus on her. "An apartment? How are you going to pay for it?"

"I'm not. You are."

He tried and failed to meet her steady gaze. After a moment he stood up slowly, like a defeated old man. Then he staggered off to get his checkbook.

TWO

❧

1955

As Frederick Yates led the way through the crowded studio commissary, conversation hushed momentarily at his approach. Small of stature, dark-haired, pale-skinned, immaculate in his London-tailored suit, Frederick nodded regally at each table he passed, ignoring the startled glances that swung from him to his unlikely companion.

Beside Freddie's diminutive form, Nicholas Picard's six feet of lean hard muscle looked even larger. His sun-bleached blond hair, combined with a tan worthy of a beach bum, gave him a glowing look of health Freddie's scowling features lacked. More astonishing to the rank-and-file studio employees, Nick's T-shirt and jeans seemed to mark him as a student in the torn T-shirt school of acting, and everyone knew Freddie never stooped to dining with the hired help.

A slight lift of Frederick Yates's eyebrow was enough to frighten off a covey of extras about to alight at one of the few remaining empty tables.

"How does it feel to be a VIP lunching with a bum, Freddie?" Nick asked with a grin, as they sat down at the newly vacant table.

Frederick Yates gave him a murderous look. "Humiliating," he complained in his pseudo-British accent. "The sooner ended, the better." He leaned over to the diners at the next table. "Do you mind?" he asked, as he reached for their menus.

They didn't.

"You could have asked for their balls and gotten the same response," Nick said, taking the menu Freddie shoved at him.

"Don't be crude, Nicholas." Freddie drummed his fingers on the table, his impatient glance darting around the packed commissary. "Why are there never any waitresses in this bloody place?"

Nick ignored Freddie's petulance, concentrating instead on the menu before him. For the past week, he had dined on peanut butter sandwiches morning, noon, and night. Freddie was paying for this lunch, and Nick intended to get Freddie's money's worth. Something as far removed from peanut butter as possible.

Freddie's drumming grew louder.

A fragile little brunette waitress hurried to their table. "Hasn't Betty taken your order yet, Mr. Yates?"

"She seems to be otherwise occupied. Perhaps you could assist us."

"Certainly, Mr. Yates." She waited, pencil poised over her pad.

"Nicholas?" Freddie prompted. "Surely you have made a decision by now."

Nick had decided to opt for volume. "Two Reubens. With extra corned beef."

The waitress glanced up. She had huge green eyes. "Two?"

"You're right," Nick told her. "Make it three."

The corners of her mouth tilted upward but her voice remained solemn as she turned to Freddie. "And you, Mr. Yates?"

"Tuna salad. Bring it quickly. I've a meeting in half an hour."

"Certainly, Mr. Yates."

Nick grinned at her. "I see my brother's an important man around here."

Her startled glance swung from Freddie's slight frame to Nick, more than a head taller and a good sixty pounds heavier. Nick could see the effort it cost her to choke back the laughter.

So could Freddie. Like a thunderclap, his frown sent her scurrying off through the lunchtime crowd. He transferred his displeasure to Nick. "Don't ever say that again, Nicholas! You're not my brother!"

"Close enough," Nick countered. It was true. For Hollywood, anyway. Frederick Yates was Morgan Gaynor's stepson from a previous marriage. And Morgan was Nick's stepfather too. Ex-stepfather, he reminded himself. The divorce was over five years old, but Nick had remained fonder of Morgan Gaynor than of any of the other men in his mother's life before or since, an affection that Gaynor returned.

That was half of what bugged Freddie.

"You always have to charm them, don't you?" Freddie's mouth twisted into a bitter line. "I don't know why I wasted a lunch in order to watch you add another scalp to your collection."

And that was the other half.

"I was just being pleasant, Freddie. You ought to try it sometime."

Freddie snorted, a delicate upper-class English snort. Poor Freddie. It pained him beyond belief that his biological father had been a stuntman with a third-grade education. When his dim-witted but beautiful mother married Morgan Gaynor, Freddie had adopted his stepfather's accent and manners as protective coloration.

Over Freddie's shoulder, Nick could see their mutual ex-stepfather winding his way through the bustling commissary, past the tables full of contract players. Tall, slender, stoop-shouldered, Morgan Gaynor had an elegance Freddie could never hope to achieve. If Morgan had glanced their way, he would have invited both of his former stepsons to join him. That was the kind of man Morgan Gaynor was.

Even though he had no desire to see Morgan today— had, in fact, every reason to avoid him—Nick still felt disappointed when Morgan disappeared through the door of his private dining room.

He transferred his disappointment to the star-packed tables around them. "What other studio has a contract list the size of this one? Someone should tell these clowns the star system is dead. Don't they know they're dinosaurs?"

Freddie flinched. "Keep your voice down."

"What do you care, Freddie? You're one of the big guys now. Look at you. Nepotism lives." Their mutual ex-stepfather was head of the studio.

Freddie flushed. "Stop calling me Freddie!"

"You want me to call you Frederick? After we shared the same bathtub for half our lives?" Not exactly true, since Freddie was five years older than Nick, but why let facts stand in the way of sentiment? "No way, man. I really do love you like a brother." Not exactly true either, but Nick loved to see Freddie squirm with embarrassment as he did now, twisting around to see if anyone had overheard that last statement.

"I want you to call me Mr. Yates. Or better yet, don't call me at all." Freddie spoke so fast he had trouble keeping the British accent. "It would delight me to be a perfect stranger where you're concerned." He paused, breathing hard, as the waitress showed up with their food. "Bring the ticket straightaway," Freddie told her, the accent in place once more.

"We were discussing dinosaurs before we got sidetracked," Nick said around a mouthful of corned beef, cheese, and sauerkraut. "The world is changing, Freddie. Maybe you haven't noticed. Especially the film world. The best movie I've seen in the past few months was *Gate of Hell*. We gave it an Oscar, but it didn't make a single best-film list in Japan. You know why? Because the Japanese considered it ordinary. Ordinary! That's the kind of standard we're up against." He shook his head wonderingly. "Wasn't that the most magnificent color photography you've ever seen?"

Freddie shrugged. "I didn't see it. Why should I?"

Nick almost choked on his Reuben. "Why should you? How about the fact that box-office attendance is still off?"

"Television." Freddie picked the pieces of pimento out of his tuna salad, one by one. "They'll get tired of watching a plywood box eventually."

"What about the art houses?"

"What about them?"

"Have you ever been to one?"

"I don't care for subtitles."

"Has it occurred to you that there are now hundreds of art houses?" Nick thought of the one where he'd seen *Gate of Hell*: small and intimate, with luxurious seats, and packed to the rafters. "Maybe your audience isn't at home watching television. Maybe they're interested in a different kind of film."

"The audience wants glamour from Hollywood. They want tried-and-true. That's why the studio isn't looking for original screenplays. We want adaptations." He lined up all his discarded pimentos in a straight row. "We want something that will play on the wide screen."

"Bullshit, Freddie! Your audience is voting with its feet. Other studios see it. Look at *Marty*. Look at *On the Waterfront*."

"The method movie," Freddie sneered.

"You didn't like that either? Jesus, Freddie! Somebody liked it. Look how many Oscars it won!"

"It was sloppy and self-indulgent."

"And they let you out without a keeper? If Morgan thinks like you, the two of you will run this studio right into the ground."

If Freddie had a monocle, he would have twirled it just then. "I'll tell him you said so, old boy. I'm meeting him right after lunch."

Nick laughed. "Tell him. I'll tell him myself the next time I see him."

"Ha!"

They had lapsed back to the level of two kids squabbling in a sandbox. "Let's cut the crap, Freddie. I'm offering you a script that will bring this studio out of the Stone Age."

"The answer is no."

"I'm trying to do you a favor."

"Some favor. Trying to make me ruin my reputation with an amateur script."

"That stung, Freddie. I'll ignore it, though. I happen to know you haven't even looked at the first page of this monumental piece of film history yet."

"Monumental piece of shit!" A passing redhead from the secretarial pool giggled, and Freddie turned beet red. "At any rate, I'm not involved with scripts. I told you that on the phone."

"This script will make your career."

"My career is doing fine without your help."

But not without Morgan Gaynor.

Nick didn't say it. He didn't have to. He and Freddie locked glances across the table.

The waitress brought the check. One glance at Freddie's expression and she departed without a word.

Freddie scribbled his name on the check and left it lying on the table as he stood up. "Why don't you go back to school?" Nick had dropped out of college last year when he turned twenty. Morgan had been upset by his ex-stepson's decision. Almost as upset as Nick's mother had been. "Or get a real job. Something that pays enough so you don't have to scrounge meals. Perhaps something in another city."

"So I won't be a source of embarrassment? Sorry, brother dear, it's too much fun seeing you blush."

"I don't blush!"

But he was blushing right now. And it made him mad. Mad enough to say, "Why don't you ask your mother to have one of her many male friends read your bloody script? She has better connections than I do. She's slept with someone from every studio in town."

The laughter died in Nick. "I don't want any help from her. You know that."

Freddie sighed. "I fail to understand you, Nicholas. You don't want any help from her. You don't want any help from Morgan. Why do I get the honor?"

"Because, dear Freddie, if I get any kind of boost from you, I'll know it's because I damn well earned it."

Freddie started to stomp away. Suddenly he turned and came back. "Give me the phone number of that dump you're in now."

"Why?"

"Why? Because if I'm interested in your script I'll call you."

Nick shook his head. "I'll call you." No way did he want that telephone number passed on to Morgan or, worse, to his mother. He'd gotten his share of phone calls when he dropped out of school. He wasn't setting himself up for another barrage.

"Really, Nicholas! You want my help and then you don't want my help. What do you really want?"

"To stand on my own two feet."

"Unlike me?"

Nick shrugged. Across the commissary, he could see Morgan emerging from his private dining room. "Better hurry to your meeting," he told Freddie. "It takes hard work to keep a studio in the Stone Age."

Freddie bit back whatever else he was about to say and stalked away.

Nick felt the same conflicting emotions as when they were kids and he finally succeeded in making Freddie truly angry. Freddie never retaliated with a zinger about Nick's mother otherwise. It was the only way he could actually hurt Nick, and he never used it except as a last resort.

"Shit," Nick muttered, as he watched Freddie leave the commissary. He really did love the pretentious little asshole like a brother, even if he had a strange way of showing it.

The fragile brunette showed up for the check and then lingered while Nick finished off the last of his Reubens. "You sure made Mr. Yates mad. Are you really his brother?"

"The black sheep of the family."

"You don't look alike."

"We had different mothers and fathers." He grinned at her.

"I get it. You're no kin at all, right? That's why he was so mad."

"Let's just say both of us wanted the same father but neither of us got him."

She frowned over that one a moment and then grinned back, dismissing it. "He's already signed the check. I could add on a couple more of those Reubens."

"Thanks, but I couldn't eat another bite right now."

"To go." She gave him a long sideways look with those big green eyes. "I could bring them to your place after I get off from work."

No use letting Freddie's tab go to waste. "Make it four of the most expensive thing on the menu."

"Four?"

"One for you." Nick scribbled down the address and phone number.

Frederick intercepted the waitress in the kitchen. "Give me his address." He had known Nicholas wouldn't be able to resist the girl. When had the son of a bitch ever resisted anything?

Her shoulders slumped. "Sure, Mr. Yates." She dug it out of her pocket.

He copied it down and handed it back to her. "Our little secret," he told her. "Go ahead and meet him. Just refrain from mentioning this."

Her eyes widened. "But—"

"What's your name?"

"Nancy. Nancy Stark."

He wrote that down too. "Good girl. There will be a bonus in your pay next week."

"Yes, *sir*, Mr. Yates." She hurried off, her rear swaying.

Frederick watched with disgust. He liked women well enough, women of his own class. Nicholas tried to fuck anything that moved.

"Freddie!" he muttered out loud, as he left the commissary. A stage hand turned and stared. "I'll Freddie you, you miserable— I know what you're afraid of."

Only he would wait a week. Give Nicholas time to forget about this encounter. Then he would unleash his revenge.

The landlady's cool hand on his bare chest woke him. "Nick? I've been pounding on your door for five minutes."

He opened his eyes with a groan. She looked too fresh and perky for the way he felt. "Have a heart, Cindy! I worked until three A.M."

"Worked! Ha! You were writing your script." She slipped under the covers with him, fitting herself to him. She was thirty-five, but the body inside her T-shirt and skimpy shorts was as taut as a teenager's. Nick felt his own body show its appreciation. "If you were really working, you could afford a phone of your own."

That woke him up a little more. "I've got a call?"

She ran her hand down his torso and over his lean stomach. "Mmmm," she said as she grasped him. "Shall I tell her you've got better things to do?"

He heaved himself out of bed and tugged on his jeans while Cindy watched. "Ever think about making a blue movie, Nick? You could wear a mask, and your friend there would be the star. You could make a few bucks. Want me to introduce you to someone?"

He grinned at her. "Try me tomorrow."

Cindy looked hurt. Today was the first of October. The rent was due. Again. Today made three months Nick owed. "It's not me, Nick. You know I'd let you have more time. George is on my case." The apartment house belonged to George. So did Cindy, when he had time for her.

Nick leaned over and gave Cindy a friendly pat on her rear. "Don't worry about it, babe," he said as left. "I'll get by."

"I'll wait right here," she called after him.

He cut through the courtyard to Cindy's apartment. George didn't believe in wasting money on gardeners. Watered but unpruned, the plantings had run wild, fighting each other for a foothold. The plant-choked courtyard reminded Nick of Hollywood itself. Someone had pointed out once that Hollywood only existed as a state of mind, not as a geographical place. Good, Nick thought, because the reality of Hollywood as a place was depressing. The ocean of apartment buildings and small hotels, bungalow courts, and cramped little houses served as transient housing for the hangers-on of the movie industry. George's apartments rented to painters, carpenters, extras, machinists, and those, like Nick, who were aspiring but unemployed. The elite had fled Hollywood long ago for Beverly Hills, Brentwood, and Bel Air—or ranches in the San Fernando Valley. Someday Nick planned to join them.

He let himself into Cindy's apartment and picked up the phone. Whoever the caller had been, she had hung up.

Nick replaced the receiver and went into Cindy's kitchen to rummage through her refrigerator. The phone rang again just as he discovered a pound of bacon. Luckily, the phone cord stretched into the kitchen.

"Nicholas?" his mother said. "What took you so long to come to the phone?"

Freddie! You son of a bitch! How did you get my number?

"What do you want, Mother?" Nick held the phone against his ear with his shoulder as he snagged a skillet and filled it with bacon strips.

"Do you realize how long it's taken me to find you? You could at least be civil!"

The silence lengthened as the bacon started to sizzle. Nick began breaking eggs into a bowl.

"I want to see you, Nicholas. This afternoon."

The clock on Cindy's kitchen wall told him it was nearly noon. "What about?"

"I haven't seen you in six months! Maybe I want to wish my only child a happy birthday." He had turned twenty-one a couple of weeks ago.

"Why today?"

"Just show up, Nicholas."

"I'm right in the middle of something. I don't think I'll be able to—"

"Come at two," his mother said and broke the connection.

Nick dished up the bacon and scrambled a skillet full of eggs. Cindy wandered in while he was eating. She pulled out a chair, sat down, and swung her long tanned legs up on the table. "Phone privileges. Kitchen privileges. What next?"

"How about bed privileges?" Nick wolfed down the rest of his omelet. He'd gone all yesterday without food.

"I thought you'd never ask," Cindy said, as she stood up and peeled out of her clothes.

Sex with Cindy was like an athletic event. Everything went by the rules. Nothing out of bounds, or she'd call a foul. And everyone ended up a winner.

Afterward, Nick broiled himself the hefty T-bone she'd been saving for George. Cindy watched with a troubled frown as George's steak disappeared, along with half a head of lettuce and a couple of juicy tomatoes. "You *are* going to be able to pay the rent this afternoon, aren't you? You know how George is."

"No problem," Nick lied. Maybe he'd hit up Freddie for the money. The little asshole owed him something. Tattling to a guy's mother! What a juvenile thing to do.

Nick went back to his own place, showered, shaved, and changed into a suit, sacrificing his last clean shirt to his mother's whim. On the way out of his apartment, he slammed his door with unnecessary force, thinking of the interview ahead.

Cindy came out of her apartment as he passed. "Don't you look nice." She straightened his tie and gave him a peck on the cheek. "Is someone picking you up?" she asked, as she shaded her eyes against the sun and peered through the archway to the garage beyond. "I don't see your car."

"It's in the shop for a couple of days."

"When you get it back, you can take me out to eat someplace besides my own refrigerator."

Nick paused when he reached the street. Anywhere else he would have seen kids jumping rope or old folks taking a walk in the sun. Not in Hollywood. Few old people and fewer children lived in the apartment houses on either side of the street. The identical red-tiled roofs and white plaster walls held only the floating population of movieland.

Hands in his pockets, Nick sauntered down to the end of the palm-lined block. When he reached the corner, he stopped to light a cigarette, cupping his hands against the breeze, and looked back the way he had come.

Satisfied no one was watching him, he loped across the street and down two blocks to the vacant garage where he had stashed his Corvette the night before. Could be his imagination, but when he drove up to the apartment house just after midnight, he thought he'd spotted a man from the bank parked across down the street in a DeSoto. Nick had discovered the vacant garage a couple of weeks ago, while painting the modest little bungalow next door, and had kept it in mind for just such an emergency. Last night, by the time he parked the Corvette and returned to his apartment house on foot, the suspicious DeSoto was gone. Still, unless he came up with some hard cash, Nick knew it was only a matter of time before the bank found him.

Not today, though. When he opened the garage door, Nick was relieved to find the little Polo white roadster still there. "Come on, babe," he said as the Corvette hesitated and then surged to life. "You're all I've got left in the world."

"Miss Chandler's in her bedroom," the maid told Nick. She accepted the newspaper he had found waiting at the end of the drive.

"Thanks." He paused, uncomfortable. Was she the same girl who had been with his mother the last time he visited? He couldn't remember. Helen Chandler changed maids like she changed dresses. Nick assumed it was to keep any one human from knowing all the intimate details of her life. "I'll show myself up."

"Certainly, sir. All the gentlemen like to do that," the maid added.

Nick was halfway up the stairs when the realization struck him that the girl hadn't known he was Helen Chandler's son. He was torn between the impulse to laugh and the urge to storm downstairs and correct her mistaken impression.

Wouldn't Freddie love to know that Helen's boyfriends were getting younger these days!

That thought made him pound harder on the door than he had intended.

"For heaven's sake, Nicholas!" his mother called. "Come in before you break the door down."

Helen Chandler's heavy drapes were drawn tightly closed, shutting out the first day of warm October sunshine. "I've been expecting you to visit me for some time, Nicholas." Her voice came out of the darkness, low and husky, as he shut the door. "I almost hired a private detective. Is this any way for a son to treat his mother? You don't know how I've worried."

"I'm here now," he said sullenly. He knew it was an act, but it worked. Just as she had manipulated audiences from the movie screen, she still had the power to jerk him around emotionally.

Helen Chandler knew it too. She gave a throaty laugh. "Don't be such a baby, Nicholas."

God, how he hated to hear that! It was what she had always said when he wanted her to stay home and act like a real mother. "Don't be such a baby, Nicholas," she would say, and kiss him on the cheek—and then run off with some man to Palm Beach or New York or Paris or London or Rome.

After she married Morgan Gaynor, Nick stopped asking her to stay home. She was still gone as much as ever, even after she finally stopped making movies, but it no longer mattered. Morgan was always there, for Nick *and* Freddie. Nick was still deeply ashamed that his mother had cuckolded a man as decent as Morgan. And equally puzzled as to why Morgan had allowed it.

During the years Nick was growing to manhood, he and Morgan had discussed almost everything under the sun, except that.

The bed creaked as she stood up. "Frederick told me you're on the edge of destitution."

"Freddie has a big mouth. Someone ought to shut it for him."

"Frederick has your welfare at heart. Just as I do." She passed in front of a faint sliver of sunshine that had escaped the heavy drapes. Her silhouette was that of a young girl. "You're wasting the best years of your life. I have a wonderful job all set up for you at the studio. Working with Vincent Tandy. Wouldn't you like that?"

Like it? To work with one of the best directors in Hollywood? Nick bit down hard on the temptation. "I don't want a job as a payoff from someone my mother is sleeping with."

"Why not? And you'd better make up your mind fast, because Vincent isn't getting any younger. His heart isn't what it used to be."

"I trust the rest of his equipment is in working condition?"

"It's just fine, dear."

He snorted in disgust. "What in hell do you want from me, Mother?"

"I want you to accept the job Vincent is offering you. He owes me, and this is a good way to collect. It will be good for you too. I know you, Nicholas. Better than you know yourself. I know what you need." That soft, seductive voice coming out of the near darkness was hard to resist.

Nick walked over to the window. He could see the long sloping yard through a crack in the drapes.

"Do it for me, Nicholas," she begged.

If I had a mistress who sounded like that, I'd be down on my knees begging her to let me do anything she wanted.

Nick yanked the drapes open. Sunlight crashed into the bedroom.

"Jesus!" his mother said, flinching from the light. "Why did you do that?"

"I didn't want to get confused." Nick turned and looked at her. She was still a beautiful woman, but her birth certificate was written in the skin around her eyes.

She had redecorated the bedroom again, but the end result was still oppressively feminine. The thick fur throw on the huge canopy bed, flung back as she rose, revealed pale green satin sheets beneath it. The French settee and side chairs by the windows had been reupholstered in a green-dominated brocade to complement the new floral wallpaper. Only the antique Savonnerie rug remained the same. "Amazing how that old rug manages to hold up to the traffic through here," he said.

"Really, Nicholas, you're acting like a child."

That, he thought, was probably true. "I have to go, Mother."

"Wait." She stood up gracefully and went over to her spindly-legged Carlton desk.

"For what?"

"This." She opened one of the top drawers and took out a check.

When she handed it to him, Nick read the sum. It was the exact amount he needed to bring his rent up to date and pay his back car payments. "How did you know?"

"Frederick did a little checking for me."

The little louse! He was probably afraid Nick would hit *him* up for the money. "You can give Freddie a message for me, Mother."

"Yes?"

"This." Nick ripped the check into pieces and let them flutter to the rug.

The maid met Nick at the bottom of the stairs. She was dabbing at her eyes with a handkerchief as she showed him to the door.

He stopped at the door and lifted her chin so that he could look her in the face. "What's wrong?"

She began to bawl in earnest, and Nick found himself with his arms around her. "Come on," he said softly. "It can't be that bad. Tell me about it."

"James Dean. He's dead," she managed between sobs. "It was . . . in the paper."

"What?"

"Yesterday. He was in an automobile accident." She bawled harder.

"Nicholas," his mother called from the top of the stairs. "What are you doing to my maid?"

The girl jumped away from him and disappeared into the back of the house.

"Nothing, Mother. I was just leaving."

Nick let himself out. When he climbed into the Corvette, he sat there without turning the key. James Dean had been the new teen idol. An imitation Brando. His second movie was opening in three weeks. Maybe he would have made something of himself, maybe not. Now no one would ever know. In a year's time, no one would remember his name.

It just went to show you, Nick thought as he turned the key. Do what you want. You might not get a second chance.

Nick barreled through the East Gate, absurdly relieved to be leaving his mother and the wooded hills of Bel Air behind him. When he turned onto Sunset, he reached for the radio knob and then let his hand fall. He didn't want to hear about James Dean dying young. What had he been, twenty-three? Twenty-four? He had seen Dean once or twice, skimming through the Hollywood Boulevard traffic in his silver Porsche.

Going nowhere fast. Just like me.

Nick eased off the accelerator, settling down to a more sedate speed. He drove toward the ocean, stopping finally at the Spanish-style gas station at the end of Sunset Boulevard to fill the Corvette's tank. Then he turned north and opened up the little roadster, enjoying the feel of the wind in his hair. Eventually he turned right, through the deep slash of Topanga Canyon, up into the hills.

It was after sunset before Nick turned back toward the coast, full dark before he came hurtling out onto the coastal highway on two wheels and began to eat up the distance between the nose of the Corvette and the tall taillights of the Chrysler New Yorker ahead of him.

Something—white, flapping, like a huge-winged crane—blossomed beside the Chrysler, billowed out, and then flew free.

Nick didn't have time to be terrified. He wrenched the wheel, trying to avoid the thing, but it came over the Corvette's windshield. Cloth wrapped itself around his face, blinding him, as the roadster skidded.

He clawed the fabric off with one hand as he fought the wheel with the other. It seemed like an eternity before he brought the Corvette to a shuddering halt in the middle of the highway. Somewhere off to the right he heard the crash of waves in the night. The Chrysler's taillights had vanished in the darkness ahead.

Nick grabbed the white thing from the floorboard where it had fallen and found it was a woman's blouse.

Idiots!

He wondered if they had any idea how close they'd come

to killing him. Had they given a moment's thought to the car behind them? Probably not. He wadded up the blouse and tossed it onto the highway. Then he gunned the Corvette angrily, sending it hurtling forward into the night.

He had gone less than a mile and over a low hill when his headlights picked up the big Chrysler stopped alongside the highway. Nick slowed. With a distinct feeling of joy, he realized he would have a chance to use his fists.

A nude woman walked out of the darkness beside the Chrysler and into the beam of his headlights.

Nick slammed on the brakes, screeching to a stop in the middle of the southbound lane. Leaving the Corvette's motor running, he opened the door and stared at her, transfixed.

A middle-aged man, old enough to be her father, climbed out of the Chrysler. He yelled at the nude woman and shook his fist at her.

The woman turned toward the man. The wind off the ocean whipped her long blond hair around her face. Her reply was too soft to carry all the way to Nick.

Nick couldn't believe his eyes. It wasn't just that the woman was naked, she was absolutely the most beautiful creature he had ever seen in his life: tall, with full breasts, and a waist so small he could probably span it with his hands. She couldn't possibly be real.

But she was.

Incredibly, she turned her back on the middle-aged man and walked toward Nick's headlights. As she approached, he saw she was not a woman but a girl.

A natural blonde.

Nick finally remembered to breathe. He got out of the car abruptly, slamming the door behind him.

The girl halted. She raised her hand, shielding her eyes from the glare of his headlights, and peered his way.

"Get back in this car, Juliet!" the man shouted.

"Juliet." Nick said it slowly, drawing it out, savoring it. "If you're Juliet, then I want to be Romeo."

The girl threw back her head and laughed, oblivious to her own nakedness.

Nick walked in front of the Corvette's headlights and held out a hand to her. She took a step in his direction.

"Juliet!" the man roared. He started toward them with murder in his face.

Another car topped the rise and caught Juliet in its headlights. The astonished driver swerved. His Buick plowed into the Chrysler.

The middle-aged man ran over to the crash and jerked the dazed driver from the Buick, slamming him against his own ruined hood.

The nude girl kept her eyes fastened on Nick.

"Juliet, I adore you," Nick told her, meaning it as he had never before meant anything in his life. "Will you come home with me?"

"I have nothing to wear," she protested.

Nick realized it was the first time he had ever heard a woman say that in utter truthfulness. He grabbed a windbreaker from the Corvette and draped it around her shoulders. "I'll get you anything you want tomorrow. Just come home with me tonight." He held out his hand again.

This time she took it.

Nick helped her into the Corvette and then raced around to the driver's side. He burned out, leaving rubber all over the road.

"Juliet, come back!" her companion called after them in utter despair.

She laughed, as the wind whipped her hair, and zipped up the windbreaker.

Nick wondered if she was a call girl. "Was that your date?"

She gave him a disdainful look, as though she could read his mind. "You think I date men that old?"

Nick blinked and concentrated on his driving. No more
questions, he decided. That might destroy the beauty and
mystery of tonight. A gorgeous naked girl had dropped into
his lap out of nowhere. He would be a fool to question his
good fortune.

The girl stretched lazily, like a tawny cat. The movement
raised the windbreaker above her shapely thighs.

This is the happiest moment of my life, Nick thought.

He couldn't believe he owed it all to Freddie.

"This is where you live?" Juliet asked.

"This is it." Nick pulled into the driveway. He hoped
Cindy had already gone to bed. He suspected sneaking a
totally naked girl into his apartment might constitute a foul
under Cindy's rules.

He parked the Corvette in the garage and then hustled Juliet through the archway. The overgrown courtyard
looked like a jungle in the darkness. "The gardener's been
away for a while," Nick said as he led her around the
worst of it.

When he turned on the light in his apartment, Juliet
took a good long look around before she turned her attention to him. Her eyes were the deepest, most vivid blue
he had ever seen in his life. "What's your name?"

"Nick. Nicholas. Nicholas Picard." He wiped his sweaty
palms against his trousers. Her skin was so fair he could
almost see through it.

"Nicholas. I like that." She switched off the light.

He heard the windbreaker's zipper.

She moved forward until her full breasts were pressing
against his chest. "Kiss me, Nicholas Picard," she whispered
in the darkness. "I like to be kissed."

When Nick awoke, he still couldn't believe it, not even
with Juliet still lying beside him in all her nude splendor.

Last night all he could do was bury himself in her, over and over.

Now, looking at her, he was already hard again.

He moved against her, drifting his lips across hers in the lightest of kisses.

"Mmmm," she said sleepily. Her eyes flew open. He had forgotten how startlingly blue they were. "You do such nice things, Nicholas."

"Let's do them again," he murmured against her neck, and then let his lips move along the slope of her collarbone.

She arched up toward him, her nipples already hard and upright.

Someone pounded on the door.

"Damn!" Nick said.

Juliet giggled.

"Nick? Are you in there?" Cindy called.

"Just a minute," he yelled back. "Stay here," he told Juliet. "Don't move. I'll be right back."

"Nick?" Cindy called again.

"Coming!" He struggled to get his jeans over his erection. Juliet giggled louder.

When he finally got them on and closed the bedroom door firmly behind him, Cindy was already waiting in the living room.

"Do we have company, Nick?"

"What's up?"

She lifted an eyebrow.

"Come on, Cindy. What do you want?"

"I've got a message from George. You have to pay every penny of the rent in full—in cash—by five P.M., or George and some of his buddies will come over and move you out."

Nick glanced over his shoulder at the bedroom door. "Can't you get him to give me some more time?"

"I've given you all the time you deserve, you rat, plus refrigerator and *other* privileges."

"Cindy, please."

She relented a little. "I really can't do anything, Nick. I would if I could. You know how George is when he's made up his mind."

Nick shrugged. "Well, thanks for trying."

"You're a nice guy, Nick. I hate to see you leave." Cindy paused at the door. "I thought you said your car was already in the shop."

"What?"

"So I wondered why the wrecker—"

"Oh, no! Oh, shit!"

He pushed past her and raced across the courtyard.

The tow truck was just pulling down the driveway with the Corvette. As it turned into the street, the bank man sitting beside the driver shot Nick a single-fingered salute.

He trudged back through the courtyard. Cindy was leaning against the door frame, watching him. She cocked an eyebrow. "So?"

"So I'll get the money. I'll have it here by five."

"In cash," she reminded him.

Over her shoulder Nick saw the bedroom door open. Juliet emerged, wearing one of his T-shirts and nothing else. She smiled at him.

"I said in cash, Nick. Nick?"

"Sure, sure. In cash."

Cindy straightened and turned, following Nick's glance. "*Excuse* me," she said with heavy sarcasm. "I didn't know I was interrupting anything." She stalked away, across the overgrown courtyard.

Nick didn't notice she was gone until she slammed the door of her apartment. He crossed the room to Juliet and took both her hands, pulling her toward him, so that he could kiss her.

"Mmm," he said after a long time. "Will you wait here for me?"

"Like this?"

"Exactly like that."

"What about my clothes?"

"I'll get you clothes. I'll get you anything you need. Just wait for me."

Juliet smiled up at him. "I'll wait."

He groaned and pulled her to him. "I'll be back as soon as I can."

Cindy opened her door just wide enough to see him standing there and then tried to slam it in his face.

"I need your car for a while, Cindy. To get the money."

"No way. George will kill me if you skip in my car owing him rent."

"I'm not going to skip. I'm going to get the money."

"Where?"

"From my mother."

"I'll bet. If your mother had any money, you wouldn't be living in this dump."

He hesitated. "My mother is Helen Chandler."

He hated the change that came over Cindy's face. "Really, Nick? Your mother is really Helen Chandler? Oh, my God! I loved her pictures when I was a kid. She's wonderful. You're so lucky to— Wait a minute," she said suspiciously. "This isn't some kind of trick, is it? How do I know she's your mother?"

He flipped open his wallet and showed her the photo hidden behind his driver's license: himself, a gawky adolescent with a sullen face beneath his blond crew cut, standing beside glamorous platinum-haired Helen Chandler. The family resemblance was unmistakable.

"Why in the world didn't you ask her for money sooner?" Cindy looked up at him, puzzled.

Nick felt his face tighten. "Can I borrow your car or not?"

"Sure. Here." She dropped the keys in his palm.

The little maid looked like a cadaver herself today. Her eyes were huge dark smudges, swollen with weeping. She led Nick through the house and outside, where Helen Chandler was having lunch in her lush flower garden.

"Tell Vincent Tandy I'll take the job," Nick said without preamble.

"After the way you treated me yesterday, how do you know I'm still willing to help you?"

He smiled at her. "After I've come crawling on my hands and knees to beg you, how could you resist?"

She looked at him shrewdly. "Why now, Nick?"

"My car was repossessed this morning, and I'll be kicked out of my apartment by five P.M. if I don't come up with the cash for my back rent. Isn't that reason enough?"

"It wasn't yesterday."

"Just write the check."

She did, but a frown line marred the perfection of her face. When she handed it back, she said, "Bring the girl over for dinner Friday night."

Nick couldn't hide his surprise. "How did you know there was a girl?"

"Isn't there always?"

Nick looked down at the check. He handed it back to his mother. "This isn't enough."

Helen Chandler laughed.

She kept laughing as she tore it up and wrote a new check for twice the amount of the first one. Her laughter followed him down the stairs.

He slammed the front door behind him. But the laughter stayed with him.

THREE

1956

HELEN CHANDLER RAISED HER WINEGLASS IN A jaunty salute to her daughter-in-law. "Has Nicholas told you anything about his father?" she asked Juliet.

"Mother," Nicholas warned.

Helen smiled, dismissing him. The immense formal dining room was designed to hold forty dinner guests comfortably. Tonight it held two—uncomfortably. Helen shifted irritably in her Queen Anne chair. Nicholas did not pretend that, were it not for her maternal urging, he and Juliet would not have fallen into the habit of dining with her once or twice a month. "Think of it as interest on the loan I made you," Helen told him after the wedding. "It's all the interest I'll ask, if you cooperate." He had come, as she knew he would. A new bride was an expensive proposition, and his studio salary wasn't large enough yet for him to repay his mother. Of course, that hadn't meant Nicholas would be civil about it.

Helen caught sight of her profile reflected in the glass of the Hepplewhite breakfront beside her and lifted her chin slightly to minimize the hint of slack beneath her jaw. She wondered if the girl realized that the eighteenth-century English antiques in this house were worth a small fortune. How crass Nicholas would think it, if the subject were brought up. Helen smiled faintly to herself. Perhaps she could maneuver the girl into doing so in front of him.

Nicholas continued to stare at Juliet with big cow eyes. After four months of marriage, he still appeared totally besotted by the girl. Helen tapped a perfect fingernail against her wineglass and listened to the crystal sing. Only a verbal bombshell would tear Nicholas's attention away from his new bride. She dropped one now. "Nicholas's father was the most beautiful man I ever saw. I knew I had to have a child by him."

"Really, Mother," Nicholas said. "That's drivel."

"And you can see I was right," Helen went on, speaking directly to Juliet. "We made a very handsome child together, Etienne Picard and I."

Juliet turned to look at Nicholas, as though verifying what Helen said.

Something about the girl reminded Helen of herself, as she had been a long time ago, a memory she did not care for. The blatant sexuality, so much a part of Juliet at first, was toned down now. That only made the girl's allure stronger—if such a thing were possible.

"Tell me about Nick's father," Juliet said now. "What was he like?"

Nicholas groaned loudly. "Not tonight," he said, as he stood up. "Tonight we have to eat and run. I have an early meeting at the studio in the morning."

Helen stood up too. "You and I will have lunch one day," she told Juliet. "I have some pictures of Nicholas as a child I'm sure you'll want to see." She smiled as Nicholas looked positively ashen at the thought of his wife and his mother comparing notes.

When they left, Helen stood at the window watching Nicholas's car, a new Chrysler New Yorker St. Regis, go down the drive. After the wedding she insisted he trade his little roadster in. He resisted, as he always did when she tried to be helpful. She prevailed finally, by pointing out that the tiny Corvette was no car for a married man. Helen chuckled dryly to herself. It was her offer to take up the payments on the New Yorker after the trade was made that convinced him.

She had waited years to find a lever that would work with Nicholas. She never dreamed the lever would come in the form of a bride.

Helen continued to stand there long after the New Yorker disappeared from sight, absorbed in the puzzle of Juliet Brittany. She had never expected Nicholas to marry the girl. If so, she might have handled things differently. As it was, she had been incautious, too delighted at finally having a way to move Nicholas into a worthwhile job with the studio. She had given the lever itself no thought at all.

A mistake.

She had made the same kind of mistake with Nicholas's father. Etienne Picard had possessed brains as well as masculine beauty. He had outwitted her at every turn. Her brief affair with him had been designed to frighten the studio with the thought that their top female star might decamp to France. Or, if not that, then kill herself flying with the daring young pilot. She never intended to fall in love with him.

God, she had loved flying with Etienne! Nothing before or since had made her feel so alive. Probably, she thought dryly, because she had never before or since been quite so close to the edge of death. Etienne was a man who saw no virtue in living without risks.

No one would believe it now, but there had been no one before Etienne. When they finally consummated their love on a heap of scratchy blankets in the hangar where he kept his plane, he was astounded to learn that at twenty-three she was still a virgin—and even more astounded when he learned how ardent a lover his virgin turned out to be.

She had been as besotted with him as Nicholas was with Juliet. She couldn't stop thinking about him, touching him, holding him.

Helen was surprised by the dampness on her cheeks. It had been years since she cried for Etienne. She had thought all the tears were gone by now.

She turned away from the window abruptly and went to pour herself some brandy, taking it with her into the dark living room. She sat down on the couch without turning on a light.

Only chance had kept her from dying with Etienne. She had been scheduled to go up with him that day. Instead she had been involved in a screaming row with her agent and the head of the studio. She had announced that she and Etienne were getting married, and those plans met with their disapproval. He was a nobody, a nothing, not even an American. They wouldn't allow her to wreck her career like this, they told her.

Then she played her trump card: she was pregnant.

They tried desperately to talk her into an abortion, telling her that a child now would wreck her career. But she would gladly give up her career for Etienne's child.

When she finally drove out to the airport in triumph, she could see a thin wisp of smoke curling into the air. It didn't mean anything to her at first. It was only after she had gone to Etienne's hangar and found it empty that she began to worry. When she reached the office, the first face she saw told her what had happened.

Even after that, her agent and the studio head tried to talk her out of having the child, but she was determined. It was all she had left.

Documents were forged to prove that she and Etienne had been married in Mexico. Her photograph beside Etienne's grave appeared in every newspaper across the country, as did the news, a few weeks later, that she carried his child.

Instead of ruining her career, the tragedy enhanced it. She found herself more in demand than ever.

Helen gave thanks for that, because she could lose herself in her work. As she submerged herself in each new role, she forgot what she had lost for hours at a time. The only thing left to remind her was the child, who looked more like his father each day.

It was years before she could look at Nicholas and not see Etienne's face: long lonely years, while she darted off to one part of the world or another, making ridiculous films that brought in great amounts of money at the box office. When the day finally came that she could look into Nicholas's eyes and see her son and not his father, she tried to draw him close.

It was too late. Nicholas had grown apart from her. He resented her leaving him alone for most of his childhood. He had no way of understanding what pain the sight of his solemn little face had brought her. Nor how much the distance between them hurt her now.

Helen finished the brandy but she continued to sit in the dark living room, with only her thoughts for company.

"If you don't want me to talk to your mother, why do you insist we have dinner with her?" Juliet asked.

Nicholas shrugged. He was driving too fast, but it didn't seem to bother Juliet. Neither did the fact that his mother was Helen Chandler. At first he had been thrilled to find Juliet exhibited none of the star-struck awe that infuriated him so much in his friends and acquaintances. Now it only irritated him. A lot of things irritated him now. Like driving this wallowing cow of a car, for example.

Nick wondered how life had suddenly become so complicated. He had enjoyed being a bum. A creative bum, but a bum nonetheless. The last thing he intended was to find himself a married man with responsibilities at the tender age of twenty-two, yet that was exactly what had happened.

He glanced across at Juliet, still every bit as lovely as the day she walked into his headlights. Then she had seemed too beautiful and mysterious to be real. Nick had been terrified she would vanish like quicksilver, too terrified to let any time go by before he asked her to marry him.

Perhaps the complications started with their wedding. Somehow he had not expected Juliet to have a family—ridiculous but true. Of course she had a family: a father, an aunt, a sullen sister, and two silent, staring brothers. He wondered why she bothered to invite them. None of them seemed to be on particularly good terms with her.

And the father—halfway through the ceremony Nick suddenly realized why Juliet's father looked so familiar. He was the man with Juliet the night Nick found her nude in the middle of the highway.

Nick never had the nerve to ask Juliet exactly what happened that night. He had been afraid that learning what it was would destroy the mystery.

Perhaps it was the loss of mystery that bothered him now. Whatever he had expected from his relationship with Juliet, it was not something so prosaic. Especially not dinners where his mother and his wife discussed his baby pictures.

Then there was the studio. It was irrational to blame Juliet for his having gone to work at the studio. He made the choice without even telling her he was considering it or how he really felt about it. But it was a sacrifice he had made for her, so he could keep her in his life. Somehow, irrational or not, that made the blame hers.

His stint with Vincent Tandy had lasted three short weeks. Then the famed director had a heart attack.

When Freddie offered him a job to replace the one with Vincent Tandy, Nick felt he had no alternative but to accept. So here he was, reporting to Freddie and remembering bitterly those three unbelievable weeks he spent watching one of the country's best directors at work. Now, instead of watching film history being made, he spent his days with budgets and contracts. And always, in the background, Freddie—smirking.

Life was depressing enough without these damned dinners with his mother. The only surprise tonight had been when she mentioned his father's name. He couldn't remember Etienne Picard's name being spoken aloud in his presence half a dozen times in his whole life. His father was a cipher, dead before Nick himself was born.

In my own way, I'm just as bad as Freddie, Nick thought, only Freddie purposely expunged the memory of his old man. Nick never had a chance to create one; his mother had seen to that. She must have really hated the bastard for knocking her up, because she had allowed no mention of him in her presence. Etienne Picard's shadowy figure had no place in Nick's life while he was growing up. As a model of manhood, he'd had no one—until Morgan Gaynor.

And yet, as that same model of manhood, Morgan was so confusing. Why had he put up with a faithless wife for so many years?

Nick could remember so well, one October morning when he was twelve, seeing the disappointment etched into Morgan's face as he read a telegram just received from Helen to say she was staying another month in Rome.

He'd seen the same disappointment on Morgan's face when Morgan learned he was staying on at the studio after Vincent Tandy's death. "This drone's job isn't meant for you, Nicholas," he had said.

But Nick had turned down Morgan's offer of an assistant director's position. Even if he had a wife to support, Nick refused to follow Freddie's example of hanging on Morgan's coattail. He would make it on his own, or not at all.

Juliet reached over and stroked his leg. A few weeks ago that might have roused him. Tonight he was so depressed he barely noticed.

When they reached the apartment, Nick went straight into the bedroom. He didn't ask Juliet if she was coming to bed.

Juliet plopped down on the sofa and looked around the living room. Then she sighed. She worked so hard, cooking and cleaning, scrubbing and polishing, trying to make this place the perfect home for Nick. No matter how hard she worked, she was always disappointed when they went to Nick's mother's house. Every time she felt just the least bit pleased with what she had done, she would remember Helen Chandler's gorgeous mansion and get depressed.

But then, if it weren't for Helen they would still be living in Nick's ratty Hollywood apartment. Juliet's mother-in-law had gone out of her way to help the newlyweds find a better place and help them set up their household.

Not that Nick seemed a bit grateful for his mother's help. In fact, he was so surly whenever the three of them were together Juliet felt as though she were balancing on a tightrope. One misstep and that was it.

Juliet sighed again. She couldn't understand what had gone wrong between her and Nick, but something had. At first, he had been so enthralled with her he couldn't leave her alone; now he barely noticed she was alive. She couldn't understand why he changed.

That made her think of her father, and every time Juliet thought of Oliver Brittany, the anger rose within her.

She got up and went in the kitchen. The counter was already spotless. Juliet put an apron over the nice dress she had worn to her mother-in-law's, took out the cleansing powder, and began to scrub it again. She didn't want to think about her father, but she couldn't shut the image of him out of her mind. Tears welled up in her eyes when she remembered how he used to look at her as though she was the most important person in the world. She had felt so special.

What a joke!

She moved out of the house the day it happened. He gave her a big check, but the money didn't last as long as it should have, not after she bought clothes for herself and furniture for her new apartment. It really wasn't her fault, she reasoned, as she dampened the dishcloth again and attacked a new portion of the counter. No one ever taught her how to manage money. So she spent lavishly, on anything she wanted, and tried to find work as an actress.

It was harder than she thought it would be. You had to have an agent, and nowhere in all the training her father paid for had anyone mentioned getting an agent.

After a while, she wasn't even sure she still wanted to be an actress. Sometimes she thought all she really wanted was to feel special again, like she had before everything changed. But she kept on trying to be an actress, because that was what Oliver Brittany had encouraged her to be, and she had finally realized she had no dreams of her own.

Juliet continued to go to her lessons. Her father must have paid for them, because no one, from the acting coach to the singing instructor, asked her for money. The rent was a different matter. She was two months behind when she realized that she would have to ask her father for the money directly. The manager wouldn't even discuss calling him up for her.

He picked her up outside her apartment the same evening she phoned him. When she climbed into the car, Juliet couldn't believe how he had changed. The trim elegant man she remembered was gone. The clothes were as expensive and well tailored as ever, but the man inside them looked like a seedy imposter. His handsome face had grown gaunt, and his eyes were hungry looking.

He had made reservations for dinner at a little restaurant up the coast. Every time she looked up from her meal, his hungry eyes were fastened on her face. To her amazement, she found she wasn't frightened of him, not even when they got back in the car and he lunged for her.

She shoved him away. "Don't do that again, Oliver, or you'll be sorry."

He pulled away and stared through the windshield at the lights of the restaurant. After a moment he turned the key.

He drove for a long time in silence. "Why did you call me, Juliet?" he asked at last, his voice hoarse.

"I told you why. I need money for my apartment. That's all I want from you."

"That's not all I want from you." He turned to stare at her for so long the car swerved from one side of the road to the other.

"Papa!" she screamed.

His gaze returned to the road. "You and I belong together, Juliet. I'll give you the money for your apartment, but you have to do . . . certain things for me." He spoke softly, in the same voice he once used to read her bedtime stories.

She turned to the window, refusing to answer. The voice went on and on, telling her the disgusting things they would do together.

Finally, Juliet could stand it no longer. She reached for the top button of her blouse. Slowly, she undid the buttons. When the blouse was open to the waist, she yanked it free of her skirt and then rolled down the window.

The sea wind whipping through the car caught Oliver Brittany's attention. He yelled at her.

Juliet paid no attention to him. She shrugged out of the blouse and held it out the window, letting it billow in the wind. Then she released it.

As it fluttered away into the night, she reached behind her for the fastening of her bra. "What are you doing?" Oliver Brittany yelled at her.

She took off her bra and released it out the window. It followed her blouse into the darkness of the highway behind them. She reached for the button on her skirt.

Oliver Brittany slammed on the brakes. "Have you gone out of your mind? What's wrong with you?"

Juliet unzipped her skirt and raised up enough to slip it off. She tossed it out the window also.

Oliver grabbed her arm. She shook herself free and threw open the car door. When she stepped out of the car, she turned and told him, "I will walk down this highway stark naked before I will let you touch me again." Quickly, she peeled off the rest of her clothes and tossed them to the ground. . . .

"Juliet!"

Juliet stirred, surprised. That was Nicholas, calling her from the bedroom. She straightened up slowly, unsure how long she had been leaning against the countertop. The scouring power had caked on her hand. How astonished Nick had been when she came walking into his headlights out of the darkness. But he never asked her a word about that night. She wondered what he had thought.

Still, she was glad he hadn't questioned her. She found it difficult to explain, even to herself, the emotional tornado that had seized her that night.

Almost as hard to explain as the impulse that made her invite her family to the wedding. Perhaps she hadn't believed they would actually come. When they did, Juliet had been terrified Nicholas would guess from their manner what lay between her and her father.

Juliet rinsed her hands and turned off the light. In the bedroom, she found Nick had called out in a dream. He was sound asleep now, his face boyish but handsome in repose.

She remembered what Helen Chandler said tonight about wanting to have the baby of Nick's father. Juliet studied Nick's sleeping face. For the first time, she thought seriously about having his child. She was alone in the world now. Her mother was gone, her father worse than gone, and the wedding had shown her she no longer had a family. All she had was Nick.

Tonight she felt she didn't have him either.

If someone had asked her why she married Nicholas Picard, she would have said it was because of the way he looked at her the night they met. As if she were the most important and desirable thing on this earth.

She gazed down at her sleeping husband. If she had Nick's baby would he look at her that way again?

Helen Chandler was surprised when Juliet called to ask when she could come to lunch, even though it had been Helen herself who suggested it. She had been so sure that the girl wouldn't respond to the vague invitation. Then Helen realized what must be behind it.

Nick had said the girl was planning to be an actress. No doubt she married Nick thinking he would help her career. Now she had realized it was Nick's mother who could help her, not Nick.

Helen prepared herself carefully for the meeting. She could still outshine any young girl in the beauty department. And she wanted to look especially lovely when she watched Juliet's face crumple in disappointment. Because she did not intend to lift a finger to help her daughter-in-law achieve her dreams.

When Juliet arrived, she made no mention of an acting career at all. She seemed perfectly content to look through the photographs of Nick as a child. She asked Helen a million questions about pregnancy and what it had been like with Nick in the early months.

When she left after lunch, Helen realized the subject of acting had never come up. It was later that night when she finally understood Juliet had been investigating what it would be like to have a child, Nick's child.

Helen frowned.

If only she had guessed sooner, she would have been much more graphic in her tales of the delivery room. The last thing she wanted was to become a grandmother. Or to see Etienne's face repeated one more time.

Nick had just left for work when Juliet answered a knock at the door and found Helen Chandler's chauffeur standing there in his stiff uniform. "A package for you, Mrs. Picard," he said.

It was rectangular, heavy, wrapped in expensive paper. She barely closed the door before she ripped into it. Inside she found a thick blue book, *Pregnancy and Birth*, by a doctor with an unpronounceable name. Juliet knelt to pick up the note that fluttered to the floor. *I wanted you to be well informed, my dear,* it read in her mother-in-law's distinctive handwriting. *I'll be happy to schedule an appointment for you with my own personal physician whenever you like. Helen.*

Excited as a child, Juliet carried the book over to the sofa and opened it.

The first full-color plate made her gasp.

The second made her stomach lurch.

Juliet slammed the book shut and went out into the kitchen to make a fresh pot of coffee. When it was brewed, she took a cup back into the living room and opened the book to page one.

It took her four days to read Helen's gift from cover to cover. At night she hid it beneath the sofa, so Nick wouldn't see it. Each morning, as soon as he left, she attacked it again. By the time she finally finished, Juliet knew every disastrous and painful complication of pregnancy a woman could suffer.

The photographs of the malformed, monstrous results of those complications were etched indelibly into her brain.

"You've been awfully quiet." Nick pushed back from the dinner table. "What have you been doing with yourself this week?"

"Reading," Juliet said as she carried the last of the dishes to the sink. "Would you take out the trash?"

He hefted the pail and glanced down, surprised. "What's in this? It weighs a ton."

"Garbage!"

Nick frowned. Her voice sounded strange. "Are you okay?" He took a good look at her. He hadn't been doing that lately. "You look kind of . . . pale. You're not . . ." His stomach did a wild flip-flop. "You're not . . . pregnant, are you?"

"Don't be stupid." She turned on the faucet.

Nick lifted the garbage pail again, his momentary panic already fading. Maybe having a kid was supposed to be the reason for getting married, but the last thing he needed now was another responsibility. Freddie was enjoying the hell out of having him under his thumb at long last.

"I'm going to bed when I finish the dishes," Juliet said.

"Fine," Nick mumbled, his mind on Freddie. "I may go back to the studio. I've got some things to wrap up before—"

A dish shattered in the sink.

Juliet stalked by him.

"Did you cut yourself?"

"No!" She slammed the bedroom door shut behind her.

Nick fought back an impulse to fling the garbage pail at the door. Marriage! It sure wasn't what he expected.

He took a deep breath and began to pick the broken

pieces of china out of the sink. When he opened the pail to drop them in, he caught sight of a big blue rectangle in the bottom of it, a book of some kind.

Curious, he reached for it. When he tried to tug it free of the pail, he dislodged a mixture of egg shells and coffee grounds over both the book and his hands.

"Garbage is right," he muttered. Whatever it was, it was ruined now.

He rinsed his hands in the sink. When he took the garbage pail out, he took his suit coat with him. No more fireworks tonight, he promised himself. Working over at the studio beat marital bliss anytime.

This time, when dinner was over, Helen watched Nicholas and Juliet leave with a smile on her face. When she sent the book, she feared it was already too late. But watching Juliet tonight, she knew that the girl was not yet pregnant.

Now she wouldn't be. Helen had chosen the book with care.

So there, Etienne. You won't torment me anymore.

FOUR

1957

NICK STARED AT THE SCREEN, FASCINATED. WHEN Juliet reached for his hand in the darkness, he took hers for a moment. Then he pulled away, leaning forward to concentrate all his attention on the screen again.

Juliet slumped back in her seat angrily. This was the fifth foreign film Nick had dragged her to in as many weeks. He worked such long hours at the studio that they hardly ever went anywhere. When they did, it was to one of these art theaters. She was so sick of subtitles she could throw up! She should have stayed home and finished reading *Peyton Place*. The steamy exposé of small-town life had been on the best-seller lists for weeks. Reading it last night, Juliet could see why. At least the lurid scenes helped her forget for a while that Nick was working late at the studio again. The only times they were together in the evenings were for the occasional dinner at his mother's or when he dragged her to one of these stupid foreign films.

What she would really have liked tonight was to see *Anastasia* again. Juliet had known better than to mention that desire to Nick. She had already talked him into seeing it three times. It had been so wonderful last month when Ingrid Bergman won the Academy Award for Best Actress for her role as the czar's long-lost daughter. Now there, thought Juliet, was a woman who did what she wanted and damn the consequences. The weeks before and after the Academy Awards the papers had rehashed Bergman's story: how she left Hollywood in 1949 because of her affair with Roberto Rossellini and how she conceived the Italian director's child out of wedlock. Nobody ever dreamed she would return to American films in triumph.

Of course, not everybody was happy Ingrid Bergman had won, including Nick. At first, he had refused to watch the Academy Award ceremonies on television with her, boycotting the program because neither *Marty* nor *On the Waterfront* had been nominated for Best Picture. But he was working at home that night and couldn't resist coming in to watch the writing awards. When Deborah Kerr announced the winner for Best Motion-Picture Story, Robert Rich for *The Brave One*, he hooted in delight. "There'll be some red faces over that," he explained to Juliet. "Robert Rich is a pseudonym for Dalton Trumbo."

"So?"

He's one of the Hollywood Ten, one of the leftist writers who was railroaded into jail in 1950."

"For what?"

"Contempt of Congress. When they were called before the House Un-American Activities Committee. You know. Communists in Hollywood. All that mess." He turned his attention back to the screen. "This serves the Academy right. They blocked Michael Wilson from a nomination for Best Adapted Screenplay for *Friendly Persuasion* because he plead the Fifth before HUAC. Declared the poor guy ineligible. They never expected this." He watched Hermione Gingold accept the Best Adapted Screenplay Award for S. J. Perelman. "Maybe Carroll Baker will win Best Actress."

Juliet had turned to glare at him. To compare Carroll

Baker sucking her thumb in *Baby Doll* to Ingrid Bergman as the Princess Anastasia was ridiculous. She bit her finger- nails until Ernest Borgnine announced Ingrid Bergman's victory.

Nick snorted in disgust. "Sentimentalism," he had de- clared.

Now Juliet shifted in her seat, wondering if this movie would ever end.

When the house lights finally came up, Nick stretched and turned to her happily. "That was great!"

"I don't know why you think so. It was dark and depress- ing. It gave me claustrophobia. Just like this theater."

"You don't understand," he said, as they started up the aisle. "The Europeans know how to make a real movie. The kind of movie I'd like to make. It would never work here, though."

Juliet's interest was caught. Nick became so excited when he talked about making movies himself that it made her thrill a little inside too. "Why wouldn't it work here? Just don't turn on as many lights on the set."

He didn't even smile. "It's not the ambiance, it's the actresses. American women don't have the honesty to admit their own sexuality."

She stopped dead in the aisle. The man behind them bumped into Nick. "What's that supposed to mean?" she asked, as the other moviegoers pushed past them.

"Come on," he said, grabbing her hand. "There's a bar down the block. I need a drink."

As soon as they left the theater, he dropped her hand. He walked fast, his shoulders hunched, hands jammed in his jeans pockets. Juliet was forced almost to a run to keep up with him, which didn't improve her mood. His remark about European women still burned. She didn't know where he got his information. The actresses in the foreign films engaged in little more sex than their American counterparts. As far as Juliet could see, the main difference between Nick's European actresses and American stars was that the Europeans looked as though they never washed their hair. But try telling Nick that.

The bar was full, with a mostly male crowd. Juliet noticed that she got several quick looks as Nick shoved his way through the crowd until he found an empty table jammed up against the wall. But no one was interested in a married woman, she thought bitterly. Not even the married woman's husband.

Nick waited impatiently for service, drumming his fingers on the table. After a moment, he said, "I'll get us something at the bar." She could barely hear him over the music from the jukebox.

She was still fuming over what he had said about European women. She could admit her own sexuality as well as any foreign bitch! Across the room, Nick leaned against the bar, still drumming his fingers. That dreamy look on his face told her he was thinking about the woman sprawled across the dark screen of the art theater. He never looked at her that way anymore.

Something clunked on the table. Startled, Juliet glanced down. Her wedding ring lay in a damp spot left by the barmaid's rag. Without realizing it she had slipped the plain gold circle off her finger. She looked at it as though she had never seen it before.

Nick's shadow fell across the table. Juliet scooped up the wedding ring and held it in the palm of her hand as he set two beers on the table. She dropped the ring in her purse.

"Little girl's room," she said as she stood up.

Nick nodded absently.

She pushed her way through the crowd toward the rest rooms. When she glanced back, Nick was staring off into space with a moody look on his face.

The ladies' room was little more than a glorified closet. Juliet locked the door, pulled her sweater off over her head, and looked at herself in the tiny cracked mirror above the lavatory. She wore a "sweater girl" bra with stiff, padded cups that transformed her breasts into two spiked cones. "Definitely not European," she muttered as she stripped it off and tossed it in the trash. Now when she slipped her sweater back on her breasts were full and sensuous beneath it. She stood on tiptoes and turned this way and that to study the effect in the mirror.

She reached under her skirt and pulled off the light girdle and half slip, tossing them in the trash with the bra. After a moment's hesitation, she took off her panties too. Someone tried the door and then knocked loudly. "Just a minute!" Juliet yelled.

She closed the lid of the toilet seat and climbed up on it, so she could see her lower half in the mirror. The prim straight skirt had turned lascivious, hugging her curves.

Pleased, she scrambled down and opened her purse, pawing through the jumble for her lipstick. Carefully, she repainted her lips, making them ever so slightly fuller.

Too bright, Mama's voice muttered harshly in her brain. *Too thick. You want to look like a whore?*

Juliet stared at her reflection angrily. "I want to look like whatever Nick wants," she told the voice in her brain.

Mama had no reply.

Juliet's hair had been fastened into a ponytail. She freed it and leaned over to shake her head. When she straightened, it fell full and loose around her shoulders.

Someone tried the doorknob again.

"All right!" she yelled. With one last look in the mirror, she unlocked the door.

Nick stared moodily down at his beer. He felt so frustrated these days. Two years ago he was bitching to Freddie about the dinosaurs, and here he was working in the boneyard. Today, Freddie told him he was up for a promotion. For two cents, he'd tell Freddie where to shove his promotion, and then he'd go back to screenwriting.

Wishful thinking. No way could he cut loose. He was a married man with a wife to support. So far no kids, though. A mixed blessing. On the one hand a kid would be another leg iron, but on the other it might be nice to be a father. Funny, he had been so hot to marry Juliet. Now he never thought of her except in terms of bondage.

He drained the last of his beer and then glanced at his watch, irritated. What the hell was taking her so long? By the time she got back to the table and dawdled over her beer like she usually did, it would be almost eleven. He had hoped to get back to the studio tonight.

He reached across the table for Juliet's beer. A buzz at the far end of the room made him pause. The mostly male bar was reacting to something he couldn't see. Then the men parted, and he understood.

The blonde who made her way to the jukebox with a sensual swaying of her rear was not to be believed. The way her ass jiggled, you could almost believe she wasn't wearing anything under that skirt.

Don't drool, he told himself and looked guiltily toward the rest rooms. Juliet wasn't in sight yet, so he gave himself over to the guilty pleasure of watching the blonde lean over the jukebox and study the selection, the skirt clinging so tightly across her rear that the outline of her cheeks stood out in bold relief.

A brief flurry of fists erupted near the bar as two drunks vied for the privilege of asking her to dance. Without waiting to see how the fistfight ended, another man, medium height, solidly built, moved forward until he stood directly behind the blonde. Then he too leaned over the jukebox. His pelvis plastered to that glorious ass, the man whispered something in her ear.

Nick shifted to ease the painful tightness in his jeans. He knew every man in the place had the same problem. The hell with Juliet. He wasn't moving from this spot until he had seen the end of the little drama.

Gogi Grant's voice died away. In the silence, it seemed as if the whole bar were holding its collective breath. The next record clicked into place. "Moonglow and Theme from 'Picnic'" swelled out of the jukebox. Perfect, Nick thought, as the blonde straightened and turned to face the man behind her.

Shock hit Nick like a body blow. The blonde with the glorious ass was his wife.

Paralyzed, he watched as Juliet tossed her hair over her shoulders, making her breasts jiggle beneath the sweater. Laughing, she moved into the man's arms and began to dance with him, pressing herself against him.

Before Nick realized what he was doing, he was on his feet, elbowing his way through the crowd. He shook off the hands that tried to hold him back and ignored the curses that followed him. His whole being was focused on the dancing couple.

He lunged the last few feet in a blind rage, grabbed Juliet by the arm, and swung her away from her partner to face him. "What do you think you're doing?"

Juliet looked at him blankly.

"Do you know this guy?" her partner asked her.

She shook her head.

"She's my wife."

Her eyes widened in amazement.

"Is that true?" the guy asked her.

"Do I look married?" she asked, snuggling up to him.

He gathered her into his arms and let his hands curve possessively around her rear, as he glared at Nick. "Get lost, asshole."

Nick grabbed the man's arm and yanked him away from Juliet. It occurred to him, almost as an afterthought, that the guy outweighed him by twenty pounds, but the killing rage was still driving him. He punched the other man in the nose so hard he felt his knuckles give.

Juliet's partner dropped to the floor, blood spurting from between the fingers covering his face.

Clutching his injured hand, Nick turned to Juliet. She was gazing at him with round wide eyes as though she had never seen him before in her life.

"Come here!" he shouted.

She backed up a step, her breasts bobbing loosely beneath the sweater.

Someone grabbed Nick by the arm. He ducked the punch and hit his assailant in the solar plexus.

Someone else broke a chair across Nick's shoulders and he dropped to the floor.

He curled up, protecting his stomach from a kick aimed his way. Through the shifting trousered legs, he caught sight of Juliet's painted toenails in her bare little sandals.

He scrambled to his feet. A riot was in progress. The bartender had disappeared. Probably calling the cops.

Juliet had retreated to the jukebox. Nick plunged through the fighting bodies and grabbed her arm. This time she came without resistance. He led her out the back way, past the rest rooms, and into the alley. When he stopped, she pressed herself against him. He looked down into her laughing eyes.

"Is this sexy enough for you?" she said, her voice low and throaty.

Something stirred in his blood. He pulled her to him and kissed her deeply, while he reached beneath her sweater. When he touched her bare breast, he groaned.

Sirens sounded in the distance.

She pulled free. "Come on," she said as she took his

hand. They ran down the alley and back to their car.

He climbed in on the passenger side and unzipped his pants. She crawled in after him and settled down on top of him. For the first time, Nick appreciated the roominess of the New Yorker. He strained upward into her, knowing he would burst if he could not find release soon. She moaned as she kissed him hungrily, her hair tumbling wildly around their faces. Nick thrust upward a dozen times, violently, rocking the car. When he exploded into her, she cried out, echoing his own passion.

He clung to her as he drifted slowly back to awareness. No one was near their car in the shadow-dappled parking lot. He realized he had not diminished within her. If anything he was larger, filling her softness completely.

Their bodies were jammed together so tightly he could barely catch his breath. Her skirt had ridden up around her waist, leaving her thighs bare and white in the moonlight. Slowly, he pushed the sweater upward, letting her breasts fall free. She pulled it over her head and tossed in the back. The shifting movements made his penis twitch and grow even larger within the moistness of her. He nibbled at her breasts. She cried out with pleasure as he took the hard little buds of her nipples in his lips.

She pressed down on him and again he thrust upward. This time he took longer. He was more deliberate, using his mouth on her breasts and his hand on the tiny knob of her clitoris. He brought her to a shuddering, screaming climax before he allowed himself to reach his own release.

Only then did he become aware of approaching footsteps. The feature had ended. Another group of moviegoers was pouring into the parking lot.

Somehow, while Juliet dissolved in giggles, he managed to slide from beneath her and out of the car. Zipping his ruined trousers, he hurried around the back and climbed in on the other side.

As he slid beneath the wheel, Juliet leaned over to kiss him. "Weren't we better than the movie?" she whispered, her breath hot against his neck, her bare breasts pressing against his arm.

"Wait until I get you home," Nick promised.

Juliet woke long after Nick had gone to work. She took a long leisurely shower, turning this way and that to view the love marks he left on her body. She had never spent a night like that before. She could hardly wait for him to get home.

When he finally did arrive, late, he was no longer the ardent lover of the night before. "Rough day," he said as he wolfed down the casserole she had made. "I've got to go back to the studio tonight."

"Oh, Nick!"

"Sorry, babe."

And then he was gone.

Juliet sat down across the kitchen table from her husband. "Nick? Aren't you going to eat?"

"Hmm?" Nick continued to stare off into space.

He had no idea where he was, Juliet realized. If that night in the bar had been the high point of their marriage, this was the low. Bleak despair washed over her. She jumped up and went to stand at the kitchen sink, staring out the tiny window, trying to hold back the tears. She hated this newest pattern of their life.

Nick was never home. He worked all day at the studio, came in only for a brief evening meal, and then rushed off again. When she complained, he claimed he had more work to catch up on at the studio. He never returned until after midnight, and then he was so drained he went right to sleep. Even when he *was* home for more than a few hours, he was so distracted he didn't know she was around. His mind was always somewhere else, even when they were in bed together.

Alone so much of the time, with nothing to do, Juliet had cleaned the apartment to hospital standards. Every surface sparkled. When she tired of that, she thought of getting a job. But what could she do? Her old dream of being an actress seemed remote now. Married women didn't do that sort of thing. Married women had babies. But every time she thought about having Nick's baby, the awful, sickening photographs from the book Nick's mother gave her came flooding back into her mind.

She even found herself thinking of her father again. If only he hadn't done that terrible thing to her, they could go back to what they had been. Sometimes Juliet believed anything would be preferable to the way she lived now.

She turned around. Nick still stared into space, his dinner untouched before him. "Nick?"

"Mmm?"

"I'm tired of this, Nick."

"Tired of what?" he said absently.

"Really!" Juliet shouted, pushing herself away from the sink. "You're impossible!"

She stormed into the bedroom and locked the door behind her. She plopped down on the bed to wait for Nick to tap on the door and ask if she was all right.

It took a few minutes for her to realize he wasn't coming after her. Maybe he didn't care that she was angry. More likely, he didn't realize she had left the kitchen. The clear cold blast of anger brought by that realization calmed her down enough to think rationally. It was time she found out exactly what was going on. Past time.

That decision made, Juliet strode over to the bedroom window, opened it, and climbed through. She hesitated for a moment before she let herself drop down to the front lawn. The living room window also looked out on the lawn.

If Nick had finished his dinner and was watching. . . .

Who was she kidding? Nick noticed nothing. That was the problem. Juliet scooted off the windowsill and dropped down on the grass. A few minutes later she had talked her portly, middle-aged landlord into loaning her his car. When Nick left the house, she followed him.

Her husband drove straight back to the studio. Juliet parked outside the gates and stared after him in amazement. Whatever she had expected, it wasn't that.

Surely Nick had a mistress? That was the only possible explanation. She had thought he was spending all these late night "work sessions" at his girlfriend's house or apartment. Now she reconsidered. He had to be seeing an actress or someone else he had met at the studio. They must be meeting in his office at night.

For a moment she considered trying to talk the guard into letting her inside the gate. She could feel her anger rise at the thought of catching Nick in the act in his office. Especially since *she* had never seen his office.

She could picture herself looking in the window (*surely* it would have a window) and seeing Nick and some woman. And then she would—

What?

Set fire to it! Let him and his girlfriend come running out of his office naked, while flames danced all around them.

Juliet realized she was gripping the steering wheel so hard her knuckles had gone white. She took a deep breath and leaned back against the seat, letting her blood cool. Then, after a few minutes, she drove home and returned the landlord's car.

When Nick got home, just past midnight, she pretended she was already asleep. In a few minutes, she was.

After that, Juliet quit trying. Sometimes she didn't get dressed all day long. She slept late in the mornings, so that Nick had to fix his own breakfast. When she finally woke, she lay around the house in her robe, her hair uncombed, listening to the radio or watching the television set that had been a wedding present from Nick's mother. The shiny surfaces of the apartment no longer sparkled.

She cooked Nick's supper in the same robe and then, when he made his nightly return to the studio, she went back to the television set again and was always asleep, or appeared to be, when he got home at night.

When the phone rang, she ignored it. Recently, getting up to walk the few steps from the couch to the phone had become too difficult.

The phone kept ringing. And ringing. Reluctantly, Juliet heaved herself up.

"Juliet? Don't cook anything for tonight. I'm taking you out to dinner."

"Nick? Is that you?"

"Who else would it be? See you later."

"Nick? Nick, wait." But the line was already dead.

Juliet hung up the phone. What was happening? Nick hadn't sounded like himself. He had sounded happy. What did that mean? Was the affair still going on? He wasn't going to ask her for a divorce, was he? She knew from the women's magazines that was how it was done. Your husband took you to a public place, like a restaurant, so you wouldn't scream or attack him.

She smiled grimly. If that was what Nick had in mind, he might be surprised.

Then more urgent concerns struck her. What to wear? What to do about her hair? It had been so long since she had been anywhere, she had almost forgotten how to put on makeup. She reached for the phone to call the beauty shop.

. . .

Juliet retucked a strand of her hair nervously as they waited for their table. The upswept hairdo she asked for had indeed made her look more sophisticated. Now she worried that it would come tumbling down in the middle of dinner. And the full-skirted black dress she chose from her closet, hoping it would show off her waist: she had forgotten the neckline was so low. Each breath she took exposed the creamy tops of her breasts. When they entered the restaurant, heads turned to watch her pass, but the only eyes Juliet cared about were Nick's.

If she had thought Nick was different over the phone, he was frighteningly so in person. His eyes were on her, all right. But there was no appreciation of her beauty in that single-minded scrutiny. He stared at her as though he were sitting in judgment on her. At the same time he kept fiddling with the lock on the briefcase he had lugged along with them to dinner. She wondered if it held divorce papers.

As soon as they were seated, Nick ordered a magnum of champagne. By the time their steaks arrived, Juliet was half drunk and totally hysterical. She could do no more than pick at her food while she waited for whatever dreadful thing was about to happen.

When the waiter cleared away the last of their dishes and poured them each another glass of champagne, Nick reached down to open the briefcase. Juliet's hand shook so badly, champagne splashed onto the table. She barely noticed. Her eyes were on the folder Nick took out of his briefcase.

"Here it is," he said, waving the folder. "I'll bet you wondered what I've been up to."

"I—I did . . . wonder."

He grinned at her. "Well, now you know."

Juliet took a hefty gulp of champagne. "Now I know," she agreed. "What do I know, Nick?"

He slid the folder across the table. "Now you know you're married to the best goddamned screenwriter in Hollywood."

She picked it up, her right hand making damp champagne fingerprints on the cover.

"Go ahead," Nick urged when she hesitated.

Juliet took a deep breath and opened it. The first page was mostly blank. "*Juliet*," she read aloud. "*A screenplay by Nicholas Picard.*" She looked at him across the table. He was grinning broadly. "That's my name." She felt a little foolish, as though there were some joke on the page she couldn't quite catch.

"It's your name, all right. Because the screenplay is about you."

Juliet's wine-drenched mind struggled with the thought. "You can't write a screenplay about your wife, can you?"

"I just did."

When they got back to the apartment, Nick brewed a pot of coffee while Juliet changed clothes. She had been tipsy in the restaurant. Nick hadn't realized that until they started to leave. Now she was sober and eager to read the script.

Nick poured himself a cup of coffee and sat across from her in the living room, watching her read, until the strain grew too great. Every time she frowned, or smiled, or sighed, or giggled, he wanted to leap across the room and see which line elicited the response. Finally, unable to stand it any longer, he ran a tub of hot water and soaked in the steam-filled bathroom, waiting for her to finish.

The idea for the script had come to him the night after the fight in the bar. That little episode had given him the urge to write the script he only dreamed of before. It was high time America grew up sexually. The Europeans were leading the way, but no one in the United States had taken up the torch.

Until now.

The woman—girl, really—in the script was Juliet, with all her dramatic qualities unchanged: a teasing, pouting nymph, not quite a woman, not still a girl. Aware of her sexuality, of the power she wielded over men, and yet not completely aware of the devastation she could cause if she wished.

Nick grinned ruefully. Like that night at the bar. It had taken weeks for his knuckles to heal.

It was a simple story, really. The film Juliet cannot control her impulses. A free spirit, her flirting, seductive ways first attract and then entrap a married lover. Finally, when her lover decides to go back to his wife, she attempts suicide.

When he finds out, her lover rushes back to her side. He stays with her while she recovers, wrecking his marriage and losing his business in the process. But when she has completely recovered, she is no longer interested in him. An emotional butterfly, she has moved on to another man. Her married lover is left with nothing.

Nick lay back in the tub, going over the script scene by scene in his head. The rising tingle of excitement he felt told him he had a winner.

The water had cooled by the time the door opened. Juliet stepped inside the bathroom and closed the door behind her. Nick looked up. "Well?"

Silently, she took off her clothes. When she was completely naked, she climbed into the tub with him, laying her body on top of his. "It's wonderful," she murmured in his ear. "I love it."

"You should." Nick turned over, capturing her beneath him with a splash. "You're going to be the star."

"I hardly ever see you anymore," Helen Chandler complained, in the curious, cracked voice she had acquired since her stroke two months before.

"We've been busy, Mother," Nick replied. Under the table, he squeezed Juliet's hand.

"Trying to make a movie star out of your wife?"

The scornful edge in Helen's voice didn't disturb Juliet. She was too happy. Her marriage had become everything she dreamed it could be. Nick spent every minute he could steal away from the studio with her, rehearsing her in his screenplay. She was the center of his universe once more. "We're trying to make a success out of Nick's screenplay," she told her mother-in-law calmly. "Surely you want that too?"

Helen didn't reply. Instead, she shoved back from the table and reached for her cane. It eluded her fingers, crashing to the floor.

Before Nick could rise, Juliet stood and hurried around the table to pick up the cane. When she placed it back in Helen's hand, she met her mother-in-law's cold glance. For a moment, she thought Helen would lash out at her with the ebony rod.

Then Helen looked away, across the table, at Nick. "Of course I want the best for Nick, Juliet. Don't be silly."

She accepted the offer of Juliet's arm to rise, her fingers biting into the soft flesh of her daughter-in-law's upper arm. Juliet refused to flinch away from Helen's painful grip. She could understand at least a part of Helen's anger. The premature stroke Nick's mother had suffered had left one side of her face frozen in a perpetual grimace and made the ebony cane a necessity. It wasn't easy for a woman whose beauty had been as legendary as Helen Chandler's to look in the mirror and see a twisted-faced crone staring back.

"Let's have our coffee outside this evening," Helen said. With agonizing slowness, she led the way to the French doors and onto the terrace. When they had settled down in the loungers and Helen's maid had brought the coffee, Helen continued as though there had been no interruption.

"Tell me, Nick, how do you plan to proceed? Rehearsing Juliet in her role over and over may be good for her performance, but do you actually intend to make a film?"

Nick sighed in irritation. "Why else would I go to so much trouble?"

Juliet allowed herself a sly smile. "It *is* fun rehearsing, though, Helen. Nick is a wonderful writer."

"And he's put in a preponderance of love scenes, no doubt." When there was no reply, Helen set her coffee cup down with a crash. "It's plain to see you're indulging yourself, Nick. I ask you again: Do you intend to make a real film, or is this exercise merely an excuse to make love to your wife?"

Nick leaned over and squeezed Juliet's hand. "I don't need an excuse to make love to Juliet."

"Have you talked to Morgan and Frederick about your project?"

"No, and I don't intend to. It will be an independent production."

Helen snorted. "Just as I thought. You're *not* serious."

"Really, Mother, I don't think you've kept up with what's happening in the business. Box office attendance dropped to thirty million a week in May. And TV reruns haven't brought it back up over the summer. All the major studios are in trouble. All of them."

Helen lifted her chin haughtily. "Morgan didn't say anything about—"

"Morgan knows as well as I do what's happening. None of the majors can face the increased production costs. RKO ceased production. Republic's out of the movie business; they're putting everything into TV. Warner Brothers has put fifteen million dollars into filmed TV. The studio system is breaking up. Morgan admits it himself."

"Frederick told me you have some rather strange ideas. I see he was right."

"Freddie sees himself as Morgan's successor. You know that. What he doesn't see is that there won't be anything left when he gets there."

"I talked to Morgan just last week. He told me he'll be moving to New York at the end of the year. Frederick will be executive vice-president in charge of worldwide productions."

"Oh, great! The little bastard will be insufferable."

"Nick! Your language!"

"You know it's the truth, Mother."

"Frederick said you could be on the board of directors too, if you would put the best interests of the studio above your own self-indulgent impulses."

"You mean put Freddie's best interests above my own. No way. I'm going to start my own independent production company."

"Where do you intend to get your financing? Not from me, I assure you."

"I'll get financing. Don't worry." But Nick himself was worried. Juliet could tell from the frown on his face.

For the first time since he had brought the script to her, so was she. Things had been wonderful between them the past few weeks. She couldn't bear the thought of returning to the sham of a married life they'd had before they began working together on the script.

"Do you still have my camera equipment?" Nick asked Helen abruptly.

"Why, yes, I believe so. It's probably in your room." She studied her son curiously. "Why?"

"I've decided a few photographs of my star won't hurt the project one bit."

"I didn't know you were a camera nut," Juliet said on the way home.

"Nut? I'm a genius with a camera, and don't you forget it."

He was, too. As well as a nuisance. He followed her everywhere with his blasted camera clicking away. "Turn this way, Juliet. Look to your right. Bend over and let your hair fall free. Stand up. Look at me. Don't look at me." And on and on until she wanted to scream.

But when he brought back the first batch of prints and spread them across the coffee table, she had to admit the results were impressive. Especially the photographs he took of her nude. Juliet had known those were for Nick alone, so she had put everything she could into them. The results made her suck in her breath. "Is that really me?"

Nick nodded. "If anything, you photograph better than you look."

Juliet frowned, unsure whether that was a compliment.

Nick wasn't paying attention to her. He studied the photographs spread across the table. "I can't wait to see what you look like on film," he muttered, as much to himself as to her. "All we need now is backing and we're on our way." He scooped up the photos. "That's going to be the rough part."

"Why don't you talk to Morgan Gaynor like your mother suggested?"

"You sound like Freddie." Nick's voice turned cold. "I don't need Morgan's help. Or Mother's."

"I understand," Juliet told him.

She didn't understand at all.

The tempo of their lives changed again. Instead of being with her every free moment, rehearsing the script, now Nick was never home. Instead, he was chasing financing.

Juliet grew so desperate she even called Helen. That did no good at all.

"He's made it more than plain he doesn't want me to interfere," Helen Chandler told her daughter-in-law.

"If you don't, he's going to drop the project!" Juliet protested.

"Then you won't be a movie star after all, will you, my dear," Helen said in her stroke-shattered voice. "What a pity."

Nick finally straggled home after seven. He bolted his dinner before Juliet could take her place across the table. "Got to get back to the studio," he said as he stood up. "I'll be late. Don't wait up."

"What about our rehearsing?"

Nick sighed. "It's a lost cause, babe. No one wants to put money in the project. Without the money we can't do a thing."

"We could rehearse anyway. Just for us. I like it, Nick. I like it when you make love to me the way it says in the script."

"Grow up," he said roughly. "It's over."

When he left, she cried until she couldn't cry anymore. It was the money, she thought as she sobbed. Only the money. Otherwise they could be together, just as they had these last few weeks. Nick would be totally involved with her again.

If only they had the money.

"Papa?"

Oliver Brittany nearly dropped the phone. "Juliet?" he asked hoarsely. "Is that you, Juliet?"

"It's me, Papa." Juliet sounded as though she had been crying.

"Is something wrong, Juliet?"

"I need you, Papa. I need your help." Desperation made her voice crack.

"Just a minute, Juliet." He got up and closed the door to his office. "Now tell Papa what's wrong," he said when he came back to the phone. He leaned back, holding the phone with one hand, massaging himself through his trousers with the other, as Juliet poured out the story of Nick's script.

"You always wanted me to be an actress, Papa. This is my chance, don't you see? I'll make you proud of me. All we need is the money. Your bank can take care of that, can't it?"

Oliver Brittany rubbed harder. "Of course it can, Juliet."

Now she did sob. "Oh, Papa, thank you. Thank you so much."

He was only moments away from release. "There will be a price, Juliet."

Silence on the other end of the phone.

Oliver felt himself begin to shrivel. "Juliet? Are you there?"

"I'm here, Papa."

"You know what the price is, don't you?"

"Please, Papa. Don't make me—"

"I can promise you this film will be made, Juliet. Only you have to pay the price."

"It's wrong, Papa," she whispered into the phone. "You know it is."

"You have to pay the price."

"You're killing me, Papa!"

He hesitated. She wouldn't commit suicide, would she? No, not Juliet. "You'll have everything you want. Just say yes."

The whisper was so faint he almost missed it. "All right, Papa."

"When?" he asked ruthlessly, afraid she might change her mind.

"Tomorrow morning. Nick will be at work."

When he hung up, he reached for the tissues in his desk drawer. Unzipping his pants, he brought himself quickly, efficiently, to a climax.

•   •   •

Oliver Brittany parked half a block down from his daughter's apartment house. He was too early and he knew it. His son-in-law never left for the studio before eight-thirty.

Nicholas Picard would have been astounded to learn just how much his father-in-law knew about him and his personal habits. Especially since they had not met or spoken since the day of his wedding, over a year ago.

That was one of the great joys of having money, Oliver reflected. Money could buy anything: the name of Nick's after-shave, the brand of underpants Juliet wore, the terms of Nick's mother's will.

The only thing it had not bought Oliver until now was the names of the other women with whom Nick was sleeping. Oliver finally realized there were no other women in his son-in-law's life. Odd, considering how many women he had had before he met Juliet.

But understandable. There was no one quite like Juliet. The thought of her made Oliver's penis throb. He took the newspaper from the seat beside him and opened it up against the steering wheel, so he could watch the front of the apartment house over the pages, yet shield his face in case his son-in-law looked this way as he left. Oliver knew he shouldn't have arrived so early, but he had been unable to stay away. He couldn't believe Juliet had finally called him. It was a dream come true. He stroked himself as he watched the neighborhood children passing on their way to school.

Nick emerged from the apartment house at eight-thirty-five and climbed into the New Yorker (purchased by Helen Chandler; Oliver had a copy of the sales receipt in his file). By eight-forty he was well on his way to the studio, never having glanced in the direction of Oliver's car.

Oliver got out of the car, shielding his erection with the newspaper, and strode up the sidewalk. Down the way, a gardener weeded a flower bed. Beside an open doorway in the next building, two women gossiped. No one paid Oliver Brittany any particular attention. When he knocked on the door, Juliet answered at once.

He had expected her to be pale, nervous, reluctant. Instead, she smiled at him with so much warmth in those intensely blue eyes he was speechless.

"Papa," she said. "Come in."

The sight of her made him tremble with desire. She paused only long enough to lock the door, and then she led the way into the living room. He could have sworn she wasn't wearing a bra.

"Sit here, Papa," she said, motioning to the sofa.

He remained standing. "Don't you think we would be more comfortable in the bedroom?"

"Not yet, Papa. I have a little performance for you to watch first. You know that Nick has been rehearsing me in his screenplay?"

Oliver frowned. "I'm not sure this is part of our agreement. I think we should—"

"Just watch, Papa. You'll see that I've become quite an actress after all." Juliet gave him a slow, sultry smile, and he sat down. "That's better," she told him.

She walked over to the dining table. He watched the movement of her hips as she bent slightly and picked up one of the chairs. "Are you watching closely, Papa?"

"I'm watching, Juliet." He realized he was still holding the newspaper in front of him. He reached beneath it and began to stroke himself.

"Good," Juliet said, satisfied. She lifted the chair up and smashed it against the window, shattering the glass.

"Juliet! What are you doing?" He was standing. The newspaper dropped from his hands and slid across the floor, scattering its sections everywhere.

She swung the chair again with such force that it went

sailing through the window and out onto the sidewalk.

"Have you gone mad?"

She turned around to face him. "Mad?" She took three quick steps and grabbed the front of his shirt with both of her hands, yanking it so hard in different directions that the buttons popped off and went flying.

"Mad?" she said again, her voice curiously calm. "You think this is mad?" She ripped her blouse open and left it hanging. Her bare breasts bounced from beneath the ruined material. She yanked her skirt open and let it fall on the carpet.

Oliver Brittany shook his head. He couldn't understand what was happening.

Juliet began to scream.

"Juliet? Please! Don't do this!"

She couldn't possibly hear him. He couldn't hear his own voice over her shrieks.

Someone pounded on the door.

Juliet continued to scream. If anything, she grew louder.

Voices rose in answer outside. After a minute, someone applied a shoulder to the door. He could see the wood give each time the body on the other side slammed against it.

Juliet continued to scream.

Oliver put his hands over his ears just as the door crashed open. A man lunged halfway across the room from the force of his entry. Two more followed him in. The first man paused for a second, taking in the screaming, hysterical woman, and then wheeled to face Oliver.

"Please," Oliver muttered, his hands still covering his ears.

The first man strode forward and punched him right in the belly. Oliver doubled over, groaning, and the two other men bore him to the ground. Unable to catch his breath, he lay there unresisting, while they pummeled him with their fists.

Juliet continued to scream.

Someone yelled that the police were on the way.

Oliver's one clear thought through the pain of the pounding fists was that he hoped the police arrived before Juliet's husband.

Half a block away Nick could see the flashing lights of the two squad cars parked in front of his apartment house. He pulled in behind them and scrambled out of the car. Police calls crackled through the air. He pushed his way through the crowd on the sidewalk. One of the chairs that belonged in his living room now lay on its side in the grass. The window above it was shattered. Nick could feel his jaw clench. If Juliet was hurt . . .

A policeman stood at the door to the apartment house. Nick identified himself to the officer. Somewhere inside the building, he could hear a woman crying hysterically.

Juliet. His stomach knotted.

"The husband," the policeman at the door announced to someone just inside.

Nick pushed past him, into his own living room.

Juliet, covered only by a man's jacket, was sobbing uncontrollably. The policeman who had been trying to restrain her released her arms when he saw Nick.

Nick caught her around the waist and lowered her to the sofa. She leaned against him, her tears wet against his cheek, her words incoherent.

"What happened?" Nick demanded of the policemen.

"We don't know, sir," one of the officers replied. "Your wife hasn't been able to tell us a thing yet. The neighbors said they heard a crash." He pointed to the shattered window. "Must have been that. The door was locked from the inside. The neighbors broke in. Found your wife like this. And him. They worked him over pretty good."

Nick turned to follow the policeman's gaze.

Against the far wall, a burly policeman on either side of him grasping his arms, stood Oliver Brittany.

Oliver saw Nick's face change as the ugly truth registered on his son-in-law. At that moment he was grateful for the policemen holding him. Otherwise he would have been a dead man.

"Know him?" the policeman asked Nick.

"My wife's father." Nick spit the words out like a curse.

"Nicholas?" Oliver said. He must have made an infinitesimal move forward, because the patrolmen's grip tightened painfully on his arms. "It's not what it—"

"Shut up, you bastard!" Nick snapped at him. He turned back to Juliet, cradling her face in his hands. Gradually her sobs subsided. "That's it," he told her softly. "That's my girl. Now tell us what happened."

"Oh, Nick," she said, burying her face against his neck. "It was so awful."

Oliver could feel all eyes in the room turn his way. The coldest, hardest glance was that of his son-in-law.

"Come on, babe," Nick urged. "Tell us."

"He . . . he said if I did what he wanted—" The sobs started again.

All the blood left Oliver's face. He felt as though he were going to faint.

"It was awful!" Juliet gasped finally. "He tried to rape me. If . . . if Papa hadn't come I don't know what would have happened."

Oliver's breath caught in his throat.

"What are you saying?" Nick asked Juliet.

"He tore off my clothes," she managed to say through her tears, "but Papa stopped him. Papa pulled him off of me and hit him. He . . . he jumped out there." She pointed to the shattered window.

Oliver managed to meet Nick's gaze. His son-in-law's eyes

measured him coldly and then turned back to his wife.

"Juliet, are you sure that's what happened? You can tell us the truth. You don't have to be afraid." He glanced back at Oliver. "No one can hurt you now."

"If Papa hadn't been here—"

Nick's voice had grown so cool and calm that he might have been a prosecuting attorney. "Why was he here, Juliet? I thought you two didn't get along."

Juliet began to cry again. "Oh, Nick! It was going to be a surprise for you. I was going to tell you tonight."

"Tell me what?" Nick's voice hadn't warmed a single degree, Oliver realized.

"That we can make the movie after all. Papa is going to arrange the financing. It's all settled." For the first time, Juliet looked straight at him. "Isn't it, Papa?"

Oliver could see the muscles bunched beneath Nick's shirt, could almost feel those hard fists slamming into his body. He lifted his head and forced a smile. "All settled," he told his son-in-law.

What other choice did he have?

Nick stared down at the parking lot, the only view from his one tiny window. His cubicle at the studio had never seemed more like a prison than today. The thought that he might be leaving all this behind made the busywork Freddie passed on to him unbearable.

Sloan Whitney's car pulled into a parking slot. Nick fought the impulse to open the window and yell down at the lawyer. He could wait the few minutes it would take Whit to reach his office, Nick told himself. No use letting the whole studio know what was going on. Especially if it was bad news.

Sloan Whitney worked in the studio's legal department. His photographic memory had made him a legend at the studio. He and Nick had met through Nick's work on contracts and become firm, fast friends. It had been Whit's support that gave Nick the idea of trying to produce his screenplay himself. The heavy-framed glasses Whit habitually wore gave him a bookish look, but the coal-black eyes behind them were sharp and alert. Nick knew the lenses were plain glass, solely for effect. Just as he knew that while Whit and he were the same age, the lawyer had used the premature thinning of his hair to claim five additional years, an age bonus that helped earn him an equally premature promotion. Nick himself was still cursed with the boyish looks that made the studio rank and file look at him skeptically. Not that the studio men bothered him, but all the money men he had approached about financing his screenplay had reacted the same way.

"Is this the office of the famous independent producer Nicholas Picard?"

Nick turned. Whit stood in the open doorway, a broad grin on his face.

"You got it?" Nick sat down suddenly, almost afraid to believe it was true.

"Move this crap out of the way," the lawyer said as he set his briefcase on Nick's desk. Nick shoved a pile of contracts aside as Whit unsnapped the case, and then the lawyer paused in mid-motion. "Did I detect a note of disbelief in your voice? When has the marvelous Whit ever been known to fail?"

"Come on, Whit," Nick begged. "Show me his signature."

Whit took a contract out of the case and opened it to the last page. "We are on our way to the big time."

Nick leaned forward. Oliver Brittany's signature was on the last line. "What did he strike out?"

Whit grinned more broadly. "Nothing."

"Nothing at all?"

"Zip. *Nada.* His pen didn't touch the paper anywhere but here." Whit tapped the signature. "What have you been holding out on me, Nick? I could have brought you his left testicle, gift-wrapped."

Nick looked up at his friend and said, "I have no idea what made him do this."

Whit's grin faded. "Too bad," he said as he took a seat on the other side of the desk. "If you knew what made him offer the financing, you could probably squeeze a little more out of him."

"For Christ's sake!" Nick exploded. "Isn't this enough?"

"Nowhere close. But that's okay, because once it's known that Brittany's backing you, we'll be able to pick up the rest. And Morgan Gaynor will give us a juicy distribution deal, you can bet on it."

"I don't want Morgan's help," Nick said sullenly.

"You don't want him as an enemy, either. If you turn him down for a piece of the action, that's exactly what you might have."

Nick shook his head, but he didn't argue anymore. Whit didn't understand the complex relationship between Nick and Morgan Gaynor. For that matter, neither did Nick. But Whit was right about one thing, Nick thought. He owed his ex-stepfather a chance. But not Freddie. No way was Freddie going to buy in. "Are you sure there's no way Brittany can wriggle out of the agreement?"

Sloan grinned. "You're looking at a genius where the law is concerned. His ass is ours." He glanced around the tiny cubicle. "It's time to start looking for office space, my lad. We're on our way."

"We?"

"Just remember, in years to come, when you have this town by the balls, that old Whit was your first and best friend."

"What's your fee for this, Whit?"

"Tonight, the biggest drunk this town has ever seen, paid for by you."

"Come on, Whit. Name a price."

Whit gave him an owlish look. "That's only the first installment. The rest of it is all your legal business from here on out."

"You've got it, but what good will it do you?"

"My lad, I know a rising star when I see one." Whit took off his glasses and slipped them in his pocket. "Now let's go celebrate."

Nick stood up and put on his coat. Whit was right. He was on his way. He could feel it. If only it weren't Oliver Brittany's signature at the bottom of the agreement, Nick thought. Anybody but him. Not that it seemed to bother Juliet.

"Hey! Don't look so grim," Whit told him. "We got what we wanted, remember?"

"Yeah. We got exactly what we wanted." Nick shoved the contract into the top drawer of his desk. "Let's go get drunk."

FIVE

❧

1958

Glamour!

Rehearsing scenes with her husband in her own apartment had been more glamorous than the actuality of a Hollywood movie set, Juliet thought. Today they were shooting outdoors: the set, a terrace outside a restaurant. They should have been through with this scene already, but clouds kept forming and re-forming, blocking out the sun.

At first Nick took advantage of the pauses to rehearse his stars.

Stars!

Juliet couldn't help pouting a little. She was the star, all right. The canvas-backed chair in which she sat had her name stenciled across the back to prove it. But making a movie wasn't at all what she expected. Reality was interminable waits for rehearsal or filming to begin, or sitting without squirming or sneezing while her face was made up and her hair curled, or doing everything over and over and over until she could absolutely *scream* with boredom. She couldn't believe this was the life Papa had wanted for her.

If it weren't for Nick, she would have stormed off the set the first day and never come back. Being directed by her husband was the most curious—and erotic—experience.

109

Naïvely, she had believed making the movie would be like rehearsing with Nick. Instead, it was different, in a way she could never have imagined beforehand. When they were actually rehearsing or filming a scene, the presence of so many other people on the set made it seem as though they were making love in public. Every move, every whisper, every nuance of emotion was magnified by the number of spectators, so that even the simplest action made her feel as though she were on the verge of an orgasm.

Juliet wondered if Nick felt it too.

Unfortunately, those times were few and far between. Most of the time she simply sat and waited for someone to call her name. Like now.

Juliet flipped idly through her copy of the screenplay. Nick said he wrote it for her, and she could indeed see flashes of herself in it. Or see the self she might have been if she were wilder. Since the first time she read Nick's script, she found herself wondering at odd moments what life would be like if she actually was the girl he portrayed on the page. Not that she was sure what the film Juliet really wanted out of life.

For that matter, she wasn't sure what she wanted herself, other than to be loved by Nick.

Juliet's chair creaked as she shifted, her skin warmed by more than the sun. She had never thought about making love to any other man besides Nick. Not until she read Nick's screenplay.

She hadn't thought of tricking Papa until then, either. It had been Nick's screenplay that gave her the idea. Perhaps she hadn't been the real Juliet that morning. Perhaps it was the Juliet of the screenplay who entrapped Papa. She couldn't help smiling when she thought of Papa's expression when she broke the window and began tearing off her clothes. What a scene *that* would make in a movie! Of course she would never dare tell Nick the truth. She had been so worried about whether he would believe what she told him about the intruder.

After the police left, her father stayed a few minutes more to assure Nick that the financing was all set. Finally, Nick had realized that Juliet still stood there, clad only in a neighbor's jacket. Oliver Brittany left then. Nick found Juliet's nightgown and helped her into it. Then he gave her a shot of brandy and put her to bed.

When he went outside, she tiptoed to the window to watch him examining the ground outside the shattered window, looking for an intruder's footprints in the soft dirt of the flower bed. Frantically, Juliet tried to think of how to explain why there were none. Her panic-stricken mind refused to function.

When she heard Nick returning, she scurried back to bed and pulled the covers up, so frightened she was trembling beneath them.

But when Nick came back in the house, he said nothing. He sat down at the dining table with a pen and paper and began to write columns of figures.

With a funny pang in her chest, Juliet realized he wasn't going to question the lack of footprints or anything else. Why should he? He had gotten exactly what he wanted: financing for his film.

Juliet heard the chair beside her creak and felt a hand on her upper thigh. Lazily, she looked over, shielding her eyes from the sun with one hand. "Hello, Lewis."

Lewis Farley, her co-star, smiled back. He kept his hand where it was. He was forty, twice her age. He had been one of the contract players at the studio until his contract was not renewed. Nick said he could get Lewis for peanuts, and he had. Juliet didn't care about that. She was sure Papa would cover any expenses.

He'd better. Or she would threaten to tell Nick the truth about him.

For just a moment she wondered what life would be like if she really could tell Nick about Papa.

"Don't frown at me like that, my sweet," Lewis told her.

"Was I frowning? I was worried about remembering my lines," Juliet improvised.

Lewis leaned forward. "I'm looking forward to the scenes without lines," he murmured.

Her breath caught in her throat. She knew which scenes he was talking about, the sexy ones she had so enjoyed rehearsing with Nick. Around the set, heads turned to stare at the two stars. For a moment Juliet felt as though she and Lewis were on some gigantic platform, acting for the benefit of the stagehands. "I . . . I'm looking forward to them too," she said.

You couldn't say that bastard Lewis didn't work to get into his character, Nick thought as he watched the actions of his two stars from across the set. Look at him, with his hand on Juliet's thigh.

Nick took a deep breath. A few weeks ago that sight would have sent him plunging across the set to knock Lewis's caps right down his throat. Not today, he realized. Today he was wondering, almost clinically, if Lewis's lust would show up on the screen.

Nick glanced up at the clouds. Was the goddamned sun ever going to shine?

Across the set, Lewis leaned closer to Juliet.

Just about time for the good stuff, Nick thought. He had held off purposefully on the sexy scenes because he knew Lewis well. The actor would build up a passion for his leading lady, a passion that would not be tempered by the knowledge she was his director's wife.

Let that passion build, then. Nick was counting on it. Because he wasn't going to let the two of them do more than shake hands until they were absolutely burning with desire for each other.

That would transfer to the screen. He was sure of it.

Sunlight gilded the set for a moment and then vanished again. Nick watched his wife smiling at another man and wondered about his own motives.

He really loved Juliet. Even when married life had started to pale, he had never doubted that. But now, every time he looked at her, it was as though he were seeing two women: the actual Juliet—and the woman she *could* be.

With just a little help, a little urging, Juliet could become the woman he had created in his script, a devastating woman where the male animal was concerned.

As her husband, he wasn't sure he wanted to see that transformation. But the director in him could see Juliet beginning to catch glimpses of that woman herself. Reading the lines of his screenplay, seeing herself for the first time on the screen in the dailies, she was, quite obviously, beginning to understand herself. And Nick was doing everything he could to hasten the process of self-discovery for her.

A selfless thing to do, he mocked himself. The noble husband thinking only of his wife's psyche.

His jaw clenched as he watched Lewis take Juliet's hand in his and saw the sideways glance she shot at the actor from beneath lowered eyelids, a glance calculated to inflame. If he was being honest with himself, Nick had to admit that any self-revelation he helped her experience could only make his film stronger.

So had he become a worse sellout than Freddie? Willing to do anything for the sake of the final product? And if he helped Juliet to discover within herself the woman *he* saw in her, what would it do to their own relationship as husband and wife? Nick watched Lewis Farley flirt with his co-star. What had it already done?

Nick was on the point of rising from his chair, of striding across the set, when the sun broke through the clouds abruptly.

He forgot everything except the scene he was about to film. "Let's go for it, people!" he shouted to the crew.

Each day of filming brought Juliet a heightened awareness of her own body. How could she help it when everyone was so concerned with her physical self: the makeup man, the wardrobe lady, the cinematographer, Lewis, Nick? All of them watched her, watched every move she made.

But the two pairs of eyes that meant the most were Nick's and Lewis's.

She had longed to be the center of Nick's world. She'd had no idea what a glorious experience it would in fact be. She had only thought she was the focus of his attention before, when they played at rehearsing. Now she knew what it was truly like. Each day on the set, it was as though he were making love to her with the camera.

At night, in bed, he would talk to her about the day's work. With the lights out, she could visualize the scenes in the darkness over the bed, seeing her body and Lewis's entwined together in front of the camera.

Nick kept asking what she thought about each scene. Was that what *she*, the real Juliet, would have done in the same situation? If not, how would she have acted?

Nick's questions made her keep examining her own motives, the *why* behind her actions. More than that, she had begun to realize that Lewis was really enthralled with her. He wasn't just acting. He was as infatuated with her as his character in Nick's script was with the film Juliet.

And she loved it! Just the sight of Lewis's hot gaze following her across the set made her feel warm all over. She kept finding excuses to stand next to him, talk to him, walk in front of him, knowing that every movement of her body made him crazy with desire.

Now she really understood the film Juliet. The Juliet in Nick's script longed to control men with sex. The real Juliet had begun to wonder if that was what she wanted too.

Nick watched the evening rushes with a rising sense of excitement that was almost like a sexual rush. By God, he was meant to be a director after all! The riveting performance of the two actors up there on the screen was all due to his direction. He found he could almost ignore the small rustling sound in the darkness that meant Lewis had reached over to take Juliet's hand. After all, that was what he wanted, wasn't it? To have his two stars fall madly in love?

Even if one of them was his wife.

The next day Nick groaned when he saw a small English gentleman, complete with walking stick, making his way across the set. "Take five, everybody," he called. "What's up, Freddie?"

Frederick Yates frowned at Nick's use of the diminutive. "Morgan asked me to stop by and see how you're coming along."

"We're coming along just fine. Disappointed?"

"Really, Nick, try not to be such a bloody juvenile. Morgan is sincerely interested. For that matter, so am I."

"Yeah. So interested you went out of your way to try and kill my distribution deal with Morgan. I can do without *your* interest, Freddie."

"Really, old boy. You have to understand that there is friendship and there is business." Freddie glanced around the set. "Are you too low-budget to furnish coffee to visitors?"

"Sally?" Nick called over his shoulder to the curvaceous brunette script girl. "Bring this freeloader some coffee." He turned back to Freddie. "So to what do we owe the honor of your company?"

"I've been hearing some interesting things about your film. I just thought I'd check them out for myself before I passed them on to Morgan."

"Verifying your gossip before you repeat it? Freddie, you've changed."

Sally handed Freddie a cup of coffee, giving Nick a long slow wink as she turned away. "A heart of gold and a body to match," Nick told Freddie. "Want me to introduce you?"

"Not my type, old boy. I prefer my female companions to be a little higher up the social ladder. You might consider that yourself." Freddie sipped daintily at the coffee and then grimaced. "Don't you think you're going overboard on your sex scenes, Nicholas?"

"What's that supposed to mean?"

"It's your *wife*, old boy."

"What about her?" Nick followed Freddie's gaze.

Across the set, Juliet and Lewis sat close together, studying a shared script that rested on Juliet's lap. Lewis had his arm draped around Juliet's shoulder. Juliet was smiling up into his face.

"Is the husband really the last one to know?" Freddie asked. "Or are you more interested in your movie than your marriage? You should hear what they're saying about you, old chum."

"Do you know what they say about *you*, Freddie? That the stepson also rises."

Freddie blinked but he didn't lose his composure. "Better that than what they're saying about you, Nicholas. I'm flying to New York tomorrow. I'll tell Morgan hello for you."

"Do that."

A few yards away, Freddie wheeled around and retraced his steps. "Here," he said, handing Nick the coffee cup. "With your budget, you can't afford a replacement."

"Lunchtime," Sally reminded him after Freddie's departure.

"Good," he told her. "I never feel like working after a visit from that little bastard."

He didn't feel like eating either. He spent the lunch break watching Juliet and Lewis laughing and talking with each other.

Even after lunch, while they worked on the next scene, he couldn't put Freddie's words out of his mind. The afternoon's film would be a total waste, he thought. The director might be on the set physically; mentally, he was absent.

By the end of the day, Nick knew Freddie was almost right. Juliet and Lewis weren't having an affair, not yet. But they were on the verge of one.

Why should he be surprised by that? He had done everything short of presenting them with the key to a motel room, hadn't he? It was a little late to start acting the outraged husband.

The question that remained was not What did he intend to do about it but Did he intend to do anything at all?

As he watched the rushes that night, Nick realized that the scene he thought was a disaster was, in fact, fine. More than fine. It sizzled on the screen: a humbling experience, since it wasn't due to his directing.

And if it wasn't his directing that was making the sparks fly between his two stars, it had to be their own attraction for each other. If he said or did anything to destroy the passion he had allowed to build, what would that do to the film?

On their way home afterward, Juliet said, "Frederick

seemed to upset you when he visited the set today. What did he want?"

Nick hesitated for a moment. One word from him and it would all be out in the open. One way or another, they would have to settle it.

"Nick?"

"Nothing important," he muttered.

Nick couldn't sleep that night. He kept wondering about his motives. Was he hesitating because Juliet's affair was adding to the movie? Was it because this was the final step in Juliet's becoming the woman she was meant to be? Or was something wrong with his own manhood?

He wanted to make this movie so badly he had shut his eyes to what might have happened between Juliet and her father. Now he wondered if that had cost him a piece of his soul.

He punched his pillow, trying not to think about Morgan Gaynor and his mother. All these years Nick had wondered why his stepfather had gone along with Helen Chandler's infidelities. Had he finally discovered the reason?

Lewis was with her all the time now. "Getting into the character," he told Nick.

Not that Nick asked in the first place, Juliet noticed. She wasn't sure anymore how Nick actually felt about her. These days he left her with the feeling that the woman he captured each day on film was more important to him than his flesh-and-blood wife. That he was more interested in watching her through the camera's eye than he was in being with her in real life. He definitely preferred to talk about the film her, rather than the real Juliet.

It seemed to Juliet that the more she resembled the woman in Nick's script—on and off the screen—the better Nick liked it. But did *she?* Juliet wondered.

She wasn't sure she had a choice. So much of Nick's energy was concentrated on making her the girl in his script that she felt as though a strong current threatened to sweep her into an entirely different life. All she had to do was let it take her.

Lewis caught her outside the makeup trailer. He pressed against her, letting his lips trail softly across hers. "Oh . . . my . . . God," he half moaned, half cried. "Do you realize what you're doing to me? You're driving me crazy."

Juliet found herself kissing him back. Only for a moment. Then she pushed him away. "Someone's coming."

They moved apart guiltily as the script girl passed. Juliet could feel Sally's knowing glance as though it were a physical touch. The whole crew was waiting for her to consummate the affair—even Nick.

Lewis had grown bolder with each passing day. Nick could hardly ignore the fact that his co-stars were on the verge of going to bed together. But he *was* ignoring it.

The past few days, after Frederick Yates's visit to the set, it seemed to Juliet that Nick was throwing his two stars together off camera as well as on: wanting her to become the girl in his screenplay, forcing her to become that girl, ignoring her when she was just plain Juliet, just herself.

Lewis kissed her again.

This time, Juliet moved into his arms without urging.

The third time, long after midnight, Juliet and Lewis made love in Lewis's bed. The first time had been on the rug in front of the white stone fireplace in Lewis's living room. The second time had been in the aquamarine waters of the pool. Now they were in the master bedroom with its glass-walled view of the LA basin.

"If you stay until the sun comes up, you can see Catalina

Island," Lewis murmured against her neck. It was the first
full sentence he had spoken to her since he let her into his
house six long hours ago. "Where did you tell Nick you
were going?"

She didn't want to talk about Nick. She wanted to give
herself over completely to the waves of pleasure Lewis's
slightest movement aroused within her.

Lewis stopped moving. "Juliet?"

She looked up into his pale face. She could feel him
beginning to diminish inside her. "I didn't tell him anything," she said impatiently, "but he's a fool if he can't
guess."

"What if he—"

"Think about me, Lewis. Not about him." She reached
between them and took his testicles in her hand, stroking
and caressing them. Lewis's member began to stiffen once
more. He groaned and began to move inside her.

She had the power, Juliet thought. Just like the film
Juliet, she could make a man forget everything but her.
The realization filled her with a mixture of elation and
sadness.

Strange, she thought, as she moved beneath Lewis, finding her own pleasure as he found his, all she had wanted
was Nick's love. She wondered if that would ever again be
enough.

1959

"Miss Brittany! Over here!"

Nick, standing to one side, watched the reporters throng
around Juliet. No one had asked him yet how it felt to
have the first film he had written and directed turn into
a smash hit. In case they did, he had a one-word answer
ready: "Great!"

A congratulatory telegram from Morgan Gaynor was

stuffed in his breast pocket. And while he knew that meant he was assured of distribution and financing for his next film, he treasured it more because both he and Morgan knew he had made it on his own.

Well, perhaps not completely on his own, Nick thought, watching his wife answer the reporters' questions. It was a good thing Juliet didn't have a literary bent. Otherwise she might complain, like F. Scott Fitzgerald's wife, Zelda, that her husband had stolen her life and was using it in his work. Because, Nick admitted to himself, that was exactly what he was doing.

The trades were crediting him with creating "America's answer to the European sex goddess." If Nick was honest with himself, he had to admit America had been ready for Juliet; all he had done was take care of the introductions. He simply gave Juliet a vehicle that would translate her personality to the screen and then directed her in a way which made that talent obvious.

The set of his photographs of Juliet that ran in *Playboy* last month hadn't hurt a bit either, although it had taken a lot of talking to convince Juliet.

Funny, as much of an exhibitionist as Juliet was, he had thought she would jump at the chance to show off that glorious body of hers.

Not that it had been Nick's idea in the first place. The publicist on the picture had caught sight of those particular snapshots while Nick was searching through a stack of photos for a head shot. "What a *Playboy* spread those would make!" he had exclaimed, practically smacking his lips at the thought. "How about it, Nick?"

It was Whit who answered. "No way, man. This is his wife."

"This is business," the publicist said with a grin. "Isn't it, Nick?"

Nick had met Whit's glance for the briefest possible

moment before he glanced away. "Business," he had agreed.

Whit took off his glasses and polished them thoughtfully. "Get a release from her," he said, after a moment. "Just to make sure everything is straight." Old Whit was a great one for getting things straight. Before he married Tina last month, he'd had her sign a prenuptial agreement.

"No problem," Nick said, although it had proved to be a long, weary process before he wore down her objections and Juliet agreed to let him publish the photographs.

Whit never mentioned them again.

Leave it to Freddie, though. Last week the little bastard had asked him how he liked the thought of men all over the nation masturbating to his wife's pictures.

But for all Freddie's nastiness, he had been quick enough to jump on the bandwagon. He knew as well as Nick that Nick could now make any movie he pleased—as long as his wife was the star of it.

Juliet turned and waved at him through the crowd of reporters. Nick waved back. He had the new script almost completed, but he hadn't shown her any of it yet. Even though the main character's name was Suzanne, it was Juliet all over again. However, this time he had taken some liberties with the character he wasn't sure Juliet would approve of—or agree to—such as having the girl motivated by a past affair with her father. Nick wasn't sure why that idea had popped into his head, but it fit the story too well to take it out.

Juliet would simply have to agree. After all, it was his film, not hers.

Filming on *Breakdown* began the last week in July.

How things have changed, Juliet thought, as she walked onto the bedroom set the third Monday in August. While they were making *Juliet*, Nick screamed over every penny spent. Not this time. Money flowed like water into everything from wardrobe to champagne for the leading lady in her own trailer. Juliet loved it.

Money was flowing into Juliet's personal life as well. She and Nick owned a house now, a low-slung contemporary tucked back in a wooded Malibu canyon. As soon as the money began coming in from *Juliet*, Nick sold the New Yorker and bought himself a brand-new Corvette convertible. He groaned when Juliet insisted she wanted a Cadillac, but he finally gave in and bought her a powder-blue Coupe de Ville with magnificent tailfins and gleaming chrome trim. When she drove it, she felt like a real Hollywood star at last.

She finally felt like Nick's wife again too.

After *Juliet* wrapped, Lewis Farley showed an irritating tendency to try and cling to something that was clearly over. The infatuation that gripped Juliet during the course of making the movie had subsided. She knew it was Nick and Nick alone she really loved.

And Nick loved her.

While he was working on the new script, they had never been closer. The only thing Juliet regretted over those months while Nick was involved with his writing was that he refused to rehearse her in any of the scenes before official rehearsals with the rest of the cast began. Now, however, she realized that only served to make the actual filming more exciting these past few weeks.

She sighed. Everything would be perfect if only she could forget how Nick had encouraged her affair with Lewis.

And those photographs.

Dinners with Nick's mother ceased the month that issue of *Playboy* was published. Helen Chandler never said that was why, but Juliet knew. She should never have let Nick talk her into letting him sell those photographs. She only agreed to do the nude shots in the first place because she believed they were for him alone. Now men all over the country had seen them.

"You're blushing," her new co-star said. Rollo Torrance was twenty-four, and *Breakdown* was his second starring role. He spent his free time combing his thick shock of brown hair and checking his reflection in any convenient shiny surface. Rollo lowered his voice, his words just for her. "Thinking about the script?"

"Thinking about my husband," she said demurely, knowing that would put Rollo in his place. He had walked onto the set expecting she would go to bed with him.

Dream on, Rollo, she told herself. Nick was the only man she needed.

Rollo moved closer to Juliet. "I love you," he whispered. "I want to know everything about you."

"Why?"

"Because I love you."

"What do you want to know, then?"

"Who was the first man who ever made love to you?"

"My father." She said the line with absolute conviction.

The two of them continued to look at each other. The camera kept rolling.

"Nick?" someone asked.

"Cut," Nick said. "Wonderful!"

The set came to life again as the crew scurried around. Nick stood where he was. Nausea gripped his stomach like a gigantic fist. He wrote that line because it sounded right for the character. Just now, hearing Juliet say it, he knew it was true. A lot of puzzling things about the relationship between Juliet and her father suddenly fell into place.

Juliet stared across the set at Nick, her heart racing. He knew! She could see it in his face.

She had argued about the line when he first showed it to her, insisting that it wasn't right for her character, that she didn't feel comfortable with it.

Nick had brushed aside her objections, telling her that he was making up a past for the character in the film. It had nothing to do with her.

Juliet knew it had everything to do with her. Panic fluttered in her stomach. Now that Nick knew the truth, he would never feel the same about her again.

"My God, Juliet, you were wonderful!" Rollo said. "I could eat you up."

Juliet turned. The adoration in Rollo's eyes calmed her. *He doesn't know. No one knows but Papa. And Nick.*

She grasped Rollo's hand as though it were a lifeline. His eyes widened.

She moved closer. "Promises, promises," she said softly, just for him.

She didn't love Rollo. She never would. But at least she wouldn't look into Rollo's eyes and see what she had just seen in Nick's.

Nick sat in the dark screening room with the script girl, watching his wife make love to another man, on the screen and two rows in front of him. Juliet giggled softly while Rollo nuzzled her ear.

If he were half a man, he would stomp down the aisle, yank Juliet out of her seat, and punch Rollo in the nose. But what would he do for a male star?

He looked up at the screen again. No one could deny the chemistry on the set was showing up on the screen. Maybe that was what kept him sitting here, the knowledge he was making another dynamite movie.

Or maybe it was the problem he was having digesting the truth of Juliet's relationship with her father. The memory of Juliet half naked and screaming that day she claimed an intruder attacked her kept nagging at him. He couldn't forget how Oliver Brittany looked when Nick walked into the apartment that morning, like a man ready to be executed.

A sick feeling gripped Nick. Why hadn't he done more that day? Investigated further? Asked more questions? Why had he simply accepted the surface story, flimsy as it was?

The answer was simple. Because he wanted to make a movie. The plain truth was that he had wanted to make a movie more than he wanted to protect his own wife.

At least Brittany wasn't in on the financing for this picture. However, he had made a substantial profit from his share of *Juliet*.

Nick shifted uncomfortably in his seat. He could hardly argue he hadn't known what was going on. Maybe consciously he hadn't recognized the truth, but his subconscious knew. Otherwise he would never have inserted that line in the script.

"Ready to leave?" Sally asked him.

"In a few minutes," Nick said. "Have you got anything to eat at your place?"

She smiled up at him in the faint light from the screen. "Your favorite dish," she whispered.

And then another argument after midnight, Nick thought sourly. Sally couldn't accept that Nick never stayed the entire night.

The evening of the day Nick finally understood what had happened between her and Oliver Brittany, Juliet had moved into a separate bedroom. Maybe she thought that way her husband wouldn't be able to monitor how often she met her lover. If so, she was wrong.

Night after night, Nick lay awake, staring at the ceiling as he listened for the crunch of that grotesque powder-blue monster of hers in the drive. He wondered what he would do if one night Juliet simply didn't come home.

That wasn't going to happen, Nick told himself. She needed him as much as he needed her. When this movie was released every man in America would envy him anew—the man who was sleeping with Juliet Brittany. Too bad it wasn't true.

The lights came on in the screening room. Juliet and Rollo had disappeared.

"Ready, lover?" Sally asked softly.

"More than ready."

SIX

1960

NAKED, HIS WILD BUSH OF GRAY HAIR CURLING ELEC-trically around his lean face, Xavier Anton sat at the concert grand piano in the living room of his sharp-angled wood, glass, and steel aerie, six thousand feet above Palm Springs in the San Jacinto Mountains. The first time he brought Juliet to his Idyllwild house he told her, "Your husband could make one of his dreadful films for what it cost me to have my piano placed in this room. Of course, moving my piano was a much more worthwhile endeavor."

Juliet lay, equally naked, on the white overstuffed couch, staring dreamily out the glass wall opposite her at the pines and big-cone spruce, while Xavier's fingers raced across the keyboard, filling the room with music all the way to the soaring ceiling.

"There," he said, swinging around from the piano. "Identify that, my sweet."

"Beethoven. 'The Emperor,' " she added, with a sly smile.

"No! No! No!" When Xavier stood up, she could count his individual ribs. "How many times must I tell you? 'The Emperor' is an inappropriate, misleading nickname. This is Concerto Number Five in E Flat, Opus Seventy-three."

"I can never remember numbers," Juliet said compla-

128

cently. "Besides, I like it better when you play it with the orchestra." He had given her an autographed recording of one of his performances.

"You shall hear me play it this summer with the Los Angeles Philharmonic, my young Philistine."

"Stop calling me a Philistine. I got rid of my Cadillac, didn't I?"

"Thank God!" Xavier said with a shudder. He had been horrified when he saw her beloved Cadillac. Now, at his insistence, she drove a sleek black Jaguar, and she had grown to appreciate its conservative British styling just as she had grown to appreciate the other things Xavier had introduced her to over the last six months.

Nick had never asked her why she wanted to change cars. "Nick's almost finished the new script," she said abruptly. "He's calling it *Women*, but it's really about one woman and the different women she becomes when she's with different men." She knew that much only because she'd overheard Nick discussing it with Sloan Whitney. He hadn't allowed her to read a word of it.

Xavier stood up and closed the piano. "Have you told him?"

"Not yet."

Xavier crossed the room to stare out the window wall.

Juliet got up and followed him. Standing in front of this huge expanse of glass made her feel as though she were on some gigantic screen, as though her film self had suddenly developed eyes and could look out at the audience. She gazed at the tops of the pines. "He'll be reasonable. You'll see."

"He won't be reasonable," Xavier said with exaggerated patience, as though he were speaking to a very young child. "With you as his star, he has his choice of films and financing. Without you, he has no career."

"Nick wants what's best for me," Juliet said stubbornly.

"You're deluding yourself. Do you know what your friend Rollo told me?"

Juliet giggled. "Poor Rollo." It had been Rollo Torrance who introduced her to Xavier at Xavier's Hollywood Bowl concert. She had gone home with Xavier afterward. Thank heavens *Breakdown* had already wrapped. A lover with the jealous look Rollo wore that night had definitely not been in Nick's script.

"Rollo says everyone believes Nick created you. No one considers you capable of being an actress on your own— without his help. He didn't create you, of course." Xavier's mischievous smile beneath the wildly curling bush of hair made him look like a wicked elf. "I know that better than anyone. Nick is just using you to achieve his own ends. But he doesn't deny the public misconception. In fact, Rollo says he encourages it."

"I don't believe you!"

"Then watch his reaction when you tell him that you want to change your image. If he truly loved you, Juliet, he would allow you to stretch, to grow." Xavier's face grew momentarily sad. "As I will when the time comes."

"He'll allow me to grow," Juliet insisted.

"Talk to him soon, then."

"Why?"

"Because my good friend Adriano Luca is coming to the States next month. Do you know who he is?"

"The Italian director?"

"The *great* Italian director. The man is a genius." Xavier motioned across the room. "His photograph is on that table. The one in the ivory frame."

Juliet went over to examine it. Adriano Luca had an arrogant Roman nose and soulful poet's eyes.

Xavier followed and put his arm around her. "I'll introduce you to him, my little Philistine. He's the director who can turn you into a serious actress." He hesitated long enough that she turned and looked at his face. "If he should choose to."

"You're nuts," Nick said. "I refuse to discuss it anymore."

"I'm merely trying to take control of my own career," Juliet said calmly. Inside, though, she was beginning to fume. Xavier had been right.

Nick paced back and forth across his office. She had made this appointment to talk with Nick through his secretary. Even though they were still living in the same house, Juliet felt as though they were strangers. It had seemed easier to broach the subject of her career in the more neutral ground of his office.

"I'm your director," Nick complained now. "I'm the one who showed you what you could be on the screen. Doesn't that count for anything?"

"Don't you give me any credit, Nick?" she asked softly.

"You're okay as an actress," he admitted. "But what makes you think you would have been the kind of star you've turned out to be without me to direct you?"

"Oh, you directed me, all right." Sudden fury gripped her. "You directed me right into two affairs. Did you do it because you thought it would help your movies, Nick?"

He stopped pacing and looked at her. "It did, didn't it?"

"Are you proud of that?"

"I'm proud of the films we made together."

"I'm glad! Because there won't be any more of them."

"Look, Juliet, we need to cool down. Think it over. All I'm asking is that you not make any public announcements yet. All right?"

"I won't change my mind, Nick. I'm going to be a serious actress. Xavier says—"

"Him! I should have known. Haven't you gotten over your hots for the great maestro yet?"

"Right! Him! You don't want me to go to bed with Xavier

because it won't help one of your movies. Well, it helps me!"

Nick clamped down on the sick rage that flooded through him. "You're angry. We're both upset. Just give me a little time. This new script is perfect for you. The financing is set. It will be your biggest hit."

"I'll think about it."

Juliet wasn't up when Nick left the house. Not that he normally saw her in the mornings. They'd had separate bedrooms for over a year. Her idea, but he had gone along with it. He had gone along with a lot of things over the past year that he never would have dreamed he'd accept before. Jesus, he wished he'd never written that line of dialogue!

Nick climbed in his Corvette, still disgruntled about not seeing her this morning. Last night she'd been out till all hours, giving him no opportunity to talk to her. He wanted to take another crack at convincing her she had gone way off course. Juliet Brittany as a serious actress? What a joke.

He'd call later and see if she was free for lunch, he decided, as he gunned the Corvette. By the time he got to his office, he was in a reasonably upbeat mood. He knew he could convince Juliet he was right, given time.

Only time turned out to be what he didn't have.

His secretary met him at the office door, a worried look on her face, a copy of *The Hollywood Reporter* in her hand.

"What's up, Peggy?"

"You better sit down and read this, Nick."

He did.

Juliet was a front-page item. She had called a press conference the afternoon before to announce publicly that she was discarding her sex-kitten image.

"You didn't know, did you?" Peggy asked.

"We talked about changing her image. I thought I'd convinced her otherwise." He glanced at the article. "She must have set this up as soon as she left here yesterday morning."

"Nick? There's more." Peggy handed him a message from Juliet. His clothes would be at the Chateau Marmont this afternoon. Her lawyer would be in touch.

Peggy patted his shoulder. "You want a drink?"

"At nine A.M.?" Nick stared down at the note. "On second thought, yes. And you better get Whit on the phone."

"He's on his way over," Peggy said as she opened the bar.

"Thanks, Peg." When she pressed a glass into his hand, he asked, "The financing for the film?"

She nodded. "I was saving that until after the drink. That's why I made it a double."

"Cheers," Nick said as he downed the whiskey.

Why in hell had he ever written that line of dialogue?

In the midst of an already overscheduled day, Frederick Yates received a call from the television department that he was needed in Douglas Larkin's office at once. Frederick had fought the idea of the television department tooth and nail at first. Now they had four series in production and the promise of three more for next season. Of course, his objections to that particular venture were ancient history, forgotten. No one who wanted to remain in a position of power with the studio would be thoughtless enough to bring up Frederick's previous reluctance to involve the studio in such a moneymaking venture.

However, making pilot films for television took a huge bite out of the studio's budget. With only three networks to sell those pilots to, and the intense competition from the other studios, any call from the television department made Frederick's blood pressure rise automatically.

"A problem?" he asked Douglas Larkin, when he reached the producer's office. A crude man by Frederick's standards,

Larkin was given to coarse humor and coarser personal habits, and that made Larkin perfect for television, a crude and vulgar medium suitable only for the masses. Larkin had shown a genius—Gad, to use the word in connection with television!—in producing the kinds of shows that led in the ratings race each week. Larkin's brand of crude vulgarity was not easy to come by. The producer was a treasure, and Frederick made an effort to treat him as such.

"Got something for you to see," Larkin said. "A real side-splitter. A perfect girl turned up for the daughter role on *The Waverlys*." *The Waverlys* was one of Frederick's pet projects for next season. "Only you won't believe what happened."

Frederick consulted his watch, trying not to let his irritation show. Because of Larkin's bloody message, he would be dining on antacid the remainder of the day. Still, it was important to keep Larkin happy. So, as he started for the door, he merely commented mildly, "I don't actually have time for this, Douglas."

"She looks like Juliet Brittany," Larkin called after him.

Frederick hesitated. "Perhaps a moment, then."

"I knew you couldn't pass up a chance to ogle a figure like that."

Frederick didn't bother correcting him. It wasn't the girl's figure that attracted him. It was the intense need to be aware of anything concerning Nick. Even his about-to-be-former wife.

When they reached the projection room, Larkin signaled the projectionist. "I could sell tickets to this screen test," he crowed to Frederick. "It's the worst I've ever seen."

The girl's resemblance to Juliet Brittany struck Frederick immediately. However, the resemblance was only superficial. The facial bones were similar, as was the figure—although the girl was carrying a good deal of excess weight—but the combination of the two left something to be desired.

She was, to put it bluntly, plain. A drab little nothing, hopeless in the extreme, at whom no one would glance twice if not for that faint, extremely faint, resemblance to Nicholas Picard's wife.

The plainness might be overcome, Frederick conceded. Makeup could do wonders to emphasize her resemblance to Juliet. Diet and exercise would expose the figure beneath the padding. However, the girl's worst fault was a fatal flaw for an actress. She had no rapport with the camera.

Frederick drummed his fingers on the armrest. Why on earth had Larkin invited him to view this disaster? Even if makeup *could* correct her essential plainness, nothing could be done about her controlled rigidity. I am an ice princess, her every movement screamed, as she recited her lines for the camera. It could grow no worse, Frederick thought.

And then it did.

The girl's hands began to tremble.

"This is where it gets good," Douglas Larkin said with a chuckle. "I can't believe my secretary talked me into giving this dud a try."

The girl faltered, began again, stuttered, stopped, stared straight into the camera—and burst into tears.

Any resemblance to Juliet Brittany vanished in the deluge.

Some women weep delicately, in a way that can touch the heart and enhance their beauty. This girl's face contorted into such a look of raw pain it turned Frederick's stomach. Any attractiveness she might have possessed was washed away by sobs so violent they left her gasping harshly for breath.

"Isn't she a total loser?" Larkin exclaimed in delight. "Doesn't that just make your day?"

Frederick leaped to his feet. "I have a million things to attend to, old boy," he said stiffly as he squeezed past Larkin. "You must excuse me."

Larkin leaned back, chuckling, as the camera zoomed in for a final shot of the girl's crumpled face. "Roll it again," he called to the projectionist. "Stay and watch this baby one more time," he urged Frederick.

"Thanks, but no," Frederick told him. *The man has no taste,* he thought as he stalked up the aisle. *No wonder Larkin's television programs were so successful. A tasteless producer for a tasteless medium.*

At the door to the projection room, Frederick paused and looked back. The short snippet of film was beginning once more. He found himself hesitating, his hand on the doorknob, watching the pale counterfeit of Juliet Brittany's face.

Larkin whooped. "Here it comes!" he called.

Frederick left, slamming the door before the girl's noisy tears could flow once more.

Frederick adjusted his tie nervously. He brushed an imaginary speck from his immaculate suit. He twisted in his chair to inspect the polish on his shoes.

"For heaven's sake, Frederick," Morgan Gaynor protested, looking at him over the rim of his reading glasses. "You're not a schoolboy in the headmaster's office."

For Frederick, his stepfather's elegant English accent took the sting out of the comment. However, it did nothing for his nervousness. The truth was Frederick felt exactly like a schoolboy each time he flew to New York. He prepared for these meetings as though he were cramming for an exam. He was more than ready to answer any question Morgan might pose on the dozens of business items in the papers his stepfather was reading through.

The fact that Morgan was so much taller did nothing to help Frederick's self-confidence. He had inherited his mother's small-boned, delicate frame. On balance, he was grateful for that. Otherwise, he might have turned into a ruffian, like his real father. According to his mother, the few times his stuntman father had actually seen him, the man had thrown up his hands in disgust at fathering such a spindly son. He died when Frederick was two, from a fall gone awry during a western. All Frederick remembered of him was the faded obituary from *The Hollywood Reporter*. Morgan was the only father he had ever known.

"There, then," Morgan Gaynor said, straightening the pile of papers Frederick had brought with him. "You're doing an excellent job," he told his stepson warmly. "But of course I knew you would."

Frederick braced himself, waiting for the exam to start. For all his cramming, Morgan's first question took him completely off guard.

"How is Nicholas?"

"Nicholas? All right, I suppose." Frederick could feel irritation rising within him. A lot of good solid accomplishments were in those papers. He wanted his due for them. "I haven't talked with him recently."

"You should, my boy. He's having a rough time of it."

"That's what he gets for marrying a woman just like his mother," Frederick snapped before he could catch himself.

Morgan gave Frederick a chilling look over the top of his reading glasses. "And what do you mean by that?"

Now he did feel like a schoolboy. He would get his knuckles rapped for this one. "Surely you've heard the rumors about Juliet Brittany. I'm surprised they stopped short of banner headlines."

Morgan took off his glasses, stood up, and walked around the desk. He stopped directly in front of his stepson's chair. Frederick started to rise. Morgan put a hand on his shoulder, keeping him in his seat. "What did you mean about Helen?"

Frederick inhaled the lemony scent of the cologne his stepfather favored. "Nicholas and I are all grown up now,

Morgan. We both know Helen Chandler is a slut who slept with half of Hollywood in her day."

Morgan slapped Frederick so hard his head snapped back. "Keep your filthy, lying tongue off Helen."

"Morgan—"

"You are no gentleman."

"And Nicholas is?" Frederick sneered. It was all he could do to keep from bawling like a child.

Morgan turned away.

After a moment, he sat down on the edge of the desk. "Listen to me, Frederick. Helen and Nicholas are the geniuses, the creative ones. They live by a different set of rules. You and I are the drones, the businessmen. You must remember that and forget this ridiculous jealousy."

"I'm not jealous of Nicholas," Frederick blurted. It sounded false even to him.

"Just look in on him." Morgan Gaynor leaned over and put his hand on Frederick's shoulder. "Offer him your support. Your friendship. It would mean a lot to me, Frederick."

Frederick blinked back his tears. "Yes, sir. Of course, sir."

"You're a pal, Freddie," Nicholas said expansively.

Frederick flushed, but he managed to keep his temper in check. "I do wish you would call me Frederick."

"Sure, Freddie." Nicholas signaled the waitress for another drink. "You want one too?"

"Not just yet." Frederick had nursed his gin and tonic through three reorders.

"Oops! There she is!" Nicholas said. "And her boyfriend too."

Frederick glanced around. Juliet Brittany had just come in with a tall swarthy-looking man. "Who is he?"

Nicholas looked surprised. "Adriano Luca."

"I'm still in the dark."

"The Italian director. Won three awards last year for—Christ, Freddie! You haven't changed a bit. Don't you keep up with the business?"

"That doesn't mean I must know the name of every scurvy foreigner who rolls into town. And stop calling me Freddie!" He paled for a moment, thinking he might have gone too far. To his relief, Nicholas wasn't paying him the slightest bit of attention. Instead, he stared greedily at Juliet Brittany as she leaned across the table toward Luca, her gown barely containing her ample assets. Indeed, half the room was focused on the couple, including the couple's waitress.

Frederick had spotted the waitress the moment he and Nicholas entered the room. In fact, if he had not intervened, they would have been seated at her table, and that would have been far too obvious. It had taken Frederick weeks to set up this night's entertainment. He would do nothing to make his careful plan go awry.

Frederick had thought of the girl on the plane back from New York after his meeting with his stepfather. A rerun of that disastrous screen test Douglas Larkin subjected him to had popped into his head. At that moment, Frederick had known exactly what to do.

Nicholas slammed down his empty glass. "You know what Luca is going to do, don't you? He'll tell her he's making a film of great social and political significance, and then he'll have her strip for every scene."

"It worked for you, didn't it?" Frederick observed dryly.

"I made her a star. Luca just wants to make her, period."

"It looks as though he already has, old boy. I suppose you'll have to find another coattail to hang onto."

"What's that supposed to mean?" Nicholas asked belligerently.

"It means you have a script but no star. And therefore no financing. Am I right?"

"I made Juliet what she is." Nicholas leaned forward. "We both know that."

"It was an accident, Nicholas. A once-in-a-lifetime fluke. You could never do it again."

"Two movies aren't a fluke." Nicholas signaled for another drink.

"Nicholas, if I believed that, I would make you a wager. A substantial wager."

For a moment Frederick was fearful he might have waited too long. That Nicholas might be too far in his cups to bite at the bait dangling so enticingly before him.

"What kind of wager?" Nicholas said finally.

"That you couldn't turn someone else into a star of Juliet's magnitude."

Nicholas's drink arrived. He sipped it more slowly than the last one. "Sure I could," he mumbled. Frederick sensed he was losing Nicholas's attention.

"I would make it a wager worth your while, Nicholas. I would give you a deal that would make you the most prominent director in Hollywood." Nicholas's bleary glance had strayed back to Juliet. "Instead of a has-been."

That caught his attention, Frederick noted with satisfaction. "What do you mean, a has-been? I'm only twenty-six, for God's sake."

"And without Juliet Brittany you're washed up. You'll have to struggle for financing again just like a beginner. Who knows," Frederick said with a broad grin, "you might even have to come back to work for me."

"Jesus!" Nicholas drained his glass. "What's the bet?"

"You take an unknown and make her a star of Juliet Brittany's quality. In return, I give you the keys to the studio."

"What unknown?"

Frederick pointed across to the waitress. "Her."

Nicholas studied the girl silently.

"She even looks a little like Juliet, don't you think?" Frederick found himself babbling nervously. "I noticed that earlier." He forced himself to stop talking. Had he given away too much?

Nicholas traced his finger around the rim of his empty glass. "I could do it, you know. I could make her a star."

"Then prove it," Frederick said brutally. "Prove it to me and everyone else in this town who's laughing at you."

Nicholas reached across the table.

Frederick flinched, thinking that Nicholas was about to punch him in the nose. Then he realized that Nicholas was offering to shake hands.

" 'S a deal," Nicholas mumbled.

And Frederick knew he had won.

Kathleen

1960–1963

Kate was a shy fawn of a girl, plain of face, awkward in her movements, unconvincing in her acting. Had I told her the first night we met that I planned to transform her into Kathleen Mallory, "the most beautiful woman in the world," she would have laughed in my face.

No one in Hollywood was less likely to believe this transformation could occur than Kate herself.

—From the unpublished memoirs of Nicholas Picard

SEVEN

1960

WHEN A HORSE THROWS YOU, YOU'RE SUPPOSED TO climb right back on the beast, Kate Mallory told herself as she hesitated just outside Douglas Larkin's office. Only she didn't want to get back on. She would rather forget about horses for the rest of her life! But Selena had insisted Kate meet her at the producer's office—and after all Selena had done for her, how could she refuse?

Kate shoved through the door with enough force that the receptionist glanced up, startled. "I'd like to see Miss Adams. She's expecting me."

"Your name?" the receptionist asked, and then recognition flashed across her face, swiftly followed by amusement.

"Kate Mallory." Kate tried to keep her voice steady. This was the first time she had been back to Selena's office since that disastrous audition. Now she wished she hadn't come at all.

"Please have a seat, Miss Mallory," the receptionist said.

Kate sank down on the sofa. She could feel her hands beginning to tremble the way they had at the audition. It was too much to hope for that Selena would be prompt for their luncheon date. Selena was never on time for anything.

When Kate glanced up, the receptionist was still staring

at her. Kate dropped her eyes and reached blindly for a magazine. She flipped through the glossy pages, not seeing a thing. Had the receptionist been at the audition too? Or had she only heard about it?

It just wasn't fair!

Kate had dreamed of being an actress for years, years she spent simmering with frustration while her family blocked her at every turn. Now she was finally eighteen and didn't need anyone's permission to do anything. And what happened? She got stage fright.

Selena had been the best friend anyone could ask for, starting with the first minute she got an advance look at the script for *The Waverlys* and decided Kate was perfect for the part of the daughter. From that moment forward, Selena arranged everything, including the clothes Kate was to wear. She even put in a good word with Douglas Larkin, the producer whose secretary she was, and personally watched as Kate was made up. That Kate would land the daughter's part seemed like a sure thing.

Until the moment the camera focused on her and she realized that, regardless of the clothes and the makeup, she was still just plain Kate. And that was that. Any hopes she had of being an actress were crushed forever.

Kate blinked back her tears as the glossy pages of the magazine swam before her eyes.

"Kate! You're always so early!" Selena set her purse down on the edge of the receptionist's desk. Pulling out her compact, she powdered her freckles and then ran a comb through her curly red hair. "I'll be back in a couple of hours, Marge," she told the receptionist.

Kate ignored the receptionist's smirk. Now that Selena was here, everything was all right. Selena had the ability to do that.

"Doug is out of the office today," she told Kate as they left. "So my time is my own. And I found this delicious little restaurant you're just going to love." When they reached Selena's trim red sports car, she stopped and looked Kate right in the eye.

"Are you okay, doll? How's the job?"

"I'm fine," Kate assured her. "And the job's okay. If I can't be an actress, at least I can watch actresses." She was a waitress at DeCola's, the new "in" restaurant.

"Now don't be a defeatist. You just had a tiny little problem with your self-confidence. We can fix that."

"I'll still be me," Kate said mournfully.

"Don't be stupid, doll. Of course you're still you." Selena unlocked the car door. "Hop in. This place has the cutest waiters you've ever seen! I've been dying to take you there."

Selena was a breath of fresh air. At twenty-three, she seemed so much more worldly than Kate herself. Best of all, whatever happened, Selena never lost her boundless optimism. Being with her always made Kate feel so much more positive about life—even about herself. Over lunch, Selena divided her time between commenting on the different waiters' physiques and encouraging Kate to try another audition.

"No way," Kate told her. "I'm already a laughingstock. Did you see the way your receptionist looked at me? I wanted to shrivel up and die." She could admit things like that to Selena.

"What do you expect from a woman with no eyebrows?" Selena retorted. She glanced at her watch. "Oops! I've got to get back. Our great leader will be calling in at two-thirty. Did I tell you I got another raise?"

"He's still hoping you'll go to bed with him," Kate said, trying to sound as sophisticated as Selena. Secretly she couldn't understand how Selena could resist Douglas Larkin, with his endless stream of presents and raises. Kate couldn't imagine what it would be like to have a man chase her with so much dedication. Or even to have a man chase her at all.

"Do you realize how much that hope is costing him?" Selena said.

They were both laughing as they left the restaurant. The good feeling Kate got from lunching with Selena lasted all the rest of the afternoon.

Kate let herself into the house at five P.M. Her stepsisters were waiting just inside the door, eight-year-old Gail and ten-year-old Cynthia. The weasels her stepmother brought with her when she married Kate's father.

Lorraine herself was nowhere in sight.

"Hello, Ratface," Cynthia said.

"Mother's going to get you in real trouble this time," Gail crowed.

"Welcome home," Kate muttered. "I've never seen such charming children."

"I'm not a child," Cynthia sputtered.

"Trouble, trouble, trouble," Gail chanted.

"Lorraine doesn't know I'm alive."

"Well, you'll wish you were dead when she gets through with you," Cynthia said.

"No, I wish you were," Kate mumbled to herself as she started up the stairs.

"Kate!" her stepmother's imperious voice rang out.

Kate turned slowly. Lorraine Mallory stood in the doorway of the living room, glaring up at her. Her stepmother was dressed for dinner in an elegant black dress that served as a backdrop for her diamonds and her silver hair.

"I hope you enjoyed lunching with your father's slut."

Kate felt the blood drain out of her face. "I don't know what you're—"

"That was a nice little restaurant. I hadn't been there before. Had you?"

"Look, Lorraine—"

"I've seen your father's slut before. Obviously, so have you. You looked like such great friends, laughing together. It's no more than I would expect from someone like you. You're your mother's daughter!" she finished bitterly.

Over Lorraine's shoulder, Kate saw Gail mouthing *Trouble, trouble, trouble.* "I've got to get ready for work," she told her stepmother, just as the front door swung open.

Joseph Mallory glanced around the domestic scene. "What's going on?" he asked his wife.

"Your daughter is getting ready to go to her waitress job," Lorraine told him. "How can you stand to let her work at something so menial? It disgraces the whole family. What would the parents of Cynthia and Gail's schoolmates think if they knew?"

Her father glanced up the stairs at Kate and then shrugged. "It's her life," he said. "When are we due at the Stevenses'?"

Kate drove along Sunset Boulevard in her ten-year-old Nash Rambler. Not much of a car but her own, she thought, as she passed the hole in the ground marking the spot where only a few months earlier the Garden of Allah had stood. Across the street the Chateau Marmont Hotel rose like a great castle above the Strip. Kate averted her eyes from the billboard for the Sahara Hotel with its forty-foot-tall Las Vegas showgirl revolving endlessly on her silver dollar.

For some reason, the showgirl always reminded Kate of her mother. Probably because her father would take one look at the forty-foot-figure and declare she was flaunting herself. That was a crime Kate was accused of with regularity. One of her father's favorite phrases, it had become her stepmother's also. When Lorraine married Joseph Mallory, she also took on the task of making sure that her then thirteen-year-old stepdaughter never flaunted herself.

Kate had tried her best to cooperate. If only there had not been so many definitions for the term. Coming down the stairs too fast. Wearing her clothes too tight—or too loose. Combing her hair back from her face—or letting it fall free. Speaking too loudly—or too softly.

Punished daily for this crime, Kate grew more and more bewildered, until finally the real definition of flaunting herself was revealed to her in one of Lorraine's tirades. It was: anything that drew attention to her physical self.

Because her physical self was a dangerous thing, indeed. It was her mother's body that had wrecked her mother's life, her father's life, Kate's life, and, by extension, Lorraine's life. According to Lorraine, it was Pauline Mallory's promiscuousness that corrupted her husband. After Pauline, Joseph could trust no woman, including his second wife. Nor could he be faithful. The affair with Selena Adams was just the most recent of many.

In the face of her husband's unfaithfulness, Lorraine Mallory had dedicated herself to stamping out all traces of his first wife from his life—and from Kate's. Kate must be guarded from any expression of a physical or sensual nature. Her stepmother's attitude, coupled with Joseph's cold admonitions not to flaunt herself, left Kate with the lingering fear there was something not quite right within her, that deep inside her lurked something, barely contained, which might slip its bonds at any moment and menace society. She knew she must keep herself under the most rigid control, must deny any hint of her own sexuality.

As a consequence, she felt both distant from and envious of other girls, other women. *They* were free to flirt, to have boyfriends, to display their bodies in a provocative manner. She was not. Because she, like her mother, was missing some vital element of morality or decency that all other women possessed.

Sometimes she hated her mother for that. Other times,

she felt a curious sadness for the only other woman in the world to have been cursed with this same unpredictable and dangerous nature.

Pauline Mallory had died when Kate was fifteen and a half, a suicide in a cheap Las Vegas hotel. It had been Lorraine who broke the news, Lorraine who told her Joseph Mallory would be flying to Las Vegas to make burial arrangements for his ex-wife, Lorraine who asked Kate if she wished to accompany her father to attend her mother's funeral.

Kate knew instantly it was some kind of trick, a test of her unpredictable nature. She refused automatically, on the spot. Her father merely grunted when Lorraine told him Kate's decision. But even though Kate passed the test, she still failed. Joseph Mallory had gone on to Las Vegas even though Lorraine clearly wanted him to leave the arrangements for his ex-wife to someone else. And it was shortly after his return that a new mistress appeared in his life: Selena Adams.

Lorraine held Kate responsible for both events, as if it were her fault Pauline Mallory died in the first place.

Kate gripped the wheel. What was she going to do about Selena? In the five years since Lorraine married Kate's father, Kate's friendship with Selena Adams was her first overt show of defiance against her stepmother. No matter what the cost, she couldn't give up Selena's friendship. If it hadn't been for Selena, Kate would never have gotten the audition. Even though it had been a disaster, Kate still felt as though she owed Selena something for giving her the opportunity.

Besides, Selena was *fun*. Her best friend. The only thing Kate couldn't understand about Selena was why in the world a wonderful person like her would ever be involved with someone like Kate's father. Even though Kate considered Selena her best friend, that was the one thing she would never dare ask her.

Kate had seen the wedding photographs of her mother, a slim, blond, pretty girl, and her father, a proud smile on his face as he looked down at his bride. It was hard to understand how the girl in the photograph could have become the woman whose blatant affairs would lose her the custody of her daughter. Or how the smiling young man could grow to hate his wife so much that he would raise the daughter but never love her.

I won't be like my mother, Kate told herself for the millionth time. I'll never be like her.

Tuesday was a slow night at DeCola's. Kate couldn't miss the good-looking man with blond hair who came in alone and was seated at her corner table. After she took his order, he kept following her with his eyes as she went back and forth to the kitchen, making her feel extremely uncomfortable.

At first she thought he was mocking her, pretending to be interested in her as a joke. After fifteen minutes, she began to wonder if he could somehow see through her careful shield to that hidden side of her she fought so hard to keep contained.

Tammy, the other waitress on her side of the room, noticed Kate's admirer too. "Aren't you going to do anything about that?" she asked Kate as they both hit the kitchen door at the same time.

"About what?" Kate asked coldly.

"Table Fifteen is *cute*! And he's obviously looking for some companionship."

"Well, I'm not!" Kate snapped as she picked up Fifteen's order.

"Then how about trading tables?" Tammy asked eagerly. "I'll give you Number Five for Number Fifteen. They're regulars. Good tippers."

Kate shrugged. Inwardly, she was relieved. "If that's what

you want." She extended the tray. "This is his order."

"I want, I want." Tammy took the tray with a big smile and walked out, hips swaying.

Number Five turned out to be a bunch of lousy tippers. Kate wasn't surprised. She never got as much in tips as the other waitresses; she couldn't bring herself to banter and flirt with the customers like they did. She was too afraid someone might take her seriously. Kate scooped up the handful of quarters and dropped them in her pocket.

When she turned, she found herself looking straight into Table Fifteen's eyes. He ignored Tammy's attempt to capture him in conversation and continued to watch Kate as she took care of her other tables.

He was waiting outside in the parking lot when her shift ended. When she saw him she ducked back inside and asked Carl, the big bouncer, to walk her to her car.

It was a good fifteen minutes before Carl was able to leave. By then Kate was sure his services were no longer needed, but she was afraid he would be annoyed if she didn't wait for him. When Carl finally escorted her out to the parking lot, she was surprised to see the man still standing there.

So was Carl. Obviously, the bouncer had only been humoring her. He hadn't really believed anyone would be attracted to her enough to hang around.

She was even more surprised when the man followed her to her car, ignoring Carl's presence.

"I'd like to talk to you, miss," the man said.

Kate unlocked her car door, ignoring him.

"Beat it, buster," Carl warned. "The lady's not in the mood for conversation."

Kate swung the door open, tossed her purse inside, and got in. "Thank you, Carl," she said. "See you tomorrow."

"Have you considered a screen career?" the man asked.

Kate stared straight ahead, her hands gripping the wheel.

Some kind of joke, she thought. One of the girls had put
him up to it. But she didn't remember mentioning her
audition to any of the other waitresses, and she certainly
wouldn't have told any of them what a disaster it turned
out to be. How had they found out?

The man took her silence for assent. He fumbled in his
pocket. "I'm a producer, and—"

"Can it, punk," Carl said, without glancing at the man.
"Drive safely," he told Kate.

"At least take my card." He tried to hand it through the
open door.

Carl blocked his access with a hamlike upper arm. "Take
off," the bouncer told Kate and slammed the door shut.

Kate accelerated. In the rearview mirror, she saw the
man arguing with Carl. As she turned into the street, he
tossed his card to the ground in frustration.

Just another Hollywood wolf, she thought. Then she giggled. He might be just another wolf to anyone else, but he
was her first one. Wait until she told Selena!

When Kate woke the next morning, she found the house
had turned into an armed camp. No one was speaking to
Kate, not even Gail to taunt her. Not much different from
a regular day, Kate thought. Lorraine had never talked to
her stepdaughter except when absolutely necessary, and her
father had not spoken directly to her within Kate's memory.

Funny, Lorraine seemed to think Kate struck up a friendship with her father's mistress just to spite her. Actually, it
was her stepmother's fault that she and Selena met in the
first place. Wouldn't Lorraine just die if she knew it had
been right here, in her own house, in Kate's room!

Kate had just turned sixteen. She'd only had her driver's
license a month, so Lorraine's crisp order to stay away from
the house that Friday night had seemed to pose no particular hardship. Until Kate learned that having a car at her

disposal made her no more popular with her schoolmates than she had been before. No one was interested in cruising the local drive-in with *her*. So she had studied at the library until it closed and then sneaked in the house the back way and up to her room, ignoring the party sounds coming from the front.

When she opened her bedroom door, she was startled to see a voluptuous little redhead with translucent skin and perfect features perched on the edge of her bed, smoking a cigarette and thumbing through that week's copy of Kate's high school newspaper.

Kate stood there, staring like an idiot.

"Isn't high school a drag?" the redhead said. "Want a cigarette?"

"I . . . I'd better not. My stepmother—"

"Isn't she just a perfect bitch? I couldn't listen to her a single second longer. That's why I decided to hide out up here. You don't mind, do you?"

Kate shook her head numbly.

The redhead took a deep drag on her cigarette. "How in the world do you take it? I can't understand why Joey doesn't divorce her."

Kate closed the door with the feeling she had just entered Never-Never Land. "Joey?"

"Joey Mallory. Isn't he your father? Aren't you Kate? I'm Selena. Selena Adams."

"He doesn't divorce Lorraine because her father is the senior partner." Joseph Mallory was an entertainment lawyer with one of the most prestigious firms in Los Angeles.

Selena whooped. "So that's why he won't marry me!"

"Marry you?" Kate sat down on the bed beside Selena and accepted a cigarette with trembling hands. "You want to marry my . . . Joey?" she asked as Selena extended a lighter.

Selena nodded, eyes sparkling with devilment.

Kate made a split-second decision. "If there's anything I can do to help," she said earnestly, "just let me know." She took a drag on the cigarette, her first try ever at smoking, and choked. She and Selena had been fast friends ever since.

Of course, Selena was no closer to marrying her Joey than before. If the redhead had actually counted on Kate's being able to influence her father, she had long since learned what a futile hope that was. They had remained friends anyway. Now that Lorraine had finally found out about that friendship, Kate had no idea what might happen next.

She soon learned. Lorraine dropped several broad hints during the day that it was time Kate moved out of the house and into a place of her own. Kate had no intention of leaving until she was kicked out. Since the disastrous audition had changed her career plans, she no longer knew what to do. The waitress job had seemed sufficient while she still had hopes of becoming an actress. But her waitress pay was not enough to cover the cost of living on her own.

Still, if her stepmother found her consorting with the "other woman" again, she might be looking for another place to live anyway. Kate realized she was going to have to let Lorraine's anger die down before she got in touch with Selena again.

When Kate came downstairs on Friday morning, she happened to see a letter with her name on it sitting on the entry hall table. She received so little mail that she seldom checked the table. It could have lain there for weeks. Picard Productions was the return address.

"When did this come?" she asked Cynthia and Gail, on their way to school.

They ignored her. The silent treatment was still on.

Kate stuck the letter in the pocket of her robe and went through the dining room and into the kitchen, where she found Lorraine instructing the maid about the day's shopping. Kate ignored their wounded looks long enough to pour herself a cup of coffee and make toast.

Lorraine sighed. "I don't see why you can't eat breakfast at the same time as everyone else. It only makes more work for Maria."

"I work until after midnight," Kate said mildly.

Lorraine didn't deign to reply.

Kate took the toast and coffee back up to her room. She had finished the toast before she remembered the letter in her pocket. She ripped it open, earning a paper cut in the process. *Dear Miss Mallory,* it read, *It is most urgent that you contact my office at once regarding work in an upcoming feature film.*

It was signed *Nicholas Picard, Picard Productions.*

Kate leaned back. Someone was pulling her leg, weren't they?

She started to crumple the letter and then paused. She took it with her to the hall telephone and dialed the number on the letterhead.

"Picard Productions," a warm female voice said. "May I help you?"

Kate hung up. Her breathing ragged, she pulled out the telephone directory and leafed through the pages. Picard Productions was listed.

It had to be a prank, she thought. Someone was still trying to make her miserable over that audition. Things like this just didn't happen in real life.

Kate stared at the telephone.

After all, if things like this really happened, then—anything might be possible. Anything.

"It's some kind of joke, isn't it?" Kate asked Selena.

"Call them and find out. Picard Productions is legit. Nicholas Picard is—was—Juliet Brittany's husband. I understand the marriage is on the skids. Call them," she urged.

Kate shook her head numbly. "I'm afraid."

"Then I'll call for you," Selena said. "Come on."

Kate followed her to the pay phone and waited, her heart thudding painfully, while Selena fished in her purse for change and then dialed the number. "Good morning," she said, in her cool, efficient office voice. "I'm calling on behalf of Miss Kate Mallory. She has been asked to contact your office. . . . Yes, I'll hold. . . . Yes, Mr. Picard, I'm calling for Miss Kate Mallory. She received your letter and—" Selena cocked her head, listening, her eyes on Kate. "Why, of course. She would be happy to. You understand, though, that a girl can't be too careful in this town. There are so many . . . right!" Selena laughed gaily and Kate found herself blushing. Selena probably thought Kate had never been approached by a man. She hadn't had a chance to tell Selena about her very own Hollywood wolf.

"This afternoon?" Selena cocked an eyebrow at her.

Kate stared back, frozen-faced.

"This afternoon will be fine," Selena said firmly. "Three o'clock. She'll be there, Mr. Picard."

She hung up and turned to Kate.

"It's all set. You'll be there if I have to drag you myself," she threatened.

In the end, Kate went alone. If she was going to have another disastrous audition, she didn't want a witness to it.

"Miss Mallory, Mr. Picard," the secretary announced as she showed Kate into Nicholas Picard's office. Kate advanced two steps and then halted in amazement as she recognized the man behind the desk.

"Good afternoon, Miss Mallory," he said, as he rose and came around the desk to take her trembling hand in his. "We could have saved a lot of time the other night if your bodyguard had let you take my card."

"Is this—is this for real?"

"You bet it is, Kate." Nicholas Picard displayed enough teeth in his smile to make any Hollywood wolf envious. "I'm gonna make you a star."

Kate's knees gave way. She sat down so hard her teeth jarred. "You're crazy, Mr. Picard. Absolutely crazy."

Freddie, you bastard! You set me up!

Everything Nick learned about the girl showed him what a sucker he had been. After the first interview with her, he almost chucked the project entirely. She had blabbered out everything, including the details of her paralyzing stage fright.

Worse than that was the girl herself. There was nothing at all to work with. Nothing except the vaguest trace of a resemblance to Juliet.

Not that he gave Kate Mallory the slightest hint of his feelings. No matter what a disaster she was to begin with, she would be his tool to show Freddie he didn't need Juliet—and to show Juliet the same thing.

So, instead of slitting his wrists, Nick cleared all his appointments for Monday and had her come back.

He spent the first hour just looking at her. Walking around the office and staring at her from different angles, as she sat in front of his desk rigid and uncomfortable.

When Peggy popped in with doughnuts and coffee mid-morning, he waved her right back out. The hopeful look on Kate's face that blossomed when she saw the doughnuts faded abruptly.

"No breakfast?" Nick asked sympathetically.

"I . . . overslept."

"Good. From now on, you're on a diet. You need to lose twenty pounds."

"Twenty? I can't possibly—"

"Maybe thirty. We'll decide that later." Nick tapped his

pencil on the desk. "And we'll do something about your hair."

"My hair?" She lifted her hand to smooth it back.

"The style's all wrong. And the color." Nick paused. An idea was forming. "Stand up."

She stood.

"Walk around."

She walked.

Sexy she was not. Rigid, cold, contained, maybe; but not sexy.

"Can't you loosen up any? Swing your hips? Something?"

She stopped dead. "What do you mean?"

Nick sighed and leaned back in his chair. Freddie, you bastard! He could just see the little asshole laughing his head off.

He leaned forward and buzzed Peggy. "Kate and I are going to the movies," he told her.

"What are we doing?" Kate asked as they took their seats in the theater.

"Watching this movie," Nick said.

"Could we get some popcorn?"

"We'll have lunch later." It would be lettuce and carrots for her, although he didn't want to mention that right now. "Watch the film."

Seeing Juliet on the screen, bigger than life, with every male in the audience lusting after her, was an almost overpowering experience for him.

He *had* made her what she was!

And *damn* but he missed her!

He tore his glance away long enough to look over at the girl beside him. Her head had nodded forward.

Nick jabbed her in the ribs. "Wake up."

"Sorry," she mumbled. "I work late."

"You just quit that job."

"I can't quit. I need the money."

"Quiet!" someone whispered behind them.

Nick lowered his voice. "You'll get a salary from Picard Productions for more than you're getting in tips as a waitress."

"My stepmother wouldn't—"

"How old are you?"

"Eighteen."

"Don't worry about it. Are you still living at home?"

She nodded.

"We'll get you an apartment and pick up the first month's rent. Then you can pay the rest out of your salary. I'll have my secretary find you something right away. We'll have you moved in by the end of the week. Peggy will mother-hen you if you have any problems. Now watch the film," he ordered.

"Yes, sir!" she said smartly. In the flickering light from the screen, he saw the smile on her face. It transformed her into something entirely different from the plain girl who had walked into the theater with him.

For the first time in days, Nick relaxed. Ah, Freddie, old boy, you were wrong after all. Your joke on me just might turn out to be a joke on you.

Nick took Kate Mallory to see *Breakdown* five more times during the next seven days. Evenings, he ran a print of *Juliet* for her in Picard Productions' projection room.

The experience affected Nick himself more than he would have guessed. For the first time the celluloid version of Juliet became more firmly implanted in his mind than the flesh-and-blood woman with whom he had shared his life.

The more familiar he became with the film Juliet, the more he began to see how, with just a few subtle changes, he could make Kate Mallory resemble her.

Almost as soon as that thought took form, he saw that Kate herself had anticipated it. Because, whether she realized it or not, Kate Mallory *wanted* to transform herself, Nick thought. It was almost as if by watching Juliet on the screen, Kate was absorbing the other woman into her own being.

But it was not an exact copy. If it worked, Nick knew that Kate would be a cooler version of Juliet. She would never be able to shake completely the emotional reserve that was so much a part of her, never become the thoughtless, reckless creature of feelings and instincts that was Juliet Brittany. Instead, where Juliet was fire, Kate would be ice—but, with any luck at all, just as explosive on the screen.

Kate dropped five pounds the first week. After that, she rebelled, gaining back two. It was a simple matter for Nick to consult a diet doctor and get her a generous prescription. After that the diet went smoothly.

Damn! Nine months of hard work and it wasn't enough.

Nick stood just behind Kate, his hands on her shoulders. He was looking not at her but at her reflection in the full-length mirror he'd had installed in her bedroom. It was all there, he thought, all the pieces. But it wasn't enough. The parts refused to add up to a whole.

Beneath his hands, Kate shifted uncomfortably, trying to turn away from her own reflection.

Nick slid his hands from her shoulders to either side of her neck and on up, until he was grasping both sides of her head, preventing her from looking away from the image of her own face.

"Don't," she protested, trying to twist out of his grasp.

Nick increased the pressure of his hands slightly, not enough to hurt her, just enough to keep her gazing into her own face. "Why don't you like to look at yourself? You know you're beautiful."

He felt the shock wave of denial ripple through her frame. "It's not real. It's not me." She dropped her glance.

"Look at yourself," he said quietly, lifting her chin with his fingers. "What do you see?"

"I see me. Kate." Nick caught the faint undercurrent of disgust in her voice. "Just plain Kate. You can dress me up in lovely clothes and surround me with beautiful things, but inside I'm just the same old Kate."

How simple it was, Nick thought as he turned her around to face him instead of the mirror. He had spent thousands of dollars on her hair, on her wardrobe, on the furnishings in this apartment, trying to turn her into the woman—the star—he knew she could be. Now he finally understood that it would only take one word to work the magic. "Listen to me," he said, as he lifted her face so that their glances locked. "Kate is gone. She no longer exists."

A soft look of bewilderment clouded her eyes. "What do—"

"Listen to me!" he commanded. "Do you know who you are? You aren't Kate. You are Kathleen. Kathleen Mallory. And you are going to stand the town on its ear, Kathleen!"

"Kathleen." Her full lips parted slightly as she breathed out the name, making him ache to lean down and kiss them. He could see her putting on the name as if it were a cloak, a magic coat behind which her other self could hide. "I'm Kathleen," she whispered as she turned to the mirror and gazed at herself.

A different person looked back out of the cool silver glass. Kate no longer existed. Kathleen Mallory had taken her place.

"Can I speak to you for a moment, Nick?"

Nick looked up. His secretary stood in the doorway of his office. "What's up, Peggy? I thought you left when Kate did."

"I wanted to talk to you privately." Peggy took the chair in front of his desk.

"You want a raise? You've got it." She was his good right hand. He had no intention of losing her.

"You may not want to give me a raise when you hear what I've got to say. It's about Kate."

Nick leaned back in his chair. "Is she cheating on her diet again? I noticed she hadn't lost as much this—"

"It's not that, it's . . . I'm not sure I like what you're doing with her, Nick."

"What I'm—"

"That girl's flesh and blood," Peggy burst out. "You're looking at her like she's a statue. She's got feelings. What will happen to her afterward?"

"She'll be a star. What happens to her after that is her business." He grinned at her, softening the words. "You worry too much, Peggy. She'll thank me for making her a star. You'll see."

"I hope so," Peggy said. "Because she'll never be able to go back to what she was before."

"What she was before was nothing," Nick said bluntly. "Why would she ever want to go back to that?"

EIGHT

1961

JULIET POURED HERSELF ANOTHER GLASS OF CHAMPAGNE. Her hotel room seemed more like a prison cell tonight. Maybe it had been a mistake to come back to Los Angeles.

It had certainly been a mistake to go to Italy with Adriano Luca. That bastard Xavier Anton had wept crocodile tears when he handed her off to Adriano, telling her a relationship with Adriano was necessary for her growth as a person. Now she realized that had been the purest bullshit. Xavier had simply been ready for a change. He lost no time replacing her with a nubile young violinist fresh from Juilliard. As for Adriano, he had claimed their movie together would be a masterpiece. Instead, it had turned out to be too spicy to play in the United States without so many cuts that the plot (what there was of it) was incomprehensible. She had refused to return to the States with Adriano for the U.S. premiere. Instead, she fled to France for six months. Alone.

She wasn't a woman who was meant to live alone, Juliet realized. Solitude did strange things to one's mind. The whole time she was in France, all she could think of was Nick. Her life, her career, everything had cratered since she left Nick, and it was all his fault.

It was certainly Nick's fault she had gone to Italy with Adriano in the first place, Juliet thought petulantly. She had been ready to go back to him, to admit she had made a mistake leaving him for Xavier in the first place. But then Frederick Yates went out of his way to let her know Nick was searching for a "new" Juliet Brittany.

Judging by the ads for *Women* in this morning's trades, he had found her. That should have been her film. Nick wrote the script for her. But that wasn't what enraged Juliet. Instead, it was the face staring up at her from *The Hollywood Reporter* on the floor beside the bed, the face that looked so much like her own but wasn't.

Who was Kathleen Mallory? Juliet wondered. Where had she come from? And how could another woman look more like her than her own sister?

Not that she had any idea what Marcy looked like now. She hadn't seen Marcy or Todd or Tony since her wedding day.

Juliet realized her glass was empty. She refilled it with the last of the champagne and leaned back against the pillows, staring moodily into space. What she wished, above all else, was to turn back the clock and be a child again, when she was her father's favorite. If only Mama hadn't died. If only Oliver hadn't turned into a monster. If only Nick still loved her.

She stared down at the picture again. Damn you, Kathleen Mallory!

She swung her legs off the bed. When she stood up, the sudden movement made her lurch against the nightstand for support. The champagne bottle teetered and fell and her glass followed it, shattering when it struck the bottle. Juliet ignored the smashed glass and knelt to pick up *The Hollywood Reporter*.

Squatting beside the bed, she ripped out the ad and stared at it, memorizing the face that looked so much like her own. "Picard Productions presents," she muttered.

She pulled herself back up and fished around through the litter on the nightstand until she found a book of matches. Then she made her unsteady way into the bathroom.

The hotel was generous with its towels. She dumped all of them into the tub. Then she pulled yards of toilet paper from the roll beside the commode and fluffed it into a nest. As she set the ad in the center of the toilet paper, she said, "Make yourself comfortable, Kathleen."

Striking the match, she let it flame for a moment and then touched it to the toilet paper.

She watched the fire until the ad caught, shriveling Kathleen Mallory's lovely face into that of a grotesque hag.

Then she went back in the bedroom, picked up the phone, and dialed room service. When the girl answered, Juliet said, "This is Room Three-twenty. Send up another bottle of champagne. And a fire-extinguisher."

Kate studied herself in the full-length mirror in her bedroom. She never tired of the miracle. Inside she was still the same old Kate, but the woman reflected in the mirror was Kathleen Mallory, film star. "Cinderella," they called her in the papers, and indeed it had been like a fairy tale come true.

But there were two sides to a fairy tale. Kate knew that now. Had Cinderella ever felt lonely at the castle? Had she missed her father, maybe even her stepsisters and her stepmother? Even if she hated them, they were her family, all the family she had.

The day Kate moved out of her father's house, Lorraine warned her that she was severing all ties with her family. Her stepmother had been more right than she had known, because even Selena had changed, dodging all Kate's invitations to get together. Selena finally confessed that Kate's father had asked her not to see Kate anymore. "I'm sorry, Kate. He told me it's him or you. I think he's wrong, but I love him."

Kate wasn't sure which was harder to understand, why her father hated *her* so much or why Selena loved *him*. All she knew was that while her family hadn't been great, she no longer had even that.

However, it was as Cinderella at the castle that Kate really felt like an imposter. Every time she dressed up as Kathleen she felt sure everyone could see right through the disguise to just plain Kate. Would there ever be a time when she didn't feel like a misfit and an outsider?

"There's my girl," Nick said, coming up behind her, still damp from the shower, a towel wrapped around his waist. He slipped his hand beneath the silk of her robe and captured her breast, teasing her nipple with his fingers.

And that was the other part of the miracle, Kate thought as she arched back against him. That someone like Nick Picard would be interested in *her*. Within weeks after they met he had become her best friend, in less than a month, her lover.

He leaned forward and captured her lips. "We have plenty of time before the party," he said after a moment.

Kate took one frightened look at the mirror. She had spent an hour turning herself into Kathleen. It would take another hour after their lovemaking to do it again. But when Nick slid his other hand down between her thighs, she moaned her surrender.

Afterward, repairing the damage their lovemaking had left on the beautiful mask that was Kathleen Mallory, Kate felt a vague sense of shame. When Nick was possessing her body, making her moan and gasp and cry, he was the center of her universe and nothing they did seemed wrong. Only afterward did she think about her mother and wonder if it had been that way for Pauline Mallory too.

. . .

The phone rang at 2 A.M.

Nick groaned and grabbed for it. "Hello."

"Nick? I need you." The voice was muffled by tears, filled with desperation. It took him a moment to recognize it.

"Juliet? Is that you?"

Kate raised up on one elbow, watching him.

"I really need you, Nick. I'm so . . . I don't know what I'm going to do. I wish I could just go to sleep and never wake up. The doctor gave me some pills, but—"

"Don't take anything, Juliet! I'll—where are you?" He motioned to Kate for something to write with.

She scrambled out of bed and returned with a pencil and pad. Nick copied down the address. "Do you want me to call your doctor?"

"I just need *you*, Nick. Please!"

"All right. I'll be right over."

He hung up the phone. "That was Juliet. I think she's . . . not well." He was dressing as he talked.

"I didn't know she was back in Los Angeles."

"Neither did I." He stopped buttoning his shirt. "Now don't get upset. This doesn't mean there's anything between us. But I was married to her for several years and she sounds like she's in a bad way."

Kate stared at him solemnly. "When will you be back?"

Nick reached for his billfold. "When I can."

Kate couldn't sleep after Nick left. Her imagination wouldn't let her.

When he hadn't returned by 4 A.M., she got up and began the slow application of the mask that turned her into Kathleen instead of plain old Kate. More promotional pictures were scheduled for this morning. When Nick set up the massive advertising campaign for *Women*, he had planned to attend to every detail himself. As she drove herself to the photographer's, Kate wondered if that would still be true this morning.

When she arrived she found she had misjudged Nick. He was already there, taking care of everything. The tired set of his jaw and the shadow of a beard on his usually clean-shaven face were the only signs of last night's activities. Just wondering what those activities were helped Kate to retreat even further behind the mask of Kathleen Mallory. On the outside she was cool, withdrawn, an icy blond beauty, just the image Nick wanted the photographer to capture. On the inside she was terrified. Was this the end of her fairy tale? Was Nick going back to Juliet?

When the photo session ended, she managed to get him alone for a few minutes. "Nick? Last night—what happened?"

"Juliet was in bad shape. She just couldn't cope. I talked her through it." He rubbed a hand across the stubble on his chin. "I'm beat, and we've still got a full day. Let's not go anywhere tonight, okay?"

"I—okay."

"Great!" He gave her a hug. "See you later."

As Kate watched him go, she had the weirdest feeling that the first round of a championship fight had just been fought between herself and Juliet.

Kate had no idea whether she had won this round or lost it.

Once or twice a month the call would come, usually in the middle of the night. Whenever the phone rang, Nick's response was always the same. If it was Juliet calling, he went. He would hang up the phone, pat Kate on the bottom, and say, "I'll be back as soon as I can."

Sometimes he returned in a couple of hours; sometimes he was gone the rest of the night; once it was two whole days before she saw him again. That was the worst. By the time he finally walked in the door, Kate had convinced herself that he was never coming back. That Juliet had won.

Tonight the call had come at 1 A.M. Nick pulled on his clothes and left immediately. If only she were really Kathleen there would be no contest, Kate thought, as she sat staring in the mirror waiting for Nick to return. But she wasn't really Kathleen; she was just plain Kate.

"Now this is the way you make an omelet," Nick said as he dumped a dozen beaten eggs into the hot skillet.

"Nick! I can't possibly eat that much," Kate protested.

"One egg's for you," he said with a great deal of satisfaction. "The rest are for me." He gave her a quick approving smile. "It's great that you don't have to diet anymore."

"Great," Kate echoed. It wasn't true. She was constantly hungry, but she didn't dare eat. Just now she had been thinking how satisfying it would be to eat a dozen eggs herself.

Except that Nick would notice. He did all their shopping, all their cooking. At first he said it was to remove her from temptation. Gradually, he had discovered he enjoyed the acts of shopping for food and cooking it. "I must have been a French chef in a previous incarnation," he often joked.

"Freddie paid up today," Nick said now, triumphantly.

Kate dragged her thoughts back from the dozen eggs, creamy and moist, with tiny bits of onion and bell pepper and mushrooms. "Paid what?"

"You know, the bet. You're a star, babe. Just like Juliet. Better than Juliet. Even Freddie had to admit it. And the little bastard came through. Now that *Women* is doing so well at the box office, we've got a great deal with the studio for the next one."

It always made Kate nervous to think about Nick's bet with Frederick Yates. She knew now if it hadn't been for

that bet, Nick would never have taken a second look at her.
Kathleen, that wondrous creation who stared back at her
from the mirror, would never have come into existence.

Nick set the skillet off the flame and gathered her in his
arms. "Let's do something to celebrate."

"Of course. What would you like to do?"

"How about getting married?"

Kate stared into his face. "Are you joking?"

"Are you turning me down?"

"Oh, no! Oh, Nick! It's going to be the happiest day in
my life!"

"Mine too. Not many guys get a chance to marry 'the
most beautiful woman in the world.'"

Kate blushed. That was a line from Nick's new script,
Diamond Lady, the one she had been working so hard to
memorize. She had protested when she came across it that
no one would believe it. They had argued for days, but Nick
refused to give in. She was Kathleen now, and Kathleen was
indeed "the most beautiful woman in the world."

"And Freddie just confirmed it with this deal," Nick said,
reading her thoughts. "So no more arguments from my star
about the script, okay?"

"No more arguments," she agreed as he shoved the skillet
back over the flame. She even forgot to be hungry.

Kate wanted a simple wedding, with just her family and
Nick's mother. Instead she got a circus.

It began when Helen Chandler insisted her son's wedding be held in the late afternoon at her Bel Air home.
Half of Hollywood was there (the timing, too, was at Helen
Chandler's insistence—she was not an early riser), including Juliet Brittany in a skin-tight silver lamé dress as Kate's
maid of honor.

That, Kate thought bitterly, was Joseph Mallory's fault.
When Kate found out her stepmother and stepsisters were

boycotting the wedding, she had asked Selena to be her maid of honor. At the last minute, under pressure from Kate's father, Selena backed out.

It was Nick who suggested Juliet. Kate had let herself be pushed into accepting her by Nick's argument that it would look odd if she had no maid of honor.

Not half as odd as having her husband's first wife, she had thought to herself. She hadn't dared say that aloud. Nick might have interpreted it as criticism of Juliet, and he was very sensitive on that subject.

Of course her father wouldn't agree to give her away. He refused to attend either the ceremony or the reception, even though the whole thing was being paid for by Nick's money and not his. Or perhaps that was the real reason behind Joseph Mallory's refusal.

Or perhaps he simply couldn't stand to see his daughter "flaunt herself" on her wedding day.

Nick had asked his stepfather, Morgan Gaynor, to give the bride away; so on the afternoon of her wedding, Kate found herself walking down the aisle on a stranger's arm while the groom waited for her in front of the altar with his ex-wife and his lawyer. Sloan Whitney had joked several times in the days before the wedding that he planned to be the best man at all Nick's weddings from now on.

No one cried during the ceremony, although Nick's mother seemed suspiciously near tears half a dozen times. Helen Chandler was a tight-lipped, twisted-faced woman, a shell of her former self. Kate had learned her new mother-in-law's physical deterioration left her prone to sudden rages, and she was terrified of the woman. At the reception, she stayed as far away from Helen Chandler as she possibly could, afraid one of those rages might break loose and cap an already ludicrous day.

When Nick led Kate out for the first dance, she was pleased to catch a glimpse over his shoulder of Helen

Chandler peacefully asleep in her chair. For the first time she dared to hope that the day wouldn't end in a farce after all.

Nick held her close. "I love you," he murmured in her ear.

Kate leaned against him, wanting to believe that with all her heart. Too bad she couldn't. She was enough of a realist to know that it was not her he loved but his creation, Kathleen. Still, she responded, "I love you too," as though it were her line in a new script.

When he held her even closer, she closed her eyes and tried to forget that Kate existed. Dancing in Nick's arms, she could almost believe that she really was the woman he loved.

Nick paused in mid-step.

Kate opened her eyes.

Morgan Gaynor was striding toward them, his face etched with a terrible grief.

"Morgan?" Nick said, releasing Kate. "Are you all right? Do you need to sit down?"

Morgan Gaynor pressed his hand to his chest. "It's Helen," he gasped. "I thought she had merely fallen asleep, but when I checked on her just now— She's dead, Nicholas."

Morgan Gaynor's knees gave way. He hit the floor before Nick could catch him.

My special day, Kate thought, surveying the remains of the wedding cake, as the caterers moved around the room, cleaning up the debris left by the wedding guests.

Frederick Yates had commandeered the limousine waiting to take her and Nick to the airport and followed the ambulance carrying Morgan Gaynor to the hospital. As soon as Nick realized there was nothing more he could do for his mother, he had gone to the hospital too. He hadn't asked Kate to come with him; in fact, she was fairly sure he had forgotten she existed.

Kate found herself wondering if Juliet Brittany had also gone to the hospital. Resolutely, she shut that thought out of her mind and went upstairs to change out of her wedding dress.

Helen Chandler's funeral was more heavily attended than her son's wedding, Kate thought, peering around at the mourners from behind the shelter of her veil. Morgan Gaynor was there, against doctor's orders, a gaunt, white-faced figure in a wheelchair. He would recover, but there was talk that even more control of the studio would pass into Frederick Yates's hands now.

After the graveside ceremony, Frederick Yates himself came charging up to Nick. Before Nick could help Kate into the waiting limousine, Frederick grabbed his arm and pulled him around. "Morgan just told me about the tombstone!" he stormed at Nick. "Did you talk him into that?"

"Freddie, for God's sake—talk him into what?"

"He's ordered a double tombstone. He's going to have himself buried beside Helen!"

Nick handed Kate into the limousine and turned back to face Frederick. "I knew it was a double plot. I didn't know about the tombstone."

"You bastard! You talked him into it."

Kate couldn't see what was happening. She heard a brief scuffling sound outside the car, a thump against the roof, and then the sound of Nick's voice, pitched too low for her to catch the words. She realized Frederick must have swung on Nick and that Nick now had him pinned against the car, trying to calm him.

After a moment, Nick released Frederick and the other man hurried off.

"Nick?" she asked as he got into the limousine. "What happened?"

Nick grinned at her. "Apparently Freddie thought Morgan was being unfaithful to his mother by wanting to be buried next to mine."

Then his face grew solemn. He didn't speak to her again on the drive back.

When Nick first mentioned traveling up the coast, Kate thought it was to make up for their canceled honeymoon in the Caribbean. She soon found it was anything but.

"It's a natural," he told her as he loaded his camera equipment into the car. " 'The most beautiful woman in the world' photographed with the oldest trees in the world."

It *was* beautiful among the redwoods. And lonely. Thank goodness. Because Nick wanted photographs of her and not her clothes.

Kate's protests fell on deaf ears. "You'll see," he told her. "It worked with Juliet. It'll work with you."

So finally Kate just blanked her mind and let Kathleen take over. Kathleen didn't mind flaunting her nude body against the bark of the gigantic redwood trees or standing all alone in the silent forest while swirls of mist encircled her. Kathleen loved it.

It was only Kate, buried deep inside, who writhed in embarrassment while the motor drive of Nick's Nikon clicked out its song like some strange insect of the forest.

Nick found her among the packing boxes in one of the upstairs bedrooms of Helen Chandler's Bel Air home.

Her home now, Kate reminded herself. All the contents of their former apartment fit easily into this one room when they moved into the house after Helen Chandler's death.

She was acutely aware of how she looked in shorts and a faded work shirt, without makeup, her hair tied back from her face with a scarf. "I didn't realize you were home," she said quickly, by way of apology, before he could mention her appearance. "I was looking for something."

Nick glanced around at the stacks of boxes. "Why don't you just unpack and be done with it?"

"I haven't had time. We've been working on a picture, remember?" It was true *Diamond Lady* had just wrapped, but she wouldn't have unpacked the boxes even if she'd had time. The accessories she had been so proud of in the tiny apartment they shared before their marriage looked woefully out of place among her late mother-in-law's priceless antiques.

"That's your department," Nick said with a shrug.

She looked at Nick suspiciously, not trusting the grin that suddenly lit his face. "Have you got something behind your back?"

"Bingo!" Nick handed her an open copy of *Playboy*. "Congratulations," he said. "You're gorgeous!"

Stunned, Kate leafed through the photo spread. I must be splitting in two, she thought wildly. There, on the magazine page, was Kathleen, glorying in her nakedness in the redwood forest. And here, in Helen Chandler's former mansion, was plain old Kate, looking at that glossy sexual creature and wishing she were dead.

"Great, huh?" Nick said. "I told you that you were the most beautiful woman in the world. Now everyone knows it." He ran his hand up under her shirt and into her bra, taking possession of her breast.

She opened her mouth to Nick's kiss, but she could feel the chill settling over her body, damping out any desire on her part.

Kathleen would love this, she thought, as Nick pulled her down on the carpet beside him. He eased down her shorts and panties and inserted himself into her. But I'm not Kathleen!

She lay there, letting Nick find his own release.

At the last minute, she panicked, afraid he would be angry, and faked her own orgasm just as Nick came.

He pushed himself off her and looked down with an expression somewhere between disgust and anger. "What's wrong with you?" he demanded. "You don't ever seem to enjoy yourself anymore."

Kate turned her face away.

After a moment she heard the front door slam, and a few minutes later Nick's car drove off.

He was in his office this time when the call came.

"Nick? I need you." The sexy whisper of Juliet's voice over the phone made him harden.

"What's wrong?"

"Franco left last night. I'm all alone." Franco was the latest of her lovers, a former busboy turned actor turned gigolo. "I'm so lonely, Nick."

It's time for you to get on with your life, Juliet. We're not married anymore. Find some other patsy.

That's what he should have said.

What he did say was, "I'll be there in half an hour."

Nick was barely inside the door of her apartment before Juliet was all over him, tearing at his clothes, kissing him, holding him, so desperate for him that her fire ignited his.

Why am I doing this? he wondered as she pulled him down to the floor beside her. It's Kate I love.

But why can't Kate be like this?

Then he groaned in surrender.

After Nick left, Juliet lit a cigarette with shaking hands. Why was it that life didn't seem complete without Nick? What was it about her that made her unable to function alone?

He hadn't been gone five minutes and already she was

plotting how she could get him back. Juliet knew she walked a fine line with Nick. At any time, he might refuse to come when she called. He might decide that his present wife was more important to him than his ex-wife.

Then what would she do?

NINE

❧

1962

KATE COWERED IN HER DRESSING ROOM. FOR THE third morning in a row, nausea had forced her to rush off the set of *Couples*. No doubt remained in her mind. She was pregnant. The thought of how Nick would react to the news terrified her. As director he would simply rearrange shooting around her changing body. But as her husband what would he do? What would he say?

Since his mother's death, Nick had grown more self-assured. Almost cocky. That change in him was mainly because of the fame he had achieved for his creation, Kathleen Mallory.

And why not? Kate thought. The fame was his doing, not hers. On her own, Kate could never have become the cool, elegant creature who moved as gracefully through the jungle of Hollywood's social life as on the screen.

Another wave of nausea swept over her.

Kate struggled to her feet and hurried into the bathroom. Her stomach finally empty, she washed her face, knowing how angry the makeup man would be to learn he had to redo his work. As she glanced at the pale, frightened face in the mirror, she thought, *That's the real me. That's Kate.*

It was foolish Kate who got herself pregnant. Kathleen would never have been that stupid.

That night several weeks ago, Kate had been afraid Nick would accuse her once again of being cold, so she hadn't told him her diaphragm wasn't yet in place. She couldn't stand it when he was angry or impatient with her, and he would have been both if she had called a halt to their lovemaking long enough to insert it. Instead, she lay there worrying, unable to respond to his kisses or caresses—and he had been angry after all.

Kate dampened a washcloth and pressed it to her fevered face. What in the world was she going to do? One thing was certain. Whatever she did, Nick would be angry with her.

"She's what?" Nick stared at the doctor in amazement. Of all the diagnoses he had expected when he realized how sick Kate had been, this was the last one.

"The lab tests will be back in a few days. However, I've been in this business too long not to know a mother-to-be when I see one," the doctor said jovially. "Congratulations, Mr. Picard. You're going to be a father."

"Where is she?"

"She's still in the examination room." The doctor pointed. "Second door on the left."

Nick hurried down the hall. When he opened the door of the examination room, Kate was reaching for her clothes. She clutched the sheet to herself like a shield as she turned around. Her eyes were huge, frightened, as she watched him close the door. "Nick?" she said hoarsely. "Are you angry?"

"Angry?" He walked over and gently tugged the sheet away, letting it fall to the floor between them. Putting his arm around her shoulder, he pulled her close. Slowly he ran his right hand over the gentle swell of her abdomen. "You've made me the happiest man in the world." It was true, too, even though the news had sent his brain into overdrive trying to figure out how to shoot the last half of *Couples* around a pregnant star. For just a moment, he was troubled by the memory of how upset he had been when he thought Juliet was pregnant in their first year of marriage. What a jerk he had been. Not this time, though. He would be the perfect husband, the perfect father. He could hardly wait.

The view of Los Angeles from the terrace of Juliet's apartment was more spectacular than usual as pinpoints of light began to dot the cool violet shadows of the evening.

Juliet sat with her back to the cityscape, lost in her own dark thoughts. Why did everyone find it so funny that she wanted to be a serious actress? Nobody laughed at Sophia Loren for trying to change her image. And look at her now, up for an Oscar for Best Actress for her performance in *Two Women*, subtitles and all.

The thought of subtitles reminded her of Nick, of that wild night long ago when they made love in their car after the foreign movie. Her glance dropped to the glass top of the wrought-iron table beside her, where a magazine lay open to an article entitled "New Role for Kathleen Mallory: Motherhood."

The Chablis in her glass had warmed to the temperature of her hand. She took a long sip of the wine and then set the glass down deliberately on the glossy full-page close-up of Kathleen Mallory's beautiful face.

What Juliet most feared had come to pass. That bitch whose coldly perfect face mocked her own had finally given Nick a reason to refuse to come to Juliet when she called him.

A knot of nausea twisted in Juliet's stomach. She had done the right thing, she assured herself. When Nick found out, he might be angry at first—but he would get over it. He always got over his anger with her. Because whether he realized it or not, she was the one he really loved. Otherwise, why would he have created this emotionless doll in Juliet's own image?

Thank God she had gone ahead with her plan when she did. If she'd had even the slightest doubt about her course of action, the confirmation lay on the table beside her.

Nausea twisted her stomach again. Juliet snatched up her wine and drained the glass. All she needed was time. Four months should be enough. Then she would call Nick, and he would come. He would tell her it was for the last time— but he would come.

Juliet stared down at the wet, puckered circle the wineglass had left on Kathleen Mallory's face. If Nick agreed to come one last time, that was all she needed.

He would be hers forever.

Kate stretched out on a lounger beside the cool aquamarine waters of the pool, enjoying the warmth of the sun, her fears of a few months ago all but forgotten. How could she have misjudged Nick so badly? When he learned she was pregnant, her life had changed dramatically, overnight.

On the set, Nick had always been a difficult, demanding director, never satisfied until something was perfect. However, once he learned she was expecting, he had been careful not to tire her with endless retakes. Since *Couples* finally wrapped three months ago, life had become one long lazy day after another. When Nick was home, he treated her like a princess, waiting on her hand and foot.

With all that tender loving care, Kate found herself relaxing for the first time since their marriage. She couldn't believe how stupid her fears had been. She had imagined that Nick would walk out on her as soon as he heard the news. Or, worse, that he would force her to have an abortion. Her change in attitude had reflected itself in their lovemaking. No longer tense and worried, she could relax and really enjoy herself, even though she was hugely pregnant now. She could even put the worry of her mother's promiscuity aside because this was different. Within the bonds of matrimony, she was free to do anything Nick wanted, to accept any pleasure he gave her.

Nick had noticed the change. "Pregnancy becomes you," he had murmured in her ear last night.

The baby kicked. Kate shifted to a more comfortable position on the lounger. She closed her eyes and let herself drift in the memory of last night's lovemaking.

The faint scuff of footsteps across the flagstones interrupted Kate's pleasurable thoughts. Her eyes flew open. She squinted into the sun at the figure looming over her, acutely aware of the blush burning along her cheekbones.

"The mail, madam," the maid said.

"Thank you, Lois."

The maid scuffled away.

She must think I'm an idiot! Kate shook her head at her own stupidity as she shuffled through the stack of mail.

Lois had handed her five bills and a square white envelope. The bills she set aside for Nick. He liked to open those himself, and Kate was quite willing to let him handle all the money matters. She didn't recognize the handwriting on the envelope. Inside, she found a card and several photographs.

"You're invited to a baby shower," the card said, although the time and place were not filled in. At the bottom, someone had written, *I thought you would want to know.* It was signed, *A Friend.*

Kate glanced at the photographs. Her hands began to tremble. They were all of Juliet Brittany, an obviously pregnant Juliet Brittany.

All the warmth drained out of her body. Nick! How could you?

The answer came back, sharp as a knife: *If you were really Kathleen Mallory, he wouldn't have.*

. . .

After dinner, Nick came around to her end of the table and put his hands on her shoulders. Kate felt herself shrinking away from him. "You look lovely tonight." He brushed his lips against her cheek. "I thought about you all day long."

And I've thought about you, she wanted to scream at him. You and Juliet. Only she knew it wasn't really his fault. It was hers, for not being more of a woman. "I . . . I think I'll go on up to bed," she said abruptly, pulling free of his hands. "I'm very tired."

Nick watched her go up the stairs. Even eight months pregnant, she was a joy to the eyes. But cold as an iceberg sometimes, and this was obviously going to be one of those times.

He walked over to the bar, irritated by her and by himself. Birth might be a beautiful experience, but it certainly left a guy horny. He wasn't sure how long he would be able to hold out.

The phone rang.

"Nick?"

The mere sound of Juliet's voice aroused him, and he realized it had been months since he last saw her. He knew she was going to ask him to come to her. He steeled himself to tell her that things were different now. He was about to become a father. His extracurricular activities would have to stop.

"We need to talk," Juliet said.

Nick hesitated, caught off guard. Usually these conversations began with her saying desperately that she needed him, and he always responded. Instead of the grand gesture of self-denial he had been about to make, he found himself asking, "Tonight?"

"Yes."

Intrigued by the change in her, he said, "I'll be there in a little while."

After he hung up, he started toward the stairs to tell Kate good-bye. With one foot on the bottom step, he thought better of it. An iceberg didn't need company or good-byes. An iceberg was sufficient unto itself.

Kate stood at the window and watched Nick's newest Corvette shoot down the drive. Inside her stomach, the baby began a lazy cartwheel. She put both hands around the undulating bulge and stood there, tears coursing down her cheeks, long after Nick's car disappeared.

Juliet didn't answer the doorbell.

Nick tried the door and found it unlocked. He stepped inside and called her name. When there was no response, he panicked. As long as he had known her, Juliet had danced on the edge of an emotional chasm. The threat of suicide had remained unspoken between them. Nonetheless, Nick's worst fear was that one day when she called he would arrive too late and find she had taken her own life.

He hurried through the apartment, frantically calling her name.

"I'm in here," Juliet called from the bedroom.

Relieved, Nick opened the bedroom door. Juliet stood on the balcony, her back to him, gazing out at the lights of Los Angeles, which were spread like a sparkling carpet across the night hills. She turned.

Nick saw her silhouette against the glow of the city. He halted in mid-step. "Juliet? Are you—how did . . . ?"

She laughed. "How did it happen, Nick? You know that as well as I do."

"Are you saying it's my baby?"

"Of course it is."

"What do you expect me to do about it?" he asked her,

stalling for time, as he tried to think.

Juliet laughed again. "I expect you to love me, Nick." She held out her hand. He crossed to her and took it, pulling her into his arms. Kate would never understand, he thought, as Juliet lifted her face for a kiss.

But Kate was cold and distant, and Juliet was warm and close. He had a momentary flush of shameful pride at having fathered a child on not one, but two such beautiful women.

"There's going to be hell to pay," he murmured as he kissed Juliet's upturned face again.

"It will be worth the price," she promised.

1963

Kate held Nick's hand as they gazed in through the wide expanse of glass at the newborns. "She's awake this time."

"She's beautiful," Nick said softly. "Just like her mother."

Kate looked up at his face. What she saw there made her lean against him. Nick put his arm around her and drew her even closer. Kate felt the icy core that formed within her the day she learned about Juliet's baby beginning to melt.

"I can't wait to take my two girls home. I've bought a few presents," Nick admitted sheepishly.

Kate thought of the baseball equipment, footballs, and wagons he had already purchased in the last month, preparing for the arrival of a son. "What kind of presents? Oh, Nick, you're not disappointed she's a girl, are you?"

"How could I be disappointed with a daughter as lovely as Danielle?"

He turned back to look at the baby. As she watched his face light up with pride, Kate made a vow to herself. Nothing was going to destroy her marriage. She no longer cared about Juliet and her pregnancy; all she cared about was Nick and her own child. She would let nothing come between them, even her own jealousy. If she had to share Nick with another woman to keep him, then she would.

Kathleen wouldn't, an inner voice nagged.

But I'm not Kathleen, she told it. *I'm Kate.* And for the first time she was proud of it.

The night her labor started, Juliet was more frightened than she had ever been in her entire life, and more alone.

Nick was out of town, somewhere up the coast with Kathleen Mallory and his new daughter. Juliet's frantic attempts to reach him had been in vain. She suspected that was the fault of Nick's secretary. Peggy must have taken Kathleen Mallory's side against her. Nick would never have ignored her messages. He knew how apprehensive she was about having this baby, and how terrified she was of being alone.

But alone she was, in the hands of unfeeling strangers, as pain after pain racked her.

Far worse than the pain were the indelible memories of the plates in the book on pregnancy Helen Chandler had given her. The fear of what all this suffering would produce was even more terrifying than what was happening to her body. What kind of monstrosity would she bring into the world?

Juliet's labor stretched on into the next morning. At 8 A.M., the doctor, growing sympathetic at last to her pleas, tried to contact Nicholas Picard.

He too met with a wall of silence.

Juliet's daughter was born at 10:24 A.M.

The nurse held up the baby, red, wrinkled, screaming.

Juliet turned her head away. She had given birth to a monster.

"Here's your daughter, Mrs. Picard," the nurse said, offering the tiny blanket-wrapped bundle.

Juliet scooted farther back on the bed. She did not raise her arms to take the child. "What's wrong with her?"

The nurse laughed. "Why, nothing. She's the most perfect baby I've ever seen." She laid the child in Juliet's arms.

Juliet looked down into her daughter's eyes, blue as her own, and fear stabbed through her. She had thought no further than binding Nick to her with a child. The reality of a baby was terrifying.

"I'll help you start nursing her," the nurse said, "and then I'll check back—"

"No!" Juliet thrust the baby back at the nurse. "I can't. I need to make a phone call."

"But Mrs. Picard, you have to—"

"I won't. I can't." Juliet began to sob. "I want Nick. Why doesn't he come?"

The nurse stood helplessly, clutching the baby as Juliet's sobs escalated, and then turned and hurried from the room.

Minutes later, another nurse appeared, along with Juliet's doctor. By then, Juliet's sobs had grown too violent. She was unable to tell them that Nick was all she needed.

She barely felt the needle's prick.

"Hello, beautiful."

Juliet opened her eyes. Sunlight was streaming in through the window of her hospital room. Someone leaned over her bed. She squinted against the glare. "Nick?" she whispered. "Is it really you?" She began to cry again.

The bed creaked as Nick sat down on the edge and gathered her into his arms. She clung to him, sobbing.

"Shall I call the doctor, Mr. Picard?" the nurse asked.

Juliet clutched Nick even more tightly. "No," she murmured against his chest.

"She'll be all right in a minute," Nick told the nurse.

When Juliet heard the door click shut, she said, "I needed you so much, Nick."

"I'm here now," he told her.

Another sob broke through. "I wanted you here this morning. When the baby was coming."

He tightened his arms around her. "That was yesterday, Juliet. You've been out since then."

She gasped. "Am I all right? Is there something wrong with me?"

"You're fine. You were just upset. The doctor gave you something to make you sleep." Nick's voice grew firm. "Now you have work to do."

She lifted her hand to her hair. "A film? I couldn't, Nick, not for a few weeks. My hair is a mess and my figure—"

"Not a film," he said patiently. "The baby, our baby. You're a mother now. You have to act like one."

"But, Nick, I don't know anything about being a mother."

"You'll learn." He held her away from him, and she saw something change in his face. "We've brought another human being into the world, Juliet. Now we have to take care of her."

"Nick, I can't!"

Nick pushed the call button. When the nurse answered, he said, "Mrs. Picard is ready to feed the baby now."

Panic fluttered in Juliet's stomach. "Nick! Don't do this to me! I don't know how."

"I'll be waiting right outside until you're finished," he said as he stood up.

Juliet wanted to shriek at him, but she was afraid he might leave her if she did.

She watched him disappear through the door. In a few minutes, the same nurse as yesterday appeared with the baby in her arms. This time, instead of advancing confidently, the nurse eyed Juliet suspiciously from just inside the room. "Mr. Picard said you wanted to try and nurse the baby."

"Yes," Juliet said hoarsely and then shut her mouth before

she could babble out anything else.

The nurse handed her the baby and helped her arrange her gown. Juliet wondered how she should start, but the baby took care of the next step herself, her greedy little mouth fastening around the nipple.

"She's going to be a healthy eater," the nurse said after a moment.

As the baby continued to nurse hungrily, Juliet found that her daughter began to fit more comfortably into the curve of her arm.

When the baby finally finished, the nurse showed Juliet how to burp her and then took her away.

Nick came in then, beaming. "The nurse told me you did a great job. I'm proud of you."

Juliet smiled, basking in his approval. "Come and sit beside me again."

"Sorry, babe. I've got an appointment this morning I can't break. I'll be back when I—"

"Nick, don't leave!" She grabbed his hand. "Stay here with me. I'm afraid."

He pulled his hand free. "You're a big girl now, Juliet. A mother. You're going to have to act like one. I'll be back as soon as I can."

Then he was gone and she was alone once more. And terrified.

Nicholas Picard was bathing his daughter. Kate stood in the bathroom doorway, watching nine-month-old-Danielle splashing happily in the tub with her father's hands steadying her, and tried not to wonder if he did the same thing with his other daughter.

Juliet's baby was six months old now. Kate had seen a photograph of her on the front page of one of the tabloids. Eden was a beautiful baby. So had Dani been, at first.

These days Kate found herself searching her daughter's

face anxiously, wondering if her own plainness would eventually win out over Nick's genes.

"There you go, pumpkin," Nick told his daughter. "Clean as a whistle." Just as he reached for the towel, the phone rang.

Kate stayed where she was.

"Aren't you going to get that?" Nick asked, as he toweled Dani dry.

"All right," Kate said. She didn't hurry. The phone had rung twelve times by the time she picked up the receiver. It was Juliet, of course, just as she had known it would be.

"Is Nick there?" Juliet asked breathlessly. "I have to talk to him. It's an emergency."

This kind of emergency happened at least twice a week. Kate put her hand over the receiver. "It's for you, Nick."

"Coming." In a moment he appeared with Dani wrapped in a towel. He handed the baby to Kate and picked up the phone.

Kate watched him for a moment and then took Dani to her room and began to dress her. She was just lacing the baby's right shoe when Nick came in.

"She's having trouble with Eden. I'll be back as soon as I can."

"What kind of trouble?" Kate asked, surprised that her voice was so steady.

"Colic, I think. Juliet's convinced it's the end of the world. Good-bye, pumpkin," he said as he leaned over to kiss Dani on the cheek.

And then he was gone.

Kate picked up the left shoe and fitted it on Dani's tiny foot. Slowly, she began to lace it. She ought to enjoy a day at home alone, she thought. It was one of the last she'd have for a while. Tomorrow she would begin interviewing housekeepers. With *Couples* being released this month, Nick had lined up a backbreaking series of promotional events for the picture. Kate would be traveling almost constantly for a while. But the truth was she was alone most of the time anyway—even when Nick was home. Even though he hadn't said anything about his next project, Kate knew he was working on something. All his free time was spent in his study, pecking away on his typewriter.

That wasn't exactly a fair assessment, she rebuked herself. Nick made sure that there was plenty of time each day for Dani.

And then there was Juliet. Or, to be more precise, Juliet's daughter.

Nick always went when Juliet called him, but nowadays Kate had the feeling it was more for Eden's sake than for Juliet's. No doubt Juliet had counted on that when she decided to have the baby.

Kate and Nick had never discussed Juliet—or Danielle's half-sister. Kate was too terrified of rocking the boat to bring it up. Still, she couldn't help thinking that if it weren't for Juliet and Juliet's child, she and Nick and Dani would actually be the happy family they appeared to be.

The lie she lived was beginning to fray her nerves.

TEN

1964

TWO MEN WERE KISSING IN THE GAZEBO.

Nick glanced at them idly as he walked by. Conrad Hilliard's parties were known for their eclectic mix of guests. Even for someone of Nick's stature, to be invited to one of Hilliard's parties meant that you had really arrived in this town. He knew for a fact that Freddie had never received an invitation—even though Morgan's retirement last year had given him complete control of the studio. That thought put an extra spring in Nick's step.

The knot of people by the pool untangled, and Nick saw his host's tall form in the center of it.

He made his way over. "Mr. Hilliard," he said, extending his hand. "Thanks for the invitation. I've been looking forward to meeting you."

Hilliard gave him a long cold stare. "I'm not sure I know your name, young man."

Nick flushed, but he kept his grin in place. He even managed not to glance around to see if anyone had overheard Hilliard's remark. "Sorry. I'm Nicholas Picard."

Conrad wrinkled his brow. "Helen's son?"

Nick's grin vanished. That wasn't his only claim to fame anymore. "Yes, sir."

"How is Helen?"

"She's dead, Mr. Hilliard."

"Oh, right." Conrad Hilliard's attention wandered to the tray of drinks held aloft by a passing waiter. "Oh, boy," he called. "Over here."

When the waiter approached, Hilliard took not one but two drinks and wandered off in the direction of the pool.

Nick met the waiter's glance. The waiter lifted his eyebrows a fraction of an inch. Nick took a drink himself and stood there, trying to regain the elation he had felt a few moments ago, but it was no use. So much for his theory about the importance of his invitation. It must have been some PR man's mistake. He drained the glass and set it down.

He should circulate, he thought. Make the most of it, while he was here. But he found he'd lost his stomach for mingling. Nick turned and walked back the way he had come.

The two men were still kissing in the gazebo. As he approached, they broke apart. One of them walked swiftly past Nick, toward the house. As he passed, Nick could see a smear of lipstick across his lips.

Nick glanced toward the gazebo.

The other man, in suit and tie, caught Nick's glance on him. As Nick watched, the man reached up and unpinned his hair. He leaned over, letting it fall free, a blond tangle in the moonlight, and combed it out with his fingers.

When the figure stood up again, Nick saw that he had been mistaken. It was not a tall slim man but a tall woman, her figure hidden by the suit: Allison Hilliard, the great man's daughter.

"Nice performance, Miss Hilliard," Nick called to her.

"Thank you, Mr. Picard." The sultry note in her voice made his spine tingle. "I wonder if I might meet you at your office sometime this week."

"Why, of course, Miss Hilliard."

"Good." She leaped over the gazebo rail as lightly as a

young boy, paused a moment to straighten her tie, and walked off in the direction her companion had taken.

Nick watched her go, wondering just what that was all about.

"I'm surprised you could find time for me." Allison Hilliard looked around Nick's office as though she were calculating the cost of the furnishings. Her glance stopped at the two framed baby pictures on his desk. "What with the demands of multiple fatherhood."

"You seem to know a lot about me," Nick said. "I'm flattered. I know a lot about you too."

"Just what is it that you know about me, Mr. Picard?"

"I know that I'd like you to call me Nick."

She didn't warm to his smile.

If she wanted this strictly business, then so be it, Nick thought. And with gloves off. "You're an actress by birth, which is a blessing and a curse. Up till now you haven't been able to shake the label of being Conrad Hilliard's daughter. Most people think you've gotten as far as you have because of your family name."

"And what do you think, Nick?"

"I think you're a damn fine actress, Miss Hilliard."

"Allison."

"Allison. But you haven't had the right director yet. Until you do, no one will realize that you're not just the great man's daughter."

"What an interesting assessment, Nick. I'll keep it in mind."

She gathered up her things and left. She had been in his office less than five minutes, Nick realized.

After a moment, Peggy came in with a fresh cup of coffee. "So what did she want?"

Nick leaned back in his chair. "I'm not sure. I think she's on a fishing expedition."

"Fishing for what?"

"Fame."

"She *is* famous, Nick."

"Not the way she wants to be."

The phone rang. "If it's dinnertime, it must be Juliet," Kate said, slamming down her wineglass.

Nick raised an eyebrow as he passed her on the way to the phone. When he came back, he said, "I have to leave."

"All she has to do is whistle and you come," Kate said bitterly. "Dani and I don't really matter, do we?"

"What's your problem tonight?"

"The same problem I have every night. I'm getting tired of sharing my husband."

Nick came around and stood behind her. He dropped a kiss on the top of her head. "Juliet's not as good with children as you are. She needs help with Eden."

"Let her hire it."

Nick drew back. "Eden is my daughter too. It wasn't something I intended, but it happened. I won't evade the responsibility."

"What about Juliet? Isn't she evading her responsibility as a mother? What if just for once you said no to her, Nick. What if you said, 'I'm having dinner with my wife and for once I don't want to be disturbed.' "

"Juliet isn't entirely stable. You know that."

"I don't know that. All I know is that you spend almost every evening with her and not with your wife."

"I have to go," Nick said.

"Then go!"

She sat where she was until she heard the Corvette squeal out of the drive. Then she stood up slowly and began to clear the table. Her plate was still half-full; her appetite had vanished the moment the phone rang.

When she finished in the kitchen, she went up to check

on Dani and found the little girl sleeping peacefully.

Kate longed to do the same. But after she got into bed, she couldn't seem to drop off. She kept wondering what Nick and Juliet were doing. No matter how hard she tried to relax, she couldn't rid her mind of the image of the two of them together.

Finally she got up and went down to Nick's study, where a pile of unread scripts had accumulated. She took the top five back upstairs with her. At least they did the trick. Halfway through the first one, her eyes grew so heavy that she switched off the light and fell asleep almost at once.

Something woke her in the night—someone moving in the room. Kate's heart fluttered painfully in her chest for a moment, and then she realized it must be Nick.

She glanced at the faintly glowing face of the clock beside her bed: 3:15 A.M. She tried not to think of what Nick had been doing until that hour of the morning.

The rustle of the sheets had alerted him. He crossed to the bed and stood over her. Unwilling to feign sleep, Kate gazed up, but she was unable to make out his features in the gloom. Suddenly, he switched on a flashlight, shining it right in her face.

"Nick!" she protested, flinging her arm across her eyes to protect them from the glare.

"Juliet?" a strange male voice said hoarsely. He grabbed her arm, yanking it away from her face.

Still blinded by the light, Kate tried to scramble out of bed.

He caught her by the shoulder, flinging her back on the mattress, the flashlight still shining full in her face.

Then the flashlight disappeared into the bedclothes, as he tried to climb on top of her. She could feel the hardness of him.

"No!" she screamed.

He grabbed the top of her gown and ripped it, baring her breasts, and at the same time tried to separate her legs with his knee.

She fought him silently, but he was bigger, stronger than she was. He lifted himself up, and she heard the sound of his zipper in the darkness. Then he was back on top of her. She felt the hard pole of flesh poking at her inner thighs.

Kate's fingers grazed something in the sheets. The flashlight! She grabbed it and hit the man as hard as she could across the back of his head.

He groaned and fell to one side.

She struck again, wildly. Her eyes still had not adjusted to the dark. She was unable to see exactly where he was.

Twice, she missed. The third time she heard a satisfying *thunk* as she connected with his head.

He half-fell, half-scrambled off the bed. He was silhouetted for a moment as he stumbled past the faint moonlit rectangle of the balcony door. Then she heard the bedroom door open and close.

Dani!

Kate scrambled out of bed, holding her torn nightgown around her, and raced down the hall to her daughter's room. When she switched on the light, she saw Danielle still peacefully asleep in her crib. Kate grabbed the toddler up so abruptly that she began to cry.

Kate clutched her daughter and tried to decide what to do. There was no phone in Dani's room. She should have called the private guard service from the phone in her bedroom, Kate realized belatedly. The thought of leaving this safe rectangle of light for the dark hall terrified her. Dani cried louder. Wet warmth flooded through her diaper to Kate's gown.

Kate steeled herself as she stepped to the nursery door and looked both ways down the hall.

It was empty, but she knew he could be anywhere in the

house. Kate held Dani to her and hurried down the hall to her own bedroom and the phone.

The private security guards arrived less than five minutes after her call. Kate had waited in her bedroom, afraid to venture down the hall to the nursery to change Dani's diaper, afraid to put her down long enough to put on something over her ruined nightgown. She met them at the door of the bedroom, reeking of ammonia and trying desperately to keep the nightgown closed while holding a squirming toddler.

"You say you didn't get a good look at him, Mrs. Picard?"

"That's right. He had a flashlight. He shined it in my face."

"That's the same flashlight you used to beat him off?"

"Yes, that's right."

"Where is it now?"

"Why, I"—Kate glanced around the bedroom—"I'm sure it's here somewhere. Unless"—she began to tremble—"unless he came back for it while I was in Dani's room."

"You were all alone in the house?"

"Except for my little girl, yes."

"Where's your husband, Mrs. Picard?"

"He's out."

The two patrolmen exchanged glances. "We'll just check the house and grounds," one of them said.

In the end they found nothing. That should have comforted her, but something about the manner of the security patrol disturbed her. It was almost as if they didn't believe her.

"I understand you have a new movie coming out soon, Mrs. Picard," one of guards said as they were about to leave.

"Why, yes."

Again that exchange of looks. And then she knew. They thought this was some kind of publicity stunt. "Thank you for coming by," Kate said coldly. She made a great show of locking the door behind them, Dani balanced on her hip.

At least they had been thorough when they checked the house. She would have been afraid to stay in it alone, otherwise. The alarm system hadn't been turned on, and that had provoked another exchange of looks between the guards, she remembered. How could they know it was always Nick who turned the system on and off? Since he hadn't been there, she hadn't thought to activate it.

She did now. If Nick came home and set it off himself, that was his problem.

After she changed Danielle's diaper and the sheet and put the little girl back to bed, she thought for a moment about calling Nick. Surely he would consider her being assaulted important enough to tear himself away from Juliet.

One brief glance in the mirror convinced Kate otherwise. Her hair was matted and tangled, her nightgown ripped, and she stank of urine.

What a ridiculous charade this marriage was, Kate thought as she turned away from her reflection. She was tired of pretending that everything was all right, that Nick could actually love her.

It was time to think about a divorce.

"Allison! So nice to see you again," Nick said as Peggy ushered the great man's daughter into his office. Not that she couldn't have picked a better morning for this appointment. It had taken him all night to calm Juliet's hysterics. He hadn't gotten home until the sun was up, and then he had to deal with one of Kate's silent moods. The housekeeper had informed him there had been a break-in last night, but she knew no more about it than that. Since Kate wasn't about to interrupt her silent treatment with a few facts, Nick had stopped to talk to the security people on the way to the office. They seemed to think it was a publicity stunt cooked up by him. He thought it was a stunt cooked up by Kate to keep him home. He and Kate were going to have a discussion about that tonight.

"I was pleased that you had time to work me in today," Allison Hilliard said.

"I always have time for you." A courting dance, obviously. But was he doing the courting or was she?

"I must tell you that my agent objected strenuously when I told him I planned to talk to you today."

"I'm glad you didn't listen to him."

"I did more than that." Allison Hilliard smiled. "I fired him."

Nick blinked. He knew Joel Edelmann. Everyone knew Joel. The old fart was an institution in Hollywood. You didn't fire him; he fired you. If Allison Hilliard hadn't been Conrad Hilliard's daughter, she wouldn't have landed Edelmann for an agent in a million years. Yet she'd had the nerve to fire him. "And what was it he objected to?" Nick asked cautiously.

"I told him I was going to put my career in your hands." Allison Hilliard leaned forward. "Everyone says you're a star maker. You've done it twice, turned nobodies into stars. I'm giving you something better to work with, Nick. I'm not a nobody. I'm already a star. Make me something more than that."

So he had guessed right about her!

Nick clamped down on his own elation. Allison Hilliard was going to be his passport to the kind of success he had only dreamed about.

"Well?" she asked.

"You've got a deal."

Allison Hilliard climbed into the waiting limousine. "Home," she told the driver, and then slid the panel shut, so that she was completely cut off and secure in her own little world. What a wonderful investment that postage stamp had been, she thought. She had known Nicholas Picard wouldn't turn down an invitation to her father's party. Nobody ever turned down an invitation to one of Conrad Hilliard's parties.

She leaned back, savoring the look she had seen in Nick's eyes just now, the look that said he planned to use her, to use her connections. She knew as well as he that, with his talent and her connections, Nicholas Picard could be something special in Hollywood.

God, the vanity of the male animal was beyond belief! It would never occur to Nicholas Picard that *she* planned to use *him*.

BOOK TWO

PUPPET

Allison

1964–1973

At second glance, the artistic eye could see a decidedly masculine component in Allison Hilliard's renowned beauty. Hollywood chose to ignore this essential clue to the real woman. Therefore, no one understood why the daughter of an acting legend like Conrad Hilliard needed my help to achieve her true fame.

Of course, I chose her roles and directed her—but those actions did not make Allison the superstar she is today.

Instead, it was my unspoken assurance that, of all Hollywood, I alone understood the real role she was born to play, the greatest role of her life—that of being a better man than her father.

—From the unpublished memoirs of Nicholas Picard

ELEVEN

1964

Hᴉs Rᴏʏᴀʟ ᴍᴀᴊᴇsᴛʏ ʀᴏsᴇ ᴀᴛ ᴅᴀᴡɴ. Fʀᴏᴍ ʜᴇʀ ʙᴇᴅ-
room, Allison Hilliard followed His Highness's progress
by the sounds of the household. First came the ceremony
of emptying the Royal Bladder and evacuating the Royal
Bowels. Then the first Royal Shower of the day, followed by
thirty minutes on the phone to New York. After that would
come the morning tennis game and, after that, the second
Royal Shower of the day, followed, finally, by breakfast on
the terrace.

Allison sat up in bed and listened as the courtiers raced
about, trying to anticipate His Royal Highness's wishes before they became commands. Heaven forbid that Conrad
Hilliard should frown.

If he should have to *ask* for something, like an ordinary
mortal, the sky might fall.

And she was the Crown Princess.

Allison grimaced and reached for her cigarettes. It was funny, she thought, as she lit one. Most actresses in Hollywood
would kill to be in her position. And there wasn't much *she*
wouldn't do to be out of it.

Her stomach growled, reminding her breakfast was at least
an hour away. She knew she was smoking far too much these
days, but without cigarettes as a crutch she couldn't possibly

hold her weight where her father insisted.

The smoke from the first of the day's cigarettes was rough against her throat, but at least her stomach didn't growl again. The empty, gnawing feeling began to settle down into something she could live with.

Allison threw the bed covers aside. Nude, she walked over to the full-length mirror on her closet door and examined the reflection of her body. She had hated being tall as a child, and even more as an awkward teen. Now, at twenty-three, she was proud of her height, proud of the advantage it gave her over other women.

And men.

A double whammy, she thought with pleasure. Being Conrad Hilliard's daughter, and tall besides. There weren't many men in Hollywood who could stand up to that combination.

A smile played across her lips as she remembered that Nicholas Picard had. Nick.

We're going to make beautiful music together, Nick. For a while.

She would use Nick to achieve what she wanted. Men used women all the time in Hollywood. It was time the tables were turned.

Of course, the danger when a woman acted like a man was that she might get trapped in her own snare and fall prey to the very person she had tried to use. Allison thought of the tender curve of Nick's bottom lip, the dancing light of mischief in his eyes. She would have to be careful. Falling in love with Nick Picard was definitely not part of the master plan.

Allison turned this way and that, studying herself in the mirror. What would Nick think about her body? At this weight, she was as angular as a boy. When she raised her arms, she could count each separate rib. Only her breasts, full and prominent, retained the soft curve of feminism.

Surprise, Conrad!

The sky *had* fallen once on His Royal Highness: the day he got a daughter instead of a son.

It was part of the family legend—how crushed Conrad Hilliard had been when the doctor came out of the delivery room and told him that the young wife he adored had been delivered of a daughter instead of the son Conrad had dreamed of, the son who would have taken his place on the boards as the fourth generation of the world's leading theatrical family.

The son he longed for was born two years later—and died only minutes after birth. Three others—stillborn— followed at two-year intervals. Until at last, when Allison was eleven, Conrad Hilliard realized that if he tried again he would lose his wife as well.

Allison knew the day, almost the hour, of that fateful decision. Because that was the day His Royal Highness finally turned his attention to his daughter. That was the day she became the Crown Princess.

Until then, Allison had been a chubby, happy child, prone to daydreams, not very bookish. She knew that her mother was sickly from her attempts to have babies and that her father was an important man, too busy for her. She was not bothered by either of those realities. Benign neglect suited her.

Becoming the Crown Princess had not. Her life turned into a grinding series of diets, tutors, acting lessons, exercises. Exhausted at the end of each day, she was continually overwhelmed by the knowledge of just how much she had failed her father—indeed, all past generations of Hilliards— by not being born male.

Conrad Hilliard generally breakfasted in the graceful white gazebo, in majestic solitude for the most part. His wife, frail and sickly, seldom left her own bed so early in the morning.

His daughter never joined him unless summoned, except on the rare occasions when she had something specific to discuss with him.

Allison followed her father's imposing figure across the lawn. If he noticed the extra place setting on the small breakfast table sheltered by the gazebo, he gave no sign of it. Nor did he acknowledge Allison's presence by so much as a nod when she slipped into the chair across the table from him.

Interviewers always remarked upon how large and imposing Conrad Hilliard's head was. That massive skull made his every movement seem of momentous significance, even the act of pouring tea from his own antique china teapot, the blend no one else was ever invited to share. When he poured the stream of dark liquid into his cup, he focused on it as if it were the most important thing on earth for that precise moment in time.

Which, of course, it was, considering that he usually suffered from a hangover of magnificent proportions. If any of the interviewers who joined the great man for breakfast over the years realized the dark liquid in Conrad Hilliard's teapot was mostly whiskey, they were kind enough not to mention his weakness. His roaring nightly drunks did not go unremarked, but somehow those, simply because they were at night, were deemed more acceptable. He was celebrated as an alcoholic in the grand theatrical tradition.

Lucky for him, Allison thought, as she poured her own black coffee. Otherwise he would be just another sad old drunk and nobody would give a damn about him. She lit a cigarette and watched her father consume his breakfast of eggs, rolls, bacon, and nearly a pint of plump fresh strawberries. It was typical that, while he knew she had a reason for being there, he would not be the one to bring up the subject. Or even to greet her civilly.

One huge strawberry, almost golf-ball size, rolled off his

plate and across the table. Allison picked it up and inhaled its fragrance. Like perfume, she thought.

She took one small delicate bite off the end and let the flavor explode in her mouth.

"Have you weighed this morning?" Conrad Hilliard asked abruptly.

"Yesterday." She put the remainder of the strawberry down in the exact center of her pristine plate. "Right on target."

"It's important that you watch your weight, Allison. You know that."

For heaven's sake, don't lose your temper, Allison told herself. She took a long drag of her cigarette and looked longingly at the remainder of the strawberry.

"Actually, you should weigh every morning. It's irresponsible not to. You're quite careless about things like that." Conrad Hilliard poured himself another cup of "tea."

Be calm!

It was no use. Something about her father always made her lose her cool. She snubbed out her cigarette on the strawberry. "I've fired Joel Edelmann. He's no longer my agent."

Her father looked at her for a moment and then went back to his breakfast.

She reached for her cigarettes and lit another. Her fingers were beginning to tremble. "Aren't you going to say anything?"

"Joel told me you called him and babbled some nonsense. We talked it over and decided you were just having one of your feminine spells. Joel will ignore it." He speared a piece of bacon with his fork. "No harm done."

Feminine! That was the worst epithet he could throw at her, and she knew it. "I did mean it! Joel Edelmann is no longer my agent. I'm taking control of my own career."

"How can you be so irresponsible?"

It was the beginning of the lecture she had heard every day of her life since she became the Crown Princess. Only she had sat through it for the last time. As the best-known voice in the English-speaking world rumbled on, Allison shoved away from the table. She jumped to her feet and strode out of the gazebo without a backwards look.

For the first time in his life, Conrad Hilliard lost an audience.

As always in times of stress, Allison's destination was the kitchen.

Just as Conrad Hilliard did not resemble other mortals, neither did his family's kitchen resemble that of other families. A huge, white, echoing chamber of sterile surfaces, its sharp edges were not dulled by anything that hinted of domesticity. It would have done quite well for a large restaurant. The message it so proudly broadcast was that eating was a business, pure and simple, with no room for pleasure or self-indulgence.

It was Allison's favorite room in the house.

She marched straight across to the large double refrigerator and threw open both doors. For a moment, she simply stood there, lost in dreamy contemplation of the crowded shelves. Then she roused herself and began to pull items out and place them on the gleaming white counters: smoked foods, spicy foods, sweet foods, crunchy foods, soft foods.

Next to the refrigerator, the walk-in freezer held all forms of frozen delights, along with its beef carcasses and chicken parts. Allison plunged in and emerged, shivering, with an armload of ice cream in assorted flavors and a variety of frozen pastries. These treasures she added to the others already on the counter.

From across the kitchen, she dragged Cook's stool over to the counter and climbed up on it, crossing her legs. She lit a cigarette and took a deep drag.

Then she began.

On her far left was half of a huge ham. Allison leaned closer to it and began to imagine, in the greatest possible detail, what it would be like to consume the whole thing, bite by wonderful bite. She gave herself over completely to her contemplation—allowing herself to feel, without guilt, the almost rubbery texture of the ham when her teeth cut through it and to enjoy the slick fattiness of it on her tongue.

Next to the ham was half a cherry pie. Allison imagined eating it: the crust, tender and flaky; the cherries, round little bombs of sweet heavy flavor.

The cigarette grew shorter, burning her finger. Allison stubbed it out on the counter and lit another.

Next to the pie was a carton of chocolate ice cream. Allison lifted an imaginary spoonful to her lips: cool, dark, silky.

Item by item, she worked her way across the counter.

"Miss Allison? Miss Allison?"

Allison looked up.

"Do you want some breakfast now, Miss Allison?" Cook asked.

Allison stood up. She reached over to stub out her cigarette in the chocolate puddle at the base of one of the ice cream cartons. "I couldn't eat a thing."

"But, Miss Allison, you—"

Allison walked past Cook and took the stairs two at a time. In her room, she stripped down to bra and panties and began to do sit-ups, over and over, until she was so exhausted all she could do was lie back on the floor and stare up at the ceiling.

"Allison? Darling? Are you all right?"

Allison turned her head.

Her mother stood in the doorway to her room, small and pretty, with an invalid's pale skin. Bettina Hilliard never had the slightest interest in the theater or in being a film star. Her only consuming passion in life was her husband.

What if I had been like that? Allison wondered. What if my brother had lived? What if he had shouldered the burden by becoming the Crown Prince, leaving her only her mother's footsteps to fill.

"Allison? Are you all right?"

"I'm fine." Allison turned her face in the opposite direction. "Just fine."

"How long is this going to last, for God's sake!" Allison lit another cigarette off the butt of the one in her hand. "All you do is stare at me! What are you, some kind of freak? Are you waiting for me to take my clothes off?"

Nick grinned. "If it makes you feel more comfortable, sure."

"We've been doing this for weeks!"

"Days," Nick corrected gently.

"We haven't gotten anywhere!"

"We have."

"You really ought to have this office redecorated. It's the most uncomfortable room I've ever been in. I don't know how you can stand it."

Nick glanced around at the pale blue walls, the overstuffed furniture, the placid prints. "I manage," he said gravely.

Allison began to pace around the room once more. "So what have you learned from staring at me?"

"You move like a marionette."

She halted in mid-step. "That's crap. I've seen myself on the screen."

"I'm not talking about on the screen, Allison. I'm talking about here. Real life. Every motion you make is jerky, abrupt." Nick leaned back in his chair, his hands locked together behind his neck. "On the screen, it's different. When you're playing a part, you forget yourself. You become whichever character you're portraying."

Allison flopped down on the sofa. "That's good, isn't it?"

Nick shook his head. "It limits your range."

"I don't see why."

"It means there's one part you can't play."

She bristled. "What part?"

"Yourself."

After Allison left, Nick asked Peggy to hold all calls, kicked off his shoes, and stretched out on the sofa, exhausted. Allison might think he was doing nothing, but it was damned hard work!

Every day they had the same argument. Why was he wasting so much time trying to analyze her? Why didn't they just get on with it? Allison knew he had been working on a script for Kate. Why didn't he let her read that?

That last had started out as a whim and escalated into a demand.

Nick refused.

The script was essentially complete, but he wasn't letting anyone know that yet. He had even lied to Whit last week, when the subject came up.

Not that there was anything wrong with the script. It was a good script. For Kate. The problem was that he didn't feel like doing another movie with Kate right now. It was the thought of directing Allison that had his creative juices flowing. The script he had written for Kate would be a rotten one for Allison, only he wasn't sure Allison would be able to see that just yet.

She had to be the most fascinating woman he had ever met. Thin, nervous, burning with energy, she had spent three weeks chain-smoking in his office without a clue as to what he was trying to do for her. Not that it was easy to put into words.

Just the thought of working with her had made him burn with excitement. He knew this time the spotlight would really be on him, not his creation. Everyone in Hollywood knew who and what Allison Hilliard was. All the speculation and criticism would center around what he, Nick, could do with that known quantity.

The fact that she'd fired Joel Edelmann had fueled speculation to a fever pitch. At first, the venerable agent had denied it. Then he launched an angry attack, backed by Conrad Hilliard, claiming Nick had misled Allison. All Hollywood was ready to laugh in Nick's face when Allison "came to her senses" and went back to Edelmann—and Daddy.

So when he scored, he would score big.

That wasn't the best part as far as he was concerned. Nick sat up and slipped his shoes back on. Maybe all this "sitting around" was driving Allison crazy, but it was only confirming what Nick had realized the first time he met her. There was something more in Allison, something that nobody else—not Edelmann, not Daddy, not all those other directors who had hired her because of Daddy and Edelmann—had seen.

But he had seen it: a glimpse of what she could be. And what Allison Hilliard could be was something very special indeed.

Nick walked over to the cabinet behind his desk and opened it. He had shown the contents to Allison this afternoon, shelves of scripts he had read through, searching for the right one for her. He hadn't found it yet, but he planned to keep looking. After all these weeks of studying Allison Hilliard, he would know the perfect project when he stumbled across it, whether he wrote the script or someone else did.

Nick sat down behind his desk and began to scribble notes to himself. When he stopped for a moment and looked up, he smiled at the two baby pictures sitting there side by side: Danielle and Eden, two beautiful little girls. He had expected a squawk from Kate the first time she walked into his office and saw Eden's picture sitting beside Dani's. He had been ready to explain to her that he was no hypocrite, that he had two daughters and planned to acknowledge it.

It hadn't been necessary. Kate hadn't reacted.

Funny. When they first met she seemed so warm and human. Now she was an iceberg most of the time, no emotions at all. It was as though that glacial screen image had taken her over.

Look at Juliet. She was all emotion—on the screen and off.

Strange that he had married two such dissimilar women and made them both stars.

"Nick," Peggy said from the doorway. "I'm leaving now. Are you going to be working late again tonight?"

Nick looked down at the few sparse notes. "Not tonight," he told his secretary. "I think I'll go home too."

Going home, he thought, as he shoved the note pad in a desk drawer. The only part of the day he didn't enjoy.

Sundays were the worst. Allison had awakened before dawn. Now, even though it was past ten, she still wore the shorts and man's shirt she had thrown on for her morning exercise. If it were Monday, she would be dressed and at Nick Picard's office by now, demanding that he do something about her career. But it wasn't Monday.

It was Conrad Hilliard's fault she hated Sundays. His Royal Highness had played priests, rabbis, and preachers in his day. Never, to her knowledge, had he attended church for real. Given the opportunity, he would filibuster for hours about the faults of religion and the problems it had forced on mankind. That wasn't why he had never been a churchgoer, though. The truth was he couldn't stand for someone else to have center stage, even long enough to preach a sermon.

At sixteen, Allison had rebelled against the endless boring Sundays. For six months, in defiance of her father's wishes, she had attended various Los Angeles churches, sometimes with schoolmates, sometimes alone. Somehow, though, no matter which church she attended, she always saw the figure in front of her as a bad actor, playing the part with much less skill than her father would have. Conrad Hilliard hadn't said anything when she stopped her religious experiments. He hadn't needed to.

Allison clasped her hands together, feeling the dampness of her palms. God, she was scared! What if Nick couldn't come through? She wondered if Nick had any idea just what she was risking by defying her father.

Her churchgoing had been a private defiance, attracting little notice. This was something all Hollywood was watching. Conrad Hilliard would never let her forget this.

Damn you, Nick! What are you doing? What's taking so long?

A hunger pain shot through her. Allison clasped her arms around her stomach. After a moment, she straightened and reached for the phone. She dialed Nick's home number, and while she listened to the phone ring on the other end of the line, she lit a cigarette. "Come on, come on, come on," she said, and, when a female voice finally answered, "Let me speak to Nick." She gripped the edge of the nightstand, trying to ignore the gnawing pain in her stomach while she waited.

"Nicholas Picard here," Nick's voice said at last.

"We have to move faster!"

"Allison?"

"No more stalling. We have to move faster!"

"Allison? Is that you?"

"I'm tired of your games, Nick. I'm tired of waiting for mystic revelations. We have to move. Now!"

She slammed down the receiver and looked around the room frantically. Sundays! Now she knew why she hated them so much. She was trapped up here. All she wanted to do was go down to the kitchen and stuff her face, but her father would be downstairs, guarding the way.

Allison threw herself across the bed, her head dangling

on one side, her feet on the other. She took a deep drag on her cigarette and then tapped it, letting the ashes drift down across the carpet.

What in the world was she going to do if Nick didn't come through?

"Where are we going?" Allison's hair whipped into her face as the Corvette sped down Conrad Hilliard's drive.

Nick glanced over at her. Behind the dark lenses of his sunglasses, his eyes were unreadable. She couldn't tell whether he was angry about her phone call this morning or not. All he said now was, "Don't you ever relax?"

"Not when I'm being kidnapped." Allison squinted into the setting sun. Her sunglasses were still lying on the nightstand beside her bed, right beside her cigarettes and lighter. She'd had no idea she would be leaving the house when she came downstairs in answer to the maid's summons. "You didn't even give me time to change clothes."

"I'm just trying to do what you asked. It's time to speed things up. To move faster."

"How do you propose to do that?"

"You'll see."

She had the uncomfortable feeling he was laughing at her. For just a moment the anger flared up, hot and bright within her.

Don't you know whose daughter I am? Of course he did. And he didn't care. That was why she had chosen him. Because only someone who didn't care whose daughter she was could help her become what she truly wanted to be: not Conrad Hilliard's shadow but a person in her own right. To achieve that, she would do whatever it took.

She inhaled deeply. "Can we stop somewhere and pick up a package of cigarettes?"

"Nasty habit." Nick didn't even glance her way. "It's time you gave it up."

Allison slumped down in her seat and stared straight ahead. Whatever it took.

Nick parked above the beach and cut the motor. "There's a blanket behind the seat," he said.

Allison remained where she was. "It's pitch dark!"

Nick pointed upward. "Moonlight. Your eyes will adjust in a minute. Get the blanket." He reached behind the seat himself and grabbed a small cooler. Without glancing her way, he started down to the beach.

Allison hesitated. Whatever it took. She got the blanket. Her flimsy sandals weren't made for walking in the sand. She broke a strap on the right one before she reached the spot on the beach where Nick knelt over the cooler.

He took out a bottle of champagne and two glasses. "Spread out the blanket," he told her.

She did, stumbling a little as her right sandal flopped around on her foot. When she had smoothed the blanket, she sat down on it and took off both sandals. The discipline her father had instilled in her made her line up both shoes with the edge of the blanket.

Nick handed her a glass of champagne. "Toast," he said.

"To what?"

"Allison Hilliard, superstar." He raised his glass.

Allison did not. "A joke, Nick?"

"She's being born tonight."

Allison drained her glass, slowly, deliberately, and set it to one side. It tipped over, spilling a few drops of wine on the blanket. "Are you trying to seduce me, Nick?" She couldn't keep the amusement out of her voice. "I'm no shy virgin, you know." She leaned over and began to unbutton his shirt.

Nick caught her hand. "No," he said softly, "that's not you. You're not the aggressor. Men come to you, Allison. You're a goddess. Men worship you with their bodies."

She almost laughed. But something in his face, in the moonlight, in the waves pounding against the shore, made the impulse die in her throat.

Gently, he pushed her back onto the blanket. His mouth came down on hers. The kiss was long, slow, unhurried at first. Then it grew more demanding. As it did, she was aware of Nick's fingers at her neck as he began to unbutton her shirt.

She thought about lifting her own hands to help him but found herself caught in a strange lassitude, and so, instead, she lay there passively as he removed her shirt, her bra, unzipped her shorts and slipped them off, and then removed her panties as well. Still fully clothed himself, he began to trace the curves and dips of her body with his lips, his tongue, nibbling softly with his teeth, teasing, tantalizing, until Allison felt herself trembling with emotion.

Still, she lay there.

Nick raised himself off of her and stood up. His silhouette against the moon was huge and male. She had never felt so vulnerable, so feminine, before.

"My God but you're beautiful," Nick said as he knelt beside her.

Allison turned her head away, as though she had just been caught in some terrible lie and could not bring herself to look him in the eye.

Nick took her head in his hands and turned her face to his. He bent down until he was staring straight into her eyes. "You have a beautiful body, Allison. A beautiful woman's body."

Once more she tried to turn her head, but she was caught in his hands. His grip, while gentle, was firm. "Beautiful," he murmured again and lowered his lips to hers. He held the kiss until she was almost gasping with pleasure, her body hot and trembling beneath him.

"Listen to me," he said when he pulled away. "You mustn't

be afraid to be a woman. You're such a beautiful woman."

He parted her legs with his knee. She opened willingly as he slipped inside her.

"You must remember," Nick whispered softly in her ear as they began to thrust together, "that's the one part Conrad Hilliard can never play."

Nude, Allison stepped on the bathroom scales. She winced as the needle zoomed to 120 pounds. Hurriedly, she stepped off. It was the most she had ever weighed in her life. If her father found out, he would have a fit.

It was Nick's fault. He was always urging her to eat, to fill out, to let her curves grow more feminine.

She walked back into the bedroom and examined herself in the full-length mirror on her closet door. She had to admit that Nick might be right. She did look good.

Actually, she thought with a grin, twisting and turning to catch a glimpse of her backside, she looked *great*! Not fat, not at all. But definitely feminine. A goddess, Nick liked to call her in their private moments together. Well, she thought as she turned again and glanced over her shoulder, maybe he was right.

But 120 pounds!

Luckily, her father was in London until just before New Year's, doing *King Lear*. He wouldn't be back until it was time to throw his traditional New Year's Day dinner for a good half of Hollywood. Which gave her plenty of time alone with Nick.

She glanced at her rear again and then turned and faced herself straight on. For just a moment Nick's vision of her body warred with her father's, like two shimmering outlines, one overlying the other. Hunger gnawed at her belly. Automatically, she glanced toward her nightstand where her cigarettes usually lay.

The pack was no longer there.

"It's all right to eat," she whispered to herself. "It's all right to be a woman." If Conrad Hilliard wanted a son, he should have fathered one. She grinned at herself in the mirror and went to get the sexy sweater and skirt set Nick had had delivered to her the day before. Tonight's party was important, the first step in the image-making process, according to Nick.

The studio's Christmas party would be the first public appearance of her new, more feminine self. Her picture would be in all the trades. There would be no going back after tonight.

Time the goddess got a move on.

"A resounding success," Nick pronounced as he drove her home.

"I hope so." Allison wondered if she should mention her encounter with Joel Edelmann. The rotund little agent had lain in wait for her when she emerged from the bathroom. "My God!" he had exclaimed, grabbing her by the arm. "Are you pregnant?"

Allison jerked free. "What kind of stupid question is that?"

"How much weight have you gained?"

"None of your business, Joel."

"Your father will have a stroke."

"Good," she had snapped as she stalked away. "Then you'll be without a client, and I'll inherit all his money."

She shifted uncomfortably as Nick sent the Corvette careening around a corner on two wheels. Joel was probably on the phone to her father right now. "Nick? Are you sure I'm not gaining too much weight?"

"The camera doesn't lie, babe. You're beautiful. And you're about to become a superstar. I've got the script."

Her skin turned to ice. "When can I read it?"

"Tonight, if you like. We can stop by the office and pick it up."

"Yes, tonight." Allison rubbed her arms, trying to bring some warmth back to them. "I need to read it tonight."

Allison started the script as soon as she got home. She sat in her bed, leaning against the headboard, the script propped against her knees, and read straight through. It was 3 A.M. when she finished. As she closed the cover, her first coherent thought was that Nick had to be crazy. No way in the world could she play the sexy temptress on these pages—it just wasn't her.

Not Conrad Hilliard's daughter.

The phone rang at her elbow, a shrill and startling sound in the silence of the mansion. It was the third time it had rung since midnight. She let it ring. It had to be her father on the other end of the line, spurred on by a call from Joel. She couldn't talk to him right now. She had to think.

Allison rubbed her forehead tiredly. How could she play the sexual creature in *A Different Light*? Maggie was a woman secure in herself, with no doubts about her own femininity.

Allison drummed her fingers against the cover of the script. She had defied her father and put her career—her life—in Nick's hands. Too late to turn back. She *had* to go along with what Nick suggested, whether she believed he was right or not, simply because there was nothing else to do.

Allison sighed. She flipped the script open to the beginning once more and began to read.

TWELVE

1965

ALLISON DRESSED FOR HER FATHER'S ANNUAL NEW Year's Day dinner more carefully than she had ever dressed for anything in her life. Nick had chosen her dress, a rich burgundy velvet gown that clung like silk to her newly acquired curves. Its neckline exposed her breasts nearly to her nipples. "Only a real woman could wear this dress," Nick whispered when she tried it on. He had leaned over to plant a kiss in the hollow between her breasts. Allison knew the dress was her declaration of independence from her father. Too bad it was New Year's and not the Fourth of July!

She had toyed with the idea of inviting Nick to the dinner. He would have come; Nick wasn't the kind of man to ignore a challenge. And since her father and Joel Edelmann regarded Nick as some kind of Svengali, they would have focused their ire on Nick instead of her—and she was expecting plenty of ire. While she found it irritating that the two of them thought her too brainless to make any career decisions on her own, it would have been amusing to watch Nick parry their thrusts.

Kathleen Mallory was the reason she had not invited him.

Nicholas Picard was a married man with a child—two children. Not to invite his wife today would have been an announcement of a relationship she wasn't sure existed between herself and Nick. Yes, they were lovers, but any conversation they had about events beyond the moment dealt only with Allison's career. After all, that was the way she wanted it.

Wasn't it?

She ran a comb through her long blond hair, letting it fall forward around her face. Not that she needed to comb it again. She was only putting off her entrance as the new improved model of Allison Hilliard. Her parents had been back for two days. When they arrived with enough bags for an army, Bettina had kissed her daughter warmly; Conrad Hilliard merely stared at her and went up to bed without a word. "He's tired," her mother explained, as she hurried up the stairs after him. "We had a long flight."

Conrad Hilliard had remained "tired," making it easy for Allison to avoid him. But after last night's round of New Year's Eve parties, he would be even more hungover than usual—and more quarrelsome. For the first time in her life, Allison was happy about the annual New Year's Day dinner. The last thing in the world she wanted today was to be alone with her father.

When Allison finally came downstairs, the guests were just going in to dinner. The appreciative male looks she received confirmed Nick's choice of a gown. So did the sidelong female glances. For the first time since Nick gave her the script of *A Different Light* to read, her spirits soared. Maybe she could play Maggie, after all!

When she found her place card, Allison saw she had been banished to the table that held the lesser luminaries: those on the way up and those who had been up and were on the way down. Normally she would have found this sign of her father's disfavor depressing. Also dull, for there was no conversation at this table. Neither of these groups could admit to the other's existence. Besides, any attempts to talk would blot out the scraps of conversation drifting over from the other tables. They all sat with ears pricked to catch any morsels that might fall from the lips of Conrad Hilliard's current favorites.

The waiters, aware no doubt of the distinction between the guests, served this table last. Inhaling the delicious aromas drifting over from the other tables, Allison discovered she was ravenous. But when her food was set before her, she was startled to see her plate held only a tiny bowl of clear soup, a minuscule scrap of baked chicken, and one stalk of broccoli. Had her father decided to starve this table as well as insult it?

She glanced around at her companions in purgatory and saw that, unlike hers, their plates were heaped with food. She motioned to the waiter. "I believe there has been a mistake," she said quietly.

From across the room Conrad Hilliard's voice thundered out as though he were back on the London stage. "There is no mistake, Allison. You have let yourself go. You have become fat as a pig in my absence. That, my daughter, is your dinner, and it shall continue to be until you regain control of yourself."

Every eye in the room was on her.

Shock held her immobile for a long moment.

Then she stood up, slowly, gracefully, and grasped her plate. With one swift movement she turned it upside down on the damask cloth and left it there, covering its sparse contents. Then, regally, she swept out of the room.

She was in her bedroom, the door locked behind her, before the icy sheath that was her skin began to burn with embarrassment and anger. By that time, she already had the first of her suitcases open on the bed and half filled.

New Year's Day.

A day for resolutions. A day for looking back over the

past year. As Nick was in the mood for neither of those activities, the day had been a wasted one. So had the year just past.

He had turned thirty in September, a milestone he didn't like to think about, and three days later Morgan Gaynor died.

God knows, he never understood Morgan, even though he loved him like a father.

And at the funeral Nick had been shocked to realize the small, graying man with the paunch entering the church just ahead of him was Freddie. If Morgan's death had saddened Nick, it had devastated Frederick Yates, aging him overnight.

That day, standing beside Morgan's grave, Nick felt the silly childhood antagonism that had kept him and Freddie from being friends all those years had finally dissolved. Freddie seemed to feel the same thing. After the ceremony, he turned to Nick and held out his hand.

Nick had ignored the hand and given Freddie a bear hug instead. "He loved us, you know," Nick told him. "Just as if we really were his sons."

When the two of them left the grave, Nick believed they were walking into a new relationship.

That was before Morgan Gaynor's will was read. Unaccountably, he had left everything to Nick. And that destroyed any chance Nick and Freddie had of ever becoming friends.

It wasn't the money. It was the fact that nowhere in the document Morgan Gaynor had drawn up before his death was the name of Frederick Yates even mentioned.

After that, Freddie had gone into a funk, almost losing control of the studio. The little bastard had grabbed it back at the last minute, though. He was tough where it counted. It was only on the subject of Morgan Gaynor that he was a little wacky.

If he was honest, Nick thought, he'd have to admit the same thing about himself. After a lifetime of wondering, he finally had the proof: Morgan loved him best. However, that raised a question which would trouble him the rest of his life: How could a man like Morgan Gaynor have been so cruel?

Nick poured a shot of whiskey just as Dani shrieked somewhere in the house. He heard the slam of a door and hurried steps as Kate rushed to their daughter. Funny. For a while he'd had the feeling Kate was ready to give it up, call it quits. Then domesticity had seized her with a vengeance. She threw all her energy into Dani and the house these days. Better still, after the last picture, she had stopped asking him when he would have a new project ready for her, which relieved him of the necessity to lie. Because he had no urge to make another movie starring Kate.

Beautiful Kate. Cold-blooded Kate.

He had succeeded beyond his wildest dreams with her, turning her into a glacial beauty that men all over the world longed for and women worshiped. The problem was that some of that glacial cold had seeped into the real Kate.

When he married her, he thought he loved her. Now he wasn't sure how he felt. Nor was he sure how she felt about him.

No more shrieks from the nursery. He ought to heave himself out of his chair and go up to say good night to his daughter. Maybe proposition his wife. Nick grinned at his whiskey glass. That would be a way to start the year off right.

The phone beside him rang so loudly in the quiet room that he started.

"I've moved," Allison said without preamble, when he answered. "I can't live in my father's house anymore." She wasn't crying. If anything, there was a strange elation in her voice.

"Have you been drinking?"

"You bet! Champagne. Want to join me?"

He scribbled down the name of the hotel. Before he could caution her to take care, she hung up.

Nick stared down at the paper with her address. If anything happened to Allison Hilliard, this past year would truly be wasted. He couldn't afford that.

He found Kate in the nursery, playing a clapping game with Dani. He watched her for a moment from the doorway. God, she was beautiful! The fact that she seemed so unaware of that beauty only enhanced it. "I've got to go out for a while," he said.

Dani, suddenly aware of his presence, squealed and waved.

Kate went on with the game. "Fine," she said calmly, without looking up or missing a beat.

That stung. "Aren't you interested in where I'm going or what I'm doing?" he snapped without thinking. He should be happy that she wasn't giving him the third degree; he didn't need a jealous wife fretting over his every absence. Still, it would be nice if she noticed he was alive.

"Not particularly," Kate replied. She might have been merely a nanny or a housekeeper. "We'll be fine."

"I'm sure you will," Nick muttered. Why had he ever thought Kathleen Mallory, ice queen, was his creation? Obviously, Kate had been a cold creature all along. She didn't care about him. She didn't care about their marriage.

Fine. Then neither did he.

When Nick left without picking her up, Dani howled. Kate stared at her daughter and wished she could do the same thing. Why did Nick keep torturing her like this? Did he expect her to beg to find out whether he was with

Juliet or with Allison Hilliard? Well, she wasn't going to. But neither could she end their farce of a marriage.

After that break-in, she had gone so far as to consult a lawyer. Consult was all she had done. The lawyer had been eager to represent her, listing all the advantages of freedom, including how much of Nick's money she would walk away with. However, when it came to setting the wheels in motion, she couldn't take the final step. Because, while she didn't have much of Nick, she still had some, and that some was better than nothing. She couldn't bear to think about what life would be like without him. Even sharing him with Juliet seemed less terrible than losing him altogether.

Dani continued to howl. Kate picked her up and held her close. Eventually she quieted, and they took up the game once more.

All the while Kate listened for the sound of Nick's return over their clapping.

When she woke the next morning, the first thing Kate did was go down the hall to Nick's bedroom. It was empty, the bed untouched.

He didn't often stay out all night, but it was not unheard of. She tried to go on with her day as usual, listening all the time for the phone to ring. Mrs. Gregory, the housekeeper, arrived at 7 A.M. and took over Dani while Kate dressed. Then Kate fed Dani while Mrs. Gregory attacked the house. Somehow, Dani and the house had expanded to fill Kate's days completely. She seldom thought of anything else, including her film career. It wasn't until Mrs. Gregory departed at 5 P.M., leaving a roast in the oven for their evening meal, that Kate began to listen for Nick's car, for the sound of the front door, for his step on the stairs.

No matter how long Kate lived there, no matter how many changes she made in the interior, the house still seemed to belong to Helen Chandler. And never more so than tonight. Every creak, every sigh, every whispery sound in the empty rooms conspired to make her feel like an alien here, unwanted.

Nick never came home.

In the morning, she rose to find his bed still untouched. When Mrs. Gregory arrived and the day's routine began once more, Kate could almost forget that unwrinkled bed upstairs, but when evening returned she kept drifting upstairs to look at it, as if simply staring at the bed would bring Nick home more quickly.

She woke in the night, her heart banging away inside her chest like crazy, and hurried down the hall. Nick's bed was still empty. The clock on the dresser said 3 A.M.

Something has happened to him!

She picked up the phone on the nightstand to dial the police—and then stopped. He wasn't missing. His office would have called a dozen times in the past two days if he hadn't been there. He simply had not come home.

Kate forced herself to replace the receiver. She smoothed a nonexistent wrinkle out of the bedclothes and then went down the hall to check on Dani, who was sleeping soundly.

Then she returned to her own bed and lay there staring at the ceiling until Mrs. Gregory came at 7 A.M.

After that, Kate seldom slept at night and never during the day. Each time she dozed she would wake suddenly, with a start, thinking Nick had returned. Then reality would flood in on her, and she would realize he wasn't coming back.

But it was all right, in a way, because no one except Kate herself seemed to notice. She still paid the bills out of their joint account, Mrs. Gregory still fixed dinners for two each evening before she left, and when people called to ask her to do things, to go places, to accept work, she told them all, "I'll have to speak to Nick about it before I decide."

Then one evening, long after Mrs. Gregory had left and Dani was sound asleep upstairs, Kate opened the oven door and found a single plate with a solitary lamb chop waiting inside. She knelt on the kitchen floor, weeping.

Nick called the next morning to tell her that their marriage was over. The last thing she remembered was hanging up the phone.

It was after 3 P.M. when Juliet finally realized that Nick's bitch of a secretary must not have passed along her message. Otherwise he would have called. Especially since she had been in Europe for three months. She had gotten back early yesterday morning and spent the entire day settling back into the house she had bought not long after Eden's birth. The first thing she had planned to do today was reintroduce Nick to his daughter. He wouldn't believe how much Eden had grown. Juliet scarcely believed it herself.

Only Peggy hadn't passed along her message.

Juliet wasn't surprised. She knew Peggy despised her. Did Nick know it was Peggy who had kept Juliet's messages from getting through the night she was in labor with Eden?

Juliet sighed. That was then; this was now. She had tried calling Nick's house last night. The housekeeper had claimed he wasn't there, obviously on Kathleen Mallory's orders.

Eden gurgled happily in her playpen. She was one and a half now and destined to be a beauty. Like me, Juliet thought smugly. Even though she was twenty-six and a mother, Juliet knew she looked better than ever before in her life. No extra ounces of flesh marred the clean lines of her body. The Mediterranean sun had painted her skin a rich golden brown and bleached her hair a tint of blond you couldn't buy in a bottle. Just wait until Nick found out there wasn't a single patch of white skin anywhere on her body. Imagining her sunbathing in the nude would drive him crazy.

Nick should see her! Now. This afternoon. Before any of her glorious Mediterranean tan could fade.

The thought no sooner popped in her head than she was gathering Eden's things together. She would be waiting for Nick when he got home. If Kathleen Mallory objected, that was just too bad.

The housekeeper was the first hurdle.

She stared at Juliet—twice her height, half her age, in a clingy T-shirt, skimpy shorts, and leather sandals, eighteen-month-old Eden balanced on one hip—and shook her head. "I'm sorry, Miss Brittany. You can't come in. Miss Mallory isn't seeing anyone."

"I'm not here to see Miss Mallory," Juliet said, shoving her way past the woman. "I'm here to see Mr. Picard."

"But Mr. Picard isn't here," the woman said frantically.

"I'll wait," Juliet replied with a great deal of malicious pleasure. She dropped the diaper bag on the immense table in the entry hall and hoisted Eden to a more secure position on her hip as she glanced around. Helen Chandler's house certainly brought back memories. Juliet thought about the pictures in the book on pregnancy Helen had sent her and clutched Eden more tightly. Eden shrieked her displeasure.

From upstairs, as if in answer, another child began to cry.

And then, to Juliet's absolute amazement, the housekeeper burst into noisy sobs as well.

Isabelle Gregory was the housekeeper's name. It took Juliet almost half an hour to extract that tiny scrap of information and to learn her original estimate of the woman's age was wrong. Isabelle Gregory was not in her mid-fifties, as Juliet had first guessed. She was almost sixty-five and terrified she was going to lose her job.

"You can't blame me!" the housekeeper sobbed over and over. "I'm doing everything I can for her. I know if I call anyone"—she looked up suddenly, fixing Juliet with a terror-stricken stare—"especially *him*, that will be it. He'll slap her in the hospital. And the baby: Lord knows what will happen to the baby. That woman won't want it. Not her. She hasn't got a maternal bone in her body."

Juliet felt a chill settle in her own bones. "What woman?" There had been no Hollywood news in the tiny French fishing village; she hadn't guessed she had a new rival for Nick's affections.

"Allison Hilliard," Isabelle said. "He left Miss Mallory for Allison Hilliard."

Juliet laughed, relieved. "That bag of bones? Nick likes women, not broomsticks."

"She's not a bag of bones now." Isabelle looked up at the ceiling. The child's cries had slackened when the housekeeper's began. Now they were beginning to build again in earnest. "I suppose you'll see that I'm fired," she said, her mouth settling into a thin, bitter line.

Juliet shook her head. "I don't see what you're so worried about. All you've done is take care of them."

"It's the checks," Isabelle blurted. "I forged her name to the checks."

"Whose—"

"Miss Mallory's name. I signed it myself on the checks. How else could we get food? Or have the pool cleaned? Or . . . or anything?"

Juliet shifted, bored with the whole thing. "Look, if Kathleen Mallory is too stupid to keep the household help from defrauding her, it's her problem. Not mine."

Isabelle Gregory began to sob again. "You don't understand. When they find out I didn't report it to anyone, I'll never get another job. Without references—"

"Report what?" Juliet thought seriously about slapping the housekeeper, not so much to bring her out of her hysteria but out of sheer annoyance with the woman's theatrics. "Isabelle!" she said sharply. "What in the world are you talking about?"

"I'll show you," Isabelle Gregory said.

Kathleen Mallory lay in the bedroom that had been Helen Chandler's while Nick's mother was alive, her eyes open, staring up at the ceiling, her face beautiful but uninhabited.

"How long has she been like this?" Juliet's voice dropped automatically to a whisper, as though she were in the presence of a terminally ill patient or someone already dead.

Isabelle Gregory wrung her hands. "Two weeks. Almost three."

Juliet swung around to glare at the woman. "And you haven't notified anyone? A doctor?"

"She's not unconscious," the housekeeper protested. "She eats. I take her to the bathroom as often as I can. She hardly ever soils herself," she offered in eager defense. "And I bathe her. Just like Dani."

Danielle was still crying somewhere down the hall.

Eden shifted irritably in Juliet's arms. "Dan," she said, which meant she wanted down.

Juliet shoved her into the housekeeper's arms. "Go feed both the girls," she told the housekeeper. She walked over to the bed. "Kathleen?" she said softly and, when there was no reply, a little louder. "Kathleen?"

"*He* calls her Kate," Isabelle said from the doorway.

"Take the girls downstairs and feed them, I said." When the door had closed behind the housekeeper, Juliet turned back to the woman on the bed and said softly, "Kate?"

There was not exactly a response but an almost imperceptible change in the still figure's slow, regular breathing.

What in hell am I doing? Juliet wondered. Go downstairs, call an ambulance, and let someone else sort this out.

"Kate?" she said again, a little louder this time.

The figure on the bed continued to lie as still as a porcelain figurine. Then the eyes blinked.

"Kate! Say something!" Juliet demanded.

"Kathleen." The voice was rusty with disuse.

Anything to keep her talking. "*He* calls you Kate. The housekeeper told me so."

"Kate, Kate, Kate," the figure on the bed wailed. "I must *be* Kate. He wouldn't have left Kathleen." The tears came then.

Juliet pulled a chair closer to the bed and waited for the flood of tears to abate. At least the girls and Isabelle weren't crying anymore.

"She was just like a zombie," Isabelle Gregory said as she wiped a dribble of cereal from Dani's face and offered another spoonful. Dani opened her mouth like a little bird as the spoon approached. "I've never seen anything like it."

Juliet balanced Eden on her lap. "Does she have any family?"

The housekeeper sniffed. "She does. They wouldn't give her the time of day. That's why I didn't call them. They'd slap her in an institution so fast. . . . She's a nice little thing, Miss Brittany. Not at all like her movie roles. I'd just hate to see anything like that happen to her."

Or your job, Juliet added silently, remembering the woman's anguished tears earlier. "Surely you don't think Nick would be as heartless as that?" she asked with real curiosity.

Isabelle's lips tightened. "They weren't getting along.

And then that Hilliard woman." Dani refused the next spoonful of cereal, turning her head away emphatically. "He's moved in with her, you know. This might be just what he wanted, an easy way out of his marriage."

That didn't sound like Nick, but Juliet wasn't quite sure enough to take the chance of phoning him. What if Isabelle was right? What if Nick came stomping in, took one look at Kate, and institutionalized her?

Why would you care?

A good question. One she wasn't sure she knew the answer to. Except that, upstairs, bending over Kate, she had the strangest feeling of déjà vu—something to do with her sister, Marcy. As though it were really Marcy she were taking care of, and not her ex-husband's present wife.

And that was the craziest thing of all. Because never, in her whole life, had she ever even thought of ministering to Marcy.

Still, looking down into Kate Mallory's face, the face so much like her own, Juliet couldn't shake the feeling of sisterhood.

"You are going to stay, aren't you?" Isabelle said as she stood up. "You'll help me take care of her for a few days? I'm sure it's just shock, him leaving her and all. If she talked to you, she must be starting to come out of it. You will stay, won't you?"

Juliet stood up too, balancing Eden on her hip. Her impulse was to gather her things and walk straight out the door. So why did she say, "Of course I'll stay"?

As the days passed, it seemed as though Isabelle Gregory was right. Kate's only malady was shock, shock that Nick had dumped her for Allison Hilliard. Pointed little items were appearing in all the columns about Nick and Allison; Juliet made sure those sections of the paper were not left nearby. Not that it made any difference. If Kate picked up a paper, she merely thumbed through it idly, not reading anything.

If Kate had continued to be bedfast, Juliet would have called a doctor regardless of the housekeeper's protests. Thankfully, she had Kate up and walking about the next day, and sunning herself by the pool the day after that. Juliet had her talking, too, about Dani, about clothes, about hairstyles. Occasionally, Juliet would catch Kate regarding Eden with a quizzical expression on her face, as though she wasn't quite sure who the child was, and at those times Juliet found herself wondering if Kate had really grasped who she, Juliet, was.

After a few days of driving back and forth to fetch things from home for Eden and herself, Juliet had moved into one of the upstairs bedrooms, bringing half the contents of her house with her, it seemed. Eden and Danielle had certainly enjoyed meeting each other, especially since it meant that their total of toys was suddenly doubled. They played together happily and shared the same bath. Watching them, Juliet couldn't help marveling over how much alike the two little half-sisters looked.

Just like herself and Kate.

At first Juliet thought she had stayed with Kate because of the possibility that Nick might come back to the house. As the days passed and her Mediterranean tan faded to a normal California hue, she was forced to realize that wasn't it.

What exactly it was, she didn't know. She knew only that she felt good for a change, better than she had in years, and it had something to do with the way she had come in and taken charge of Kate Mallory's life.

Kate woke on a Tuesday, at exactly 7 A.M., and realized she was finally well. Not that she had thought herself sick—the truth was, she hadn't thought at all. She had merely existed for weeks and weeks, as though she were wrapped in cotton, sheltered from the world. It was only now, waking to wellness, that she could perceive the illness that had grasped her for so long.

Someone was singing in the hallway. A light tap sounded on her door, and then Juliet Brittany burst in. "Are you awake, Kate? Good. Isabelle has the food ready. You haven't forgotten we're taking the girls on a picnic, have you?"

Kate grappled with the separate problems presented to her all at once. Isabelle: Was that Mrs. Gregory, the housekeeper? The girls: Dani and . . . Eden? And Juliet Brittany here in Kate's bedroom, the face that looked so much like Kate's own, only with a beauty Kate knew an imitation could never achieve: When had she and Juliet become friends?

Kate realized that *when* didn't matter. She needed a friend. She swung her legs out of bed and stood up, glancing at Juliet just in time to catch the look of immense relief on the face of her husband's first wife, as though Juliet hadn't quite believed Kate would be able to leave the bed by herself.

"It's okay," Kate told Juliet. "I'm all right. Really I am. Thanks to you." Kate hugged the woman she had never thought she would like, the woman who had become her very best friend in the world.

Oliver Brittany dodged behind a rack of frilly children's party dresses. After a moment, he leaned forward and peered cautiously across the aisle.

Juliet stood in front of the mirrors, watching two little girls in matching pink while the saleslady simpered.

"I'll take these two also," Juliet told the saleslady. Once more she disappeared into the dressing room with the children.

Oliver straightened, conscious of his aching feet. This

was the third store he had followed his daughter through today, watching her choose clothes, shoes, and toys for the two little girls. Watching her bend and turn and twist in the tight, mid-thigh-length dress. Watching the way her hair fell forward, shielding her face. Watching the way her breasts moved beneath her bodice as she walked. His hand strayed to his crotch.

"May I help you, sir?"

Oliver jerked his hand away and turned to face the saleswoman who had appeared at his elbow. "I—I was just looking for something for my granddaughter."

The saleswoman's eyes, sharp and suspicious, registered disbelief, and Oliver realized he was clutching the shoulder of one of the frilly dresses with his other hand.

He released it abruptly. The hanger swung wildly and then clattered to the floor.

Juliet, emerging from the dressing room with a child's hand in each of her own, stopped dead and stared straight into his eyes. Then she bolted out of the children's department without her selections, ignoring the anguished cries of the saleswoman who had been assisting her.

Kate heard the front door slam even before Isabelle Gregory's glad welcome, a sound she had become pleasantly accustomed to over the past few months. Juliet was back from shopping.

However, the first thing Kate saw as she went downstairs was a look of alarm on the housekeeper's face. Mrs. Gregory was holding Dani by the hand, while Eden climbed over the packages heaped in the entry hall. Juliet was nowhere in sight. "Where is she?" Kate asked Mrs. Gregory.

"She went to the kitchen," the housekeeper said. "I think . . . she must not be feeling well."

Kate went out to the kitchen herself, where she found Juliet, her face pale, pouring herself a large tumbler full of red wine. "Was shopping with the girls that hard?" she asked lightly, trying to mask her concern.

Juliet tossed back a healthy gulp of wine. "Medicinal," she told Kate, kicking off her shoes. "I don't know why I'm so upset. It was just that I saw . . . some crazy old pervert staring at us, and I was worried about Dani and Eden."

"How awful!" Kate poured herself a smaller glass of wine and sat down at the table. After a moment, Juliet joined her. "Do you want me to call the police?"

"No. That won't be—" Juliet broke off as Mrs. Gregory appeared in the kitchen doorway. Her eyes fastened on the store name on the bag the housekeeper was holding. "Where did you get that, Isabelle?" she asked, her voice tight with strain.

"An elderly gentleman asked me to give it to you. Very nicely dressed, he was. He wouldn't give me his name."

"Juliet? Was that him?" When Juliet didn't answer, Kate took the bag from Mrs. Gregory and looked inside at the little girl's clothes: dresses, slips, panties. A receipt fluttered out on the floor.

"Burn them." Juliet downed the last of her wine and went to pour another glass.

"But Miss Brittany"—Mrs. Gregory waved the receipt at her—"they're all paid for. It says so right here."

"I don't care, Isabelle. I won't have the girls wearing those clothes. Burn them!"

"Do what she says, Mrs. Gregory," Kate said quietly. When the housekeeper left, she said, "Are you sure you don't want to call the police?"

Juliet shook her head.

"Or talk about it?"

Juliet shook her head again.

Kate finished her own wine. "Would you like to stay here tonight?" Juliet was living in her own home now and had been for several months, although the two women and their daughters spent almost equal amounts of time at each other's houses.

"Oh, Kate, would you mind? I'm sure he's completely harmless, but he gave me the willies."

Kate went around the table to hug her. "You idiot! I wouldn't mind at all."

THIRTEEN

❦

1966

Allison Hilliard about - to - become - Picard glanced in the three-way mirror and felt a moment of sheer panic as she saw the curves that even the yards and yards of heavy white satin could not hide.

What if Nick was wrong?

What if her body was not female but fat? What if her father's vision of her—boyishly lean and bony, with concave stomach and washboard ribs—was indeed the ideal? She had forced herself to swallow her breakfast this morning, had fought off the nicotine craving she thought she had conquered over a year ago. Now she felt that if she did not have a cigarette she would throw up on the spot.

In the tiny chapel, the organ began to play. Hurriedly, Allison blotted her upper lip. The only blessing was that if she fainted from sheer tension, less than half a dozen people would be there to see it. She hadn't invited Conrad Hilliard to the wedding; he wouldn't have come. Nor would her mother have attended her only child's wedding without her husband's permission. Allison's maid of honor was her stand-in on *For Richer, for Poorer*, the movie she had just completed, her second with Nick.

She still hadn't achieved what she hoped to by Nick's involvement in her career, Allison thought. But she had gotten *something*. She definitely wasn't the superstar Nick claimed he would turn her into, and yet she was more than Conrad Hilliard's daughter. No one had to append that tag to her name to identify her these days. So everything was going as she had wanted—except for today. Marrying Nicholas Picard had definitely *not* been part of her master plan.

She couldn't claim she was being rushed into wedlock. It had taken time for Nick to convince Kathleen Mallory to give him the divorce, long enough for Allison to have changed her mind a dozen times. So why hadn't she?

"It's time," Linda, her maid of honor, said softly, and then sighed explosively.

Allison glanced up, surprised.

"I wish it was me walking down that aisle," Linda said. "What a dreamboat!"

Allison wondered what Linda would say if she knew the bride was considering calling the whole thing off. So why didn't she? Allison asked herself.

Because I've fallen in love with Nick Picard, and that wasn't a part of the plan.

"I'm ready," Allison told Linda. As the girl opened the door, she caught a glimpse of Nick at the front of the church.

Allison took a deep breath and stepped through the doorway.

Kate drove herself to the appointment, trying to ignore the incipient panic bubbling just beneath her calm surface. She had made up her mind and she intended to go through with it, even though it was a strange feeling to be contemplating a film career without Nick to guide it. Kate wasn't sure it was even possible. Still, time was hanging too heavily on her hands these days. Now that Dani was three, she took up much less of Kate's time; in fact, to Kate's chagrin she actually seemed to enjoy being away from her mother.

But it was the divorce's becoming final that had jolted Kate out of her rut. She had cherished the fantasy that Nick would come back to her, especially if she became enough like Kathleen Mallory. So she had lost the pounds she gained after Dani was born, let her hair grow out to the length Nick had decreed was the most flattering when he was first trying to shape her image, and even hired a new agent—because Kathleen Mallory would not have waited timidly for her ex-husband to come back to her. Kathleen Mallory was a woman who would get on with her life.

When her agent called to set up this appointment last week, Kate accepted it. If he had called a day later, she probably would have declined, because the next day was when she learned of Nick's marriage to Allison Hilliard.

It was ironic, Kate thought, as she parked the car. After all her worries about trying to act without Nick to guide and coach her, the first offer hadn't been for a movie at all.

"The Car People," her agent, Michael Bond, had christened them, and when he introduced her to them in his office she saw how apt that name was. The gentlemen from Detroit were all sleek, finely tuned specimens, their motors humming, ready for the race.

Why in the world had they ever wanted her? she wondered, as she took the seat Michael offered her.

They answered her unspoken question immediately by uncovering a large poster on an easel at the far end of the conference room. The Javelin was long, low, and as sleek as any of these Detroit executives. In large letters, the poster proclaimed, THE MOST BEAUTIFUL WOMAN IN THE WORLD DRIVES A JAVELIN. And the woman, blond and beautiful, at the wheel of the car—

"But . . . but that's me," Kate stammered.

"It's just a mockup," one of the executives explained hurriedly, misunderstanding her dismay. "The ad agency fixed it up with your head on the model's body so that we could get an idea of what the campaign would be like."

Michael Bond shot her an encouraging smile. "Don't worry, Kathleen. We'll certainly make them pay for the privilege of using your face."

The Car People laughed appreciatively. As the laughter died away, one of them leaned forward and said earnestly, "I can't tell you how honored we are to have your beauty representing the Javelin, Kathleen."

Not Kate. Kathleen. Kathleen Mallory. Remember that, Kate cautioned herself. No one would pay Kate to represent their product. No one would believe that the line from *Diamond Lady* referred to Kate either. But Kathleen? They would believe anything of Kathleen. Because Nick had made Kathleen "the most beautiful woman in the world."

Nick!

She couldn't allow herself to think about Nick or how he had disappeared from her life. She couldn't afford to feel like an imposter. She was an actress and she had a part to play: Kathleen Mallory. Kate took a deep breath and slipped into the role as easily as if Nick were directing her.

"Great work, Kathleen," Michael Bond told her when the papers were signed and the Car People had finally left. "I want you to know I really earned my ten percent on this one."

"Oh? How?" Kate asked calmly, still in her Kathleen role.

"Allison Hilliard was up for consideration too." Michael turned to pour himself a drink, missing her wince at Allison Hilliard's name. "I convinced them that what they really needed to promote the Javelin was class. That's what you've got, Kathleen Mallory."

He handed her a snifter of brandy.

"It should be champagne," he apologized. "I had no idea they'd make up their minds so quickly. But they love you. And not just them, the big guys back in Detroit do too. Class." He saluted her with his own brandy. "Classy beauty. You've got them in the palm of your hand for as long as you want."

Kate sipped her brandy. If that's true, she wondered, why don't I believe it?

"Perfect!" Nick said, and then added, "Mrs. Picard," which caused Allison to break into a smile just as the Nikon's shutter clicked. They were alone on the white sand beach. Behind her, the incredibly blue Caribbean stretched out to the horizon without a boat in sight.

Allison wore only Nick's white shirt, which covered her to mid-thigh, and thin leather sandals. The rest of her clothes had been discarded on the sand earlier when they made love: for the second time that morning, she recalled with a delicious feeling of satisfaction that made her want to stretch like a cat. Surely Nick felt the same way. But once he picked up a camera he seemed to forget anything else. This session had been going on for almost an hour.

"Walk into the water," Nick called to her now.

Allison kicked off the sandals and obeyed. When the waves were deep enough to lap at her upper thighs, she turned. "How's this?"

"Perfect!" he said again, wading into the water toward her as the camera clicked away. When he paused at last, she started back toward shore. "Wait a minute. Let's try something else. Wet yourself all over."

"Nick! Not my hair!" she protested. "Besides, this shirt will be transparent if it's wet."

He grinned. "I know."

When he got that devilish gleam in his eye, there was no arguing with him. Allison took a deep breath and lowered herself beneath the waves. She came up sputtering, her hair streaming wetly down her shoulders. Nick snapped photo after photo.

When he finally stopped, she glanced down at herself. The shirt had indeed turned transparent. Her nipples stuck out, huge and hard beneath the fine white cotton. Her navel and the tangle of her pubic hair were clearly visible. "Nick! Those shots will be obscene."

Nick waded toward her. "Those shots, my lovely, will be art."

Holding the camera well above water with one hand, he grasped the back of her head with the other and pulled her lips to his. His sudden passion took her breath away. She could feel his hardness pressing against her stomach through the wet fabric of the shirt.

"Mmmm." Nick pulled away and glanced over her shoulder. "Company."

A brilliant white sail had blossomed in the limitless blue.

"Passersby," Allison retorted, but as the sail moved relentlessly closer, she and Nick began to wade toward the shore.

Nick glanced over at her as they reached the sand. "A penny for your thoughts."

Allison gave him a provocative smile and began to help gather up their things, trading his shirt for her own clothes. "I was wondering how quickly we could get back to the hotel," she lied. "I hate interruptions." In reality, she had been considering a puzzling image that popped into her mind as Nick kissed her in the surf. Sex with Nick had been good, great, actually the best she had ever experienced, except for one time, the memory of which caused her cheeks to burn even now. She had been fourteen, hard-muscled as a boy, when she was enrolled in an English girls' school for six months while Conrad Hilliard played *Othello* in London. Her roommate had been a curvaceous and ultrafeminine French girl. Within a week they were best friends and, within a week more, lovers. For each of them, it was their first sexual experience. Their mutual experiments had been wonderfully fulfilling. However, when Allison left school at the end of the six-month period, she had made no effort to stay in contact with Martine. A relationship with another girl was simply too bizarre to consider. As soon as she returned to the States, Allison had thrown herself into a series of relationships with boys her own age and older. But until Nick she had not experienced fulfillment on the same level she discovered with Martine.

However, she thought as she bounced along in the jeep beside Nick on the way back to the hotel, something about this afternoon had reminded her of that time with Martine. Only the images had become confused. With Martine, she had been the one who was taller, leaner, and more muscled; Martine had been shorter, fleshier, more female. With Nick, the images were reversed. He was the taller, more masculine figure, and while that might be the way nature intended it, Allison thought with a bewildered shake of her head, the upshot was that she had felt as though she were making love to herself.

No one had known or guessed about her and Martine, thank goodness. She wondered what Nick would do if she told him. Laugh, probably, and then make love to her. And if she didn't tell him, he would still make love to her.

What would her father have done? She had absolutely no idea. But that reminded her of something else. "Nick?"

"We're almost there."

"What are you going to do with those photographs?"

"Enjoy them."

"Nick?" She balled her fist and struck him on the arm. "I don't want those shots published. Do you understand?"

"I would never publish them without your permission."

She slumped down in her seat, staring straight ahead, as the jeep bounced along the rutted road.

He glanced over at her. "Allison, I'm your husband. Trust me."

"Well, just remember that you don't have my permission," she said aloud. Inside, she was wondering desperately why in the world she had agreed to get married, why she had turned her career over to Nick, and, most important, what Conrad Hilliard would think if he ever saw those photographs.

FOURTEEN

1967

KATE LEANED BACK IN THE LOUNGER, SIPPING HER wine and watching the tea party in progress on the precisely manicured lawn. The four-year-old "ladies," their mothers' frilly dresses hitched up by belts to allow them to walk, their mothers' summer hats made even more outrageous by additional flowers and feathers, giggled as they poured each other Kool-Aid "tea."

Amazing how much alike they looked, Kate thought, as she watched Danielle and Eden at the tiny table Juliet had set up on the lawn for them. She glanced over at Juliet. Too bad that similarity of appearance didn't carry over more to the girls' mothers. Kathleen Mallory might resemble Juliet, but right now, in her sundress, with windblown hair and no makeup, Kate herself looked nothing like the public Kathleen. She wondered if Juliet had been as shocked as she was to see the most recent photographs of Nick's third wife. Allison Hilliard had grown to look strikingly like Juliet. Tactfully, she decided not to ask. She had no desire to discuss how closely Nick had imitated Juliet in creating Kathleen Mallory.

Kate turned her attention back to the girls. Danielle and Eden had accepted their relationship as half-sisters without question. Perhaps the similarity in their appearance made that easier. But while physically they might be similar, their two personalities were already separate and distinct. Even though Dani was three months older, she was clearly the follower. Eden was the leader, the center of attention.

And the prettier of the two, although Kate would never have admitted that aloud.

Eden stood and began a graceful little dance on the lawn. When Dani started to join her, Eden, bossy as always, ordered her to keep her seat and watch.

It was Juliet who intervened, scolding Eden, encouraging Dani. Neither of the girls resented Juliet's intervention. Eden exchanged her scowl for a sunny smile, and Dani—sometimes Kate felt that Dani would pick Juliet as her mother, given the choice.

Eden hugged Juliet around the waist and then ran to help Dani to her feet. Both girls danced on the grass, laughing as they tripped over the trailing hems of their mothers' dresses.

Juliet poured Kate another glass of wine. "Do you know that I paid five hundred dollars for that dress? I can't believe it looks better on a four-year-old than it ever did on me." She paused for a moment as she watched the girls pirouetting on the lawn. "Dani should take dancing lessons too. I checked with Mrs. Marsh. There's an opening in Eden's class."

"Dani's so young," Kate protested.

"Older than Eden. It would do her good." Juliet smiled. "You have to let her grow up. That's what's really troubling you, isn't it? I know it's bothered me. But look how much good it's done Eden."

"I don't know. . . ."

"You won't have to do anything except sign the checks for the lessons," Juliet said quickly. "I'll take Dani when I take Eden. She'll enjoy the company."

How could Kate refuse a generous offer like that? "I—all

right. I have to be out of town next week. More filming on the Javelin campaign."

"I'll keep Dani," Juliet said promptly. They traded off keeping the girls for each other. Dani and Eden each regarded the other's house as merely an extension of her own. "Kate? We need to think about something else."

Kate was startled by the serious look on Juliet's face. "About the girls?" she asked, suddenly anxious.

"About Nick."

His name was like a blow to Kate's stomach. "What about him?"

"We're not being fair to the girls. We need to arrange for Nick to see them on a regular basis. They need a father."

"I haven't found a father all that useful in my life," Kate protested.

Juliet remained silent for a long time, watching the girls dancing on the grass, so long Kate thought she had decided to drop the subject.

"Nick would be a good father," Juliet said at last. "To both of them."

Juliet was in the shower when the phone rang. By the time she scrambled out and wrapped herself in a towel, it had fallen silent.

She shoved her wet hair out of her eyes and wondered if it had been Nick on the other end of the line. As soon as she had Kate's agreement that Nick should visit his daughters, Juliet had contacted his office. Now, with a bubbly sense of excitement, she was waiting for him to return the call. Nick might refuse to see Eden alone. He wouldn't refuse to see both of his daughters.

Wrapping her hair in another thick towel, Juliet sat down at her dressing table and began to put on her makeup. She hadn't lied to Kate; the girls did need to know their father. However, her motives hadn't been entirely innocent. She needed to see Nick too. It had been a long time. Far too long.

The phone rang again. Juliet knocked over a perfume bottle as she grabbed for it. "Hello?"

"Juliet?"

It wasn't Nick; it was her father.

"Juliet? I want to see you." She could hear his heavy breathing. "I want to talk to you. Just talk. That's all. I promise."

"No."

"Juliet, please. Please just let me be around you sometime. Just—"

"No! I've seen you following me! I've seen you. I want you to leave me alone. Just leave me alone or I'll call the police."

She slammed down the phone and stood there trembling. She was breathing heavily herself, as though she had just run a footrace.

After a moment, she picked up the phone again and dialed Kate's number. "Where are the girls?" she said when Kate answered.

"Why—here, of course."

"Can you see them?"

"No, they're down in the kitchen with Mrs. Gregory."

"Go and make sure."

"Is something wrong, Juliet?"

She felt like screaming, but she managed to keep her voice steady. "I had a crank call. It's probably nothing to worry about. Please go and make sure."

"Just a moment."

There was a thump as Kate laid the phone down, followed by what seemed like endless waiting. Juliet was panicked enough to think seriously of rushing downstairs in her towel and driving over to Kate's.

Kate finally came back on the line. "Juliet? They're fine.

They're baking cookies with Mrs. Gregory. They've got more cookie dough on themselves than the cookie sheet. They insisted I try one of their creations. It wasn't half bad."

Juliet exhaled explosively.

"Juliet? Are you all right?"

"I'm fine. I just—I was worried. Do me a favor, Kate. Keep a close eye on them today. There's probably no reason to worry, but I do."

"I know," Kate said. "So do I. I'll watch them. Are you coming over later?"

"Maybe. I'll give you a call."

Juliet hung up and sat down heavily on the bed. Just the thought of Oliver watching her made her stomach lurch. If he went near Eden or Dani—

The phone rang right beside her, startling her. "Hello?" she said cautiously.

"Juliet?" She breathed a quick sigh of relief. Nick's voice was on the other end of the line this time. "It's been a long time. I got your message that we needed to talk."

"We certainly do," Juliet said, happy to hear no hint of her recent panic in her voice. "Kate and I have come to a decision."

"You—and Kate?"

She almost giggled. She could just see the incredulous look that must be on Nick's face right now.

"Yes, Kate and I. The mothers of your children, Nick. We think you should see your daughters."

Nick hung up the phone and leaned back, his hands clasped behind his head. When had Juliet and Kate become so thick? If there had ever been two females on the face of the earth who couldn't stand each other, it was his two ex-wives. He never would have suspected they were even speaking to each other, let alone making plans for him to visit his daughters.

His daughters.

What a curious-sounding phrase that was. He wondered what they were like. How old were they now, four? Five? He wrote out a check each month for each of them, or rather Peggy did, but he hadn't seen either of the girls since they were babies. Hadn't even seen a photograph of them since then.

Nick buzzed the outer office. When Peggy picked up, he said, "Have either of my ex-wives sent me photographs of my daughters recently?"

"I beg your pardon?"

"My daughters, Peggy. Do I have any recent photographs of them?"

"Not that I know of. Shall I—"

"No, never mind. I'll take care of it myself. By the way, I have an important appointment Wednesday at one o'clock. I'll be out of the office the rest of Wednesday afternoon."

"I'll jot that down," Peggy said efficiently. "If someone asks where you are, what shall I say?"

Someone was Allison. She resented any of his time that was not expended directly on her career. "If anyone should ask, tell her I'm visiting my daughters."

"Your daughters?"

"It's time, don't you think?" Nick switched off the intercom and leaned back in his chair again. What a curious feeling it was to know that there were small bits of himself alive on the planet. How had he managed to forget?

"I'm a buttercup," Danielle said shyly, twisting the hem of her skirt. She had yet to emerge from the shelter of Juliet's arm.

Eden sat on Nick's knee, playing with his tie. "I'm the Queen of the Buttercups," she announced loudly. "Are you coming to my play?"

"Eden! You're a plain buttercup, just like Dani," Juliet

scolded. "There are no queens. And it's Dani's play too."

"Mommy says I'm *her* queen," Eden told Nick, unabashed by the criticism. "Are you really our father?"

"Really and truly," Nick told her. He held out a hand to Dani. "Don't you want to sit on my lap too?" She came slowly and climbed up on his other knee. She reminded him very much of Kate, just as Eden reminded him of Juliet. Funny. He could see nothing of himself in his daughters, not yet anyway.

"Where is Kate?" he asked Juliet.

Was that a frown? he wondered. As quickly as it appeared, it was gone.

"Upstairs," Juliet said. "She thought you would be more comfortable with the girls alone."

And I can tell you're lying, Nick thought. She didn't want to see me. I can't blame her, not after the way I left her for Allison.

Just thinking of Allison was a distraction. He had promised her he would make her a superstar; small wonder that she was growing impatient.

So was he.

Eden tugged on his tie. "What are you thinking about?"

"You," Nick told her.

"You liar! You were not!"

"Eden!" Juliet laughed in spite of herself.

"I think, Nick, that I will follow Kate's example and leave you to deal with these two angels alone." Juliet went upstairs, leaving an uneasy silence behind her.

Nick looked down into the two small faces. Two sets of bright blue eyes stared back at him. He felt a momentary urge to call Juliet back. He knew nothing about little girls—or children in general, for that matter. He had never been around children much, even while growing up himself. Except Freddie, of course, but Freddie was older and didn't count. At least Nick hoped not. He would

hate to have a lifelong feud with these two little "angels."
"Well," he said, suddenly uneasy, "I'm certainly glad to see
you both."

"Why haven't you ever come to see us before?" It was
Dani who asked that uncomfortable question.

"I've been pretty busy."

Dani didn't even blink. "Mommy said Juliet was making
you come. She said she wouldn't have any part of it."

Her eyes looked suspiciously moist. Something grasped
Nick's heart and twisted it painfully. He tightened his arms,
hugging both his daughters close. "I'm truly sorry to hear
that," he told Dani. "And I'm sorry I haven't been more of a
father to you. I'll make it up to both of you, I promise."

"Really?" Eden asked.

"Cross my heart and hope to die," Nick told her solemnly. "How shall we begin?"

Eden looked so much like Juliet at that moment it almost
took his breath away. "I know," she said. "You can buy me
a horse."

"Come right in, Kathleen," Michael Bond said. "Have
you met Barry?"

Kate looked at the tall dark-haired man and shook her
head.

"Barry Inman," the stranger said with a warm smile that
made her think of Nick in one of his better moods. "I handle the literary side of the agency. If you ever decide to write
a book, I'll be glad to handle it for you, Miss Mallory."

"I'll keep that in mind," Kate told him.

He excused himself as she took her seat, and she felt
ridiculously sorry to see him leave.

Michael immediately launched into one of the laudatory
speeches that always made her want to turn and twist in
her chair in embarrassment. She wished she'd had the presence of mind, when he first became her agent, to tell him

she preferred to be called Kate in private. Now it was too late. It was also too late to tell him she hated all his fulsome comments about her beauty. She couldn't shake the feeling she should correct him, tell him, "That's Kathleen Mallory you're talking about, not me. I'm just plain Kate." The horror of being thought a nut had kept her silent and embarrassed. Like today.

She was relieved when the session was finally over, so relieved that she came barreling out of the office and crashed right into Barry Inman.

"Hey," he said, holding her upright. "Are you okay?"

"Yes, I'm okay," Kate said, blushing furiously. "I *am* sorry. I didn't mean to—"

"I always suspected Michael mistreated our female clients. Now I'm positive."

Kate gave him a startled look and then caught the twinkle in his eye. He laughed, and she joined in.

"Lucky for me, he does," Barry Inman continued. "I was trying to think of a way to see you again. Would you have dinner with me, Kathleen?"

Kate smiled up into his face, feeling whole again for the first time in ages and absurdly touched by his offer. "I'd love to," she said. "Only, please call me Kate."

FIFTEEN

1969

ALLISON CLUTCHED NICK'S HAND TIGHTLY IN THE darkness as they watched the rushes of *Special Lady*. After all this time, her gamble of defying her father and going with Nick's judgment had paid off. *Special Lady* was going to be a winner; she could feel it. And her own performance—she had never been better.

Nick leaned close to her in the darkness. "This is it, babe," he whispered. "I promised you I'd make you a superstar. *Special Lady* will do it."

Allison relaxed then and leaned back in her seat. For the first time ever, she didn't try to pick apart her own performance as her father had taught her, didn't try to find the flaws. She knew full well that Conrad Hilliard would consider the whole movie flawed, because the "special lady" in Nick's script was the most sexual creature Allison had yet portrayed on the screen. She felt an almost insane urge to call Conrad Hilliard on the phone and say, "You belong to another Hollywood era, dear old Dad. *Special Lady* will drive the nails in your coffin."

The lights came on then, and Nick turned to her. "I think this calls for a celebration, Mrs. Picard. Alone. Just the two of us: a magnum of champagne and a king-sized bed."

Before she could answer, they were surrounded by other members of the cast and crew who had been on hand for the rushes. Nick smiled at her ruefully. "Later," he whispered to her as everyone clamored for a celebration party. "Enjoy your triumph."

"And yours," she replied generously. But she knew, as Nick must, that although he had written the script and directed it, it was she who had come alive on the screen, had come fully into her power at long last.

Take that, Daddy dear!

"Miss Mallory?"

Kate looked up into the mirror of her dressing table. Mrs. Gregory stood just inside the door of her bedroom, ringing her hands worriedly.

"What's wrong?"

"It's Miss Danielle. Miss Brittany is here to pick up Eden, and Miss Danielle won't let her go."

"For heaven's sake, Mrs. Gregory!" Kate slammed down her hairbrush. "I would think you could manage to handle a six-year-old!"

"It's just that she's so upset, Miss Mallory. I know you wanted Mr. Inman to see her in her new outfit, but I wondered if you wouldn't let her go home with Miss Brittany instead. The girls were having so much fun today."

Kate glanced at the clock on her dressing table as she shrugged into her robe. Barry would be here in twenty minutes, and she wanted to be calm, collected, and beautiful for him. They had been dating for almost two years. She found him comfortable to be with. His only flaw, if it might be called a flaw in a bachelor, was that he didn't particularly care for children. Kate made certain he saw Dani only when her daughter was on her best behavior. She certainly didn't want to have him walk into the middle of a domestic crisis involving screaming six-year-olds. That would confirm his worst suspicions about children.

"Sorry to disturb you," Juliet called as Kate came down the stairs.

Juliet was holding Eden by the hand. Dani stood beside Eden, her arms wrapped tightly about her half-sister's waist. "I don't want her to go," she blurted as Kate reached the bottom of the stairs. Her face was blotched and swollen from her tears.

"Dani, Barry's coming tonight. I wanted him to see you in your pretty new dress."

"I don't care. I don't like Barry. I like Eden."

"Please, Aunt Kate." Eden spoke up. "Can't Dani come home with us? Mommy won't mind, will you, Mommy?"

Eden gave Juliet a charming smile that made Kate cringe inside. Why in the world couldn't Dani look like that? Kate thought about Barry. The last thing she wanted was for him to see the disparity between Dani and her half-sister. She had to get Eden out of here fast, before Barry arrived. "*Would* you mind, Juliet? I hate to impose, but—"

"Certainly not. That is, if Dani wants to come with us."

"Oh, please," Dani begged, her pleasure transforming her face into something approaching beauty for the first time since Kate had come downstairs.

"I think she actually prefers your house to mine." Kate tried to make it sound like a joke, but it wasn't.

Juliet had knelt while she was talking to Dani. Now she stood up in one graceful motion. "I love having her, and so does Eden. You know that. Now come along, girls," she ordered, with a wink at Kate. "Danielle's mom has a hot date."

Mrs. Gregory, having no doubt how the confrontation would end, had gone to pack Dani's things. She reappeared now, overnight bag in hand, and followed Juliet and the girls out to the car.

Kate went back upstairs slowly. Maybe the fact that

Barry didn't care for children was one of the things they had in common. She wasn't sure if she cared for them either. She always felt so helpless, so uncomfortable, dealing with Dani. Juliet had a natural warmth and spontaneity where children were concerned. Kate certainly did not. Because of that, Kate found herself letting Juliet keep Dani more and more. Dani made no secret of the fact that she loved staying at Juliet's house—perhaps even better than living in her own home.

If Kate didn't know Juliet better, she would suspect Juliet of trying to undermine her, to steal Dani's affections from her. That was stupid, Kate thought. If anything, it was she who took advantage of their friendship by pushing Dani off on Juliet more than she should.

As Kate entered her bedroom, she glanced at the clock on her dressing table. Barry was due in five minutes, and he was never late! Kate tore off her robe and dressed hurriedly. She was just running a comb through her hair when the doorbell sounded.

She took a deep breath and checked her image in the mirror. The woman who stared back was calm, collected, and beautiful—just the way Barry liked her. Not having to worry about how Dani would act in front of him had smoothed out the tiny tension lines on her forehead. Kate smiled at her reflection and then went downstairs.

"So how did it go last night?" Juliet asked when Kate came on the line. "Did Mr. Inman pop the question at long last?"

"Oh, Juliet!" Juliet rolled her eyes at her reflection in the toaster as she buttered toast for the girls' breakfast. She knew Kate well enough by now to know that particular inflection meant she was blushing furiously. "Barry and I are just good friends."

"Even good friends get married, Kate." Juliet sincerely hoped that was true, because if Kate remarried, Juliet wouldn't have to worry about her getting involved with Nick again. To Juliet's dismay, each time Nick visited the girls, he was full of questions about Kate. Juliet stuck her tongue out at her reflection in the toaster and began to butter another slice of toast. "So what did you and the dashing Mr. Inman talk about last night?" She grinned wickedly at herself. "Or didn't he give you time to talk before he swept you into bed?"

"Juliet!" To Juliet's great amusement, any hint that Kate might have a sexual nature always embarrassed her. "We talked about Nick, for one thing."

Juliet dropped the toast. It landed, butter side down, on the floor.

"Juliet? Are you there?"

Juliet stooped to pick up the toast and tossed it in the trash. "You talked about Nick?"

"Barry says everyone is talking about Nick's new picture. It's all over Hollywood. Barry says it's the best thing Nick has ever done. In fact he says *Special Lady* is going to make Allison Hilliard a major-league star."

Juliet stared down at the smear of butter on the floor.

"Juliet?"

"I . . . I've got to go. I dropped something, and the girls are going to be in here in a minute wanting breakfast."

"Thanks for keeping Dani. I'll send Mrs. Gregory for her later."

Juliet hung up the phone and knelt to clean up the butter. Strange. Kate's success as the Javelin woman hadn't bothered her. But hearing about Allison Hilliard's triumph, she felt a dull red rage. She wiped mechanically, until the smear of butter was gone.

Who was she kidding? she thought, as she went back to buttering toast. She hadn't had a film role since before Eden was born. No wonder Nick was no longer interested in her.

She had made the girls the center of her whole life, losing herself in a fantasy in which Nick noticed what a wonderful mother she was—much better than Kate—and came back to her. The reality was that she had turned into a drudge, a housewife, and no one was going to be interested in her. Especially Nick.

So what was she going to do? She couldn't just sit and vegetate. Juliet stared at herself in the toaster. Her vegetative days were over, she decided. It was time she got back into the world again.

Juliet's first blow was how long it took her to get an appointment with an agent. Her old agent wasn't interested. It was only because of Kate that she managed to get Kate's agent, Michael Bond, to represent her. Not that she wanted to ask Kate, but by that time Juliet was so desperate she would have accepted help from anyone.

The second blow was the size of the film role for which she was auditioning. She had leafed through the script she had been given, certain there was a mistake, and then in a fury she phoned Michael Bond.

"You can't expect to go in at the top after all these years," Michael told her calmly. "You have to work your way up again."

Juliet almost ripped up the script and told him to go to hell. But she didn't. Getting back into the world had become too important to her.

However, the morning of her audition, events conspired against her. She had begun subscribing to *The Hollywood Reporter* again, and the copy beside her breakfast plate had a lead story on the prerelease interest in *Special Lady*.

If that wasn't enough, as she was driving herself to the audition Juliet caught sight of her father's car tailing her through the traffic. By the time she arrived at the studio, she was a nervous wreck. She couldn't stop thinking about

Oliver, wondering why he was following her and how long he had been watching her.

She balked at turning herself over to the hairstylist when she saw the hair of the actress who had just emerged from his clutches. The casting director insisted. The hair stylist, having heard the argument, yanked Juliet's hair hard enough to bring tears to her eyes and then stoutly denied the whole thing.

By the time she was seated in front of the camera for the screen test, Juliet was on the edge of hysteria. She stumbled over the first line, and when the casting director asked that she start again she burst into tears.

All it needed to make the day perfect was the sight of her father's car in the rearview mirror, following her home.

Oliver Brittany stayed up until midnight, working on his files. He used a fountain pen filled with jet-black ink and made meticulous notations in tiny block letters. Rather like a scientist keeping records of his research subjects, he thought proudly. When he finished transcribing the notes of his surveillance of Juliet today, he added those pages to the thick notebook labeled JULIET, 1969 and put it on the shelf beside the others, one for each year of her life. The first notebooks were thin things, barely worthy of the name. However, in the current ones Oliver had, in addition to his own observations, thousands of dollars' worth of private detectives' reports on every aspect of Juliet's life.

He sighed contentedly, proud of his work.

Then he turned his attention to the next shelf, where the notebook labeled KATHLEEN MALLORY, 1969 awaited his attention.

When she bought the new desk and typewriter, Kate had them placed originally in front of the window, where she had a gorgeous view of the pool and the sloping lawn beyond. Halfway through the first week, she realized her mistake and had them moved into the windowless dressing room just off her bedroom. For the past month, she had spent every morning, unless she was required to appear as the Javelin Woman, pecking away on the typewriter keys. So far, she had managed to avoid telling anyone exactly what she was doing. Even Juliet, observant as she was, had not guessed Kate's secret.

Barry Inman had been her inspiration, although he too had no idea what was going on. From their first date, he and Kate had talked endlessly about his work with book authors and screenwriters; he had ten years of experience and the most amusing and insightful stories to tell. Sometime during the last few months, Kate had begun to listen more carefully, to ask questions about the authors themselves and about their working methods. Her interest in his work pleased Barry. He had even teased her about writing a novel herself, so he could be her agent.

That was exactly what she planned to do.

Rolling a new sheet of paper into the typewriter, Kate spaced down to the center of the page. It wasn't going to be any good, she thought. It was going too fast, too easily, and the story itself was clichéd: a young girl destroyed by Hollywood and fame.

But yesterday she had thought of a twist: the girl comes back to take her revenge on the town and the people who destroyed her. Corny, maybe, but she felt a funny little tingle inside every time she thought of it.

Corny or clichéd, she planned to finish the manuscript. She had a desperate need to do something concrete, something that didn't feel as though it might vanish without warning. She was twenty-seven now and already learning to hate looking in the mirror. Every faint trace of a beginning wrinkle meant she was that much closer to losing the contract as the Javelin Woman. "The most beautiful woman in the world" could not grow old. As soon as her age became visible in her face, Kate knew she was finished.

Look at Juliet. Beautiful as she still was, she had been turned down for every role for which she auditioned. That wasn't going to happen to her, Kate vowed. If this story didn't work, she would simply try again. She had talked to Barry enough to know how long success at writing could be in coming.

CHAPTER FOUR, she typed, and then forgot Barry, Juliet, and everything else except the page before her.

"I'm only thirty years old! Since when is that over the hill?"

"Now, Juliet," Michael Bond began calmly. "No one said—"

"No one has to say! Do you believe I can't tell what you think from the miserable little roles you send me to audition for?" Juliet knew she was losing control, but she couldn't hold back her anger. Part of it was the lousy job Bond was doing as her agent, and part of it was Oliver. Her father had called her five times since midnight, begging her to see him. This morning, she caught sight of him behind her on the freeway again. She couldn't make a move without him spying on her.

"I told you before, it's not easy to come back after a long lapse in your career."

"What about Kate? A lapse in her career didn't seem to hurt her any!"

Michael Bond smirked. "Surely, as Kathleen's friend, you can see she's something different, something special. Her kind of beauty and talent never ages or goes out of style. You have to be a realist, Juliet. You're too old for the parts you want to play."

Juliet picked up the heavy glass ashtray at the end of the agent's desk and heaved it as hard as she could at his head. It missed by only three inches, shattering the floor-to-ceiling window behind him instead.

Michael Bond stood up.

So did Juliet.

His secretary rushed in from the outer office. "Mr. Bond! What happened?"

"I believe Miss Brittany has just exercised her option to cancel her contract with this agency," Michael Bond said, as Juliet flounced past the secretary and out the door.

SIXTEEN

1971

IT WAS MUCH HARDER THAN HAVING A BABY, THE most excruciating agony Kate had ever experienced. For the hundredth time that weekend, she lifted the receiver on the phone beside her bed to call Barry; for the hundredth time, she replaced it without dialing.

She had delivered the manuscript of *Fortune's Gambit* to his office on Friday afternoon, too impatient to wait for their date that night to hand it over. Even then, she had been too shy to give him the book in person. She had dropped the manuscript box on his secretary's desk and fled.

Barry caught up with her in the parking lot. "It's a novel, isn't it?" he said, with a peculiar light in his eyes. "You've done it, haven't you."

"Just read it, Barry. I know you're going to tell me it's awful, so go ahead and read it and get it over with." She pulled away from him and opened the door of her Javelin. "I'll see you tonight."

"No, you won't."

She hesitated. "Why not?"

"Because I'm going to be curled up with what I hope is a very good book. I'll see you when I'm finished with it." With that, he turned and marched back inside, leaving her clinging to the car door, afraid she might faint.

How she made it home after that, she had no idea.

When Sunday afternoon passed with still no word from Barry, Kate panicked. It couldn't be taking him this long to read the manuscript. Unable to bear the suspense, she packed a bag for herself and dropped Dani off at Juliet's without explanation.

Kate felt guilty as she drove away. She could tell from Juliet's drawn face she should have stayed to chat. Ever since the run-in with Michael Bond two years before, Juliet had been abnormally quiet and withdrawn. She should have gone out of her way to be friendly, Kate thought guiltily. After all, Juliet had been there when Kate needed her.

Then Kate forgot about Juliet as another thought surfaced, a sudden unpleasant vision of Barry turning the pages of *Fortune's Gambit*, scanning the words—and laughing at them.

Kate drove all the way to Carmel before she stopped. It was Wednesday morning before she thought to call Juliet and let her know where she could be reached.

"For heaven's sake!" Juliet said crossly. "Where have you been? I have a stack of messages for you from Barry Inman. Did you have a lover's quarrel?"

Kate felt her heart banging against her ribs. "What do the messages say?"

"All they say is *Have Kate call me*. There must be a hundred of them here, and Isabelle has as many at your house. What did poor Barry do, anyway?"

"He didn't do anything," Kate said slowly. "It was something I did." Obviously, Barry wanted to deliver the bad news in person. "Tell him I'll be home sometime tonight."

"Don't you want me to give him your love?" Juliet inquired with a touch of her old spirit.

"Just give him the message." Kate managed to hang up before the tears came. It was one thing to say she was prepared to keep writing regardless of what Barry thought of the manuscript; it was quite another to face the reality of being told her work was unpublishable. The thought of starting all over again on page one of a new novel was too overwhelming to contemplate.

It was a weary and depressing drive back from Carmel. When Barry appeared at her door late that evening, he insisted she shower and change so he could take her out to dinner. He refused to discuss the manuscript of *Fortune's Gambit* at all.

When he delivered her back to her door after midnight, he didn't ask to come inside. Instead, he said, "Don't worry about the manuscript. I'll have some news for you in a few days."

"What kind of news?" Kate demanded.

Barry shook his head. "You'll find out soon enough."

When Barry hadn't called by late afternoon the next day, Kate dialed his office.

"Oh, Miss Mallory," his secretary said. "Mr. Inman is in New York. He said he would contact you the minute he returned."

"He didn't leave a message or a number for me?" Always before, when Barry flew to New York on business, he had let her know where he could be reached.

"I'm sorry," the secretary said.

Kate hung up and stared dismally at her bedroom wall. Why had she ever given the manuscript to Barry? Obviously, it was so bad he couldn't bring himself to tell her the truth about it.

Kate had not realized how big a part both writing and Barry had come to play in her life until both were gone. She tried to fill her days by spending more time with her daughter, but Dani had plans of her own, all of which centered around Eden and Juliet. Juliet made a point of inviting Kate to accompany her and the girls on all their jaunts, but Kate refused. Right now she wasn't up to seeing how much better Juliet got along with Dani than she did.

When the bell at the service entrance rang at 3 P.M. on Wednesday, Kate realized with some irritation she would have to answer it herself. She had loaned Mrs. Gregory to Juliet for the day to help with a picnic for the girls.

Whoever it was didn't appreciate the delay. The buzzer sounded again and again as she made her way downstairs.

"All right!" Kate said as she threw open the door, and then she froze in astonishment.

Barry stood there, a huge grin on his face, holding a huge bunch of red roses.

"Barry! What on earth?"

He turned and shouted, "Hurry that up!" Over his shoulder Kate could see a caterer's van being unloaded in the drive.

"Barry!" A wild exuberance filled her. "What are you doing?"

"Celebrating. Let's see," he said as the caterers passed him on the way into the kitchen. "Champagne. Caviar. Chocolates. Have I forgotten anything?" Barry slapped his head in mock anguish. "The guests! They should be arriving any minute."

Stunned, Kate realized that cars were pulling up in front of the house and disgorging men and women in cocktail attire. "My hair!" she squealed and ran upstairs, leaving Barry to open the front door.

When she reappeared thirty minutes later, the party was in full swing. "Here she is," Barry called when he caught sight of her.

All conversation stopped. Everyone turned to stare. A flash went off, and Kate gave thanks for the amazing transformation she had managed to accomplish in the last half hour. Javelin would have canceled her contract if photographs of her as she had been when she first went to the door had been published.

Barry pushed through the crowd and placed a glass of champagne in her hand. "Congratulations, Kate!"

"Congratulations for what?" That was the question tormenting her all the time she was upstairs. Did it have something to do with her book? It must have!

"*Fortune's Gambit* was sold at auction for the largest advance ever for a first novelist."

Kate could feel the smile frozen on her lips, could feel herself retreating behind the protective mask of Kathleen the ice queen. "Is this a joke?"

"It's no joke, Kate. *Fortune's Gambit* is going to be a best-seller."

It was the queerest sensation. She could swear she felt absolutely nothing, yet tears were pricking her eyes and little tremors of excitement were dancing in her stomach. Terror that she might either faint or throw up gripped her. "You sold it? Someone bought it?"

Barry nodded proudly. "Yes to both questions."

"I had no idea you intended to show it to anyone," Kate said weakly.

"I'm a literary agent, remember? What did you expect me to do with it?"

"Read it, give it back, and tell me it was trash," Kate said promptly.

Everyone around them burst into laughter. "What a sense of humor you have," someone murmured.

"Now before we let the party continue," Barry said, raising his voice to silence the crowd once more, "there's one more thing."

Kate felt as though she were in Wonderland. How could there be one more thing when she hadn't absorbed the first?

Barry pulled a small jewelry box out of his breast pocket

and handed it to her. When Kate opened it, she found an engagement ring inside. She looked up into Barry's delighted eyes.

"Marry me, Kate?"

"Oh, Barry!" She threw herself into his arms. Champagne splashed out of her glass, anointing the surrounding guests.

By midnight, when Kate and Barry left for the airport and the chartered plane he had waiting, the party was still going strong.

They were married the next day in Las Vegas.

SEVENTEEN

1972

"**A**BSOLUTELY NOT!" ALLISON SCREAMED.

"Calm down and listen," Nick told her. "These are very artistic photographs. No one will—"

"I won't have it!" She hated it when he barricaded himself behind his desk and became Picard Productions instead of her husband. He thought he could just hand down a business decision and she would accept it without question. Well, not this time! "I swear I'll sue you if you dare."

"Why do you get hysterical every time something new comes up? Have you ever wondered that?"

"You're not being fair, Nick! This is different."

Allison sat down on the sofa, folded her arms across her chest, and glared at him. Of course she had been upset when she read the script for *Impressions*. If she had thought *Special Lady* hovered on the edge of pornography, *Impressions* crossed the line. Nick had really lambasted her when she said that. But for someone who always believed she would eventually follow her father onto the stage, the thought of starring in a racy little comedy where she ran around in a constant state of undress and slept with all the other characters was definitely a shock. After reading the script, Allison had flatly refused to do the movie.

It wasn't that she didn't realize each of Nick's decisions

had advanced her career one giant step after another. Still, it had taken him three weeks to talk her into starring in *Impressions.* Allison was willing to admit that judging from the excitement on the set this week she had made the right decision, but this! This was something else!

God, she wished she had a cigarette! Every time she and Nick had a fight, which was at least once a week these days, she wanted to start smoking again. "You can't use them without my permission," she said stubbornly, "and you don't have it."

"How can a woman who grew up in Hollywood be so provincial?"

That stung! "Those photographs were private, a personal record of our honeymoon. They were not for publication!"

"If you're worried that being in *Playboy* will hurt your career, don't. It certainly didn't harm Juliet or Kate. In fact, it gave them both a boost when they really needed it."

"Answer me one question, Nick: Why do you want to display your wife's breasts and pubic hair in *Playboy*? Do you have some kind of crazy complex?"

Nick grinned. "Would you prefer *Penthouse*? Hef would never forgive me."

"Most men—"

"Most men aren't trying to make their wife into a superstar."

Allison stared at him steadily for a moment. "I guess the real question is: Why are you? Have you ever thought about that, Nick? Ever wondered what it is that drives *you*?"

A faint trace of scarlet burned along his cheekbones. "I'm a businessman."

"And your wife is a product?"

"This has nothing to do with your being my wife."

Allison stood up and began to pace around the office. "I wonder if that's true."

"This is a purely business decision. A photo spread in *Playboy*, timed to appear when *Impressions* is released, will do more for the movie, and for you, than any amount of paid advertising. Everyone will be talking about you. They'll beat down the theater doors."

"Because they think they'll see even more of me on the screen?"

"Maybe they will," Nick said smugly. "I'll decide that when we edit the film."

"You're not going to make me into a porno queen! I won't let you!" To her rage, the tears came then. She dropped back down on the sofa and buried her face in her hands. This wasn't her, she thought wildly. She never cried. Crying was a sign of feminine weakness. Still, she couldn't stop.

Nick came around the desk and sat down beside her. When he put his arm around her shoulders, she resisted. He pulled her to him anyway, until she was sobbing on his shoulder. "Why don't you tell me what's really wrong?" he said softly, stroking her hair.

"They'll laugh at me," she gasped out between tears. She hadn't realized what she was going to say. The statement startled her enough that her tears slowed.

Still holding her arms, Nick pushed her away slightly, so that he could look into her face. "Why will they laugh at you?"

"Because—they'll look at me and know I'm not a real woman."

Nick leaned forward and kissed her damp cheek. "Oh, babe," he said. "Don't feel like that. You have a beautiful body. You have the most beautiful body in the world." His lips drifted lower, down her neck, to the hollow at the base of her throat.

"Oh, Nick." She sighed.

"Let me show you how beautiful it is," he said, as he began to unbutton her blouse.

"Allison!" Conrad Hilliard thundered.

Why did the sound of her father's voice on the phone always reduce her to a quaking six-year-old? She took a deep breath. "Yes, Father?"

"How long did you think you could keep it a secret from me?"

The photographs! Oh, my God! He's found out Nick sold them to *Playboy*!

Calm down, Allison told herself. You're not a child; you're a thirty-one-year-old woman. But somehow the words to defend herself wouldn't come.

"Everyone is talking about it," her father went on. "That film is sheer filth. I won't have my daughter making smutty pictures." For the first time, Allison heard the whine of age in his voice. Someday he's going to die, she thought. It had never occurred to her before.

"I'm not sure I understand the subject of this conversation," she said and was astounded at the calmness of her own voice.

"That pornography your husband has written. That you have the sheer gall to be exposing yourself in. Literally exposing yourself!"

"Are you talking about *Impressions*, Father? If you are, I assure you, you have the wrong idea."

"Filth! If you don't stop making pornography, you and that husband of yours, I'll see you're stopped. I'm not without influence in this town, as you well know. Don't make me use that influence against my own daughter." He stopped, gasping for breath.

"Really, Father, you—"

"I am ashamed of you!" he roared and slammed down the receiver.

Allison replaced her own receiver more gently and sat there, shaken, unsure if she was going to laugh or cry. All

Conrad Hilliard's performance had lacked was that immortal line, "You'll never work in this town again."

I trust Nick, she told herself. Everything Nick has done has worked. This is going to work, too.

"Great performance," she said aloud. "I just hope it's the truth."

Allison snatched the September issue of *Playboy* off the newsstand and then had a moment's panic, wondering what she would say to the cashier. She needn't have worried. The bleary-eyed woman scooped the bills into her cash drawer without looking at her customer's face.

Allison all but ran out to her car. As soon as she slipped behind the wheel, she opened the magazine and flipped to the article about herself.

The reality of her own image on the glossy page made Allison gasp. Was that really what she looked like? So womanly?

Hardly daring to breathe, she traced the form on the page with her fingertips, enjoying the rich, slick feel of the paper.

Why, I'm really beautiful! she thought.

Thank you, Nick.

"You slut!" Conrad Hilliard was almost incoherent with rage, but those words came across the phone line loud and clear. "Do you realize how many generations of Hilliards you have managed to disgrace? How could you resort to nudity instead of relying on your own talent?"

"I take it you didn't approve of the *Playboy* spread." Allison caught the edge of her lip with her teeth, trying to hold back a giggle. "Nick is a genius with a camera, don't you think?"

"My son-in-law is a whoremonger! And my daughter—"

"Really, Father, this isn't the London stage. We're not

doing Shakespeare. This is Los Angeles, the twentieth century, remember? With the help of that article, *Impressions* is raking it in at the box office. You should be proud of us."

"You are forcing me to take an action I don't relish, Allison. If you and Nicholas Picard don't stop making your pornography, I will see that you never work in this town again!" There it was at last. All the Hollywood tyrants who ever lived were rolled into that one line.

It was too much for Allison. She was still laughing when her father hung up the phone.

Why did she keep putting herself through this? Juliet wondered, as she waited in the producer's outer office for his snippy secretary to announce her presence.

The answer was simple. She couldn't sit back and watch the successes Kate and Allison Hilliard were having. Compared to them, she was a failure. Oh, she had been offered roles, all right. There wasn't a dumb-blonde-with-more-tits-than-brains role in the past three years she couldn't have had.

An *older*-dumb-blonde-with-tits, she fumed. It infuriated her that everyone seemed to think she was too old to be a star anymore. She was only thirty-three. Three years older than Kathleen Mallory, Javelin Woman and best-selling author. Only two years older than Allison Hilliard, the hottest star in Hollywood right now.

And Nick's wife.

She was still chewing on that when the secretary ushered her into the producer's office. "Miss Brittany," he said, coming around his desk as the secretary exited. He put his arm around Juliet's shoulder, his hand dangling just above her right breast. "I know we're going to enjoy working together." He gave her breast a squeeze. "Night and day."

For a just a moment, Juliet teetered on the edge of the most violent eruption that ever threatened. "If I had a gun, I would shoot you dead on the spot," she said quietly.

His grip loosened and she pulled away from him. A framed picture of a woman and three small children sat on his desk; she wondered what he would do if she threw it at him.

For a moment, just a moment, she let herself enjoy the sound of shattering glass in her mind. Then she clamped down on the impulse.

"If you will excuse me, I have other appointments," she told him. "With men. Not maggots."

He was still standing in the same spot, an astonished expression on his face, when she shut the door behind her.

The phone was ringing when Juliet walked in the front door. She lunged for it. "Hello?"

Hoarse breathing, then: "Juliet? Let me come over."

"Papa? Papa! You leave me alone, Papa! Don't you ever call me again, ever!"

"Juliet, just let me see you."

"No," she screamed. "Leave me alone! Just leave me alone!"

She slammed down the phone and took the stairs two at a time. When she reached her bedroom, she threw herself across the bed and bawled like a baby.

Isabelle Gregory arrived with the girls at 8 P.M. "I'd stay and help you get them settled, but Miss Mall—I mean, Mrs. Inman has something for me to do when I get back."

Ordinarily, Juliet would have pumped Isabelle for the information she knew the older woman was dying to give, but tonight her heart wasn't in it.

Isabelle gave her a funny look when she was leaving. Juliet wondered if it was obvious that she had been crying—

and drinking. Before Isabelle arrived with the girls, Juliet had finished a bottle of wine in her room.

After the girls went off to bed in Eden's room, to giggle and gossip under the covers instead of sleep, Juliet went up to her own room. This had to have been one of the worst days of her life, she thought. She would be glad when it was over. Tomorrow was a new day. New appointments.

New producers to squeeze my breasts.

That thought was disgusting enough to send her downstairs for a fresh bottle of wine. But the new bottle was bad, it had to be. Because once she had opened it and filled her glass, all she could think of was Oliver and Nick and everything she had lost.

Tomorrow will be a new day, she told herself again. And the sooner it got here, the better. She went to the bathroom for her sleeping pills. When she finally found the bottle in the back of the medicine chest, she carried it back to her bed and opened it. Then she looked around for her wine, but when she reached for the glass, she spilled the sleeping pills all over the bed.

She might have taken two as she was picking them up. Or she might have taken two when she was trying to count them back into the bottle. But if she did, they were having absolutely no affect. Or at least not as much as the wine she used to wash them down.

The bottle slipped from her hand again, and pills scattered everywhere. This time when she gathered them up, Juliet popped a handful into her mouth.

The wine had set her head to spinning. Juliet lay back on the pillows. It was uncomfortable, though, with all the pills beneath her, biting into her body like hard little rocks. Almost as uncomfortable as the thought of the girls, sleeping together in Eden's room. Nine-year-olds needed supervision, and she wasn't in any shape to give it.

"Need a father," she mumbled. She was just on the

verge of passing out when she managed to dial Nick's number.

Nick almost beat the ambulance. Allison had climbed in the car with him when he left the house, but she lagged behind when he raced across the lawn and through Juliet's open front door.

Upstairs, he hesitated only long enough to make sure Juliet was still alive and the medical personnel were working on her. Then he went down the hall to Eden's bedroom. Before he reached the door, it opened. Not one but two blond heads peeked out. "Daddy?" Eden said. "What's happening?"

"Hello, Eden." He knelt down and hugged them both. "Hello, Dani. I didn't know you were here."

Dani always seemed like a little adult in a child's body. "I'm spending the night. I spend the night as often as Mother will let me. Is Juliet sick?"

Nick nodded. "We're going to have to take her to the hospital. I want you girls to stay here and be very, very good, all right?"

"By ourselves?" Dani asked.

"My wife is here. She'll stay with you until I get back from the hospital."

They were good kids, Nick thought, as he went in search of Allison. They were frightened, but they were going to be all right. The ambulance had left with Juliet while he was talking to them. He found Allison in the kitchen pouring herself a drink. "Eden and Dani are both upstairs," he told her. "I want you to stay with them until I get back from the hospital."

Allison threw her head back in a way that reminded him unpleasantly of her father. "I'm not a baby-sitter."

"I don't have time for your theatrics right now!" he snapped. "Juliet is very important to both of my daughters, and they are important to me. Please go upstairs and stay with them until I get back."

"Why don't you call Kathleen Mallory?"

"I don't have time to wait for her to get here. Stay with the girls. I'll be back as quickly as I can."

He left without waiting for her reply. But as worried as he was about Juliet and as irritated as he was by Allison's attitude, he still had time to wonder, for the first time in this marriage, why he and Allison had never discussed having a child of their own.

The second time Juliet woke, Nick was standing beside her bed. "Oh, God!" she said. "I feel awful."

"That was really stupid of you," he said. She had never heard so much anger—so much disgust—in his voice. "You were counting on my showing up in time to rescue you from your little stunt, weren't you? Well, five more minutes and you couldn't have reached me. Did you ever think of that possibility when you planned this farce?"

"Farce?"

"Grow up, Juliet," he said wearily. "We both know this was just another of your little ploys to get my attention."

"No, Nick. I just had too much to drink. I wasn't trying to—"

"You've got my attention, now, Juliet," he said, leaning on the bed. "I don't think you're going to like the results. You went too far last night. You scared the girls." He straightened up. "My God, didn't you even give a thought to the fact that there were two nine-year-olds asleep down the hall?"

"Nick, please." Tears trickled down her cheeks. "It wasn't like that. I—"

"One more episode like this, one more midnight call, and you are going to be in for the custody battle of your life."

"Custody?"

"I'll take Eden away from you so fast you won't know what happened. I can do it, Juliet. I *will* do it if I have to. For Eden's sake. And I'll talk to Kate about letting Dani stay at your house so much. You're not a fit mother. You won't be until you grow up and start thinking about someone else's needs besides your own."

She had wakened to a nightmare, Juliet thought. How could this be happening? "Nick, you don't understand!"

"I understand perfectly. I hope you understand too. One more stunt like this and you won't see Eden or Dani again. Is that clear?"

Juliet managed to nod.

"Fine. I have to leave now. To see about the girls."

"You didn't leave them by themselves, did you?" Juliet said, her alarm cutting through all her other emotions in that moment.

"It's a little late for you to be worrying about that, isn't it?" Nick said cruelly.

When the door shut behind him, Juliet felt more alone than she ever had in her entire life. She wasn't sure which was worse, the thought of losing all contact with Eden— and with Dani, whom she loved almost as much as Eden— or the realization that Eden was her last tie to Nick.

If she lost Eden, she lost Nick too. Forever.

Juliet's house was silent and empty. Nick searched through all the upstairs rooms, his heart racing. Downstairs once more, he picked up the phone and called his own home. The sheer relief he felt when Allison answered vanished almost immediately in a burst of anger. "What the hell are you doing? I told you to wait here with the girls!"

"I'm sleeping." Allison yawned hugely. "What else would I be doing at 7 A.M. on a Saturday morning?"

"Are the girls with you?"

"I sent them to Kathleen Mallory last night in a taxi. If they have any brains—which I doubt, considering who their mothers are—they're probably asleep too."

"For God's sake, Allison! You don't have a maternal bone in your body!"

"I refuse to have my maternal instincts criticized by a man who only remembers he's a father a couple of times a year!" Allison yelled back and broke the connection.

A good thing they were talking on the phone, Nick thought grimly, as he dialed Kate's number. If Allison had been here he would have been sorely tempted to break her neck.

The phone rang twice, and then a man's voice said, "Hello?"

"Who is this?" Nick demanded gruffly.

"Barry Inman. Who's calling?"

"Uh . . . sorry, Barry. This is Nicholas Picard. Is Kate there?"

"She's gone to the hospital to see Juliet." Inman's voice was cool.

"What about the girls? I just found out that Allison sent them over to you by taxi last night while I was at the hospital. Are they all right?"

"Kate was miffed about that." Inman's voice thawed a little. "She thought it was your idea. And the girls were upset because you said you'd see them after you got back from the hospital. But Mrs. Gregory got them settled down. As a matter of fact, they may not even be up yet."

"Would it be all right if I came by to see them later today?" It rankled to ask Kate's new husband for permission to see his own daughters, but Nick was determined to do whatever was best for them.

"Sure. No problem," Inman said heartily.

Too early to visit the girls, Nick thought, as he closed

Juliet's front door behind him. If he went home, he would only continue the fight with Allison and turn it into something that would last a week. The office was the best place for him this morning.

Juliet was sobbing so hard she had given herself the hiccups. Kate patted her on the back, feeling absolutely helpless. "Do you want me to call the nurse?"

"No," Juliet gasped, clinging to her arm. "Don't do that. They might tell Nick."

Juliet had told Kate the story of Nick's visit in one garbled burst when she first walked into the hospital room. Really, Kate thought, he had no sense at all, threatening someone in Juliet's condition. But right on the heels of that came the worry of what in the world she would do if she couldn't turn Dani over to Juliet a good three quarters of the time. Barry was sweet about it, but he just wasn't any good with children. And Dani was so stiff and unfriendly around him. They both felt the strain when she was home. "He just misunderstood, Juliet."

"It really was an accident," Juliet repeated for the hundredth time. "If I hadn't been drinking, I never would have miscounted my pills." She clutched Kate's arm again, and Kate knew that she would have bruises there tomorrow. "You know I wouldn't try to kill myself, Kate. You know me better than that."

"Of course I do."

"And you know what it would mean to me to lose Eden. And Dani."

And to me! "I do know," Kate said aloud. "You'll get this straightened out with Nick. But Juliet, maybe it would be better if you didn't call him for a while. Just for a while," she added hurriedly when she saw the expression of dismay on Juliet's face.

Juliet stared over her shoulder.

Kate turned.

A tall, stoop-shouldered elderly man in an expensive suit stood in the doorway. He advanced, hand outstretched. "I'm Oliver Brittany," he said. "Juliet's father."

"I'm Kate Mallory." His hand was faintly damp, but Kate made a point of holding it long enough to be polite. "I'm glad to see Juliet has some family to be with her."

She turned, smiling, to Juliet as she said it. To her surprise, Juliet seemed to have grown smaller. She was huddled against the pillow, her legs drawn up, her arms clutching them, her eyes darting from Kate to her father.

"Well," Kate said, suddenly nervous. "I guess I'll leave you two alone."

"Oh, no," Oliver Brittany said graciously. "Don't rush away on my account. Juliet's friends are my friends."

Juliet's heart hammered against her chest as she watched Papa glance from Kate to her and then back to Kate again. She had never been as frightened as she was at this moment. All Nick's threats seemed puny compared to the abyss that had just opened at her feet.

She had forgotten how very much she and Kate resembled each other. Nick's fault! she thought wildly, watching Oliver focus on Kate. Nick had made his precious Kathleen Mallory into a carbon copy of her.

Juliet clenched her fists until her fingernails bit into her palms. Was she going crazy? She had wanted nothing more than for Oliver Brittany to vanish from her life, but as she watched him staring at Kate in utter fascination, she was shaken to her very core by the fear that she might have lost his attention forever.

"I really had better be going," Kate told Juliet. "The girls are both at my house, so don't worry about them."

"I'll walk you to your car," Oliver Brittany said quickly,

before Juliet could respond. "I wanted to ask you something about my granddaughter."

The door shut behind them before Juliet could find her voice.

His granddaughter?

He didn't care about Eden. Juliet knew it was her he loved—and her image re-created in Kate. She could feel a scream bubbling around inside her, a desire for violence that yearned to break free. But if it did, she knew Nick and Eden would vanish from her life. So she sat, trembling, in her hospital bed, as hate and love and loneliness formed a turbulent vortex inside her.

Juliet packed her bag slowly and wondered who she should call to take her home. Isabelle Gregory had delivered a bag filled with Juliet's things the morning she was admitted to the hospital: Kate's doing. However, remembering how Kate had left her room with Oliver, Juliet had no desire to call on her for help. Kate had returned to visit Juliet twice more after that day. Although Juliet couldn't bring herself to tell Kate what was wrong, her feelings had been obvious enough to kill any of their attempts to find a mutually satisfying topic of conversation. Kate offered to bring the girls to visit her, but Juliet refused. She had no desire to have Eden and Dani see her in the hospital. The less they were reminded of this whole episode the better.

Nick had not reappeared.

Last night, unable to stand it any longer, Juliet had dialed his home number. Allison Hilliard answered, and Juliet hung up without saying anything.

So now what was she to do?

The door swung open as a nurse entered. "Going home, are we? Glad to see you're feeling better, Miss Brittany."

"Thank you." Juliet put the last nightgown in and closed the lid of her suitcase.

"Is someone here to take you home?" the nurse asked.

The door opened again before Juliet could answer. Oliver Brittany stood there in his finely tailored suit, his face gaunt and hungry as ever.

With a curious sense of the inevitable, Juliet said, "My father."

In the car, on the way home, Papa tried to put his hand on her knee. Juliet stared down at it as though it were a loathsome spider. "No, Oliver," she said firmly, and he snatched his hand away.

When they reached her house, she said, "Bring my bag," and went inside without looking back.

Kate must have sent Isabelle over while she was in the hospital, Juliet realized. Everything smelled of fresh wax and cleaning solutions.

When Oliver appeared in the entry hall with her bag, Juliet barely glanced his way. "Take that upstairs and put my things away," she told him and went out to the kitchen to mix herself a drink.

The doctors hadn't said anything about her drinking, she thought with amusement. Perhaps they thought she had learned her lesson. In that case, they were wrong. She had finished her first drink when Oliver reappeared, standing silently in the doorway as though awaiting fresh orders.

"All you want is to be around me, isn't it?" she asked him. "All right."

"You'll let me be with you?" He started toward her.

"No!" she said sharply. "If you touch me or come near me, I'll throw you out. The only way you can stay is as my slave."

"Juliet." His voice broke. "Anything. I'll do anything you want."

"I'll tell you what to do," Juliet told him, "and you'll do it. Otherwise you leave right now." She turned to the counter to freshen her drink. When she turned back, the hungry eyes were still fastened on her. "Do you accept my terms, Oliver?"

"Of course," Oliver Brittany said. "What do you want me to do?"

It was the strangest outing Kate had been on in her life. She lay on her towel on the beach, watching the others as if they were actors in an avant-garde play and wondering why she had let Eden talk her into this.

She frowned. That still rankled. Juliet's daughter had acted as though it were of supreme importance that Kate accompany them to the beach. But her own daughter— Dani didn't seem to care if Kate was alive, let alone on the picnic.

Physically, Juliet seemed to have recovered completely from her accidental overdose. Mentally, though, she was like a sleepwalker. She went through the motions and made all the right responses, but Kate had come to know her well. The animation that had previously been such an integral part of Juliet's personality was gone.

As for Oliver Brittany, he was the strangest member of the expedition. Kate glanced up the beach to where the father and daughter were unpacking the picnic basket. She found the relationship between Juliet and her father puzzling, almost as puzzling as the relationship between Oliver and his grandchild. Eden seemed oblivious to her grandfather's presence, and Dani followed her lead. It was as though Oliver existed in a little oasis of silence in the midst of the group. He had driven the car to the beach, unloaded it, and carried the picnic items to the sand, but no one spoke to him or acknowledged his presence. Not that it seemed like deliberate rudeness; it was more as if Oliver Brittany were a ghost figure, drifting through their lives without making contact.

Kate directed a few polite words of conversation his way initially but soon gave up. It wasn't just Juliet's reaction—she had seemed almost jealous when her father talked to Kate—it was more that when Oliver Brittany turned his attention Kate's way, it made Kate herself uneasy. Even now, when she glanced up the beach again, she found him looking at her.

Kate turned her eyes back to the waves and tried not to think about how many hours remained before she would be safely home with Barry once more. He had tried to talk her out of accepting Eden's invitation. "You'll be bored out of your skull surrounded by all those kids," he warned. Kate had laughed at his description of two nine-year-old girls as "all those kids." However, one of the things she appreciated about Barry was that he didn't expect her to automatically enjoy the company of children just because she had given birth. Sometimes, watching Juliet with the girls, she felt so inadequate. It didn't matter that Barry was always telling her loyally that her career had far outstripped Juliet's. Her success as the Javelin Woman and as a writer seemed to pale when she measured herself as a mother against Juliet.

Kate wondered what Nick thought. She had made it a point never to be present when he visited Dani. Still, Kate couldn't resist asking Juliet if Nick ever inquired about her on those visits. She had not been surprised when Juliet, her eyes wide with surprise, said, "No. Why would he?"

Why would he, indeed?

Thank heaven for Barry, Kate thought. Sweet, uncomplicated Barry. If the negotiations on her new novel went as well as expected, Barry was talking about leaving the agency, much to Michael Bond's dismay. But, as Barry had explained to her, all his work now consisted of dealing with her business affairs. Why not keep it all in the family?

The girls came out of the water, shaking themselves like dogs. Kate squealed and rolled away from the spray.

"We're starving," Eden told Kate.

Kate scrambled to her feet. "Let's go see how the food is coming." She was touched when Eden took her hand and launched into a lively description of school, and irritated that Dani trailed them by half a dozen steps, sullenly kicking at the sand. "Aren't you hungry, too?" Kate called over her shoulder when Eden's torrent of conversation slowed for a moment.

Dani gave her a blank stare, as if she had been a thousand miles away. "No," she said at last, somehow contriving to make that one word sound so insolent Kate wanted to shake her.

When had this stranger moved into her daughter's body? Kate wondered. It had to have something to do with her marriage to Barry. Barry tried, but the best he had been able to achieve with Dani was an uneasy truce. I'll have to try harder myself, Kate thought, as she and Eden, with Dani still trailing behind, reached the blanket where Juliet and her father had spread out the food. "Shall I make you a hot dog?" she asked Dani brightly. Not waiting for a reply, Kate knelt, picked up a bun, and began to spread it with mustard.

The sudden silence made her pause in mid-stroke and look up. Juliet, Eden, and Dani were staring at her.

"What is it?" Kate asked.

"Dani hates mustard," Eden blurted. "Everybody knows that."

"Kate is fixing that bun for herself," Juliet said quickly. "You girls are too big to be waited on hand and foot. In fact, you should be fixing our lunch. Right, Kate?"

Dani didn't say anything. She didn't have to. She knows it too, Kate thought. We're not mother and daughter anymore. We're strangers.

Oliver Brittany finished making his own hot dog and began to eat it, secluded in the little bubble of silence that surrounded him.

Kate choked down a hot dog on the mustard-covered bun as she watched the girls, under Juliet's guidance, build their own. She ought to ask Juliet if Eden could spend the night with Dani tonight, she thought. If she didn't, Dani would simply go home with Juliet and Eden without bothering to ask her mother's permission. It was becoming harder and harder to keep up the pretense that the girls were visiting back and forth, that Dani wasn't simply living at Juliet's with her half-sister.

But when the moment arrived on the way home when she might have spoken up, Kate remained silent. Barry would hate having the girls in the house, she told herself, and the truth was, she disliked the noise and commotion almost as much as he did. This long afternoon had given her enough family togetherness to last a while.

EIGHTEEN

1973

"GOD, BUT HE SOUNDED DESPERATE!" ELSA SAID. IT was a good thing the prospective john hadn't been able to see the the woman on the other end of the line. Elsa was almost forty, five feet four, and weighed 225 pounds. When she reached across the battered desk to replace the receiver, the fat swayed beneath her arm.

Gwen, Elsa's sister, was in her mid-forties and rail thin, with a face too sharply intelligent to arouse lust in a man. The two of them were experts at finding out just what their customers wanted—and supplying it. They were also experts at making sure the johns weren't vice cops; for that, their girls were grateful. "Which one was it?"

"The one who's looking for a young Juliet Brittany. He would pay through the nose if we found a girl who fit that description."

"So would a lot of other men," Gwen said, making a note to herself on the three-by-five pad in the leather cover that she carried with her everywhere. "I'll keep my eyes open."

Gwen had a degree in accounting from UCLA, which she had acquired with dogged persistence and sheer force of will after an ego-shattering divorce. They worked out of Gwen's apartment. It was she who kept the books, managed the various payoffs necessary to stay in business, and scouted for new girls—a constant process, since most young women didn't realize how well off they were with a stable organization like Gwen and Elsa's, and were apt to disappear. It was a business like any other; their success was that they ran it that way.

The john who was looking for a young Juliet Brittany called back three times in the following month. Each time, Elsa jollied him along, telling him they were searching for a girl to fit his specifications. She offered him any of their other girls, but he refused. Only a young Juliet Brittany would do.

"You're sure he's legitimate?" Gwen asked, after Elsa hung up from his last call.

"Positive. When am I ever wrong?"

Gwen nodded. Elsa had a sixth sense where trouble was concerned that was almost as keen as Gwen's grasp of figures.

"So what have you come up with?" Elsa asked her sister.

Gwen consulted her three-by-five pad. "Very little. The closest is a street kid I've seen a couple of times around Hollywood and Vine. About fifteen, the right height, the right shape. The face is so close, but . . ." She frowned, hating the thought of all that money slipping away.

"Plastic surgery?"

"It wouldn't take much," Gwen admitted. "A little work on the nose. The tiniest lift of the eyes. But do you think we would get a big enough return on the investment?"

"You should hear him. The man is desperate. And there have to be others."

"I'll get some quotes from plastic surgeons," Gwen said cautiously. "Check the figures. If it looks good, I'll approach the girl."

"You're a genius," Elsa told her sister fondly. She stood

up. "I've got to go. Mack will be home by the time I get there." Her husband was a truck driver. He found it amusing that his wife and her sister ran a call-girl operation. If he knew that, thanks to Gwen's shrewdness with figures, Elsa and her sister could buy and sell his boss's trucking firm a dozen times over, he would have been less amused and more demanding. But Elsa had learned from her sister's disastrous marriage; all her profits were in her own name, invested wisely according to Gwen's directions. As far as Mack knew, they lived on his salary.

Gwen was already thumbing through the yellow pages, jotting down the numbers of plastic surgeons on her three-by-five pad.

As Elsa let herself out of the apartment, she had no doubt they would make a profit on this little side venture. Gwen would see to it.

Joel Edelmann was not accustomed to being kept waiting in Hollywood. Especially on the set of a movie that featured the intimate sex scenes, profanity, and nudity he considered more appropriate for hard-core pornographic films. The rotund agent told Allison Hilliard so in no uncertain terms as he followed her from the set to the door of her trailer. "No clients of mine are working on filth like this," he proclaimed piously while he waited for her to open the door.

Allison shrugged, and the pink satin robe she wore slipped down, revealing one shoulder. Joel Edelmann averted his eyes. "Then we're both glad I'm no longer your client," she said as he followed her inside.

"For heaven's sake, Allison," he protested, mopping his face. "I've known you since you were a baby. Do you realize how it distresses me to watch you prostituting yourself in front of the camera?"

"No, Joel," she said, letting her voice drop into a lower register. "How much did it distress you?"

Joel went scarlet. "Allison!"

Allison laughed. "Fix yourself a drink, Joel." She sat down at her dressing table. "I've got to get this makeup off. And get that, would you?" she added as someone knocked at the door.

"Gladly," Joel said.

When he opened the door, Allison glanced in her mirror and saw Frederick Yates standing there. "Frederick," she said. "What a surprise!"

"I asked him to come," Joel told her. "We have something very serious to discuss with you."

Allison swung around so that she was facing them. "Should I call my agent? Or my lawyer."

"No jokes," Joel said, as Frederick took a chair. "I have a message from your father. He wants you to leave this picture." He waited for her reply. When there was none, he continued. "Conrad is completely serious, Allison. You have stretched his patience to the limit in accepting a role in trash like this. If you defy him, he is prepared to turn all his resources against you. You cannot continue to exist in Hollywood if he takes that step."

"This picture? *Love Notes*? The one directed and produced by my husband? The one Frederick there is distributing?"

"This is no joke, Allison. He expects your answer today."

She turned to Frederick. "And you're on my father's side?"

"I'm on your side, Allison." Frederick's delicate lips curled in disgust. "You're a fine actress. You have a family tradition to uphold. You don't need trash like this."

She raised one eyebrow. "And it doesn't bother you that Nick would lose a bundle if I walked off the set? I thought you were stepbrothers or something."

Frederick stood up. "We're not related at all," he said

coldly. "And this discussion has nothing to do with Nicholas. You're the one whose career is in danger."

"In danger from what?" Nick asked from the doorway.

Frederick Yates started violently. "Haven't you learned to knock?" he demanded.

"On my wife's door?" Nick walked over and gave Allison a kiss on the cheek. "You did a great job, babe," he told her. "What are these two clowns hassling you about?"

"Nothing important," Allison told him. "They just want me to walk off the picture."

Nick straightened. "Any particular reason?"

It was Frederick Yates who replied. "Conrad Hilliard has threatened to use all his influence against Allison if she continues with this project."

"Jesus, Freddie! You're still worried about the dinosaurs. What can Hilliard do?"

"He can wreck his daughter's career. Don't you care about that? Or are you so selfish that all you think about are your profits?"

"I'm no more selfish than you, Freddie. I believe the studio pays you to worry about profits. This would be a good time to start. Kick this fat little clown off the lot and ignore Hilliard. He's yesterday; Allison is today."

"Stop calling me Freddie!"

"Really, Mr. Picard," Joel Edelmann protested. "Surely as Allison's husband you can see—"

"As Allison's director, I can see that she has to get ready for her next scene. Clear out, both of you."

When they had left, Allison stood up. "I thought we were through for the day."

"With your scenes out there, yes," Nick said. He pulled her close. "Not with your scenes in here."

Nick sprawled on Allison's daybed and watched her remove the rest of her makeup. "I didn't want to bring it up while the Morals Squad was here, but I've decided to shoot several different versions of the bath scene."

"Oh?"

She had a way of doing that, he thought with irritation. Nailing you with a single syllable. "This has nothing to do with them. Or your father. It's the new Supreme Court edict. According to the nine old guys in Washington, there is no longer a national standard for obscenity. Every Podunk in the country will now be able to decide what it thinks is obscene. So it's just common sense to cover ourselves."

"That's not what you said last month. What brought on this change of heart? My father's threat?"

"*Carnal Knowledge.* I just found out a little while ago that the Georgia Supreme Court upheld an obscenity conviction of the theater operator for showing it."

"But it was R-rated."

"*Love Notes* will be too." Nick shrugged. "But an R rating made no difference to the Georgia Supreme Court."

Why didn't they make movies like they used to? Joel Edelmann thought as he climbed out of his car. This modern-day trash was beyond him. Why did Allison Hilliard want to expose herself like that? He had been mortified while he waited on the set for her. He kept remembering how she had looked at six in a pretty pink party dress. It had been difficult to hold that image in his mind when she began making love to a young male actor under her husband's direction.

Joel mopped his brow. He certainly didn't want Conrad to guess that he had found the sight of Conrad's daughter so erotically stimulating.

Old movies. A scene from *The Private Life of Henry VIII* flashed into Joel's head: Charles Laughton as the king, strangling the actor who had just told him that his wife, the Queen, was unfaithful. Joel found himself wishing devoutly that it was someone else bearing the news about his daughter to Conrad Hilliard.

Bettina Hilliard met Joel at the door. "He's in his study reading a new script," she told him, "and I'm on my way to lunch."

Bettina had been a child when Conrad married her, Joel thought, as he trudged down the hall to Conrad's study. She still looked young enough to be his daughter. Young Picard had been right. He and Conrad were *both* dinosaurs.

As if to confirm that depressing thought, he found Conrad not reading but dozing, his mouth open, snoring lightly, his face an old man's death mask. Joel wondered if he too looked that way when he slept. Of course not, he chided himself. Conrad Hilliard has a noble profile; you're fat as a walrus. "Conrad?" he said softly, hoping not to wake the sleeper. I came but you were sleeping, he would say.

Conrad roused, dashing Joel's hopes of escape. "What is it?" He raised his massive head and focused on the agent's face. "What did she say?"

"She said no."

Conrad sat there a moment, like a monolith. "Well, then," he said at last, "that leaves me no choice. Thank you for coming by to tell me in person, Joel."

Joel blushed slightly, remembering his reluctance to do so. "Are you going through with it?"

Conrad seemed surprised that he would ask. "Of course."

"But to end her career like this? She's so young."

"She had her chance," Conrad said. "Now she must pay the piper."

After Joel Edelmann left, Conrad Hilliard stared at his phone, reluctant to make the first call. She was his daughter in spite of everything.

But the Hilliard tradition demanded he do something.

If only, he thought as he began to dial, if only he'd had a son.

Conrad waited exactly seven days before he summoned Joel Edelmann to his home. One look at Joel's drawn face confirmed his suspicions. "I don't understand. Each one of them promised me they would withdraw their support from her."

"Maybe they did." Joel sat down heavily. "But she's bigger than we thought." Bigger than the dinosaurs, but he couldn't explain that remark to Conrad without bringing on a coronary. "Like a natural force. You don't stop something like that with a few phone calls."

"I could have. In the past."

Joel nodded. "In the past."

Not now. And they both knew it.

"He called everyone in Hollywood!" It was the third time Nick had told the story in the past half hour, this time to Sloan Whitney, and he was beginning to embellish it.

Not that it needed much embellishment, Allison thought, as she went to freshen her drink. Conrad Hilliard hadn't called everyone—just everyone important. All the numbers listed in the burgundy leather phone book in his study, the movers and shakers in the movie industry. She knew he had dialed those numbers fully confident that he was wrecking his daughter's career.

It was no fault of his that he hadn't done just that.

Over the rim of her glass, Allison watched the mob of people swirling around the pool. The party tonight was Nick's idea, organized on the spur of the moment. She would have preferred a quiet evening alone. A wake.

If Conrad Hilliard had succeeded, she would have been drinking to the demise of her career. Instead, she was drinking to the death of her father's influence in Hollywood.

Nick was still giving the lawyer a blow-by-blow. "Why don't we give it a rest, Nick," she said, turning away from the pool. "Whit can't be that interested."

"Oh, but I am," Whit said. "It's about time that old bastard got his comeuppance."

"That 'old bastard' is my father," Allison said stiffly.

"He's not acting like it," Nick said. "When has he ever acted like it, Allison? Don't let that stiff-necked Hilliard pride blind you to the humor of the situation."

Nick's reference to the Hilliard pride stung. "I'm afraid I don't see much humor in a man being humiliated so badly."

"It's just like I told Freddie. Hilliard is a dinosaur. He's not living in the twentieth century. He doesn't realize what an important person you've become in this town."

Nick walked over and took her hand in his.

"You don't need Conrad's help. You don't need anyone's help anymore. Your career is snowballing. Nothing can stop you now." He half turned and winked at Whit. "Next thing you'll decide you don't need my help anymore, either."

He dropped her hand and went to fix himself another drink, leaving Allison to wonder why he thought that last line was so funny.

Toby

1973–1989

Where money is concerned, Toby is totally prag-
matic. This essential feature of her personality
was one I was slow to grasp—which is why
I no longer own a controlling interest in the
production company that bears my name.

Ah, Toby! Even in my uncensored memoirs
I dare not tell everything about you. But
rest assured, my sweet, I can tell enough
to make you squirm.

*—From the unpublished memoirs
of Nicholas Picard*

NINETEEN

1973

THE MORNING TOBY CHECKED INTO THE CLINIC with that scrawny old bag Gwen at her elbow was the scaredest she had been since she left Texas after murdering a man. Nobody would guess it though, she thought proudly, as the nurse ushered them down the hall to the examination room.

When the plastic surgeon came in, he treated her like visiting royalty, nodding and humming to himself while he looked over her face, just the most pleased old boy in the world. Then he turned around to Gwen and told her there wasn't going to be any problem at all.

Toby kept her eyes sharp to see if any money changed hands. As far she could tell, none did. She had made the best bargain that she could: five hundred in cash advanced against her earnings when she went to work for the old bag, plus new clothes. Old Gwen put up the cash for the operation, and Toby put up the face.

A pretty good deal. Two years of living on her own had made Toby sharper than most fifteen-year-olds. She knew that while old Gwen might renege on the cash, the percentage of her earnings, or the clothes, she, Toby, would own the face.

And the face was Toby's ticket to success.

The evening Gwen approached her on the street, Toby almost puked—because she knew that whatever the old bag suggested she had to go along with it. She had been with men and women both in the last couple of years. While she had learned what to do to make a woman happy, she preferred men. She preferred eating regular even more, though, so as Gwen walked up to her, Toby decided on the spot she'd just close her eyes and do whatever it took to get money out of the old broad.

The nature of Gwen's proposition had been a surprise, but it hadn't taken Toby two seconds to grasp the benefits to herself. Ironing out the details had taken longer, because they were both businesswomen. Gwen had come away from the bargaining convinced it was the cash advance and clothes that sealed the agreement.

She was wrong; it was the face.

Toby didn't know what planet the old hag lived on that she didn't realize how much Juliet Brittany looked like Kathleen Mallory. It didn't take any smarts to figure out that if some fancy doctor made Toby look like Juliet Brittany, a has-been as far as Toby was concerned, she would also look like Kathleen Mallory.

And Kathleen Mallory was anything but over the hill. True, she hadn't made any movies for a while. But she was still the Javelin Woman. Every time you turned on the TV, she was slinking up to that sleek old car and laying her body across the fender.

Kathleen Mallory was a writer, too. Even though Toby wasn't much of a reader, she had stolen a copy of *Fortune's Gambit* off the newsstand. The sexy parts were easy to locate. Toby dog-eared the pages so she could find them again without reading through all the he-saids and she-saids.

Old Gwen just thought she was buying a copy of Juliet Brittany's face; Toby knew she was really getting a Kathleen Mallory Deluxe Special.

Old Gwen had told the doctor she was Toby's mother. To keep up the pretense, she went with Toby when the nurse took her to her room. Old Gwen had brought along a little bag when she picked Toby up. When Toby unpacked it, she found the woman had brought her a toothbrush, toothpaste, deodorant, tampons, a nightgown, and a robe—just like Toby's real mother might have done.

Toby didn't like thinking about Momma too much; it always made her sad. However, late that night, alone in the room with the lights out and everything so quiet, it was either think about Momma back in Texas or about the knives waiting for her in the morning.

Toby was from Mesquite, just outside Dallas, but she never told anyone that. Or that her last name was Gilmer, not Flynn like she had told the old bag. She wouldn't have admitted she was from Texas either, except that, try as hard as she could, it kept coloring the way she talked. Now, scared and shaking in her lonely little room in the clinic, she looked back at Mesquite and thought it must have been paradise.

They hadn't had much, just a rented trailer house on a sun-baked little lot with more weeds than grass, but it was home. Toby was good in school. She always read straight through her textbooks when she first got them. Mostly she made A's, which was why a lot of the other kids didn't like her. Momma sewed for the public. Toby liked to look through her mother's pattern books and the magazines customers brought in to show Momma what kind of dress they wanted. The magazines helped her to dream about what it would be like to live somewhere besides Mesquite, but she had never thought about leaving Momma behind. In her dreams, it was always Momma and her both, together in some fancy place.

It was just her and Momma for real in Mesquite. Toby's daddy died before she was born, or at least that was what

Momma always said. The one time she asked Momma if she could look at her marriage license, Momma gave her a funny look and put her off. Toby never had the nerve to bring up the subject again.

Momma was little and still pretty, and there were always men around. That was okay because Toby knew how to flirt with them and get what she wanted, which was extra money for candy and sometimes even enough for material so Momma could sew her a pretty new dress. When Momma's boyfriends gave Toby money, Momma would say, "Oh, you're spoiling her!" Then she would laugh in a way that let Toby know she was proud she had a daughter men liked.

That was before Big John came into their lives.

Big John wasn't all that big, really. He was just lean and hard and downright scary. "Mean as a snake," Toby heard one of Momma's other boyfriends mutter one night as he came charging down the front steps of the trailer to get away from Big John's anger that another man would dare to call on Momma. After that, when she wasn't looking directly at Big John, Toby always thought his pale eyes must look like a snake's—with vertical reptile's pupils instead of black dots like human eyes. He had moved in the night of his first date with Momma, so it wasn't long before all Momma's boyfriends stopped coming by. So did Toby's school friends.

The first time Toby tried her flirting ways on Big John was also her last. He gave her a cold look with those pale, mean eyes and said, "Don't ask for something if you don't want it, little girl."

It scared her so bad she went and sat on her bed and didn't come out the rest of that evening, even though it was hot as an oven in her little cubicle.

That was when she was eleven. When she turned twelve, she began to fill out, and Big John started following her with his scary eyes everywhere she went.

He didn't work. At least, not after he moved in with Momma. Momma supported all three of them with her sewing. A lot of days, Big John just lay around the house. Sometimes at night he would disappear. To Toby's disappointment, he would always be back the next morning. It seemed to Toby that Momma wasn't as pretty as she had been before she met Big John. He was still hard and mean, but Momma had gotten soft and scared looking. Whatever Big John wanted, Momma just said, "Yes, darlin'," and did it.

When Big John wasn't there and Momma was busy or gone, Toby would prowl through Big John's things. Maybe she thought she could figure out what he did at night. It was a game to her to make sure no one knew what she was doing, so Toby always put everything back the way she found it.

Except for the day she opened the drawer of the nightstand beside the bed and found the snubbed-nose Smith and Wesson revolver inside it. She knew it was Big John's; Momma never had a thing like that herself.

Toby had been so scared she almost hadn't heard Momma come in. The drawer stuck when Toby tried to push it shut, because the nightstand was part of the cheap furniture that came with the rented trailer. Toby hadn't pulled it out for a second try. Instead, she hurried down the little hall to the bathroom, pulled down her panties, and jumped on the pot, so Momma wouldn't question what she had been up to.

When Big John came home, he accused Momma of going through his stuff. He hit her once really hard and told her not to touch his things again, that he didn't hold with women going through men's things. It scared Toby so bad she didn't go in the room he shared with Momma again for almost a month.

She only did it then because she was so bored.

She was home all alone on a Wednesday evening. Momma had gone to somebody's house to give them a fitting, and then she was going to stop off at church for prayer meeting. Momma had been going to church a lot recently. Toby wondered if it had anything to do with Big John. He was gone, probably for the night, so Toby had the whole property to herself.

Not that the sun-baked little lot and shabby trailer house were such a prize in the heat of a late August evening. The trucking company next door was digging a hole right next to the property line so they could put in some kind of big chemical tank. Their bulldozer had been growling and scraping at the dirt all afternoon. The grit it threw up still hung in the air, even though the noise of its digging had finally stopped.

Toby thought about going outside anyway, but there was nowhere left to play. She used to have a swing in one of the trees on the company land next door—there weren't any trees big enough to hold a swing on Momma's lot—but the bulldozer had taken that tree on its first pass.

She was so hot and bored she finally went into Momma's bedroom and started looking around. It wasn't five minutes before she found one of Big John's shoes jammed under the bed with a wad of cash stuffed into the toe. When Toby located the second shoe, there was another wad of bills inside it too.

Toby whooped like she just found an Easter egg. There were hundreds of dollars in each roll of bills. She was counting the treasure in her lap when a sound at the door made her glance up.

Big John stood there.

He had stripped off his shirt like he always did when he came in on a hot day. She could see the jagged scar that started somewhere below the waistband of his jeans and went on up to his chest and across to his left nipple. "I guess you're in here because you want something," he said.

She felt like she didn't have a stitch on, the way he looked at her. "I'll put it back," she blurted, and started stuffing the bills back in the shoes.

Big John wasn't looking at the cash. He was staring at her breasts beneath the skimpy cotton of her T-shirt.

Toby tried to scramble off the end of the bed.

Big John was too quick for her. He grabbed her legs and threw her back down on the mattress. When he raised up enough to unbuckle his belt, Toby kicked at him as hard as she could. One foot connected with his crotch.

He grunted and toppled backward, against the wall of the cramped bedroom, clutching himself. Toby lunged at the nightstand and clawed the drawer open.

Cussing like crazy, Big John lunged forward.

Toby held the revolver with both hands and blew a hole right through his chest.

He jerked backward, against the wall. Then he tumbled forward, across the bed.

Toby jumped backward and retreated to the bedroom door, still holding the gun with both hands, staring at the huge, gory wound in Big John's back. He looked like a cockroach scrabbling at the sheets as blood pumped out of him. He was making incoherent noises that weren't words, weren't anything. His eyes looked straight at her, but they weren't seeing anything anymore.

Then he died, just like that.

He stopped moving, and the blood stopped pumping, and Toby was all alone in the room.

The silence made her tremble. She dropped the revolver and stumbled into the bathroom. Kneeling in front of the toilet, she threw up until there wasn't anything left; then she threw up again after that, over and over, until the muscles of her stomach ached from all the futile heaving.

After a while, when she was able to stand, she got a washrag out of the cabinet and washed her face. She brushed her teeth, too, to get the taste of vomit out of her mouth.

When she went back in the bedroom and looked at Big John on the bed, she knew she was going to be in a lot of trouble if she didn't do something quick.

Momma hadn't bothered to make up the bed with the bedspread in place ever since Big John had come to live with them, because he liked to be able to crawl into bed anytime he wanted, day or night; so all Toby had to worry about were the sheets. She pulled the sheets free of the mattress and wrapped them around Big John's body, rolling him into kind of a cocoon.

When she shoved him off the bed and onto the floor, she saw that his blood had seeped through the sheets to the mattress. Toby got a wet towel from the bathroom and mopped that up as best she could, which wasn't very good. She put the towel into the cocoon with Big John and then, with a lot of trying, managed to turn the mattress over. Momma wasn't likely to turn it back, not by herself.

The bloody mess on the wall finally yielded to a good scrubbing with the bathroom cleanser. That left the problem of the bullet hole. The bullet had punched right through the thin metal after it left Big John's body. Toby found a picture of Jesus and the twelve disciples that Momma had brought in from Sunday school last week and Scotch-taped it over the hole.

After she remade the bed with clean sheets, Toby debated whether to put the bedspread back on and finally decided she would. It took her a while to find it where Momma had stashed it in the back of the tiny closet. It was wrinkled and didn't smell as good as Toby remembered. She put it on the bed anyway. Then she stood there, her hands on her hips, surveying the room. Everything looked as it ought to now, with the exception of the big cocoon of sheets beside the bed that held Big John.

Toby picked up the revolver and stuffed it in the cocoon too. Then she went and put on her tennis shoes. When she came back, she managed to drag the cocoon over to the back door of the trailer. She left it there while she went down the steps and pulled the big wheelbarrow out from under the trailer house where Big John had hidden it. He had borrowed it one night after dark from the trucking company next door. With a lot of heaving and straining, Toby finally managed to get the cocoon out the door, down the steps, and into the wheelbarrow.

By that time it was dusk, with long purple shadows everywhere, although still hot as blazes. Toby stopped for a minute, listening, but she couldn't hear a whisper of sound from the trucking company. She wheeled Big John across the yard and over to the pit the bulldozer had dug for the chemical tank. When she got there, she just dumped him into the hole without ceremony. Two shovels were leaning on a shed beside the hole. Toby took one and crawled down after him.

She started shoveling the loose dirt over the cocoon. If she was lucky, she thought, as she paused to wipe the sweat away from her forehead with her arm, they were finished digging the pit. Tomorrow, they might just lay that chemical tank right on top of him. She wasn't going to count on it, though. She had never been that lucky.

When Toby finally finished covering up the cocoon, she climbed back out of the pit and dumped a shovel full of dirt into the wheelbarrow to soak up the blood. Then she put the shovel back where she found it. She rolled the wheelbarrow over there too, thinking it only fitting that, since Big John had borrowed it, Big John had brought it back.

When she got back to the trailer house, Momma still wasn't home, so Toby cleaned up the smears of blood the cocoon had left on the trailer floor and the back steps. After that, she showered and changed and packed her clothes. She left three hundred dollars of Big John's money for Momma under the salt shaker on the table. The rest she took herself, thinking she would need it more, since Momma had a trade to support herself and Toby didn't.

She walked down to where she could catch the bus for Dallas. At the big downtown bus station, she bought a ticket for Los Angeles, since that was the place she read about the most in the magazines Momma's customers left. She fell asleep as the bus pulled out of the station. When she finally woke up, the bus had crossed the New Mexico state line.

By the time Toby thought to look at a newspaper, it was a week later and she was in Los Angeles. She couldn't find any articles about a body being found in Mesquite, Texas. Sometimes she still wondered about Momma, about her losing both Toby and Big John on the same day, about which one Momma missed more. Toby hadn't tried to get in touch with Momma since she left Texas. She figured not hearing from her would hurt Momma less than having her daughter tried for murder.

That was the only thing that made the thought of knives in the morning bearable. With a different face, it would be even harder for somebody to track her down for Big John's murder.

May he roast in hell, Toby thought, punching her pillow into a more comfortable shape. And with that cheerful thought, she finally drifted off to sleep.

Life just couldn't be any better, Kate thought. She treated herself to a long, luxurious stretch. When the paperback copy of her book hit the best-seller lists, just as the hardcover had done, Barry had managed to free her from the rest of her Javelin Woman contract.

For that, she would be eternally grateful. Nick's line about her being the most beautiful woman in the world had always embarrassed her. To have it repeated fifty times a day, in newspapers, in magazines, and on television, was torture. While Barry might not have understood exactly why she felt as she did, he was sensitive enough to understand she didn't like it.

That was the key to Barry, she thought fondly, as she gazed at his sleeping face on the pillow beside her: his sensitivity. Even in the sexual part of their marriage, he was sensitive, much more than Nick had ever been.

It was the one thing about getting married again that had worried her. Because of her movies with Nick, and those Javelin Woman ads, she had been afraid that Barry would think she was some kind of high-powered sex machine.

Like my mother. The thought came unbidden.

But of course she wasn't. If anything, what she had learned about her mother had taught her how destructive unleashed sexuality could be. She was careful to keep herself under control. Not that she didn't enjoy sex with Barry; she did. Sex with him was warm and comfortable, like Barry himself, with no violent passions, no torrential emotions, nothing that might shake her emotional control. No wonder she loved him so much.

"You look thoughtful," Barry said sleepily.

Kate started. "I didn't know you were awake."

"Just barely. Are you going to write this morning?"

She was supposed to be working on a new novel, but somehow the words just wouldn't come. "Do I have to?" She pouted. "It's going to be such a lovely day. Can't we do something together, just the two of us?" Dani was spending the week with Eden. Not that it made that much difference, Kate thought with just a trace of annoyance, because even when Dani was home, she never acted like they were a family. If Juliet wanted the irritation of two ten-year-olds around the house, she could have it forever as far as Kate was concerned.

"We'll do anything you want," Barry told her, indulgent as always.

Great, Kate thought jubilantly. One more day she didn't have to stare at the typewriter.

It was all Toby could do to keep her hands off her new face. Every time she looked in the mirror, she wanted to pat and stroke it, just to assure herself it was real.

When the bandages first came off, she had thrown a walleyed cat fit. The bruised, swollen thing that lay beneath them looked more like a rotten peach than Kathleen Mallory's famous face. It had taken the doctor and old Gwen quite a while to calm her down and reassure her that the bruises and swelling would eventually disappear. Toby's imagination hadn't been able to stretch far enough to guess what she would look like when that happened.

Old Gwen had come through on the advance and the clothes. She had even helped Toby find a tiny little apartment and a television set, which was good because Toby spent a lot of the days while she waited for the swelling to go away flipping from channel to channel to catch Kathleen Mallory doing her Javelin Woman ads. She got pretty good at mimicking Kathleen Mallory's voice, too. She could go for whole sentences without the tiniest trace of Texas slipping into her speech. When old Gwen dropped by to visit, she noticed immediately and encouraged Toby to keep working on erasing her accent.

As soon as the swelling had gone down enough that Toby didn't look like she just walked away from a car wreck, old Gwen took her to have her hair cut and dyed exactly the right color. When the plastic surgeon finally said she could wear makeup again, Gwen took her to a makeup artist, who showed her how to make herself look even more like Juliet Brittany and Kathleen Mallory.

Gwen was so impressed with the results of her investment that she took Toby to the little apartment where she ran the escort service with her sister, the fattest woman Toby had ever seen in her life. "You're going to be a real moneymaker for us," Elsa told Toby when Gwen introduced her.

The night Toby was finally all healed up and ready to go with the john whose request had set everything in motion, Gwen and Elsa fussed over her like a couple of old hens about to send their chick off for the first time. They were so proud of the change in her they just kept congratulating each other over and over.

Toby was pretty excited herself. The transformation had turned out even better than she expected. As she walked up to the motel room where she was to meet the john, she actually felt like she was "the most beautiful woman in the world."

That feeling lasted only until she reached the door. It was ajar, and the room beyond was black as tar. She rapped lightly with her knuckles. A man's voice said, "Come in." She stepped through the door and somebody shut it, hard, behind her.

Right then, she knew she wasn't Kathleen Mallory anymore; she was just scared little Toby Gilmer, fifteen years old and wishing she was back in Mesquite with Momma.

The man grabbed her by the arm and marched her over to the bed. He shoved her down on the mattress with one hand while he reached over and switched on the bedside lamp with the other. Blinded by the sudden glare of the light, Toby lay there blinking while he looked at her. Suddenly, he grunted in satisfaction and switched off the light.

When Toby reached for the buttons of her blouse, he knocked her hand away and began to unbutton them himself.

Lying there like a dolly didn't turn Toby on, so she asked, "How do you like me?" shaping the words carefully so that she sounded just like Kathleen Mallory in the Javelin commercials.

The john stopped what he was doing. "Juliet?" he asked hoarsely, uncertainly.

Too bad she hadn't been able to listen to any of Juliet Brittany's films, Toby thought. She didn't dare speak aloud again; she always reverted to Texas when she was upset. So she just nodded, a barely perceptible motion in the dark room.

Still he hesitated.

"What are you going to do to me?" Toby whispered, trying to urge him along.

The answer was more than she bargained for. He slapped her so hard she saw stars for a moment. Grabbing the front of her blouse, the one old Gwen had paid $29.95 for, he yanked it open, sending the rest of the buttons shooting all over the room. The skirt was next, ripped right down the front. Gwen had popped $39.95 for it, Toby recalled with a small portion of her brain. If she could talk Gwen into reimbursing her for the clothes, she'd ask for cash; she could get much better bargains for the same amount of money.

He gave her another teeth-rattling slap. "What do you have to say now, Juliet?"

Toby was beginning to worry about all her expensive plastic surgery. She knew she would never be able to talk Gwen into another face if this one got ruined. "I . . . I'm sorry," she gasped, hoping like hell that was the right answer.

It must have been because the john yanked down her panties and plunged into her. Toby didn't have time to point out he was supposed to wear a rubber. He just bucked away at her, sobbing and calling out "Juliet, Juliet" and twisting her right breast every now and then hard enough to bring tears to her eyes.

When he finally came, all she wanted to do was run to the bathroom and get rid of the sticky mess between her legs. But he collapsed on top of her, moaning and gasping so hard she was afraid he might be having a heart attack.

"Mister?" she asked softly after a minute. When he didn't answer, she tried to push him off. He was too heavy for her, though, and she had to let him lie there until he woke up from his little nap.

By that time, she was so sore and stiff she could hardly breathe. He was a different man from the bully who had slapped her, all nervous now and afraid to meet her eyes.

She knew he had already paid Gwen heavily for the privilege of fucking Miss Juliet Brittany, but she hit him up herself anyway, hoping she could get some cash she wouldn't have to account for to Gwen and her fat old sister. When he handed her five hundred dollars, she nearly fainted. Even the slaps were worthwhile if she could turn this kind of profit—and get Gwen to reimburse her for the torn clothing, she reminded herself.

"Just give old Gwen a call when you want to get together again," she told him.

The way he was scurrying around, putting on his clothes, she wasn't sure if the words registered or not.

That was okay. There were plenty of other johns where he came from.

Gwen and fat old Elsa seconded that opinion. They had her working her tail off day and night while they patted themselves on the back, crowing and cackling about how well their "investment" had turned out.

That was okay, Toby told herself. The sisters didn't know she was making a lot of extra money in tips, and she wasn't about to tell them. Especially since she knew something they didn't: their little experiment had a brain, for thinking of her ownself, and two legs, for walking away when the time was right.

One of her johns left behind a copy of *The Hollywood Reporter*. After she read that issue, she got into the habit of buying it regularly. It was *The Hollywood Reporter* that gave her the idea. As soon as she worked out the details, Toby planned to tell the sisters she needed some time off. When they asked why, she was going to tell them "for a career move."

It was time the sisters' investment starting making money for herself.

Allison shoved off from the end of the pool into her fifth lap. Usually by this time her irritation with Nick had dissipated; tonight was different. She still burned with fury every time she thought of their conversation at breakfast this morning. Who did he think he was?

After she had flown across the continent to talk to him in person, he refused to take one day off from business to discuss her career. He was still sulking because she had taken the role in the Broadway play without consulting him. Why couldn't he understand opportunities like that didn't come along often enough to take a chance on their slipping by?

Being away from him most of the past few months had given Allison an opportunity to think about where she really wanted to go with her career. She knew it was time for a different kind of film. She could feel it in her bones. My Hilliard bones, she thought, as she cut through the water with strong, sure strokes. Nick had been right about the previous scripts, and he had indeed made her into the superstar he promised. But now he was trying to typecast her, to stifle her, to prevent her from growing as an actress. It was time to try new things and she knew it, with the instinct that came from being Conrad Hilliard's daughter.

That had really pissed Nick off.

Because as soon as she mentioned her instinct, Nick had reared back in his chair and said, "It worked for Juliet, it worked for Kate, and it will work for you. They're grateful for what I did for them. You should be too."

Worked, hell! She finished the fifth lap and began the sixth. Couldn't Nick see that both Juliet Brittany and Kathleen Mallory were stuck like glue in the images he had created for them? The fact that they were grateful had nothing to do with it. Allison was grateful for what he had done so far, and she had no trouble telling him so. But as far as she was concerned, this wasn't the end of the line. It was only the beginning. Allison wanted more out of life than Juliet Brittany and Kathleen Mallory ever dreamed of having.

The pool lights had come on in the dusk. Allison barely noticed. She rarely swam this late or this long, but her rage was fueling her energy. At the end of the sixth lap, she paused, treading water for a moment, trying to judge if she had cooled down enough to climb out of the pool.

Not yet, she thought grimly, and launched into her seventh lap.

That was when it happened.

A tangle of ropelike arms suddenly enveloped her, dragging her down to the bottom of the pool. Allison thrashed wildly, caught without a breath of air at the moment she needed it most, as the weight of the thing held her down.

It was only seconds, but it felt like an eternity before she was able to break free of the octopuslike arms and shoot for the surface.

When she broke through the water into the blessed air, she saw a man silhouetted beside the pool, staring down at her. Her strength almost gone, she raised one arm weakly and tried to call to him. He remained standing where he was, making no effort to come to her aid.

Allison summoned her last reserves and swam for the edge of the pool. It was only a few feet away, but it seemed like the width of an ocean. She almost didn't make it. When she finally reached the pool's edge, the man took to his heels and bolted into the shadows.

Her lungs aching, Allison clung, gasping and coughing, to the side of the pool. It was at least five minutes before she felt strong enough to heave herself up out of the water. Standing at last on the flagstones, she peered into the water to see what had nearly drowned her.

A tangle of garden hoses lay on the bottom of the pool.

Frowning, Allison remembered seeing the hoses earlier where the gardener had left them, up the slope from the pool, the same slope where the intruder had been standing.

She dropped down into a lawn chair and stared across the pool. A peeping tom, she thought, and felt her skin crawl, as though she had been violated. The man must have accidentally dislodged the hoses while he was watching her and then been too frightened to do anything about it.

Watching her? Allison threw on her robe and hurried into the house.

Nick finally came home around midnight. Allison went downstairs when she heard his car pull in and waited for him.

"Still up?" he said as he caught sight of her.

"I wanted to talk to you. Something happened to—"

"Tell me about it tomorrow," Nick said with a yawn. "I'm beat." He went on past her without slowing down.

What was it, Allison wondered, some forgotten instinct that only women had? Some extra sense? Had she caught the scent of another woman's flesh still clinging to her husband? Because before tonight, it hadn't crossed her mind that Nick was seeing another woman. Now, as she watched him disappear up the stairs, she knew without a doubt that he was having an affair.

"She's young," the private detective said. A plain manila envelope lay on the desk in front of him. Allison supposed that it contained photographs. He had made no move to open it as yet.

"How young?"

"She claims to be eighteen." The detective was a thin, colorless man, with little expression to his face. Still, he managed to convey disbelief with the slightest curl of his upper lip, the tiniest lift of his right eyebrow. The actress in Allison stored that bit of information away, while the wife part of her wanted to shriek with anger and disappointment.

"Does my husband have any idea how young she is?"

"He's so infatuated he wouldn't notice if a truck hit him." The detective realigned the edge of the envelope with the edge of the desk. "She looks like you," he offered, as if that were an excuse for Nick's infidelity.

"Let me see."

He handed her the envelope and she opened it, very conscious of his probing glance. Then she forgot the detective, everything, as the first photograph slid out onto her lap. It was not her own face staring back at her, it was Kathleen Mallory, or Juliet Brittany, or—

"You think she looks like me?" she asked the detective, a rising note of anger in her voice that took them both by surprise.

"Younger, of course, but—yes."

Allison glanced down at the photograph again. So this was what Nick had tried to do to her: make her into another of his clones. He was no better than her father, really. Only his methods were different.

And here was yet another clone, waiting in the wings.

Quickly, she leafed through the rest of the photographs and then stuffed them back into the envelope. "I'll want that list of their meetings for my lawyer," she told the detective as she stood up.

Nick lay back on the pillows heaped against the headboard, grinning lazily, as he watched Toby Flynn, standing naked in front of the mirror, brushing her hair. "I love the way your breasts look when you raise your arms like that," he told her.

"You're sweet, darlin'." Over the past month, he had helped her eradicate a lot of the Texas accent from her speech. That "darlin' " was one of the few clues remaining.

She laid down the hairbrush and walked over to pick her clothes off the chair where she had tossed them earlier.

Nick leaped out of the bed. "No, not like that." He grabbed the damp towel on the floor beside the bed—they had showered before making love—and wrapped it around himself. "Remember how I showed you to walk."

She flashed him a quick smile, looking so much like a young Juliet Brittany in that moment that he felt a sharp pang of lost youth.

"Sorry. I forgot."

Still nude, she strolled across the room and then back again, remembering to hold her head up with Juliet's natural grace, to move her hips as Juliet had done—and as he had taught Kate to do.

Nick watched her, entranced. He could do it again, he thought. It would be so easy. She had a natural talent and the looks to go with it. It would only take a little shaping, a little molding. It wasn't that he needed another success, not with Allison's career in overdrive. But he found his hands itching to take control again, to play Pygmalion once more.

Strange how they met, almost as if fate had taken a hand. He had been scouting locations for his next film with Allison. *The Hollywood Reporter* had run a little paragraph on where he would be, and each place he stopped was crowded with would-be actresses. When Nick looked across a sea of faces and saw a young Juliet looking back at him, he had plunged into the crowd without thinking.

"Juliet?" he whispered when he reached her.

She looked up into his face, a puzzled light in her eyes. "I'm Toby. Toby Flynn. Who are you?"

She hadn't known what all the fuss was about, she said. Drawn by the crowd, she had stopped to watch.

He should feel guilty, he thought. But somehow Allison didn't arouse that emotion in him. If he had been cheating on Juliet or Kate, he would have been full of self-recrimination. Allison was too self-sufficient. She had made it clear, early in their marriage, that she didn't need a traditional husband-wife relationship. He had no idea if she had cheated on him. But he had fallen into several casual affairs over the last ten years.

Still, he had never mixed business with pleasure. Now he was tempted, more than tempted. He had told Sloan Whitney to get a contract ready for Toby to sign. He was ready to play Pygmalion again.

And Toby was more than willing. In every way.

She walked over to him now and hooked a finger through the top of his towel. "Do you really have to go?"

"Not yet."

She pulled Nick's towel loose, and it slipped to the floor. Nick made no move to retrieve it.

.   .   .

"She's what?" Nick stared at the lawyer in disbelief.

"Fifteen years old. Jailbait. If you want to hear it in the crudest possible terms, you're fucking a minor."

"You can't be serious, Whit."

"I'm serious, all right. When you told me to get the contract drawn up for her, I did a little checking. If you don't want to be in the most serious trouble of your life, you have to kiss this little dish good-bye. And for God's sake, don't put anything in writing. As far as I've been able to find out, she's on her own with no anxious mother in tow. If she did have, your goose would be cooked but good. As it is, I don't think anyone can prove you've been with her."

"The motel?"

"Taken care of."

"All right," Nick said slowly. Then, explosively, "Damn!"

"What?"

"I really wanted to work with her."

"I'll tell her to get back to you in three years."

"Did you tell him it's Toby calling? Toby Flynn?"

"I've passed along each one of your messages, Miss Flynn," Nick's secretary told her.

"Then why hasn't he called back?"

"Miss Flynn, many young women leave their numbers for Mr. Picard. I can assure you he returns very few of their calls."

Toby wished she were close enough to yank that snooty secretary's hair. "But what about my contract?"

"What contract is that, Miss Flynn?"

"Nick said he was fixing up a contract for me to sign."

"Miss Flynn, you must have been involved with someone impersonating Mr. Picard. Young girls are often taken advantage of like that."

"You're saying there's no contract?"

"That's right, Miss Flynn. There is no contract for you with Picard Productions."

With that, the snooty secretary hung up.

What in hellfire was going on? Toby wondered. Last week Nick couldn't get enough of her, couldn't wait to get her signature on the dotted line. Now she couldn't even get him on the phone.

It had happened without warning. Instead of Nick showing up for fun and games on Thursday night, a dozen roses arrived at her apartment with the message *It's over* but no signature. Since then she hadn't been able to get him on the phone, hadn't been able to get in to see him.

She had been spending the money she got from Gwen and Elsa like crazy, not wanting Nick to think she needed anything from him, because she was counting on signing a contract with his production company. Now his snooty secretary was saying there was no contract.

What had gone wrong? Had he found out she'd been a hooker? Big deal. Half the actresses in Hollywood probably started out that way.

As if that wasn't enough, she was coming down with some kind of flu bug. She had spent half the morning puking up her guts and the other half trying to get Nick on the phone.

Hell of a way to celebrate her sixteenth birthday, she told herself.

Nick sat in the audience waiting impatiently for the curtain to fall. Not that it wasn't a good play. Allison had the Broadway audience in the palm of her hand. But tonight was the last show and he was anxious to talk to her. He hadn't been pleased that she took the role in the first place, but he had gone along with it. If she hadn't been so involved in the play, he might not have gotten mixed up with that kid, he thought ruefully. It was a shame he'd had to slam the door in Toby's face. Peggy told him how many times Toby called his office. His regret wasn't simply at hurting her feelings. He hated to lose such great raw material.

Watching Allison tonight reminded Nick he didn't need raw material anymore. He had one of the most beautiful women in the world to work with. Not the most beautiful though. Not like Kate. There was too much of Conrad Hilliard's determined jaw in Allison's face for real beauty. But the talent Hilliard had passed on to his daughter more than made up for that. She had become an even better actress over the years they had been married. In spite of his desire to see the curtain ring down for the final time, he was moved to tears twice during this last act. So was the rest of the audience.

Allison had been restless recently. He hoped the play had gotten some of that out of her system, because he wanted her full attention. The script was ready to go, and so was he.

The last time he had flown to the East Coast was for the 1972 New York Film Festival, Nick recalled, as the curtain came down. *Last Tango in Paris* had premiered. Just the thought of Bertolucci's X-rated masterpiece made Nick champ at the bit to get started on the new film. Pauline Kael said once that movies are both behind and ahead of the culture. Bernardo Bertolucci had taken a giant step ahead with *Last Tango in Paris*; Nick didn't intend to be left behind.

Allison's dressing room was crowded with well-wishers and overflowing with flowers. Nick could do no more than kiss her chastely on the cheek. There was no hope of exchanging a private word.

The cast party afterward was a madhouse, but Allison showed no desire to leave. It was well after dawn before the two of them finally reached the apartment she had leased for the run of the play.

Nick tossed his tie over a chair. "I hate New York parties," he said wearily.

"Do you?" Allison took off her earrings. "I wonder why."

Nick grinned at her. This was the first time they'd been alone together since he flew in yesterday, and he could feel his need for her. "Probably because I can't get any work done at them."

"Why not?" She unhooked her necklace. "I did."

Nick thought of how good it was going to feel inside of her in a few minutes. "What kind of work?" he asked indulgently.

"I accepted a part in Tory Farb's new film."

Nick felt as though his lungs had just collapsed. "You can't do that. I have a script ready for you."

"It's too late, Nick." She might have been talking to a child—explaining the inevitable to a mind too young to grasp it.

"What do you mean?"

"I *am* grateful, Nick. You accomplished exactly what I wanted you to. Oh, I'll admit it took a little longer than I expected, but the results were worth it, don't you think?"

"Allison—"

"Let's be fair, Nick. You did even better than I hoped. You made me into an entirely different woman. Perhaps not the woman I envisioned myself as, but a damned good screen image for this part of my life. Unfortunately, this part of my life is over."

"Don't give a performance," he snapped. "Just tell me what the hell you're talking about."

"It's time for both of us to move on, Nick. I understand you have another protégée under your wing, so you shouldn't find it too hard."

Nick exhaled. "So that's it. She's history, Allison. It didn't mean anything."

"I'm truly sorry to hear that. I had hoped she would be around to comfort you." Allison gathered up her jewelry. "I've booked you a suite at the Plaza. Your bags are already there. My lawyer will be in touch with Whit tomorrow." She started for the bedroom.

"Wait a minute. Can't we discuss this?"

"Sorry." She didn't look it. "I've got to meet with Tory later this morning and take care of a hundred other things." She closed the bedroom door. Nick heard the click of the lock.

He poured himself a whiskey and stood there drinking it, staring at the door, trying to decide if it was worth it to kick the damned thing down.

Instead, he opted for a second whiskey and then went downstairs to flag a cab.

All the way to the Plaza he kept thinking that it just couldn't happen this way. He had created her, by God. The clay doesn't do that to the sculptor.

"You're pregnant, Miss Flynn." The doctor leaned forward, looking a little like a television preacher. "I hope you won't be tempted to do anything foolish."

"You mean anything more foolish than what I've already done?"

"I'm glad you've kept your sense of humor, young woman. You're going to need it." He frowned. Now he's getting to the hellfire and brimstone part, Toby thought. "Keeping this baby in your situation would be an extremely selfish thing to do."

"Who said I was going to keep it? I haven't decided anything yet. Maybe I'll just get rid of it as fast as I can."

"That would be even more foolish. Many couples want children, but nature has denied them that privilege. You're young and healthy, and your child will more than likely be just as healthy. I want you to think about giving one of those couples a new lease on life."

Toby grabbed her purse. "I'm going to think about myself first."

Toby paid the receptionist for the office visit even though her cash was starting to run low. One of the things she'd splurged on while Nick was romancing her was a little Chevy with a knock in its engine. The knock was worse today. Fixing it was going to make an even bigger hole in her finances. As much as she would have liked to drive around, she decided to save her gasoline and pointed the Chevy's nose for home.

When she got there, Toby fixed herself a tuna sandwich for lunch, but then all she did was sit and look at it. The truth was, she didn't know if she was happy or sad about the baby. She didn't want a baby, not by a long shot, but she was smart enough to know that this little bundle of joy in her belly might be enough to get her past Nick Picard's snooty secretary and back into his life again. Especially since that wife of his was dumping him. At least, that was the headline in *The Hollywood Reporter* yesterday.

Toby's heart had been set on becoming the next Kathleen Mallory. But if she couldn't get that contract out of Nick Picard, she would settle for cold cash.

Easier said than done. The barriers between Toby and Nick stayed firmly in place. The last time she got that snooty secretary of his on the phone, Toby really gave her a piece of her mind.

"Smart," Toby told herself as she hung up. "What do you think that accomplished?"

Within an hour, she found out. Nick's lawyer appeared at her door. "Sloan Whitney," he said, flashing his card.

And then he proceeded to tell her that her next visitor would be a policeman if she didn't lay off Nick.

Toby was horrified to find out how much information the lawyer had managed to gather about her. Not the worst thing, of course. Toby knew if Nick's uptight lawyer had learned she murdered Big John, she would be on her way back to Texas in handcuffs.

Still, it wouldn't hurt to try for a little cash. "I'm pregnant," she told him. "It's Nick's baby. What do you expect me to do about it?"

"Get an abortion."

"What am I supposed to do for money?"

"The same thing you were doing before you met Nick," Sloan Whitney told her. "The same thing you'll be doing for the rest of your short, miserable life."

And that was that.

Only somehow Toby couldn't bring herself to make the phone call to the sisters that would set things in motion. She knew Elsa and Gwen would not only arrange her abortion, they would finance it. But then she would be back in their stable, working for them instead of herself.

As for the baby, she didn't give it a second thought. Not until the doctor called.

"Miss Flynn, let us be frank. I know you have no desire to keep the child you're carrying. I have a patient who . . . She and her husband are desperate for a baby."

"How desperate? In figures."

"All your expenses until the baby is born, if you agree to the conditions."

"And?"

"Ten thousand dollars. When you sign the adoption papers."

Toby exhaled. "What's your cut, Doc?"

"I'm simply trying to help two very nice people achieve their heart's desire."

Bullshit! There's some kind of payoff. "What are the conditions?"

He outlined them for her, and as she listened Toby realized she had been given a second chance. She would be leaving town until the baby was born, staying at the couple's summer home in Carmel, instead of their house in Los Angeles. But she would be back. With money, next time.

And best of all, Toby thought, she still had the face.

Juliet waited in the tiny room just off the chapel, arranging and rearranging her veil in the postage-stamp-sized mirror. How many other brides had tried to catch a glimpse of themselves in that tiny scrap of a mirror? she wondered. She had spent the morning in a daze of anticipation. Instead of concentrating on the hundreds of last-minute wedding details, she moved dreamily through the chaos, wondering if Nick would be at the wedding. She had addressed his invitation personally, generously adding "and guest," now that he and Allison had split up. Writing his name on the envelope, her hand trembled with the first doubts since she accepted Hugh's proposal.

Hugh hadn't minded her sending that particular invitation. That was because he looked upon Nick as one more prospect. To Hugh, everyone was a prospect, even his bride-to-be's ex-husband.

Mrs. Hugh Odeham. It seemed strange that she was going to be taking another name after so many years. Strange that she was marrying someone who had nothing at all to do with the movie business. Hugh was in real estate; in fact, Hugh *was* real estate where Los Angeles was concerned. Juliet would never have to worry about money again, thanks to Sloan Whitney.

Funny, Juliet thought: she never expected to become friends with Nick's lawyer, but somehow it had happened. When Whit learned about her upcoming marriage, he insisted she have Hugh sign a prenuptial agreement. As crazy in love with her as Hugh was, that seemed silly, but Whit insisted.

Too bad she hadn't been able to ask Whit to give her away, but there Hugh balked, insisting it should be Juliet's father who walked with her down the aisle. For the first time in their six-month-long relationship, neither tears nor tantrums would change his mind.

"You look lovely, Mama," Eden said, as she burst through the door, with Dani right behind her. "How do we look?"

"Prettier than the bride," Juliet said, gathering them both into her arms. Now that it was too late to do anything about it, she could see that dressing the girls identically had been a mistake. She had chosen the pale pink dresses, frothy with lace, while shopping with Eden alone and had been too rushed by other things to attend their fittings. Now she could see that while Eden looked like a delicate little porcelain doll in dress, Dani looked awkward and uncomfortable. Something less ruffled, more tailored, would have suited her better. The girls still resembled each other, but during the past few months Dani had begun to shoot up like a bean stalk.

For a moment, Juliet was angry with Kate. Dani's mother was too caught up in her own life to have any time left for her daughter.

Her anger with Kate never lasted, though. Juliet realized quite clearly that if Kate had been a better mother to Dani, instead of giving all her time to her husband and her career, it would have been Juliet's loss. "I love you both so much," Juliet said, squeezing them fiercely. She glanced at the mirror, proud of the way they looked standing there together, a mother and her two daughters.

Nick's children.

The funny little tremor that shook her when she wrote his name on the invitation gripped her again. Was he here? No, the girls would have told her if he was.

"You're shaking," Dani said, concern shadowing her face. "Are you all right?"

"Stage fright," Juliet told her.

"They're ready to start. Oliver is waiting outside." Eden never called him grandfather. When Juliet realized that, she asked Eden why, afraid Oliver might have made some advance toward her. But Eden had said that the reason she didn't call him grandfather was because Dani couldn't.

"Let's go, then," Juliet said brightly, trying to ignore the sinking feeling that threatened to overwhelm her. She picked up her bouquet while Dani opened the door and signaled the organist.

Papa was just outside the door. His expression reminded Juliet of a funeral director's. When he took her arm, she felt her skin crawl. A mistake, she thought with each step down the aisle. I'm making a mistake. But whether the mistake was having her papa at the ceremony or the wedding itself, she wasn't sure.

Hugh waited at the front of the chapel. Juliet studied his face as she drew closer, looking for whatever had drawn her into this marriage. He was a salesman above all else, she realized, as she reached the altar on her father's arm. Hugh had sold her on the idea of marriage by overwhelming all her objections.

I can call Whit in the morning and have him start divorce proceedings, Juliet thought as the minister began.

"Who gives this woman?" the minister asked.

"I do." Oliver Brittany's voice was barely more than a whisper. Instead of releasing his daughter's arm and stepping aside, he continued to grip her elbow as the minister read the words of the ceremony.

When Juliet said, "I do," she knew with a depressing certainty that while she could remove Hugh Odeham from her life with Whit's help, she would never, ever, be free of Papa.

Until death do us part.

"Please, Barry, don't be like that," Kate wheedled. "Let's do something fun today. Something different. It's too pretty to sit at a desk and stare at a typewriter."

"We've done something fun and different every day this month," Barry said in the calm, reasonable voice that meant he was in his business mode, the literary agent dealing with a recalcitrant writer. "That's why we're here." *Here* was a red-roofed white house with every amenity on Eleuthera in the Bahamas, a writer's dream escape. One of Barry's former clients owned it. Barry had brought Kate to the island in hopes the change of scenery would break what they had both come to realize was a writer's block, although neither of them had spoken the term aloud. "You know you have more than one book in you. I know you have more than one book in you. But now you have to get something on paper."

"I don't see why." Kate pouted. "We have plenty of money. You said so yourself."

"We agreed we would have a working partnership. Otherwise I would never have resigned from the agency."

"I thought you wanted to resign. That you wanted to be with me."

"You were very persuasive, darling. But gigolo isn't a role that suits me. I resigned to handle your work. It's time you started producing some."

"I can't!" Kate cried, startling them both with her vehemence.

"Kate, Kate," he said, holding her close as she began to sob. "Don't do this to yourself."

"I want to go home," Kate said through her tears.

"There's no home to go to, yet," Barry reminded her, reasonable as always. They had sold Helen Chandler's house, which had become Kate's after her divorce from Nick, and the new home they were having built was nowhere near completion. Their plan had been to spend a year traveling, so Kate could research and write her second novel while the new house was under construction. "If it's Danielle you're missing, we can have her come out here for a visit."

"No," Kate said sharply. She should have thanked Barry for the offer; she knew how much it cost him to make it. But Dani wasn't the solution to her problems. In fact, Kate knew that seeing her daughter's melancholy face each day, as Dani moped around wishing she were back with Juliet and Eden, would only add to her depression. Kate received letters from Dani *and* Eden at least once a week. Their looping girlish handwriting was almost identical. Both envelopes were always addressed in Juliet's flowing hand. The girls were happy with the new house Juliet had moved into after her brief marriage to the real estate magnate. They had separate but adjoining bedrooms. Juliet had sent photographs of both rooms. Looking at those photographs, Kate realized that for all intents and purposes Dani had become Juliet's daughter. She wasn't sure how it had happened or what to do about it, if anything. "I don't want Dani here. I want to be in Los Angeles. We can rent a house or stay in a hotel. I don't care which, as long as we go back."

Barry started to object. Sometimes he was no better than an accountant, Kate thought, and then was instantly ashamed of herself. "I need Los Angeles," she went on before he could begin reciting figures to her. She couldn't tell Barry the real reason she wanted to go back. She wasn't entirely sure of it herself. She only knew that it had something to do with Nick.

She had been glad to give up the role of Javelin Woman.

She had never felt completely comfortable with it anyway. But she was having trouble slipping into the new role of Kathleen Mallory, best-selling novelist.

That was where Nick came in. It was Nick who had created Kathleen Mallory. It seemed to Kate that the farther from Los Angeles and Nick she was, the more feeble his creation became.

If something happened to Kathleen, Kate would be left with only herself. And she knew, with certainty, that no one would want Kate, plain and unadorned. Even Barry.

"Please, Barry. Take me home." Back to Nick, although she couldn't say it. And Barry would never know, because she didn't intend to see him. Just being in the same city with Nick would give her the strength she needed to be Kathleen Mallory. "Please."

"All right," Barry said, holding her close. "You know I'd do anything for you."

TWENTY

1974

ALLISON SIPPED HER CHAMPAGNE AND WATCHED Wilson Keating work the crowd at the Republican Party fund-raiser. Wilson stood out here as he did in every group. At six foot four, he looked enough like Raymond Massey playing a young Abe Lincoln to have been Massey's son. The resemblance to Honest Abe was invaluable politically; Keating was leaning heavily on the "Honest Wilson" approach.

Wilson Keating was definitely a charmer, she noted, as he bent over women's hands or raised them to his lips. If he were running for office this year, the female votes here tonight would clearly have been his.

Allison couldn't help feeling a flush of pride as she glanced around the crowded room. Half of Hollywood was here, and that was due solely to her own efforts. In the past few months, she had discovered she had a knack for organization and campaigning, and she had been furiously putting it to use for Wilson's benefit.

"There you are," Wilson said. While she had been occupied in her own thoughts, he had crossed the room to her side. He kissed her on the check. "The most beautiful lady in the room."

"Save that for a live one," she said, smiling up at him.

345

"You already have my contribution nailed down."

"I'll make sure of that later," he said softly. "Oops, there's Senator MacLaren. Back to work."

She watched him cut through the crowd to intercept the big bearlike senator at the bar. Senator MacLaren smiled at Wilson and then turned to raise his glass in a salute to Allison. Allison waved back. She was happy, she realized suddenly, happier than she had been in a long time. And it was all because of Wilson Keating.

She had seen him at yet another Hollywood party and was immediately attracted to him. But before she could wangle an introduction, he had taken care of the formalities himself. Within a month she was deep in preparations for his political future. The first step was for Wilson to embed himself deeply in the party apparatus. That way, when Wilson made a bid for governor of California in 1978, he would have enough favors to call in to assure the nomination. Judging by tonight, that strategy was already well under way.

And after he became governor—no one could claim that Wilson Keating didn't dream big. Wilson had confessed to Allison that his eventual plans included a try at the White House. Senator MacLaren, the most powerful man in California politics, had done nothing but encourage those plans. With MacLaren's support, Wilson was virtually assured of victory in the race for the gubernatorial nomination, and perhaps beyond.

At first, Allison had been apprehensive that the film image she acquired under Nick's tutelage might prove a handicap in dealing with the more conservative members of the party. Instead, she had found that the identity she worked so hard to shed, that of being Conrad Hilliard's daughter, made her more than acceptable to the party regulars. It made her their glittering treasure, a gem who could fill a fund-raiser with heavyweight contributors by virtue of being the daughter of one of the most respected actors in the world. Even her father approved of her new role, tottering out himself occasionally, as his health permitted, to lend his presence to the cause.

Her fame and money and the sheer glamour of her being a Hilliard were of obvious benefit to Wilson Keating in achieving his goals. Allison wondered if Wilson realized the benefit of their relationship to her.

Probably not. Men seldom looked beneath the surface. Even Nick—her mind shied away from that subject. It was too painful. She'd had no idea how much she would miss Nick, both personally and professionally. Half a dozen times, she had wondered if there were some way she could regain what she had tossed away. Even if her pride had allowed her to contact Nick, she doubted that it would have done any good. He would not have forgiven her for dumping him.

Besides, she still wasn't sure whether she had done the right thing in letting Nick push her career in the direction he had chosen for her. In spite of the pinnacle of success she had achieved, she couldn't shake the fear that perhaps her father had been right after all. That was one reason she had thrown herself into Wilson's campaigning and fund-raising plans. Those activities gave a deeper meaning to her life. She was tired of trying to live up to the salacious roles Nick had cast her in—and Tory Farb had continued, in the picture she had done for him. Instead of the intellectual film she had hoped to make, she had found herself doing a simple rehash of her last screen role in *Impressions*. Not that *Mood Music* wasn't a success; all her films were a success. The question that haunted her was whether they were successes for the right reasons.

Although she had allowed herself to fall briefly into a relationship with Tory, it hadn't been a satisfactory one. Tory was too pliable, too yielding, too careful to get her opinion before advancing his own.

Allison knew a lot more about herself now. At the ripe old age of thirty-three, she had finally come to terms with the fact that she needed a strong man in her life. She wasn't a woman who felt comfortable being responsible for herself. Nick, like Conrad Hilliard, had been another dominating man for her to hide behind. When she left Nick, she lost the sense of security he gave her.

Wilson had given it back, along with a direction for her life. Right now, Allison honestly didn't care whether she ever made another movie. It was more important that Wilson Keating be elected governor of California.

Wilson gazed at her from across the room, lifting one eyebrow and nodding slightly in the direction of a pudgy widow dripping with diamonds. Go to work, his look said, as plainly as if he had spoken.

Allison set down her champagne glass, sketched a mock salute in the air, and obeyed.

Toby stood on the deck of the Carmel house, gazing out to sea. The breeze from the ocean whipped her dress around her legs and made the huge bulge of her belly even more prominent.

"Wouldn't you like to sit down now, dear?" Toby didn't have to turn to know that Beth Wescott was wringing her hands nervously, absurdly anxious to take care of Toby, to please her. "How about a nice cup of tea, some of that nice herbal blend we picked up yesterday?"

"Now don't fuss over her," Lee Wescott scolded his wife. "It won't hurt a thing if Toby just stands there quietly."

"I *know* that, Lee. I'm just trying to make sure she's comfortable," Beth scolded right back.

Toby smiled to herself, enjoying the couple's gentle bickering. The last six months had been like heaven, she thought, as the salt spray stung her cheeks. The best time she'd ever had in her life. She didn't even miss Momma so much anymore, not with Beth catering to her every wish before she even got the words out of her mouth. She felt exactly like a princess.

Not at all like a murderer.

The thought of Big John lying on her momma's bed with a hole shot right through him flashed into her mind. Toby shivered.

Beth gasped. "Oh, my goodness! I told you she was going to get too cool out here, Lee." Before Toby could say a word, Beth had jerked off her shawl and wrapped it around Toby's shoulders. "Lee, you go put the water on for the tea," she ordered. "We've got to take better care of this young lady."

Toby let herself be hustled off the deck and into the spacious den. Only when Toby was settled into the most comfortable chair, with an afghan tucked around her legs and a cup of hot tea in her hand, did Beth herself relax and accept a cup of tea from her husband.

Toby sipped the warm, honey-sweetened tea, watching the couple over the rim of her bone-china cup. Such nice people, she thought. Sometimes, like now, it was easy to forget just why she was here.

The baby in her stomach might be the reason Beth and Lee had brought her into their home, but it still wasn't real to Toby.

Sometimes, like now, it seemed that it was Toby herself the Wescotts were adopting, not the baby.

Toby snuggled back farther into the chair, trying to ease the twinge of a backache. Even though it wasn't the first time she had felt that twinge this evening, she hadn't mentioned it to the Wescotts yet. When she did tell them, Beth would scurry around frantically trying to make her more comfortable, while Lee phoned the doctor to find out if the twinge of pain meant the baby was coming. Toby knew that was how it would be because that was exactly what had happened at least once a week for the past six weeks. Braxton Hicks contractions, the doctor had called them.

But tonight was different, she thought, as the emphatic pain returned to her lower back. Tonight, whether she was ready or not, the baby was on its way.

"Beth," Toby began. Then she hesitated.

"What is it, dear?" Beth asked. "Did you want something else?"

"No." Toby took a deep breath and shifted in the chair, determined to enjoy the moment as long as she could. "Everything is perfect just the way it is."

Not the season for babies, Toby thought as she gazed in the window of the nursery. Only five of the cribs were occupied, and none of them bore the name of either Flynn or Wescott. Toby made her way slowly to the nurses' station, feeling the stitches of the episiotomy. "Where's my baby?" she asked the nurses on duty.

The women exchanged glances. After a moment, the older nurse said, "The Wescotts had her transferred."

"Was she all right?" Toby demanded. "There wasn't anything wrong with her, was there?"

"Nothing was wrong, Miss Flynn. The Wescotts simply wanted her elsewhere." The older nurse dropped her glance to the paper in front of her, effectively ending the conversation. The other nurse began shuffling through a stack of folders.

Toby stood there a moment longer, but neither woman looked up again. She finally shuffled back down the hall to her room. Just as she opened the door, she heard a soft ripple of laughter from the nurses' station.

She let the door whisper shut behind her and sat down on the edge of the bed. She hadn't seen the baby when it was born, but she had heard the obstetrician say, "It's a girl." Toby wondered if it looked like her.

A phone book was in the drawer of the bedside stand, and the Wescotts were listed. As Toby dialed the number, she could feel the icy numbness in her heart starting to thaw. Beth had been so good and kind. Just the thought of talking to her on the phone was enough to make Toby feel better.

"Beth?" she said, when Beth Wescott answered. "It's Toby. I just wanted to find out how the baby—"

The connection was broken.

Puzzled, Toby began to dial again. This time the phone rang and rang. She tried the number off and on again for the rest of the afternoon. Sometimes it was busy, but most of the time, it just rang with no answer. She had almost decided to call the phone company and ask if there was a problem, when someone knocked on the door of her room.

"Come in," she called, and was relieved to see that it was Mr. Burns, the Wescotts' lawyer. "I've been trying to call Beth," she told him, "but I can't get through. There must be something wrong with the Wescotts' phone."

"And why were you calling Mrs. Wescott?" Mr. Burns asked, as solemnly as if she were on trial.

"Because I wanted to see the baby, to see what she looks like," Toby said, suddenly unsure of herself.

"Perhaps you have forgotten, Miss Flynn, that you signed a legal agreement. In return for the sum Mr. and Mrs. Wescott are paying you, you have agreed not to contact them again."

"But that was before we met. Beth is my friend. She wouldn't mind; all these months she was so nice to me." Toby could feel the tears beginning to trickle down her face.

"Mr. and Mrs. Wescott consider you as nothing more than the vehicle which delivered their child to them."

"You make me sound like a bread truck!" Toby yelled at him.

"Your description, not mine, Miss Flynn. You have signed a legal contract. The Wescotts intend to hold you to the letter of it. Don't try to contact them again. If you do, you will find yourself in serious trouble."

Toby stared down at her feet, at the lovely pink bedroom slippers Beth had bought her. "What about the things I left at the Wescotts?" she asked sullenly.

"You'll be released from the hospital day after tomorrow. I've reserved a hotel room for you for two weeks." The lawyer handed her an envelope. "Your things will be waiting for you at the hotel. As we agreed, your expenses will be paid during the two-week period. After that, you must make your own arrangements."

"What about my money?"

"The money will be delivered to you when you leave the hospital." He frowned at her. "Do we understand each other now, Miss Flynn? You won't try to contact the Wescotts again?"

"I understand, all right," Toby said bitterly.

"Fine." He turned to leave.

"Mr. Burns?"

"Yes?"

"What did they name her?"

"Really, Miss Flynn! You just said you understood."

"I just want to know. I promise I won't bother them. Just tell me what they named her."

"Catherine," he said after a moment. "They named her Catherine, after Mrs. Wescott's mother."

"Catherine," Toby said, savoring the name. "That's awfully long for a baby. Will they call her Cathy?"

"Cat," he said slowly, as though each word that escaped his lips pained him. "They will call her Cat."

After Mr. Burns left, Toby sat on the bed and stared into space until the nurse, entering with a dinner tray, roused her.

When the nurse set the tray on the stand in front of Toby, it reminded Toby of Beth fussing over her. She had to blink away the tears.

"There you are," the nurse told her. "Eat up. You need to get your strength back."

Toby looked down at the hospital food: a pork chop, creamed potatoes, green beans, a roll, a pat of margarine, a cup of coffee. She picked up the roll and began to spread it with margarine, while she tried to focus her thoughts on the ten thousand dollars. Her nest egg.

She wasn't going to spend a penny of it she didn't have to, Toby told herself. That money was going to get her what she wanted out of life—and what she wanted, more than anything else, was never to be poor again. Never again was she going to be at somebody else's mercy. "A bread truck!" she muttered.

Toby thought about little Cat, with Beth fussing over her, worrying about her, hugging and loving her. The tears welled up in Toby's eyes once more.

She concentrated fiercely on cutting up the pork chop. When she took the first bite, she found it just as dry and tasteless as it looked, but she chewed and swallowed it anyway. The nurse was right; she needed her strength back.

When the doctor came by this afternoon, she would ask him how long it would take the episiotomy to heal. She needed to get back to work as soon as possible.

Toby stuck another piece of pork chop in her mouth. Wouldn't Gwen and Elsa be tickled pink to find out their investment was going to pay off some more?

Cat Wescott. In a little pink gown and pink booties probably. Pink was Beth's favorite color.

Toby continued to chew as the tears rolled down her face. She wasn't sure if she was crying for Cat or for herself.

.   .   .

Barry Inman felt like a fool.

The idea that had seemed so brilliant before he left home
looked less than that now, as he sat in the comparative safety
of his car watching the ladies of the evening parading their
wares on the sidewalk across the street. Try to look at it
objectively, he told himself. You're in a research library.
The only decision you have to make is which volume to
check out.

That literary allusion made him feel better, since it was
the world of books that had sent him out into the night
on this particular mission. Kate's writer's block had become
so bad it was driving him insane. She spent half her time
dreaming up crazy excuses to get out of the house, away
from the typewriter, and the other half weeping because
she wasn't getting anything accomplished.

Tonight's tears had been the last straw. Barry had decided
to take action. He had been a fool to resign from the agency,
he thought grimly. But Kate had been so persuasive when
she talked about how much fun they would have traveling
together while she wrote and researched. And he had known
he would do his share for their partnership by handling her
work. Only there wasn't any work. Just tears, tears, and
more tears.

Ever since they returned to Los Angeles, he had been
aware of how his reputation had suffered. To his old friends
and clients, he was no better than a gigolo, living on Kate's
money. Tonight, he had decided it was time for action.

Still operating in the literary metaphor, Barry decided the
juvenile section looked most promising for his purposes. The
youngest of the prostitutes—in stiletto heels, black fish-net
stockings, Day-Glo orange satin hot pants, and a black
leather halter—could not have been more than fifteen.

" 'Girl of My Dreams,' " Barry muttered to himself as he
left the shelter of the Mercedes.

As he approached the sidewalk where the hookers congregated, it seemed to him their ranks thinned abruptly. The young prostitute he had chosen stood her ground.

"Excuse me, miss," Barry said when he reached her. "Could I talk to you for a moment about a business arrangement?"

She looked him up and down. The face beneath the makeup was that of a child. Barry revised his estimate of her age downward. Twelve, he guessed. No more than thirteen. A touch of nausea troubled his stomach. "You got an ID?" she asked.

He nodded.

"Show me."

He took out his billfold and flipped it open.

She shuffled through it deftly, extracted his driver's license, and held it up to compare the photo with his face. "Okay," she said. "Now that you finally got up enough courage to quit looking and come over, what do you want?"

That unnerved him. He hadn't realized the hookers were aware of his watching them. Of course, they would be. Jungle animals, he thought, eternally spied on by predators from the underbrush. Their sense of danger must be keen. "I want you to meet my wife." Barry faltered in the light of her shrewd green eyes. If he told her she was nothing more than a research volume, she would probably stalk away, insulted. "I'll pay you," he added quickly.

She smiled, amused. "I know what you want." She looped an arm through his. "And you bet you'll pay."

Barry could feel the dull red flush heating his face as they crossed to his car. He wondered if it was obvious in the streetlights. He wondered if anyone he knew would see him. He wondered if the police were watching this corner. Most of all, he wondered why he had ever come up with this crazy idea.

When they got in the car, he noticed the ladies of the night had returned to the sidewalk. "Why did they all leave?" he said, as the motor of the Mercedes purred to life.

"They thought you were a cop." She held up a candy bar she had discovered on the car seat. "Mind if I eat this?"

"Go ahead." Barry glanced sideways, watching her chew with enthusiasm. "And you didn't think I was a cop?"

"I didn't care. If you arrest me, Jonah will get me out."

"Jonah?"

"Jonah Rome." She turned to him with a wide chocolate grin that made her look even younger. "If you were a cop, you would know that."

"And who is Jonah Rome? Your pimp?"

"More than that." She crumpled up the candy wrapper and tossed it into the back seat. "Just don't damage the merchandise tonight, and you won't find out what a mean bastard Jonah can be. Or what kind of connections he's got."

Barry wondered if his little brainstorm had really been such a good idea after all.

"So," the girl said. "Have you and your wife ever done a threesome before?"

Barry gripped the wheel harder and wondered if she could see him blushing in the darkness of the car's interior.

Whoa, Christie Beck told herself. You're pushing this old dude way too hard. If you don't let up on him, he'll put you out right now, and you'll be the one Jonah is pissed at.

Christie stared out the window at the big houses whizzing by in the darkness. She'd hit a live one, all right. It had been worth the gamble.

And it had been a gamble. She had lied to the old dude about what the other girls thought. He was too much of a geek to be a cop. They all spotted that at first glance. They figured he was a fruitcake. A nut who might use a working girl for a punching bag. And they thought Christie was a fruitcake herself for going with him.

She wasn't scared, though. She meant what she said about Jonah. He'd have this guy's balls if he hurt one of Jonah's girls. But she wasn't counting on Jonah to pull her out of any tough spots. She hadn't counted on anyone but herself for the past three years, ever since she turned fifteen.

She always accepted offers from johns the other girls backed away from. She loved the taste of danger, of having to get out of a situation by her own wits—and still make a profit.

Like tonight. She would just bet this was the first time the old dude had ever hired someone to play three in a bed with his wife. In fact, he probably hadn't even warned his old lady what was on his mind.

Wouldn't it be a blast to see the expression on his old lady's face when little Christie came bopping in the door with him? Christie leaned back, anticipating.

In the end, though, it was Christie herself who received the biggest shock when Barry Inman parked his Mercedes beside the huge mansion and led the way inside.

Christie followed, busily calculating the worth of all the possessions she passed, ready to take it all into consideration when she set her price. She wasn't prepared for the identity of the woman sitting beside the empty fireplace. When that famous face turned her way, Christie stopped dead on the middle of the oriental rug. "You're her," she said, amazed. "The woman on TV. The one with the car."

The woman shrugged helplessly. "You see," she said to Barry Inman. "I'll never be able to shake that image."

"Wow!" Christie bubbled on. "I've never done it with a celebrity before."

"It?" the woman questioned Barry Inman.

"Now, Kate," he said, spreading his hands helplessly. "I didn't really have a chance to explain."

"You mean you let her think—?"

"Kathleen Mallory," Christie crowed triumphantly. "That's your name, isn't it?"

"My friends call me Kate." The beautiful face smiled at Christie. "And I hope you'll be one of them."

"Oh, I will be." Christie grinned. "I've done these three-in-a-bed scenes before."

"Barry!" Kate protested.

"Look, ah—what's your name?" Barry asked her.

"Christie. Christie Beck. From Sacramento," she volunteered.

"Look, Christie," he began again. "I haven't made it clear why we wanted to hire you."

"You mean you just want to watch? That's okay."

"Barry, please! You're only making it worse," Kate complained.

"Kate just wants to talk to you, Christie."

"If you brought me all the way out here to stiff me, Jonah will have something to say about that," Christie said angrily. A night's work wasted would be hard to explain to Jonah. He just might think it was her fault. Christie didn't like to think about what that might mean.

"Who's Jonah?" Kate asked.

"Her pimp."

"He's not my pimp. He's a very important man, and if you don't pay me, he'll be—"

"We will pay you, Christie," Kate interrupted. "We'll pay you very well."

"For talking," Barry chimed in. "You see, my wife writes books. She's thinking about writing a book about a girl like you. Maybe you've read her novel, *Fortune's Gambit?*"

Christie shook her head. "I don't read books. And I'm not doing anything kinky for less than three hundred bucks."

"Is talking considered kinky?" Kate asked her.

Christie glanced from Kate to Barry. "Yeah," she said belligerently. "It is."

"We'll pay you five hundred dollars," Barry Inman announced, running his hand through his hair.

Christie relaxed. That was more like it. "For five hundred bucks, I'll do anything you want. Anything."

"Talk," Kate said weakly. "All we want is for you to stay here tonight and talk to us."

To Christie Beck's complete astonishment, that was exactly what happened.

As Juliet watched warily, Frederick Yates circled her white and gold living room, picking up objects, examining them, putting them down. She had decorated this room herself, without benefit of an interior decorator, filling it with things she enjoyed and that she thought the girls would like. After her hasty divorce from Hugh Odeham, she had been interested in pleasing no one except herself, Eden, and Dani. However, seeing each item in the room subjected to Frederick's intense scrutiny made her uneasy. Perhaps her taste would appear unsophisticated to a man like him.

Frederick came to a halt in front of the framed photograph of Nick on the grand piano. His hands clasped behind his back, he reared back on his heels, studying it. "He has aged more gracefully than I."

True, Juliet thought. Even though he was only five years older than Nick's forty, Frederick Yates already looked like an old man. However, one didn't say that about the head of a major Hollywood studio. Especially if one was an out-of-work actress, still hoping to return to the screen one day. So she replied, "You dress so much better than he does. I've always admired your suits. The tailoring is impeccable."

Frederick gave her a swift up-and-down glance and turned back to the photograph. "You still love him, don't you, Juliet? Otherwise, this wouldn't be here."

"He *is* Eden and Dani's father. The girls like to see his photograph when they practice their piano lessons." Or while Dani practiced. More times than not, Eden merely plunked aimlessly on the keys. Still, it was Eden who usually managed to shine more brilliantly at their shared recitals— but Frederick would not be interested in any tales of domestic life. He had never married, never had children of his own. He dated brittle sophisticates who wouldn't dream of spoiling their figures with childbirth if they did marry. Not that her figure was spoiled, Juliet thought proudly. At thirty-five, she was still slim as a girl.

Frederick had picked up the photograph to examine it more closely. "Nicholas fascinates me, you know. He always has. I could never understand why Morgan preferred him to me."

"Frederick, that was years ago. You shouldn't—"

"Don't waste your sympathy, Juliet. At any rate, that's not what I'm here to discuss." He sat down on one of the plump gold sofas. "Have you considered my offer?"

"Considered it, yes. I don't need money." Whit's advice on her prenuptial contract with Hugh Odeham had been excellent. This house and all its furnishings were paid for, and she still had enough that she would never need to worry about the girls or herself.

"You didn't need money in the first place. Something else drives you. Decorating this house"—he glanced around the room—"in such a charming manner might have occupied you for a time. Now you need more than the company of two eleven-year-olds."

"I'm an actress, Frederick, not a producer."

"You *were* an actress," he said gently. "Your efforts to

return to the screen proved futile. We both know that."

For just a moment the rage simmered within Juliet. Then curiosity overwhelmed it. "Why, Frederick? Why me? Why now?"

"When Morgan headed the studio, he was really the head. That era is past. We're part of a conglomerate now. The real power is in New York. They dictate studio policy, not I. However, I am allowed a few small projects of my own. I want you to work with me on one of them. You see, Nicholas once accused me of being a dinosaur. While it may have been true at the time, I don't intend to continue in that vein. I would like to develop a project or projects for the female audience."

"Why do you want me involved?"

"Perhaps, like you, I enjoy collecting beautiful things." He sighed explosively. "Or perhaps I want you to act as producer simply because I know it will irritate Nicholas beyond belief to see you developing projects while he is unable to do the same."

Juliet knew what Frederick was talking about. When Allison Hilliard left Nick and Picard Productions, Nick had been unable to come up with another star of sufficient quality to satisfy his backers. He had yet to make another movie. "If I accept your offer, I would expect this to be a legitimate position. Not just some trumped-up thing to carry on your feud with Nick."

"Why, certainly, my dear. All my feud, as you call it, with Nicholas does is assure that however unpromising the project you develop, it will nevertheless be translated to the screen."

"Good," Juliet said. "Then I accept."

Frederick insisted that they drink a toast to their new association. When Juliet came back with their drinks, though, he downed his hurriedly and departed.

. . .

After Frederick left, Juliet had a momentary attack of panic. What if she made a fool of herself? She knew nothing about being a producer.

That wasn't important, Juliet told herself. The important thing was that Frederick had offered her the opportunity to produce solely to taunt Nick—and that was why she had accepted.

She saw Nick frequently when he visited the girls or dropped them off, and while seeing him was the high point of her week, he never seemed to notice her presence. He was still wrapped up in self-pity over Allison Hilliard's withdrawal from his life.

While considering Frederick's proposal, the thought had come to Juliet that if it irritated Nick because she was producing films while he was not, he would at least remember she was alive.

"Is he gone?"

Juliet looked up. Oliver Brittany stood in the door of the living room.

"Don't spy on me, Papa! I won't have it!"

"What did he want?"

"None of your business." She glanced at her watch. "It's almost time for the girls to be home."

"Juliet, please."

"I don't want you around them."

When Oliver Brittany trudged out, his head bowed, Juliet tried to gain control of herself. Frederick was wrong about her being alone with two eleven-year-olds. She wasn't alone. Papa was always there. When Juliet bought this house after her divorce from Hugh Odeham, Papa had sold his own home, the French country-style house where Juliet had grown up, and moved into the servants' quarters.

If he would only die, she thought wildly. Drop dead of a heart attack in the night.

"Juliet, we're home! Wait until you hear what happened today," Dani exclaimed as she and Eden came bursting through the living room door.

Eden dropped her schoolbooks on one of the sofas. "I'll let you tell your version, and then I'll tell Mother the truth," she said with a wicked little smile.

"Juliet knows I *always* tell the truth," Dani countered.

"I know both my girls are truthful," Juliet said as she hugged the two of them.

Eden pulled away before Dani. Grabbing her music from her books, she ran to place it on the grand piano. "I get to practice first tonight."

"Wait until you hear how good she sounds on the new piece," Dani said loyally, pulling Juliet toward the piano. "Play a little of it for us now," she begged Eden.

The frame holding Nick's photograph was lying face down on the piano top. Juliet reached to set it up again—and found that the glass had shattered.

"How did that happen?" Dani asked.

"I had a visitor earlier," Juliet said hoarsely. "He must have knocked it over accidentally. I'll have the glass replaced tomorrow," she said more calmly. "Go ahead and play your piece for us, Eden."

All the while her daughter played, Juliet stared at the sharp shards of glass on the shiny wood of the piano and wondered if Nick had any idea just how much Frederick Yates hated him.

The first time Kate met Jonah Rome, the sight of him took her breath away.

He was deeply tanned, with a sharp, predatory look about his face that said, This man is dangerous. The sexual feeling his look aroused in her was so powerful she could barely catch her breath.

He stood up behind his desk as Christie Beck led Kate

and Barry into his office. Neither the room nor the man himself were what Kate had expected after all her long talks with Christie. Jonah Rome's suit was impeccably tailored. His office furniture and the art on the walls were as expensive as that of any studio executive. It was hard to believe this man was involved in any way with a teenage prostitute like Christie Beck. Or that he was the mobster Kate's preliminary research showed him to be. For a horrifying moment, Kate had the feeling she had wandered into the wrong office.

"Miss Mallory." Jonah Rome came around the desk and took her hand. "I'm one of your fans, you know. I couldn't believe it when Christie told me she had met you."

"Nor how she had met me?" Kate's nervousness demanded she get that out of the way immediately.

"She told me you were researching a book, yes." Still holding her right hand in his left, Jonah Rome reached out with his right to greet Barry. "Let Christie fix you a drink, Mr. Inman. While I monopolize your lovely wife."

It was so much an order Kate was surprised Barry didn't bristle. Instead, he followed Christie to the far end of the room, where the teenager expertly mixed him a drink and then one for herself.

"How about you two?" Christie called.

Jonah still held Kate's hand. "Not just yet." His eyes had not left Kate's. She felt as though she would never be able to breathe again. "May I call you Kathleen?" he asked her.

"Kate," Kate managed to say at last. "My friends call me Kate."

"I do want to be your friend, Kate." Jonah Rome leaned closer, lowering his voice for her ears alone. "Next time, come by yourself."

Kate looked into his eyes. Jet black, they gave away nothing, not even a hint of light. "Yes," she said, and she knew she was her mother's daughter after all.

They didn't speak.

As soon as Jonah closed the door, Kate was in his arms, returning his hungry kisses with a hunger of her own. The tiny portion of her brain that was still capable of rational thought realized it was always like this. As much as they were together, as many hours as they stole for themselves alone, they never seemed to get enough of each other.

Jonah disentangled himself from her arms just long enough to remove her dress and his own clothes. Then, scooping her up into his arms, he carried her into the bedroom of the suite. Just before he laid her on the bed, she caught sight of herself in the mirror. Jonah had slipped some catch within her, releasing the sensual nature she had tried so hard to damp down. Her stepmother had always been sure Kate would be no better than her mother. Lorraine's predictions had come true, Kate thought.

Jonah groaned with desire and buried himself inside her.

Kate forgot everything, her mother, her stepmother, her father—even her husband, waiting patiently at home—as she gave herself over totally to Jonah's lovemaking.

Afterward, they showered together. Jonah amused himself by lathering every inch of Kate's body with soap. Then, aroused once more, he lifted her up until her back was pressed against the tile wall, warm from the shower spray, and inserted himself in her again.

This time, when she came, she sobbed aloud.

It was only when the heat of her passion had finally cooled and she was toweling herself dry that Kate remembered Barry. The shower spray had made a wreck of her hair. When she glanced in the fogged mirror, she could see it hanging in wet coils down her back. Jonah came up behind her, pulling her against him, so that her rear tucked neatly against his loins. "I have to go," she whispered, reluctant even now to break their embrace.

"Barry?"

She nodded.

"Don't worry about him. I sent Christie over to entertain him." Jonah reached for another towel and began to dry her hair.

Strange, Kate thought, my husband is with a prostitute, and I don't care at all. It wasn't the first time that Jonah had called Christie Beck in to keep Barry occupied. And poor Barry seemed grateful for the attention, she thought guiltily. She and Barry had had intercourse infrequently during their marriage, and even that ceased the night she met Jonah Rome. Within the week, she had moved her things into a separate bedroom. Barry had not protested. Jonah, when she told him after the first time he made love to her, had only nodded in agreement, as though he had expected no less.

"Let's get married," Kate said. It was a subject she brought up at least once a week.

He leaned past her and swabbed at the mirror with the towel he had used on her hair. "You know I can't."

"Won't."

"Won't," he agreed. "I love you, Kate. I won't put you in danger."

She jerked away from him impatiently. "How much danger can I be in by simply marrying the man I love?"

"You know what I do for a living. There are a lot of"— the expression on Kate's face made him pause to search for another word—"of my business associates who would like to take me out. I don't want you taken out with me."

"I hate it when you talk like that!" she burst out, and then began to cry.

"Come on, Kate," he said, turning her so that she was sobbing into his bare shoulder. "You're a big girl now. You know the score. I don't like having to sneak around to see you, but I don't want you identified with me either."

It was an effort, but she blinked back the tears. "I know why you feel like that," she said, trying to lighten her voice as she twisted around to stare at her reflection in the mirror once more. "I look like a hag."

He put his arms around her waist and drew her back against him. "You look gorgeous. In fact, if you needed a job, I could put you to work."

"What kind of a job?" she asked playfully. "Like Christie's?"

"Better. Christie's kind are a dime a dozen. I have guys that work the bus station every week looking for new talent." Kate kept her face carefully composed. This was the side of Jonah she didn't want to think about. "No, I could make big money with you," he mused. "Especially if you were Christie's age, instead of an old broad of thirty-two." He slapped her on the bottom. "There's a guy here in LA who pays a bundle to have sex with young girls who look like you."

"Me?" She was so surprised, it came out a squeak.

"And Juliet Brittany. I understand a call girl operation bankrolled one of their girls to plastic surgery just for this guy."

Kate had regained her composure. "So why don't you put me to work?"

"Because I love you. And because he's a mean bastard." Jonah's face was somber. "He beats his playmates afterward." He caressed her cheek. "I wouldn't want anything to happen to this pretty face."

"Why doesn't somebody have him arrested?" Kate asked indignantly.

"You don't get far in this business turning your clients over to the cops." He tipped her face up for a kiss.

Kate responded, but her mind was still on the client who liked girls who looked like her—and Juliet. What kind of man would act like that? For some reason an image of Nick popped into her mind. She had never seen Nick really angry. Would he turn violent like that man? Juliet had told her how furious Nick was the night Juliet overdosed on sleeping pills. Could he ever hate Juliet enough to pound some poor girl with his fists, just because the girl looked like her? Or like Kate? Of course not, Kate told herself. Not if she looked like me. He didn't even care enough about me to ask Juliet why I was never there when he visited Dani and Eden.

"What about Barry?"

For a moment, Kate thought Jonah was suggesting her mild-mannered husband as a possibility for the sadistic john he had just described. "Barry?"

"Think he's tired of Christie yet? I know I'm not tired of you."

As he nuzzled the hollow at the base of her neck, Kate realized she didn't care if Barry was tired of Christie. She didn't care about Barry at all.

TWENTY-ONE

1975

PEGGY HESITATED IN THE DOORWAY, HOLDING something behind her back. "Are you busy, Nick?"

Nick chuckled wryly. "Of all people, you should know the answer to that, babe." Allison's defection had dropped Picard Productions into a hole. His main accomplishment since then had been to dig the hole deeper. "What have you got there?"

"This." Peggy laid an open magazine on his desk.

Nick glanced at the full-page photograph. It took him a moment to realize the small elderly man in the picture was Freddie. And the gorgeous blonde, towering over Freddie in her heels, was Juliet. He scanned the accompanying article quickly. It was a puff piece on a television movie-of-the-week Juliet had produced that was coming out next month. Nick felt his jaw muscles stiffen. "No way, Peggy."

"You could just talk to him," Peggy pleaded.

"No."

"Look at her," she said, her mouth wrinkling in scorn. "She hasn't got a bit of talent for producing or directing, yet look at the budget he gave her. Call him, Nick."

"I don't need Freddie's help."

"You need someone's help," Peggy said mournfully. "I don't like to see you this way. You have too much talent to sit here idly."

He grinned at her. "Thanks for the vote of confidence. Now why don't you take the rest of the afternoon off?"

"Nick! I get off at five anyway. That's less than fifteen minutes."

"So? Don't ever say I'm not a generous boss. Hey," he said as she started out. "Don't you want your magazine back?"

"Don't ever say I'm not a generous secretary," Peggy replied smartly.

After she left, Nick sat there staring at the photograph, not at Freddie but at Juliet. It had been a long time since he'd seen her, he realized suddenly. And even longer than that since he'd really taken a good look at her.

God, she was still gorgeous! What was she now, thirty-six? She didn't look it. For a moment he was tempted to follow Peggy's advice and call her, not because he wanted her help but because he wanted to see her.

He couldn't do that, though; Juliet would think he was trying to use her connections with the studio. Or if she didn't think that, Freddie would.

Her eyes were still the vividly brilliant blue he remembered from their first night together.

Two lousy words, he thought: "My father." If it weren't for that line of dialogue, they might still be together. Why in the world had he ever written it?

Nick shoved back from his desk. He would be as generous with himself as with Peggy and knock off a few minutes early. Peggy had already left when he emerged from his office. He was locking the outer door when he suddenly decided to go back for the magazine. Maybe he *would* give Juliet a call tonight—congratulate her on her new project. When he left the office, his step was lighter than it had been in some time.

As he reached the street, he saw that a limousine was double-parked at the curb, blocking Nick's brand-new Corvette convertible. Nick walked around to the driver's side and tapped on the window with the magazine.

The window slid down, revealing a uniformed driver. "Sir?"

"Move it," Nick said. "That's my car."

"You'll have to speak to my employer, sir."

"Just move it, buddy. I'm in a hurry."

The driver opened the door and got out.

Nick stepped back, curling his hands into fists, ready to block a punch.

The driver walked past him, back to the passenger door, and opened it.

From inside the limousine, a voice said, "Hello, Nick." Toby Flynn leaned forward, smiling at him. "I'm back."

The magazine slipped from his hand, forgotten.

She was too good to be true, Nick thought as he listened to Toby run through the scene. Only a few weeks with a coach had removed the last traces of Texas from her speech. Melissa Carroll was good, one of the best, specializing in standard speech—mid-Atlantic, as Melissa was always pointing out. Nick had seen Melissa work her magic before, ironing the last limiting regionalism from an actor's voice. Never so quickly, though. Melissa told him yesterday she had never before seen as eager a pupil as Toby Flynn.

Neither had Nick. He had made three women stars and he planned to do it a fourth time, but even if he succeeded, using exactly the same methods, Toby was different. She had something, call it raw determination, that the others, even Juliet, had lacked.

Nick itched to get started. The plan was worked out to the smallest detail. He had admitted, but only to Whit, that it was a shameless rip-off of everything he had done before for each of his three famous ex-wives, right down to an erotic photo spread in *Playboy*, which he would time to coincide with the release of Toby's first film.

Toby wasn't a girl who required a safety net, he thought wryly. She had thrown herself into everything Nick suggested with an abandon that left him almost breathless. Instead of blanching or hesitating when he brought up the subject of photos, she was quick to point out possible poses.

Whit had been the only objector. "For God's sake, Nick!" he had exploded. "Isn't it enough that we got you out of a possible jam the first time she showed up? Why do you have to take another chance?"

Whit hadn't given any reasons for his apparent dislike of Toby besides her extreme youth, so that was the one Nick countered. "In four months she'll be eighteen," he told Whit. "Legal. That's when we'll get started."

Only he hadn't been able to wait. To Whit's disgust, Nick had gone ahead with the project, hiring the best speech coach in the business, a makeup artist, an acting coach. Nick smiled ruefully. Whit was still giving him hell.

That was nothing compared to what the lawyer's reaction would be if he found out Nick was sleeping with Toby again. That had been Toby's idea, not his. He'd like to see Whit walk away if an underage girl launched the kind of determined onslaught on him Toby had launched on Nick.

Melissa Carroll laid down the script. "Letter perfect, I would say, Mr. Picard."

Toby glanced at him hopefully.

"I'd say the same thing," he told Melissa. Toby, her face wreathed in smiles, bounced across the room to give him a hug. Nick hugged back. "You're a miracle worker," he told Melissa. "I'll see that your check reflects it."

"Thank you, Mr. Picard." Melissa had frowned slightly at Toby's display of affection. Nick's mention of her check smoothed the furrows away.

When Melissa left, Nick pulled Toby closer and kissed her urgently. He released her finally and looked down into her face. She looked so much like a young Juliet she took his breath away. "I love you, Toby Flynn."

"I love you too," she said, a smile crooking the corner of her mouth in a way that was distinctly Toby.

"No, I really love you," he corrected her. "The happily-ever-after kind of love. The will-you-be-my-wife kind of love."

She continued to look at him, slightly puzzled.

He gave her a small shake. "Well?"

"Well what, Nick?"

"I'm proposing, damn it!"

"Oh."

"Is that all you have to say?"

"Yes," Toby said, hugging him tightly. "I say yes."

They were married on November thirteenth, Toby's birthday. Whit was best man, but only after a fight. He had argued long and hard for a prenuptial contract. Nick refused to even broach the subject with Toby. "She's not marrying me for my money," he explained patiently for the fiftieth time, an hour before the wedding.

"My God, Nick! When a man has been married as many times as you have, you'd think he'd grow up a little. Or at least start looking out for his own interests. Women are like tigers on the prowl where men with assets are concerned. You should know that by now."

Nick straightened his tie. "She's eighteen years old today,

Whit. How predatory do you think an eighteen-year-old can be?"

"She won't always be eighteen. Or in love. If she is in love," Whit added bitterly.

But when Toby took her place beside him at the front of the chapel and lifted her veil, Nick noticed that even Whit drew in his breath at the sight of her lovely face.

1976

"Okay," Whit said. "Uncle. Does that make you feel any better?"

"You betcha," Nick told him. "It's not often you're wrong." Whit had argued loud and long about everything to do with *Tomorrow Morning*, from the fact that it starred Toby to the distribution deal Nick had cut with Freddie. Nick poured them both another glass of champagne. "If it makes you feel any better, I was flying blind a lot of the time. But it worked before. I didn't see why it wouldn't work with Toby too." And it did. The box office figures had made even Freddie happy. Not an easy thing to do.

Whit drained his glass in one gulp. "You had too much of your own money tied up to suit me."

Nick nodded. Nobody else had believed he could work his magic again, nobody but Toby. She was a wonder, all right, the most willing pupil he'd ever had. She always knew what he wanted before he could say it. She had even shown a grasp of the business side of moviemaking, something in which none of his other wives had been the least bit interested. It had been a relief to turn part of the details over to someone he could trust. Nick finished his own glass. "I wonder when our star will be ready," he said, pouring them both refills.

"Women," Whit said. "Here's to them." His date giggled.

She looked as though she were fourteen or fifteen but she had to be eighteen, Nick thought. Whit was scrupulous about things like that. Just as he had been several years ago about having his own bride-to-be sign the kind of prenuptial contract he'd nagged Nick about before Nick's wedding to Toby. Tina had emerged from her marriage to Whit without a nickel.

Nick flushed uncomfortably at the thought. If Whit knew that Nick had bankrolled Tina for the past year, Whit would really give him a hard time.

"Here she is, at long last. Our star." Whit raised his glass as Toby emerged from the bedroom. She wore a slim white jersey sheath—and apparently nothing else. Nick had chosen it himself. Looking at it now, and at the reaction on Whit's face, he almost regretted his choice.

Business, he reminded himself. Business before his personal feelings.

Toby sauntered over to him. "Hi, Pygmalion. What do you think?" She turned slowly, letting him have the full benefit of the dress, front and back, and then held out her hand for a glass of champagne.

"Pygmalion?" Whit said, his words beginning to slur. "Where did she learn that? Did you send her back to school?"

Toby shot him an irritated glance. She had realized on her own how much the lack of a high school education hampered her. One of the first things she had done after their marriage was hire a tutor. However, it wasn't a topic she liked to discuss.

"I think she's smart enough," Nick said, giving her a playful leer.

"Smarter than both of you," Toby snapped. She wasn't smiling.

Allison slipped off her glasses and massaged the bridge of her nose. The script she had been reading flipped closed

and slipped off her knees onto the bed between her and
Wilson.

He glanced up from the sheaf of papers he had been
going through. "What do you think of it so far?" he asked
eagerly.

In truth she was too tired to concentrate on the words.
The whirlwind pace of fund-raising and campaigning left
little extra time for her career, yet her career demanded
just as much time as it ever did. The only difference their
marriage of two months ago had made was that Wilson
expected even more of his wife than he had expected of
his lover. "I think it has possibilities. I'm only about a third
of the way through it. There are some problems."

"Now don't get technical on me," Wilson told her. "It's
got a good patriotic theme. That's what's important."

Allison slipped her glasses back on—Wilson hated them;
he said they made her look like a schoolteacher—and stared
at him coldly. "A film's politics is not always the most
important concern, Wilson. Its entertainment value has to
be considered also. Otherwise you'll never get your message
across."

Wilson's look reminded her somehow of her father.
"I really expected better from you, Allison. That kind
of attitude is exactly what is wrong with this country.
We've become a junk culture. Anything goes as long as
it's entertaining."

"Wilson, please," she said wearily. "I helped you write
that speech. For heaven's sake, don't lie there and quote
it back to me."

"I believe I should. You seem to have forgotten what we're
working toward here. We have a responsibility. . . ."

His voice rambled on, but Allison was too exhausted to
comprehend the words. Not only that, she had an early
call tomorrow, while Wilson's first appointment was a noon
luncheon with Senator MacLaren.

They might both be working for the same cause, that of getting Wilson elected governor of California, but Allison had noticed some workers' days began earlier than others.

Gwen put her hand over the mouthpiece of the phone just as Elsa came back from the kitchen with a plateful of sandwiches. "It's him." No matter that their customers ranged into the thousands after their years in the business. Both of them knew immediately who "him" was. "What have we got for him tonight?"

"You have a choice. Here are the new ones." She pushed a list over to her sister.

Gwen skimmed the names quickly and made tick marks beside three of them. Back on the phone once more, she described the candidates, listened for a moment, and then made a star beside one of the names.

"Good," Elsa said, when Gwen replaced the receiver. "That takes care of this month's profit." Elsa had been very concerned with profits for the past two years, ever since her husband found out what she was really making from the business. When he totaled up the figures, Mack had immediately sold his truck and turned the wage earning over to Elsa.

Gwen waved the list. "At this rate, we won't have any trouble keeping him in girls for the next ten years." Toby Flynn's movie had hit with such popularity that every girl on the street wanted to look like her. "Can you believe we bankrolled her?"

"Her" needed no more identification than "him."

"She paid us back," Elsa pointed out reasonably. "She didn't have to do that."

"Sure she did. She was afraid we'd try and blackmail her."

Elsa shook her head, but she didn't waste any breath arguing. She didn't waste much breath on anything these days, not with her ribs taped as tightly as they were from her last "discussion" with Mack over profits.

Mack didn't know that one of their girls had turned into the most popular movie star in the country. Neither sister was about to tell him. They had a nice little business going, and neither one of them wanted Mack messing it up with his bulldozer ways.

"It won't be long," Gwen blurted. "I talked to Oscar again yesterday."

"No!" Elsa put her hands over her ears. "I don't want to know."

Only when Gwen nodded vigorously and pantomimed crossing her heart, did Elsa remove her hands. A good thing too, because the phones were beginning to ring. Busy as they were, Gwen had trouble keeping her mind on her work. For all the years they had been in business, the sisters had been essentially law-abiding, bending no more rules than were absolutely necessary to run the kind of operation they had set up.

Now they had decided to take a fateful step, and it was all Mack's fault. Mack had made both their lives a living hell, because by making one of them, Elsa, miserable, he had made them both miserable. Divorce was out of the question; Mack would never give up all the easy money Elsa was bringing in. That was why Gwen had decided to call on Oscar for help. She didn't know if Oscar was going to kill Mack himself or have someone else do it. She didn't want to know—anymore than Gwen did.

Whatever he was going to do, she wished Oscar would go ahead and do it. Otherwise, she would be tempted to take care of Mack herself.

1977

"That old fart was trying to look down my dress!" Allison whispered heatedly to her husband, as the offender moved on down the receiving line.

"Allison!" Wilson Keating whispered back. "For God's sake, watch your—" He broke off as another potential contributor took his hand. "Hello, Mrs. Manville," he said in a normal voice.

When Mrs. Manville left off twittering and cooing over Wilson, she grabbed Allison, ignoring Allison's outstretched hand, and hugged her close. "My dear, I knew your father so well. So sad about his passing. But I'm sure he was very proud of you."

Allison recoiled. "Why would you think that?" she demanded bluntly.

"Why, because you're working so hard to support the party, you and your wonderful husband." Mrs. Manville smiled at Wilson. "Our next governor of this great state." She paused and looked more closely at Allison. "Aren't you feeling well, my dear?"

Wilson jabbed her in the ribs before she could reply. "She has a headache," he told Mrs. Manville.

"Why, my dear, surely not on this lovely occasion. Let me give you some aspirins." She opened her purse.

Allison took the two tablets and managed to force out her thanks from between clenched jaws. "I'll just get some water," she told Wilson and bolted out of the line before he could object.

She had almost reached the French doors leading to the garden when they swung open as another woman entered. "Excuse me," Allison said, starting to push on past her, and then stopped dead.

Kathleen Mallory laughed. "Should we introduce ourselves? I feel as though we already know each other, don't you? We ought to form some sort of club: the ex-wives of Nicholas Picard."

Allison laughed too, then. "You know what I wonder?" she said. "How long will it be before Toby Flynn is eligible to join?"

Kathleen Mallory was staring at her intently. "I hadn't realized just how much—"

"We look like each other! Nicholas Picard's two clones of Juliet Brittany." Allison's bitterness gave her laugh a high brittle sound. "Three, actually. Do you realize how much Toby Flynn looks like you, Kathleen?"

"Since she's fifteen years younger, I'm flattered to think so. And please, call me Kate." She glanced around the room. "How's it going in here? Are you raking in lots of donations?"

Allison grimaced. "Big bucks. I should be getting a percentage. With hazard pay based on the number of pinches and hugs I've had to endure from political fossils!" She felt almost intoxicated with the giddy feeling of finally being able to share her thoughts about tonight. What it was about Kate Mallory that made her feel that way, Allison wasn't sure, unless it was the uncanny sensation that she was merely talking to her own reflection. Tired as she was, Allison realized that what she needed most in the world was a friend. She had a strong sensation that Kate Mallory could be that friend. "I've got to have some fresh air. How about ducking out into the garden with me?" she offered abruptly. "I'll give you the lowdown on all the political intrigue involved in running for governor. Maybe you can turn it into another blockbuster novel."

"Shall we reinforce ourselves first?" Kate asked, as she stopped a passing waiter and plucked a glass of wine off his tray.

Allison reached for a glass too. As she started to lift it to her lips, Wilson grabbed her arm. "If you will excuse us, Miss Mallory," he said in a tone that allowed no room for dissent. Before Allison quite understood what was happening, he was pulling her across the room.

"Wilson!" She tried to jerk free of his grasp but only succeeded in spilling wine on the rug.

"Keep walking," he said. There was a violent undercurrent to his voice. He led her out of the room and down the hall to a small anteroom.

"Have you gone crazy?" Allison exclaimed when he slammed the door behind them.

"I was just about to ask you the same question. Why on earth were you consorting with that woman?"

"You mean Kathleen Mallory?"

"That is exactly who I mean. I don't know what has gotten into you tonight, Allison. You seem determined to do as much damage to my career as you can in the shortest amount of time."

"I have no idea what you're talking about. Kate Mallory happens to be a former wife of my ex-husband. We were just exchanging a few pleasantries."

"It's bad enough to emphasize the fact that you were once married to a man like Nicholas Picard. But to deliberately link yourself with a gangster!"

"What on earth are you talking about?"

"I don't suppose Kathleen Mallory got around to telling you who her current boyfriend is?"

"She's married to Barry Inman." Allison found herself longing desperately for a cigarette. "The literary agent. She has been for several years."

"She's having an affair with Jonah Rome. Do you know who he is?"

Her lips were suddenly dry. "He was in the news recently. Something about bribery?"

"Bribery of a federal judge, as a matter of fact. He's a criminal, Allison. He makes a habit of buying political figures so that he can dangle them from his watch chain. I can't afford to have my wife associated with him in the slightest way." Wilson straightened his tie, making an obvious effort to regain his composure. "We've got to get back."

    .   .   .

At dinner, Kate found herself seated across the table from
Allison Hilliard. However, this Allison was no longer the
warm woman Kate had met earlier in the evening. Now
she was nervous, twitchy, abrupt, playing with her food
without actually eating it. Never once did she look Kate's
way or acknowledge her presence at the table.

When the waiter whisked Allison's still full plate away,
her dinner partner made some remark, too low for Kate to
catch.

"Actually, I need to lose weight," Allison replied.

It was a strange comment, Kate thought, from a woman
whose figure would make a high fashion model feel flabby.

TWENTY-TWO

1978

Toby glanced up as the door to her office opened. "I'm really busy right now, Nick," she warned. "I'm supposed to go over these figures with the CPA at two, and I haven't finished."

"What do you expect me to do, make an appointment to see my own wife?"

"That would be nice." And wouldn't it just kill Nick's snooty secretary, Toby thought with a vicious little thrill. Old Peggy might not realize it, but her days with Picard Productions were numbered. She might be peaches and cream now, but Toby would never forget how Peggy rejected all her attempts to get in touch with Nick.

"I've created a monster," Nick said as he dropped down in the chair in front of her desk.

He said that a lot these days. It was beginning to get on Toby's nerves. She shoved the papers she'd been going over aside. "What do you want, Nick?"

"I feel like a pimp," he said, anger deepening his voice.

Toby stared at him steadily, willing herself not to react. "What's that supposed to mean?"

"It means that we're churning out films with no artistic value, simply for the money."

"Making money is what this business is all about, isn't it?"

"Twenty is too young to be a cynic," Nick told her.

"I'm not a cynic. I'm a realist." She understood exactly what was wrong with Nick. *Tomorrow Morning* had been Nick's biggest hit, doing better at the box office than any of his other pictures. After that, things had gone downhill fast. Toby's next two movies had made good money, but not on the scale of *Tomorrow Morning*. That wasn't what was eating Nick, though, Toby thought, tapping her mechanical pencil on the desk. His problem was with the reviews. All the critics claimed Nick had lost his touch. That Toby herself was a simply a caricature—and a poor one, at that—of Nick's other creations. Nick had decided he was an artistic failure. "You can't take a review to the bank, Nick. We're still making money. Maybe the ROI isn't as big as—"

"Jesus! You're starting to talk like an accountant instead of an actress."

"Maybe I don't want to be an actress anymore."

"That's just great." Nick stood up. "The critics are saying you weren't one in the first place. When you decide what you do want to be, let me know." He stomped out of her office, slamming the door behind him.

Toby shrugged and went back to the figures. She already knew what she wanted to be: head of Picard Productions.

Maybe today wasn't the best time to mention that.

1980

It was the same old argument, and Kate was thoroughly sick of it. "I think we should just call this whole thing off!" she said, leaping up from the bed. She grabbed her black lace teddy and stepped into it.

Jonah, a lazy smile on his face, grabbed her hand and pulled her back down to him. "Why is getting married so important to you, Kate?"

"It's not," she said and burst into tears.

"Don't, Kate," he murmured, holding her against his chest. "What's a ceremony when we have each other?"

"It's the *reason* you won't get married," she blurted. "Do you think I like knowing you could be murdered at any time? You won't marry me because you feel it would put me in too much danger. How do you think that makes me feel about you?"

"Kate, Kate." He covered her face with kisses.

"You won't even come back to a place like this because—" Her voice broke. She pulled away and glanced wildly around the cabin. She loved it here, isolated, in the mountains, away from Los Angeles, away from Jonah's illegal activities. It had taken a major effort on her part to get Jonah to break his ironclad rule of not meeting in the same place for the third time in a row, but he had finally given in. She knew from that small victory he would eventually give in on the other things too. Would marry her. Would even eventually leave his criminal activities behind him.

"I just want the best for you, Kate." He pulled her close once more. "You mean so much to me. More than anyone else ever has, ever could."

"Then marry me!"

She felt his arms tighten convulsively around her. Then he pushed her gently back, until he was looking into her face. "All right," he said.

For a moment, the tiniest moment, she couldn't believe she had won at last, and then she was laughing and crying at the same time—and so was he, because they both knew what that victory meant.

"Get dressed," he told her at last, when they had both calmed a little. "I'm taking you back to LA. We're gonna buy you the biggest damn engagement ring in southern California."

She was touched. "Jonah, you don't have to."

"I want to." He patted her on the rear. "Get some clothes on, woman. I'll put our things in the car."

Now that he had finally given in, Jonah seemed like a new man. He hustled around the cabin, packing their suitcases, gathering up all the personal items they had brought with them.

"Can't you hurry it up?" he said, when he turned and caught her watching him instead of fixing her makeup. "Why are you grinning like that anyway?"

"Just happy, I guess."

"You can be happy on the way into the city," he said as he carried the suitcases outside.

Kate lingered for one last look at her face. "Thank you, Nick," she whispered as she gazed at the image in the mirror. "Thank you for giving me Kathleen Mallory's face." She leaned forward and planted a swift kiss on the cool silver surface and then hurried out the door after Jonah.

He was already in the driver's seat. "Hurry up," he called. "You don't want to give me a chance to change my mind, do you?"

Kate laughed as she knelt to slip the key to the cabin under the mat.

In the silence of the forest, the explosion sounded like the end of the world. The force of the blast flung Kate against the cabin door.

She scrambled to her feet, still clutching the key in her hand.

The car was gone. In its place was a huge bonfire, thirty feet tall.

"Jonah!" she screamed. "Jonah!"

The crackle of the flames was the only answer.

Freddie's limousine, the studio logo emblazoned on the side, pulled away from the curb just as Nick arrived at his office. When Nick went inside, he found Peggy busily transcribing notes. "What's up?"

He was surprised to see her color faintly. "Mr. Yates and Miss Flynn just finished a meeting."

"A meeting about what?"

"Distribution."

"They had a meeting about that? Why wasn't I notified?"

"I'm sure it was an oversight, Nick."

"It was no oversight," Toby said from the door of her office. "Frederick and I work well together. You make him irritable. We got everything settled in an hour."

"Just the same, I don't like you cutting me out of the negotiations." He glanced at Peggy, and the expression of pity on her face made him even angrier. "Damn it, Toby! You act like you're running things."

Toby stared at him for a moment. "I am running things, Nick. Get used to it." She went in her office and closed the door.

"Nick," Peggy said urgently.

He ignored her, striding across to the door of his own office. When he flung it open, he halted. A man was sitting across from his desk. Not a man, a bum.

"Nick," Peggy said quietly, "I tried to tell you. It's Barry Inman. He said it was important."

"Nick!" Barry Inman stood up, came toward him.

Nick was so startled by Barry's appearance that he just stood there, not even extending his hand until the last moment.

"I hate to barge in like this," Kate's husband said. "But I need your help."

He had been one of the neatest men Nick had ever seen, neat in his personal habits, neat in his choice of clothing. Now he was unshaven, his shirt spotted, his tie awry, his suit badly in need of cleaning and so rumpled it looked as though he had slept in it. And his smell. . . .

"Have you heard from Kate?" Barry asked.

"Kate? Why? Is something wrong? Is she all right."

"She divorced me." Barry began to cry silently, his shoulders heaving.

Nick jerked his head at Peggy to leave them, which she did, closing the door behind her. Ignoring the man's sour smell, Nick put his arm around Barry's shoulders and guided him over to the sofa.

Slowly Barry regained control of himself, hiccuping slightly as the tears slowed. "You probably think I'm crazy. I don't care. The worst thing I ever did was let her meet that man."

Jonah Rome. Nick had seen the stories about his death and his involvement with Kate in the papers. "I tried to call her several times after the murder. I couldn't get through to her," Nick said.

"I couldn't get through to her either," Barry said bitterly. "And I was right there. She shut me out. She shut everybody out."

"Where is she now? What's she doing?"

"I don't know." Barry sank back on the sofa, closing his eyes. "I would have taken care of her, but she didn't want me around her anymore."

"Look, Barry, your troubles with Kate—"

"It wasn't my fault I got involved with that girl. He set me up. He wanted me out of the way so he could screw my wife!"

"Barry. . . ."

He sat up, his eyes pleading. "I need a job, Nick. Nobody will give me a job. If you could just put in a word for me."

Apparently Barry hadn't gotten the word that Nicholas Picard was no longer anyone of importance. Nick sighed.

"I'll work hard, Nick. All I need is a chance."

"It's all right, Barry. I'll help you find something." Even, he thought grimly, if he had to ask Toby to put in a word with Freddie.

Barry pumped Nick's hand. "I can't tell you how much this means to me." He scrambled to his feet, visibly relieved.

Nick stood, too, and reached for his billfold. He extracted two fifties. "Gasoline money," he explained when Barry shook his head. "A loan."

"I don't need money. I just need to feel like a man again. A man doesn't live on his wife's money. Or his ex-wife's money. Get me that job, Nick. That's all I need."

Nick stopped at Peggy's desk after walking Barry out to his car. "I need to talk to Toby about something," he told her. "Is she free?"

"I'm sorry, Nick. She's got meetings the rest of the afternoon."

"Who with?"

Peggy turned the appointment book around so he could read the names himself. She didn't say anything. She didn't have to.

Two years ago those men would have been meeting with him. Not today. It might still be called Picard Productions, but Toby was firmly in charge. And doing a damn fine job, Nick reminded himself. He should be applauding her. Somehow, though, he didn't feel like it.

1983

It felt funny being here alone, without Jonah.

An irrational feeling, Kate told herself, as she got out of bed, but one she experienced every morning nonetheless. She and Jonah had been in this place for less than two weeks total, the three times they had come here. She had already lived here by herself for three years.

She still missed him.

Kate had slept in her long underwear. Now she pulled jeans and a heavy wool sweater on top of the long johns and went to start the water boiling for coffee. While the coffee was brewing, she scrambled herself an egg and made toast. She liked to pretend she was making breakfast for both of them, that the jeans and sweater, bought purposely too large, were his.

Pretend. If only she could pretend he was still alive.

She washed the dishes and then put on a heavy down jacket and went outside to chop wood in the chill morning air. By the time she finished, the sun was well up and she was warm enough to discard the jacket. She carried the wood, armload by armload, and piled it on the porch, then went inside to wash up.

The typewriter waited for her on a table by the window. A square of sunlight fell on the stack of pristine white paper beside it. Kate had bought the typewriter and paper yesterday, when she drove out for supplies. When she returned she had spent a good hour finding just the perfect spot in the cabin for a workplace. Last night, before she went to bed, she had laid the typing paper out, so that everything would be in readiness this morning.

The sight of the ream of blank white paper made her stomach knot with panic. What could she find to say after all these years of saying nothing?

She forced herself to sit down in front of the typewriter and insert a piece of paper. "Jonah," she whispered. His presence was very strong in the cabin at that moment. Suddenly, Kate knew what it was she wanted to write about, had to write about.

She spaced down to the middle of the page and typed CHAPTER ONE.

.   .   .

It was well past midnight, but Toby was still in her office going over the long lines of figures. She had brushed aside Nick's offer to drive her home hours earlier and dismissed Peggy with a wave of her hand. She had something to celebrate, and she knew neither one of them would appreciate it.

Her net worth.

She gritted her teeth, thinking of all the fun Sloan Whitney had poked at her for taking classes in her spare time: accounting classes, bookkeeping classes. She could hire somebody to do that, Nick had told her; she didn't have to bother herself. Neither one of them understood how important it was to her that she understand what was going on in the business. Her business, as of today—and Nick didn't have a clue.

He had turned everything over to her, all the details, and she had accepted the work gladly. Old Whit had been too juiced and too involved with his parade of teenage girlfriends to worry much about the legal side of things, so Nick had given her more and more authority.

It might still be called Picard Productions, but as of today it was hers—and worth more money than she ever dreamed existed when she was back in Mesquite, Texas, living in Momma's trailer house.

Toby reached in the drawer of her desk and took out the envelope she had placed there earlier in the day. Peggy had brought it in to her this morning, a puzzled look on her face. "Did you send this?" she asked as she laid it on the desk.

"Yes, I did," Toby said calmly, while her heart hammered away in her chest. Peggy had already slit it open. Seen the check inside.

"Someone you knew?"

"A long time ago," Toby told her, in a tone that invited no further questions. It had taken her years to get to the point where she felt safe sending money to Momma, even if the check was from Picard Productions and her signature was illegible. Toby was still frightened that she might somehow be connected with Big John's murder. She could have sent the money anonymously, could have left off the return address. But her yearning to connect with her mother after all these years had been even stronger than her healthy instinct for self-preservation.

In the midnight quiet of her office, Toby balanced the envelope in the palm of her hand and wondered whose hand had written the word that returned it to her a month after she mailed it.

It didn't matter.

She turned the envelope over and read her momma's name where she had typed it herself. And, beneath that, the one-word message: *Deceased.*

Toby stuck the envelope back in her desk and pulled out her business checkbook. She turned to the stub for the check she had written Momma and wrote *Void* across it. Then she leafed forward to a fresh check and wrote in Peggy's name. The amount she had sent to her mother would be just the right amount of severance pay for Nick's snooty secretary, she thought, as she filled out the check.

And when Nick came crashing through her office door demanding to know why she had fired his secretary, Toby would give him his walking papers too.

1986

Barry patted the manuscript box on the banquette beside him. "I can't wait to read it. More wine?"

While he signaled the waiter, Kate took a moment to really look at him. Had she made a mistake in turning her manuscript over to him? He was not the same man she married, not even the man she divorced, but a stranger, thin, pale, and sickly looking. Perhaps that came from his living in New York now. For her part, Kate was eager to get this over with and get back to California.

"I can't tell you how glad I am you thought of me, Kate. This will be quite a coup." He leaned forward a little tipsily, and she wondered if he had indulged in a few drinks before lunch. "I can tell you my career hasn't been going as well as it might have." He patted the box again. "This will make the difference," he predicted.

Kate felt uncomfortable. He wasn't the first agent she had contacted or even the fifth. She had been out of the public's eye for so long the publishing industry had written her off. She had come to Barry only as a last resort. Thank goodness he hadn't guessed.

Barry smiled at her almost coyly. "I should have some news for you within the week. Will you be staying on a few days?"

"I'm flying to Los Angeles this afternoon. I have things to do." Some threads of her life to pick up. But those threads didn't include her ex-husband.

Barry's face fell. "I had hoped—well, perhaps next time you're here."

Later, on the plane, Kate found herself wondering why she ever married Barry in the first place.

Because he was safe.

Better safe than sorry, the old saw went. But she would rather be sorry a thousand times over than to have missed a single moment of her time with Jonah. She fumbled for her sunglasses and got them on just in time to hide the tears welling up in her eyes.

Juliet was waiting right outside the gate when Kate got off the plane. "I've missed you," she said, hugging Kate fiercely. "It's been too long."

"Are the girls with you?"

"They both have dates tonight, but we'll see them tomorrow. Now come on." Juliet tugged at her. "Let's get your luggage. We have so much to catch up on." Juliet looked wonderful, the sleek, polished studio executive. Kate felt dowdy beside her.

Strange that it was Juliet she had called when she decided she was moving back to Los Angeles, Kate thought as they rounded up her luggage. But Juliet had been delighted to help her with all the details of moving and had located her a house to rent. She even insisted Kate stay at her home while the rental house was being repainted.

"So is this a permanent move?" Juliet asked when they were finally in Juliet's Jaguar. "How could you stand to live out in the woods by yourself for so long? I would have gone crazy!"

"It was what I needed," Kate said slowly. "But now I need something else. My daughter, for one thing. I've got a lot of catching up to do with Dani."

Juliet looked at her doubtfully. "If you're planning on mothering her, Kate, I think you're a little late. Both girls are used to going their own ways. They're not children anymore."

Juliet had written faithfully, keeping Kate informed on all the girls' activities. Dani was working for a casting director. Eden was acting; she had already had several bit parts in movies.

Kate stared down at her hands. "I know she's all grown up, but I have to try."

It was three days before Kate could catch Dani alone—and then only by demanding Eden give them a few minutes.

"That was rude, Mother," Dani complained. To Kate's dismay, the sullen set of Dani's face made her daughter look more plain than usual. "After all, it's Eden's house."

"She has her own apartment. And she has been deliberately trying to keep us apart!" Kate realized how strident she sounded. "I'll apologize to her later, but I need to talk to you, Dani. Really talk."

"Don't bother apologizing." Dani dropped down on the sofa, extending her long legs. She must have gotten her height from Nick, Kate thought irrelevantly. "Eden was sticking like glue because I asked her to. I wasn't in the mood for any maternal lectures."

"What made you think I was going to lecture you?" Kate asked calmly, determined not to show how hurt she was.

"Really, Mother, what else have I ever gotten from you?"

"That's not fair, Dani. Perhaps, I've been—"

"You haven't been anything. Except away, for most of my life. With your husband. And your gangster boyfriend. And then sulking in the woods by yourself. Do you realize Juliet has been more of a mother to me than you have?"

"I realize you chose to view her that way from a very young age," Kate said stiffly. "I can't compete with Juliet in a lot of areas, but I am your mother, Dani, your real mother. I want to act like it for a change."

Dani stood up. "I'm twenty-three years old. Did you realize that? I doubt it, because you didn't even send me a card on my birthday, let alone call. Juliet didn't send a card, either, because she never sends cards. Instead, she baked a huge cake and gave me the same kind of birthday party she always gives me—just like Eden's. She has always treated me like a daughter. You never have. It's too late to start now."

When Dani stalked out, Kate remained seated. She couldn't decide who she hated more, Juliet for acting like Dani's mother or herself for acting like anything but.

1987

"I'm Frederick's golden girl now," Juliet crowed over the phone. "Thanks to you."

"You were doing fine without me," Kate told her. It wasn't false modesty, either. Juliet had become a personage to be reckoned with at the studio.

"If you hadn't put in a word with Barry, I'd never have gotten the dramatic rights to *Means and Ends*." Juliet had launched an intense campaign to acquire the rights to Kate's novel before publication, planning to turn it into a miniseries. Frederick had been lukewarm on the topic, but Juliet had been so enthralled by what *Publishers Weekly* had called "searing revelations about prostitution and gangsterism" that she had put her position with the studio on the line with her bid.

In spite of that, Barry had refused Juliet's offer until Kate's intervention. His plan had been to sell the book as a feature film instead of as a miniseries. Kate had asked him to sell Juliet the rights for just one reason—Dani. She had hoped this sign of her cooperation with Juliet would ease some of the tension between them.

It had not.

"I've got to run," Juliet said. "I've still got a million wedding details to take care off. I can't believe the big day is only a month away." Eden was marrying a young French director—over Nick's objections, according to Juliet. "You're coming, aren't you?"

"I wouldn't miss it." A lie. The last thing Kate wanted was to see Dani as Eden's plain and gawky maid of honor. She would think of some excuse not to be there.

When Juliet hung up, Kate slumped back in her chair. The call had been a welcome interruption in a boring day.

For the past six months she had been coasting along on a wave of acclaim for *Means and Ends*. The hardcover had been on every best-seller list in the country. The paperback was timed to publish with the miniseries. Things couldn't be going better, except for one tiny detail.

Now that she finally had the leisure to go back to work on a new book, Kate had discovered she couldn't write a word.

1988

This time they had to keep him waiting for almost three weeks while they lined up a new girl. "I told him," Elsa grumbled to Gwen. "I told him if he didn't treat them so mean, they'd be willing to come back for seconds."

"I don't like it," Gwen said. "He mistreats our girls. I don't care how much he pays."

"But they care," Elsa reminded her. "If we warn them beforehand and it's their decision, it's their problem if anything goes wrong."

Elsa would never have said anything like that in the old days. But after Mack died—a hit-and-run accident, the papers had called it—Elsa blossomed. She had lost 109 pounds, revealing a svelte and striking woman beneath all that padding.

Elsa didn't care as much about the quality of girls they used anymore, either. She was always raving to Gwen about how the world was changing and they had to change too. So some of their girls were strung out on cocaine, some on other things Gwen didn't like to think about. She also didn't like to think about how nervous Elsa was sometimes, like maybe she needed a fix herself. Or how much of Elsa's money just seemed to vanish into thin air. Or, more likely, up Elsa's nose.

It had been Elsa who located tonight's girl for him. Gwen had talked to the girl, trying to explain what she might be in for, but the girl had been so high on something, Gwen was afraid she hadn't gotten through.

"It's the woman with him," Elsa said abruptly. "He wasn't as bad when he was alone. All the girls say she's the vicious one."

Gwen nodded. The woman had become a standard part of the arrangements two years before. A masked blonde, she seldom spoke but she took part. In fact, most of the girls claimed it was the woman who took the lead. "We ought to tell him nothing doing when she's part of it."

"We can't," Elsa said. "We need the money. I need the money." She stood up. "I'll be right back." She grabbed her purse and disappeared down the hall. Gwen heard the bathroom door shut. In a few minutes, Elsa would come back totally wired, and Gwen would pretend she didn't notice a thing.

Sometimes, Gwen thought, she almost wished Mack were back. Because that would mean the old Elsa was back too.

She missed the old Elsa.

TWENTY-THREE

1989

ALLISON SHOVED THE SCRIPT AWAY AND REACHED FOR another. It was hard to find a suitable role these days. There were so few decent roles for actresses to begin with. On top of that, she had to choose each part she played with an eye as to how it would affect Wilson's career as well as her own.

At least she was no longer having to juggle the role of governor's wife too. After two terms as governor, Wilson had decided to follow Ronald Reagan's example and not seek a third. He planned to follow Reagan's example in another way: he wanted to occupy the Oval Office in '93.

Allison threw down the second script, aware that it was not the fault of the words on the page. Wilson and Senator MacLaren were having a council of war in Wilson's study and it irked her beyond reason that she had not been invited to sit in, particularly since she was expected to turn over most of the money from her acting career to Wilson's campaign. He would be asking for her inheritance from her father's estate next, she thought angrily.

Everything they owned, including this huge Spanish-style stucco house, and everything Wilson had attained politically had been due to the funds she furnished. Yet

Wilson still viewed her as a detriment to his career. That angered Allison more than anything else.

It was what brought her to her feet and sent her striding down the hallway to Wilson's study. Too late, she found when she reached it. Senator MacLaren was on the verge of leaving.

"Allison! So good to see you." The senator paused only long enough to hug her to his huge bearlike chest before he lumbered out.

Allison followed her husband back into his study. Wilson sat down at his desk and looked up at her with a puzzled expression. "Did you want something?"

"I want to be in on your campaign plans," she said without preamble.

Wilson scowled. "Impossible. Don't you think I have enough trouble smoothing over the difficulty your career causes? Those movies you made with Picard." He shook his head. "Do you think Senator MacLaren would give me the kind of support he does if he was constantly reminded of the kind of actress you've been?"

Allison felt as though he had struck her. "How can you say that?"

He came around the desk and took her hand. "I know what you're thinking, Allison. You want to help me get in the White House. The best way for you to do that is to continue doing exactly what you are doing. I realize I'm being blunt, but I think we owe it to each other to be honest. If it were not for the amount of money you channel into my campaign, Senator MacLaren would withdraw his support. Being married to you means I have to walk a very straight line where he's concerned. And that doesn't include inviting you to our discussions." He reached for his briefcase. "I've got an appointment now, but we can talk more about it tonight, if you like."

Allison followed Wilson to the door and watched him

stride down the hall, "Honest Abe" on his way to Pennsylvania Avenue. If Wilson Keating were ever forced to choose between his wife and the White House, Allison knew which one he would pick.

The girl was very young, fourteen or fifteen, and very high. "How many of you?" she asked for the second time, as though the number of people in the room kept doubling and redoubling.

"You were paid," the man said. "That's all you need to know."

"How many?" the girl mumbled.

"Shut up," the woman said.

The girl looked at her. "Who are you?"

"Aren't you going to start?" the woman asked the man.

"She's not right," the man whined. "She doesn't look right."

"I look like Toby Flynn," the girl blurted. "That's what you wanted."

"No. Juliet. Juliet Brittany," the man protested.

The girl blinked. "Who?"

The woman turned to the man impatiently. "What does it matter? Aren't you going to start?"

"I can't. She doesn't look right."

"Then I will," the woman said.

"How many?" the girl said.

The woman struck the young prostitute so hard across the face that the girl's lower lip split. Blood welled up in bright red drops.

"Not the face," the girl said.

"Oh, yes," the woman said, as she raised her hand again. "Particularly the face."

Gwen almost missed the small item in the back pages of the *Los Angeles Times*. She read it with growing horror, knowing now why the girl they sent out last week had never collected her money.

"It doesn't have anything to do with us," Elsa said when Gwen showed her the article.

"What if it was him?" Gwen demanded. "What if he was the one who killed her?" Her stomach lurched as she thought of that poor girl, her face beaten beyond recognition.

"She could have met a dozen other johns that night."

"There was that girl last year. Marla. She never showed up again either. What if—"

"You don't know. You're just guessing. It's not our business to guess."

"We shouldn't do it anymore. When he calls, tell him no." Gwen shuddered. "Especially if the woman will be with him. Tell him no."

"We need the money," Elsa said. "*I* need the money."

"Not that way," Gwen cried.

Elsa looked at her sister with cold, hard eyes. Stranger's eyes. "Any way I can get it," she said.

Toby picked up the receiver and then put it down again. She had the number right in front of her. It had been on her desk for a solid week, and yet she couldn't bring herself to dial it.

It had been easy to find out what Nick's other ex-wives were doing. Allison Hilliard was always in the paper for something or other to do with politics. And Toby saw Juliet Brittany several times a month at the studio or at parties. But Kathleen Mallory was a mystery lady. That might appeal to a man like Nick.

Everything she always wanted, Toby mused. She thought that was what she had when she took over Picard Productions. She had been so sure of it. But recently she had begun to realize what it was she really wanted. What she had let slip through her fingers.

She opened the desk drawer and took out the worn envelope with her mother's address on the front. Six years ago, when it was returned to her with the scribbled word *Deceased* across it, Toby had believed it was time to start a new life. She had felt she didn't need Nicholas Picard anymore.

Professionally, that had been true. Picard Productions, unhampered by Nick's artistic pretensions, had become a real moneymaker. But personally? That was something else. She needed Nick, needed his love. It was time she got him back.

The only problem was Nick's rage where she was concerned. He never forgave her for tossing him out of his own production company. For the first few months, his wild threats had filtered back to her. Then he dropped out of view. When he lost Picard Productions, he became a nonentity. No one was interested in where he was or what he was doing.

Except me, Toby thought.

Kate tried not to let her puzzlement show as the housekeeper ushered Toby Flynn into the living room. She had no idea why Toby had asked for this meeting. "Would you like something to drink?"

"Coffee," Toby said.

When the housekeeper had poured their coffee and left, Kate found Toby studying her with curious eyes.

"We really do look alike, don't we?" the younger woman said.

Kate touched her own face, wondering if her skin still looked as good as Toby's. "I'm almost old enough to be your mother."

"If you'd had a child at fifteen." Toby's laugh was harsh,

a painful sound. "You really don't look like the type, Kathleen."

"My friends call me Kate."

"I'm not exactly a friend, am I? How *do* you classify your ex-husband's ex-wife?"

"I suppose," Kate said slowly, "it depends on why you came to see me today."

Toby launched into a pitch for a new movie that she claimed was perfect for Kate.

Kate listened skeptically. Something wasn't quite right here, she thought. No one else in Hollywood was urging forty-seven-year-old women to return to the screen. When Toby paused for breath, Kate said as much.

"That's been the problem with having the industry dominated by men," Toby told her. "They make movies for eighteen-year-old boys to take their dates to. I want to make a movie that will bring women back to the theaters again."

"You're talking to the wrong person. Why don't you try Juliet Brittany? She's only three years older than I am, and she's always wanted to get back into films. Or Allison Hilliard."

"Juliet's a producer now, not an actress. And Allison Hilliard's husband wants too much control over any project she's in. You're what I had in mind for this film. With your literary background, I thought perhaps you and Nick could work on a script idea together."

"Nick?" Kate's heart made a funny little double beat. "Would he want to?"

"You're not in touch with him?"

"No. I haven't spoken to him in years." Kate smiled self-consciously, trying to mask the hurt caused by that simple statement. "Not since our divorce."

"Oh." The enthusiasm seemed to go out of Toby Flynn all in a moment.

She left soon after that, leaving Kate wondering what the real purpose of her visit had been.

The question stayed with Kate the rest of the day and then evolved into a more complicated one: Had Nick worked as hard to create the image of Toby Flynn as he had that of Kathleen Mallory?

If he had, who was the real Toby Flynn?

Whoever she was, she had definitely not been what Nick expected. Otherwise she would never have been able to oust him from Picard Productions.

For just a moment Kate felt a trace of sadness, thinking about Nick and about what it must have been like for him to lose the company he had founded. It had been—my God, it had been twenty-four years since she had seen him! At first it was because she didn't trust herself around him. She had been too devastated when he left her for Allison. And afterward there had been Jonah.

Kate glanced at her typewriter, untouched for so long. For the first time in a long while she felt a flutter of anticipation, a desire to place her hands on the keys once more.

Whatever reason Toby had for coming today, it might have an effect she hadn't planned.

Ten minutes after she got the call from Gwen, Toby was in her car. She didn't wait for Kate's housekeeper to announce her. She pushed past the woman and strode down the hall, finding Kate in her study. "What the hell do you think you're doing?" she blazed.

"Hello, Toby," Kate said calmly. She switched off the typewriter. "How nice of you to drop by. If you had called first, I would have had the coffee ready."

"Cut the bullshit," Toby told her. "I know what you're doing. Stop prying into my life."

Kate lifted an eyebrow. "I'm afraid I don't—"

"Look, you bitch! If you don't stop poking your nose into my business, you're going to get hurt."

"Are you threatening me? If you are, perhaps I'd better call my lawyer."

"I'm warning you," Toby raged. "Leave me alone, or you'll be sorry!"

"What are you so frightened of, Toby? Do you have something to hide?"

Toby stared at Kate and then turned and rushed from the room. When she reached her car, Toby turned and looked back at the house. Kate Mallory was watching her from the window.

Something to hide? You bet I've got something to hide, you bitch. And you'll be sorry if you don't stop prying. I'll make you sorry.

The information Kate was waiting for came later that same afternoon, delivered by hand in a plain manila envelope. It was hard to see why Toby had been so worried, Kate thought, leafing through the papers. Very few people would have had the connections to discover her link to a call girl operation. Even fewer would be able to uncover what Kate held in her hands. The private investigator she first hired had drawn a complete blank. It was only after she went to Jonah's friends that Kate had been able to learn Toby's little secret.

Too bad she wasn't a blackmailer, Kate thought. The information she held was explosive enough that she could ask any price from Toby Flynn and get it.

The drive to Carmel was beautiful. Kate took her time, loafing along the way. "I'm so glad you could see me," she told Beth Wescott when she finally arrived at the Wescotts' summer home.

"I just couldn't believe that a famous person like you

would want to interview me," Mrs. Wescott babbled. "How did you ever find out about us?"

"As I told you on the phone, I'm researching a book about adoptive parents. I was given your name in confidence. I certainly won't reveal your real name without your permission if I decide to use your story in my book."

"That's good," Beth Wescott said. "Lee, my husband, is dead now, but his parents are still alive and he never wanted his parents to know that our daughter was adopted."

"Catherine is what—fifteen?"

Beth Wescott nodded. "We call her Cat." She frowned. "She should be home soon. I don't know how *she'll* react to all this. She's moody sometimes."

Moody wasn't quite the word for it, Kate thought, when Cat Wescott finally appeared. There was something different—very, very different—about the girl. And at the same time, something hauntingly familiar.

The girl's beauty was overwhelming. Her eyes were china blue, her hair a silken blond, and she had a model's figure and a dancer's grace. Cat Wescott would be a cinch to star in one of Toby Flynn's films if she were only a little older. Kate wondered if Toby knew what a gorgeous creature her daughter had become.

Kate had been there over an hour when, almost reluctantly, Beth pleaded an appointment as Kate had asked her to do and left the two of them alone.

When Kate suggested a walk on the beach, thinking the girl might be more forthcoming out of the house, Cat agreed, but with no particular enthusiasm.

"Did your mother tell you why I'm here?" she asked the girl.

"She said you're writing a book." Complete disinterest.

"About adopted children." Kate took a deep breath. "Have you ever wondered about your parents?"

"What about them?"

"Who they are? Why they gave you up for adoption?"

"It's not so hard to figure why my mother gave me up. They paid her."

"What about your father? Do you ever wonder who he was? What he was like?"

Cat looked at her without a trace of curiosity in her glance. "Why would I care about that?"

With Beth Wescott's intervention, Kate was able to see the Wescott lawyer the day after her drive back from Carmel.

"You understand I wouldn't be talking to you without Beth Wescott's permission. Frankly, I don't understand why she would want any of this aired." Peter Burns was certainly not overawed at being interviewed by a celebrity writer, Kate noted. In fact, he was downright hostile.

"Mrs. Wescott told me that there was some unpleasantness after Cat's adoption. Something to do with the physician who recommended the mother to them."

"You have to understand that Lee was quite a bit older than Beth and absolutely foolish about her. When Beth found out she couldn't have a child, she was devastated. Otherwise, he would never have been interested in adopting Cat. The doctor who told the Wescotts about the mother gave them a totally false picture of her. When Lee found out the truth—"

"The truth?"

"She was a prostitute. A beautiful girl, but then she'd had a very expensive plastic surgery job."

"How do you know that?"

"Lee saw the scars after the girl moved in with them, while they were waiting for the baby to be born. That was when he had me investigate her more thoroughly. When he found out the truth about her, he wanted to call the whole thing off, but by then Beth was too hooked on the idea of the baby."

"Do you know who the father was?"

Kate had been making notes, her pen racing across the pad. The sudden silence made her glance up.

"Yes, I do, Miss Mallory. The father was one Nicholas Picard." The pen dropped from Kate's fingers. "I understand that name is familiar to you," Peter Burns said.

"Are you sure?"

"The girl was underage at the time. She tried to get in touch with Mr. Picard. She found it impossible to do so. That was why she agreed to give the baby up for adoption."

So that was why Cat looked so familiar. A lot of things suddenly fell into place for Kate. "Did Nick know about the child?" she asked as she retrieved the pen.

The lawyer shrugged.

"Does the girl, Cat, seem a little strange to you?"

"She has a screw loose somewhere," Burns declared flatly. "Cat was sleeping around by the time she was twelve. She started with high school boys and moved on to Lee's friends and business associates. That's what drove Lee to an early grave. Beth has refused to face the facts."

"Which are?"

"She should be institutionalized. Lee knew that. I know that. You'd know it if you talked to her for more than five minutes. Beth is the only one who can't seem to grasp what the girl is really like. She's been working as a prostitute here in LA. That's why they're in Carmel now. Beth thinks if she keeps Cat away from the Evil Big City, her little girl will turn out all right."

"Do you?"

"I think Cat Wescott is rotten to the core."

Outside the lawyer's office, Kate sat in her car and flipped through her note pad. No wonder Toby had warned her off.

It was an explosive piece of information, affecting both Toby and Nick.

What was she going to do with it? Kate asked herself.

She had no idea what the answer was.

It was a party Juliet would just as soon not attend, let alone host herself. But Eden and Dani refused to listen to her objections, especially since Eden had flown in from France for the event, leaving her husband behind. They had thrown themselves into the arrangements with such fervor Juliet had no choice but to go along.

The girls swept through her wardrobe like a whirlwind, tossing dresses around the bedroom, and finally declared she had nothing suitable to wear for such a momentous occasion. The three of them spent a week shopping for the perfect dress. No sooner did they settle on her dress than new discussions began on her hair. Then her makeup. Then her nails.

No detail was too small for the two of them to argue over. Not with Juliet, with each other. Juliet was just the amused bystander.

She had to admit the results were worth it, Juliet thought, as she glanced at the glamorous woman in the mirror one last time.

"Come on!" Dani called from the doorway. "Everyone is here!"

"I was just trying to decide if I need a cane to hobble downstairs," Juliet said, grinning.

Dani hugged her. "You'll never need a cane. You're never going to get old."

As they went down together, hand in hand, Juliet saw Eden waiting for them at the foot of the stairs. How strange, she thought. The last thing in the world I ever wanted was a child, even Nick's, and here I've ended up with two of them. Two daughters.

When she reached the foot of the stairs Juliet took Eden's hand, while still holding Dani's, and drew them both close. "I love you both," she whispered. "Very, very much."

"Here you are!" a triumphant female voice cried, as a camera flash went off.

"Leonie," Juliet said. "How wonderful to see you." A lie, of course. It was never wonderful to see the petite redhead. But Leonie Denton's column in *LA Today* made her a very important woman. That was why the girls had invited her to Juliet's birthday party. Juliet gave no sign that she had just received a pinch from Eden and a jab in the ribs from Dani, reminding her of that fact. She stepped forward to peck the air beside Leonie's cheek and receive a similar gesture in return.

"You look awfully good for someone who just hit the half-century mark," Leonie observed.

Juliet groaned. "Do you have to put it in those terms, Leonie? You make me sound like a monument."

"Now, Leonie," Eden said briskly, "we invited you to have fun, not to torment Mother."

"It's going to be your family's day in my column tomorrow." Leonie paused coyly. "It's been awhile since your father was an item."

"Daddy?" the girls said together.

Only they weren't really girls anymore, Juliet thought, her mind not really on Leonie's teasing remark. They were women: Dani twenty-six last month and Eden only two months away from the same birthday. The time couldn't be far off when she would be not only fifty but a grandmother as well, Juliet thought, with something approaching alarm.

Leonie's voice broke into her thoughts. "I'm wondering what you'll think when you see the item, Juliet. After all, it's about you too."

"What item?"

"On Nick. Tomorrow," Leonie repeated with exaggerated patience. "I just got a wonderful scoop. He's writing his memoirs."

Juliet's hands had gone icy cold. "His memoirs?"

"Word is that he's already got an agent. The book will be a blockbuster. Everyone will want to read about the man who married four of America's most beautiful women and made them superstars." The redhead grinned at Juliet. "Now we'll know all your secrets."

"Mother?" Eden said urgently. "Our other guests—"

"Certainly," Juliet said. "If you'll excuse me, Leonie."

As they walked away, she asked the girls, "Is your father going to be here tonight?"

"We sent him an invitation," Dani said, "but he didn't reply."

"You know how he is," Eden said. "He never knows what he'll be doing in the next twenty-four hours. Oliver is here, though."

Of course he would be, Juliet thought bitterly.

Nick's memoirs.

A passing waiter offered her a glass of champagne. Juliet watched the liquid tremble in the glass and wondered how she was going to get through the rest of the evening.

You can't tell everyone about me and Papa, Nick! I'll die if you do. If you tell, I don't know what I'll do!

Leonie was at her elbow again. "You don't want to tell all before Nick has a chance, do you? I'll give you a whole column to do it in."

Juliet didn't answer.

Leonie laughed. "That's all right. You'll get the headline tomorrow anyway: FORMER FILM STAR TURNS FIFTY."

Juliet upended her glass of champagne on Leonie's vibrant red hair.

.   .   .

"Juliet?" Kate glanced at the clock in amazement. It was 5 A.M. in California. She couldn't remember Juliet ever getting up so early before. "How was the party? Sorry I couldn't be there." She leaned back against the headboard, the tray from room service on her lap.

"I'm in disgrace." Juliet's voice from across the continent sounded muted, totally unlike her. "If the girls give you a party on your fiftieth birthday, try not to dump a glass of champagne on Leonie Denton's head."

Kate gasped. "You didn't! My God, Juliet!"

"She kept reminding me I was fifty years old. I finally had enough of it. Of course now neither of the girls are speaking to me."

That Kate doubted. No matter how outrageous Juliet's actions were, they only seemed to endear her more to Eden—and Dani. "How is Dani? I haven't talked to her in a long time."

"She's fine."

There was a brief silence. Kate found it astonishing that Juliet didn't fill it with all the details of what Dani and Eden were up to, as she usually did.

"Is something wrong, Juliet?"

"You mean aside from the fact that I'm in disgrace?" Juliet's harsh laugh was unsettling. "As a matter of fact, there is. Nick is writing his memoirs. Leonie told me last night that he already has an agent lined up."

Kate knocked over her coffee.

"Kate? Are you there?"

"Can I call you back? I've had an accident with the breakfast tray."

Kate hung up. Flinging the damp sheets back, she rose and hurried to the mirror. She hadn't combed her hair yet, hadn't performed the elaborate cosmetic ritual that turned her from plain Kate into Kathleen. "The most beautiful woman in the world." What a laugh! She looked so ordinary no one would give her a second look if they passed her on the street.

When Nick told the world how he created her, everyone would know Kathleen Mallory was an imposter. She would be just plain Kate Mallory to everyone. The memory of that disastrous television audition so many years ago came rushing back.

Everyone will laugh!

"Jonah?" she whispered. There was no longer any comfort in his name. Jonah was gone. She was all alone.

Allison woke before dawn as she always did these days. It was the only way she could get a few moments to herself before the day's demands began. It was tough enough managing one career; she had to handle two.

She dressed quickly in her running clothes and let herself out of the house. Thank heavens she had talked Wilson into moving to the Malibu house. If it weren't for her beach run every morning, she wouldn't get any exercise at all.

When she got back to the house, Allison showered, put on a thick terry bathrobe, and went into the kitchen for her breakfast: a cup of nonfat yogurt and one piece of dry whole-wheat toast.

Wilson came in while she was eating and gave her the kind of disapproving look that always reminded her of her father. "Is that supposed to help you lose a few pounds?"

"I haven't gained any weight," she said mildly, and she hadn't. Her body was as hard and angular as it was in the days before she let Nick Picard remake her into his "love goddess."

"You photographed heavy in those last pictures," Wilson said as he splashed milk into his cereal.

Allison felt her throat muscles tighten and knew she

wouldn't be able to force another bite of breakfast past them. She shoved the yogurt aside. "What's on your agenda today?"

"Don't try to change the subject. You know what's coming up." Encouraged by Senator MacLaren and MacLaren's political machine, Wilson was busy making plans for his try at taking the presidential nomination away from Bush. "We both need to be in our best shape."

"All *right*, Wilson!" she said as she stood up. "I got your subtle hint."

"Where are you going?"

"To dress. I have a busy day myself."

"Well, add this to it." He handed her a newspaper clipping. "One of my staff spotted it."

It was Leonie Denton's column from *LA Today*. The headline read PICARD MEMOIRS TOO HOT TO PUBLISH?

"Your ex-husband wouldn't have any dirt on you, would he?"

"Of course not," Allison snapped as she left the kitchen. She hurried down the hall to the bedroom, the crumpled clipping in her hand, trying not to think about Nick publishing all her doubts about her body and, perhaps worse, her father's humiliation at her hands. Allison detoured to the bathroom. She barely made it before her stomach rejected the yogurt.

Oh, Nick! she thought, as she rested her face against the cool porcelain of the toilet bowl. How could you?

The private investigator's report really made Toby's day. She'd had Nick followed for two whole weeks, and the investigator's consensus was that he was seeing no one at the moment. That left just one little problem: how to approach him.

Their parting had been less than amicable. Although Nick was still on the Picard Productions payroll for a hefty sum, he did no actual work for the company. Nor did he seem particularly grateful for Toby's largess.

The direct approach, Toby thought, and reached for the phone. Before she touched it, it rang.

"Did you see my column today?" Leonie Denton asked by way of greeting.

"I have it right here, ready to read as soon as I have a break," Toby lied.

"You really should read me first thing in the morning, dear. Especially when you're mentioned."

"Me?" Toby hadn't sent Leonie anything in weeks. Her curiosity piqued, she eyed the paper across the room.

"All of Nicholas Picard's ex-wives, in fact. He's writing his memoirs, you know."

"No, I didn't know." Toby could feel the *thud-thud* of her heart. "How did you find out?"

"Common knowledge, dear. Everyone in Hollywood is speculating on just how much he'll reveal about all you gorgeous ladies."

Toby forced a laugh. "All the law allows, I suppose. That's what he did in *Playboy*."

"I'm glad to hear you're taking it so well. I understand the other ladies are a trifle upset. Especially Juliet."

She's fishing, Toby thought. "I've got to go now, Leonie, but I'll let you know if I think of any delicious gossip about Nick that will even up the score."

"You do that, Toby. We'll give him a run for his money."

Toby hung up, her impulse to call Nick totally forgotten as panic took her.

He couldn't know. There was no way he could possibly know. No way anyone could link Toby Flynn, Hollywood producer, with Toby Gilmer, teenage murderer from Mesquite, Texas.

Was there?

The security precautions for the meeting were more elaborate than any ever dreamed up by a spy. "All we need is for Leonie Denton to get wind of this," Toby Flynn had declared.

It was Toby who had come up with the idea of the meeting, Toby who had insisted it take place at Juliet's house, and the rest of them had gone along with her plans.

The other three had driven themselves to Juliet's, so chauffeurs wouldn't be able to report on their destination, and at night, so passersby wouldn't see them turning into Juliet's drive. They arrived at staggered times, just as Toby had suggested.

Juliet had champagne chilled. "Why not?" she asked with a shrug. "It may help us think."

When they were all finally settled in Juliet's white and gold living room with their drinks, silence fell, as though, now the moment of reality was upon them, no one wanted to commit herself.

Kate glanced at the others curiously. They all seemed like strangers now, even Juliet. And yet, at the same time, so familiar. As though she were looking at her own face through a distorted glass. "What are we going to do?" she asked them, and it was like asking the question of herself.

"I see we've skipped right over the 'Should we do anything?' question," Allison Hilliard said dryly. "I suppose that means we all have something we'd rather not have exposed by Nick."

"And there's no need to go into the details," Juliet said, with such violence that the other three turned her way. She colored. "But how can we stop him?"

Kate glanced around the room. "If we simply ask him not to—"

"I already tried that," Allison said. "I called him yesterday."

The others turned to stare at her.

"Why not?" she said. "It was the sensible thing to do."

"What did you say to him?" Juliet demanded.

"I asked him not to publish his memoirs. I told him none of us wanted him to use the material about our lives." She paused. "He laughed at me."

"You should have waited," Toby told her. "We could have decided together what to say."

"We could offer him money," Juliet said. "If we all chipped in—"

"He's not doing it for money," Toby said, "so it won't do any good to offer him any."

"How do you know he's not doing it for money?" Allison asked her.

"Because I made him a very generous settlement when I took over Picard Productions. He doesn't have to lift a finger to draw a salary most people in this town would kill for."

"Is it revenge then?" Kate asked. "Against you, for taking over his company?"

It was Toby's turn to flush. "Maybe. But I'm not the only one mentioned in Leonie's story. So why does he hate the three of you?"

Allison shrugged. "Like Juliet said, the details don't matter. The question is, what ammunition do *we* have against *him*?"

Toby turned to Kate and Juliet. "How about his daughters? He wouldn't want to hurt them, would he? I always got the impression he cared quite a bit about them."

"He does," Juliet agreed. "But how would his memoirs hurt them? The circumstances around Eden's birth were thoroughly publicized at the time. Neither she nor Dani give it a second thought, and Nick knows that."

"There has to be something!" Toby said with such desperation that the other three turned her way. "Think!"

"I suppose suing him is out?" Juliet asked.

"My God!" Allison cried. "That would only make things worse."

"We can't sue," Toby said. "I'm sure we're all agreed on that. We have to find some other way."

They spent the next hour sipping champagne and trying to come up with a plan of action. By the time they opened the third bottle of Dom Perignon, the plans had become wild enough for an action/adventure script.

"This is it for me," Allison said abruptly as she stood up. "If we drink anything else, we'll be arrested for DWI on the way home. Wouldn't that look great in Leonie's column?"

"But we haven't come up with anything," Juliet protested.

"We won't at this rate." Toby gathered up her things too. "Please call me, any of you, if you come up with something. Something workable."

Kate picked up her own purse in silence. She found herself staring at the other three, wondering what their secrets were. What made them as hysterical as she was at the thought of the publication of Nick's memoirs?

Juliet was absolutely crushed. She caught Kate at the door. "We have to think of something," she said. "We can't let him do this to us."

"We'll try," Kate told her, patting her hand. Of them all, she would have thought Juliet had the least to hide. Juliet had lived her entire public life on the edge, in full view of the press. What revelation of Nick's could she possibly fear?

Allison's car was just pulling out when Kate reached her own. Allison's problem was easy enough to understand. Like Caesar's wife, the wife of Wilson Keating, undeclared-as-yet candidate for the presidency, must be above reproach. No doubt Keating was in a quandary over this. Allison's money could finance him all way to Pennsylvania Avenue; her former marriage could slam the White House door right in his face.

Just as Kate turned the key in the car door, Toby Flynn stepped out of the shadows and grasped her arm, making Kate gasp in surprise. "What do you think you're doing?"

"If I thought for one minute it was your poking and prying into my life that gave Nick the crazy idea of writing his memoirs, I'd make you sorry!"

"Look, Toby, we're all in the same boat."

"No, we're not! I'm warning you."

"Kate?" Juliet called from the doorway. "Is that you? What's the shouting?"

Toby wheeled and ran to her car. She jumped in and burned down the drive with a shriek of rubber.

"Kate? Are you all right?"

"I'm okay," Kate called back, even though her hands were shaking.

Juliet walked out to the car. "What happened?"

"Toby just wanted a few last words with me."

"Did you think of something to stop Nick?" Juliet asked her.

Kate felt a slow smile spreading over her face. "As a matter of fact, I believe I just did."

"Kate?" It was Juliet on the phone. "Where on earth have you been? I've been calling you and calling you!"

"I decided to take a few days for myself," Kate said. She stretched the phone cord so she could sit down on the bed beside her suitcase. "Has something happened?"

"*Nothing* has happened!" Juliet was obviously in one of her technicolor moods. "No one has done anything. Leonie's still running items in her column about Nick's memoirs. If I get close enough to her again, I'll pour a whole magnum of Dom Perignon over her!"

"Do you really think that will help?"

"It would help me," Juliet said and, surprisingly enough, giggled.

"Just be patient a while longer. We'll think of something to do." Actually, something had already been done, but Kate didn't dare tell Juliet that. She didn't dare tell anyone.

It was several minutes more before she could disentangle herself from Juliet. When she hung up the phone, Kate turned on the bathwater, leaving her suitcase still unpacked. Let the housekeeper do that tomorrow, she thought. She needed a bath more than she needed anything else. Maybe the scented waters would wash away the unclean feeling she'd had ever since yesterday morning.

As she slipped into the water, Kate thought how horrified Barry would be if he knew what she had done. Poor Barry. They were never meant for each other.

Not that she approved of her own actions herself. Instead of triumph, she felt nausea.

But Nick could be stopped. That was the important thing. All she needed was a month, possibly two, and the result of her hastily conceived plan would give her something she could barter with Nick for his silence.

The old Jonah, the man Jonah had been before he asked her to marry him, that Jonah would have approved of her methods. Kate found no comfort in that thought.

Time, she thought as she soaped herself. That's all I need.

It was a Wednesday morning only three short weeks later when Kate saw Nick's name in the headline of Leonie Denton's column: PICARD PLAYS PYGMALION FOR FIFTH TIME? Kate had not read beyond the first paragraph when the phone rang.

"Did you see it?" Juliet demanded when Kate answered.

"Just now," Kate told her.

"That bitch! If she calls me a 'former film star' one more time, I'll set fire to her house!"

Kate scanned the item quickly. Leonie had no facts, only rumors and speculations. From that, she had woven an artful case that Nick was working his magic on what she called "another beautiful unknown." He would, in Leonie's gushing phrases, "become a star maker of renown for the fifth time." Nowhere did it mention his memoirs. Kate pointed that out.

"Nick is almost finished with the manuscript. Dani was over there yesterday. She said he's going to send it to an agent on Friday."

"He didn't—she didn't read any of it, did she?" The thought of Dani reading about her, about Nick's creation of her, made Kate's skin crawl.

"No, but Kate, we have to stop him."

"Maybe he won't tell the things I—that we don't want known."

"He's exposed us in every other way. Why would he stop now? You said you had thought of some way to keep him from doing this to us," Juliet accused. "What happened?"

"I don't think it's been long enough. I need more time."

"Maybe the others," Juliet said desperately. "Maybe they've thought of something by now. Somebody has to think of something."

It was noon when Juliet called back. "They read Leonie's column too."

Kate's heart thudded painfully. "Did they have any ideas?"

"Nothing. Kate, we can't let Nick do this to us!" Juliet cried, her voice rising to a wail. "What are we going to do?"

Neither of them had an answer.

· · ·

The woman woke with a start at 4 A.M., her heart racing with panic. Nothing to worry about, she soothed herself as she lay staring at the ceiling. Nothing at all.

But the lie couldn't slow her galloping heart. If she didn't do something, everyone would know the truth about her. She couldn't bear that.

How could Nick do this to her? Kate Mallory had tried to stop him, but it hadn't worked. Now it was up to her, and she knew what she had to do. As she made her plans to get the gun, the tears began to trickle down her cheeks. "Oh, Nick," she sobbed suddenly. "I'm so sorry."

Finally, the sobs slowed. Exhausted, she raised herself to a sitting position, leaning back against the headboard. The truth was, she realized in a sudden burst of clarity, the fault was not hers. It was Kate Mallory who had set the tragedy in motion.

"Not my fault, Nick," she murmured, like a child begging forgiveness. She licked the salty taste of tears from her lips. "Not my fault at all."

Then her face hardened to a cruel mask.

Kate's fault. Kate would pay. She would make sure of that.

Lieutenant Gil Arquilla arrived just as the paramedics were loading the victim into the ambulance. He spared barely a glance for the unfortunate man. His mind, instead, was on the house, and this one was a beauty. A lifelong Angeleno, Gil's passion was these dowagers from another age. This one was a picturesque half-timbered Tudor-style mansion with a slate roof.

Gil hadn't bothered to bring his well-thumbed copy of *The City Observed* from the car. Bel Air lovelies like this one hadn't been covered in his favorite book because most were hidden from view by the landscaping. Their drives were guarded by iron gates that swung open only to admit the occupants, their guests, and the hired help.

Or the police.

If he couldn't be an architect, the next best thing was to be a cop. Before he left, he would see every room in the place. After all, it fell under the heading of official duties.

Sergeant Litton, efficient as always, caught up with Gil at the large oak front door. Litton knew Gil well enough to realize that once he got inside the house he wouldn't be interested in hearing any details of the case for quite a while.

Gil sighed. "What have you got?"

Litton consulted his notebook. "Victim's name was Nicholas Picard. Producer. One or more gunshot wounds to the chest. Still alive but probably won't make it."

Gil's glance strayed to the mullioned windows. Resolutely, he pulled his attention back to Litton. "Any statement from the victim?"

"He told the paramedics his wife shot him."

"Fine." Gil reached for the doorknob. "I'll question her in a minute."

"We got a little problem, lieutenant." Litton turned and waved to the man who had been standing a few feet away. "This is Sloan Whitney, the victim's lawyer. He found the victim. Tell Lieutenant Arquilla what you told me, Mr. Whitney."

The lawyer's eyes flashed behind his glasses, almost as if, Gil thought guiltily, he could tell the lieutenant had other things on his mind. "Go ahead, Mr. Whitney."

"I told the sergeant here that Nick doesn't have one wife. He's got four."

Gil found his attention fully engaged at last. "He's a bigamist?"

"No, lieutenant," the lawyer said with heavy sarcasm.

"He's divorced. Four times. The last one in 1983. He could have been referring to any of them."

Gil's mood brightened. And here he had thought it was a simple case of domestic violence. Four suspects meant it might drag on for a while. He would have to visit the beautiful old mansion again. Next time, with his camera. But for now he had waited long enough. "The sergeant will take your statement, Mr. Whitney," he told the lawyer. Before Sergeant Litton could object, Gil was inside the house.

The sergeant caught up with Gil in the hall. "What *is* it, Litton?"

"I didn't want to mention it in front of the lawyer, lieutenant, but I've got something to show you in the study."

The study was as good a place to start as any. "Show me," Gil told him.

"He was shot while sitting at the desk," Sergeant Litton said unnecessarily. Blood marked the spot, as well as where the victim had fallen. Too much blood. It was definitely going to be a homicide, Gil thought. "The lawyer says the victim was working on his memoirs. Should be a pile of manuscript pages there by the typewriter. They're gone."

"Maybe they're somewhere else in the house."

"Maybe." Sergeant Litton knelt by the desk. "The lawyer missed this."

Gil knelt beside him. Under the desk, written in the victim's blood, was a word. "Dust the desk and then move it and get some good pictures of this."

"Right."

Gil studied the letters. They formed a woman's name. "Is that one of the wives?"

"Don't you know who this guy is?" Sergeant Litton asked, astonishment in his voice.

"Producer, you said."

"He was married to some of the most beautiful broads in the business. She's not a dead architect, but maybe you've heard of her anyway. Kate is Kate Mallory. Short for Kathleen Mallory."

So much for four suspects, Gil thought. He'd better get back out here later in the afternoon with his camera. It looked like an open-and-shut case.

BOOK THREE

VICTIM

Nicholas

1989

But where, you ask, is Nicholas Picard in all these meanderings? Just as I am the missing element in these pages, my father was the missing element in my life. I knew nothing about him as a child. My mother would have had me believe I was the product of an immaculate conception. It was as though he never existed. Only recently have I begun to wonder what kind of man he was.

It astonishes me to realize that my daughters are now the age Etienne Picard was when he died. Did he know he had left a child behind in my mother's womb when he met his fiery death?

At any rate, fate left me to my mother to raise in her haphazard, mostly absent, fashion: Helen Chandler, supreme ruler of the silver screen. My world revolved around her like some ancient, goddess-worshiping society of the East. Is it any wonder that I turned my hand to creating film goddesses of my own?

I wonder—what would my father think of me? Of the man I have become?

—From the unpublished memoirs of Nicholas Picard

TWENTY-FOUR

PLEASE, GOD! LET IT BE HIM! IF IT IS, I SWEAR I'LL never date another married man as long as I live!

Leonie Denton hurried down the hospital corridor as fast as her stitches would allow. Heads swiveled as the petite redhead in the filmy black negligee rushed past. Leonie didn't notice. Thanks to her rotten appendix, she was going to get the scoop of the year—and save her job in the bargain. The thought made her smile as she followed a pimply-faced hospital orderly into the elevator.

Until a few minutes ago, Leonie hadn't been that grateful for her appendicitis attack. The vague discomfort in her belly had begun three days ago in a Mexico City hotel. Because of it, she canceled out on dinner and dancing at a Zona Rosa night spot. Her lover, Mark Maxall, had not been pleased.

Keeping Mark pleased was very important to Leonie, since he also happened to be her editor at *LA Today*. For the past two years, Leonie and Mark had been, in the language of Leonie's column, an "under-the-covers item." Leonie wanted more. They were still unpacking when she offered her first bland hint that it was time Mark divorced his wife.

Mark didn't respond. He didn't have to. Leonie saw the expression on his face before he turned away. She knew she had blown it. Permanently.

It didn't matter how popular her column was. Mark would try to bump her off the paper as soon as they got back to Los Angeles. Someone else would be living the good life at Hollywood parties. Someone else would be feasting on all the delicious gossip she grazed through every day. Someone else would be sharing the couch in Mark's office after hours.

That was bad enough. Worse lay ahead.

They were about to leave the suite when Leonie realized the uneasy feeling building in her stomach had nothing to do with her dashed hopes.

Mark blew up. How could she spoil his trip with something as unappetizing as diarrhea? Furious, he stomped out of the suite. He didn't return until after the lavish midnight show at Casablanca.

By then Leonie's uneasy feeling had become actual pain. It was now centered in the lower right-hand part of her abdomen. Still, she knew Mark's temper. When he stripped off his sweaty clothes and climbed into bed with her, she didn't dare refuse.

Screwing was sheer agony. The slightest pressure on her stomach increased the pain beyond belief. Her whimpering didn't stop Mark, and she couldn't fight him off. Finally, she screamed so loudly that someone pounded on the door of the suite, yelling in Spanish.

Cursing, Mark rolled off her. He grabbed his wallet and opened the door just wide enough to pass a wad of pesos through it.

Leonie lay on the bed, sobbing and clutching her abdomen. When she finally got through to the bastard what was wrong, Mark threatened to put her in a Mexican hospital.

Leonie was having none of that. It was the good old USA or *nada*.

Nada it was then, Mark agreed. He left to catch the flamenco dancing at Gitanerias.

Alone, trembling and feverish, Leonie ignored her nausea. Somehow she managed to get herself dressed, packed, into a taxi, and on the next Aeromexico flight back to Los Angeles. All with no help from Mr. Maxall.

She remembered little of the trip back. She remembered even less of the ambulance ride from LAX to the hospital. But burned permanently into her brain was the clear image of the disgust in Mark Maxall's face when she lay writhing and sweating on that Mexico City hotel bed.

Good-bye, Mark. Good-bye, column.

After recuperating for a day, Leonie began to amble through the hospital corridors. To her joy, she found that here, just as at any Hollywood party, she had a currency of information—gossip, dirt—she could exchange for the same. From the nurses, she learned all sorts of interesting tidbits about patients, present and former. But no tales she could use to placate Mark until a few minutes ago, when she overheard one nurse whisper to another about the famous patient who had just come into the intensive care unit.

Leonie eavesdropped long enough to guess his identity. Unfortunately, the two nurses clammed up when she tried to question them. Leonie knew from experience that neither would be likely to tell her anything. Not when the other one would know who leaked the information. But she had no time left for subtleties.

The pimply-faced orderly leered at her from across the elevator.

Leonie crossed her arms in front of her plunging neckline. Earlier this morning she had slipped on the provocative black negligee she hadn't had a chance to wear in Mexico City. Then she phoned Mark, begging him to come to the hospital. It was only after she hung up that Leonie realized why he had agreed so quickly. He planned to fire her without giving her a chance to come back to the paper. After that trip back alone, from Mexico City, she no longer wanted to marry Mark Maxall or even sleep with the bastard. But she did want to keep her column. So when she guessed the identity of the man in ICU, Leonie hadn't wasted precious minutes changing into something less revealing.

She glared at the orderly. He smirked back.

When the elevator doors slid open on the fifth floor, Leonie bolted out, ignoring the painful pull of her stitches.

Thank heavens, the orderly stayed on the elevator. She had Mark to worry about. She could only deal with one horny son of a bitch at a time.

Hastily, she positioned herself so she could watch the double doors that led into the intensive care unit. When she caught sight of the woman hurrying down the corridor, long blond hair hidden behind a scarf and face masked by sunglasses, Leonie knew the ache of her stitches was worth it. Kathleen Mallory was on the way to visit her ex-husband. It *was* Nicholas Picard inside the unit!

Nicholas had been the subject of several interesting items in Leonie's column the past few months. Now she thought, Please, God! Just one more. And don't let it be something as ordinary as a heart attack! Not unless he was fucking someone important at the time. Leonie had nothing against Nicholas Picard personally, but an ordinary item wouldn't save her column. She needed a really juicy scandal for that.

Kathleen Mallory halted outside the entrance of the unit. She didn't glance Leonie's way as she pressed the buzzer outside the double doors and announced herself as Nicholas Picard's wife.

Normally, Leonie would have pushed forward, brashly demanding to know what had happened. She would be certain of a reply, too. Most public figures were more afraid of what Leonie might print out of spite, than of the truth— however damaging the truth might be.

But when Kathleen Mallory removed her dark glasses,

Leonie could see how vulnerable she was at that moment. Some people, Leonie among them, believed Kathleen Mallory was the only one of Nicholas Picard's wives he had really loved. Whether or not that was true, Leonie had only to look at the distress on Kathleen Mallory's lovely face to be sure that *she* was still very much in love with Nicholas Picard.

Leonie was almost moved not to intrude on that private suffering. However, if she had the tiniest shred of normal human emotions, she wouldn't be in the business of flaying reputations, she reminded herself.

Before Leonie could step forward, Juliet Brittany shoved past Kathleen Mallory to push the buzzer for herself. She too announced herself as Nicholas Picard's wife and received the same instructions as Kathleen Mallory: "Wait. Someone will be out in a few minutes."

Better and better, Leonie thought. Instead of an item, she now had a whole column. However, the memory of how humiliated she had been when Juliet dumped a glass of champagne on her during Juliet's fiftieth birthday party kept Leonie from rushing over to interview the two women. Pacing now in front of the ICU, Juliet looked as lithe and wild as a tigress. The last thing in the world Leonie wanted was to have all that pent-up emotion directed her way.

Allison Hilliard and Toby Flynn rushed up to the double doors, arriving at almost the same moment. They jockeyed with each other to be first at the buzzer. Old and New Hollywood together, Leonie thought happily. The column was writing itself!

Allison Hilliard suddenly gave way graciously. It was a maneuver designed to make the younger woman look awkward.

Instead of being thrown off balance, Toby Flynn seized the opportunity before it could be retracted. She stabbed the buzzer so hard she broke a fingernail. In a loud, clear voice, she announced herself as Nicholas Picard's wife. Then she moved aside with a mocking smile so that Allison Hilliard could repeat the same words.

Each of them was instructed to wait.

How well the little playlet had defined their characters, Leonie thought.

With either Allison or Toby she might have made some headway. They both realized the power of personal publicity. But with all of them there, Leonie knew she didn't have a chance.

Watching the four women, Leonie realized that each actress symbolized a decade in Hollywood's history. Juliet Brittany was the icon of the fifties, just as Kathleen Mallory typified the sixties. Allison Hilliard's career began in the sixties, but she had changed and grown with Hollywood; it was the seventies *she* represented. Just as Toby Flynn was the quintessential eighties woman.

What interested Leonie was that one man had the foresight to discover just the right woman for each of those decades. Considering where Nicholas Picard was this morning, the question had to be, Would he ever do it again? Although her column had hinted, based on an item planted by Nicholas himself, that Nicholas Picard might be playing star maker one more time, Leonie had not taken the possibility seriously. That lightning would strike four times was unbelievable. Five times was impossible. However, the volume of mail that column drew, complete with photographs and résumés, had let Leonie know there were many women in Los Angeles who took the possibility very seriously indeed.

A nurse finally bustled through the double doors. The four women all pushed forward at once, startling her as they each demanded admittance.

The nurse protested that only the immediate family would be allowed to see the patient. She seemed confused as she glanced around at the four women. It was uncanny how much the four of them resembled one another despite the eighteen-year difference in age between the oldest and the youngest.

Their famous voices rose as they argued violently over which of them was closest to the man in ICU. Overwhelmed, the nurse called for a doctor. When he arrived, the discussion resumed on a softer note.

Leonie edged nearer.

"There you are, Miss Denton," a nurse said. "We've been looking all over for you. What in the world are you doing here? You have a visitor in your room."

"Let him wait," Leonie told her. "Can you help me find a telephone?"

"There's one in your room."

"Not that one." This nurse was very young, with wide blue eyes and a dusting of freckles across her nose. Leonie gave her a charming smile. "I need to call in my column for tomorrow morning." She smiled even more charmingly and lowered her voice. "Can you tell me why Nicholas Picard was brought in? Confidentially, of course."

"Well"—the young nurse glanced at the group outside ICU—"an orderly told me that the police said—"

"The police?" Delighted, Leonie grabbed her by the arm and pulled her a few steps down the corridor. "Let's find a phone where we can have some privacy. We need to talk to my managing editor." She'd fix that bastard Mark! She'd go right over his head. Just let him try to fire her after this.

The girl hung back. "Not me, Miss Denton! I'm just a nurse."

"Yes, you," Leonie said firmly. "And you're not a nurse anymore. You're a hospital spokesperson who prefers not to be identified."

"You mean you'll use what I say in your column?"

"You bet," Leonie assured her. "Buy tomorrow morning's *LA Today.* I'll autograph it for you."

"Where were you last night and early this morning, Ms. Mallory?" Lieutenant Sattler asked.

Kate resisted an urge to gasp for breath. The tiny office the lieutenant had commandeered for their conversation seemed suddenly airless. When the lieutenant walked into the small conference room that Cedars-Sinai had set aside for the former wives of Nicholas Picard and singled her out, Kate had realized immediately what that meant. If she had not, the faces of the other three women would have warned her. The police thought she was the one who had tried to kill Nick.

It was difficult to worry about herself, Kate found. She was too caught up in her fears for Nick's survival and the guilt she felt. All the time Lieutenant Sattler was walking her down the hall to this office, she kept wondering if it was because of the plot she set in motion to stop Nick from writing his memoirs that his life had almost ended. Yet she knew it was important she not allow herself to be arrested, that she not let the whole thing be swept aside, an open-and-shut case. Because if she did, that would leave Nick vulnerable to the real killer.

"Well, Ms. Mallory?" Lt. Sattler prompted.

"I believe from my research on *Means and Ends* that you have skipped a step, lieutenant."

"And what step is that?"

"Aren't you supposed to read me my rights?"

"You're not under arrest."

"Nevertheless, I would like to have my lawyer present," Kate said.

"Very well. Call your lawyer. Then we'll continue this discussion." The lieutenant pointed to the phone on the desk in front of her and stepped out of the office.

Kate hesitated, her hand on the receiver. Then, swiftly, before she had time to change her mind, she dialed Sloan Whitney's office.

"For God's sake, Kate! Don't you realize I'm going to end up as a witness if Nick—if this thing goes to trial?" It had only taken Whit five minutes to appear; he was already in the hospital, waiting as she was for news of Nick's condition.

"Just sit with me," she pleaded. "I want you here while the lieutenant talks to me." Inspiration seized her. "Nick would want you here."

"Nick is too goddamned sentimental for his own good!" Whit exploded. But he walked to the door and invited the police lieutenant back inside. "I'm here as a friend of the family, not as a lawyer," he told the lieutenant.

"Ms. Mallory is not under arrest. Did she explain that to you?"

"Ms. Mallory isn't quite sure what's happening," Kate pointed out. "Suppose you tell her."

"All right." The lieutenant sat down on the edge of the desk. As if taking his cue from the policeman, Whit offered one of the two chairs in the tiny office to Kate and took the other himself. "I understand that your nickname is Kate, Ms. Mallory, although you are known professionally as Kathleen?"

"Actually, Kate is my real name. Nick christened me Kathleen when he made me a movie star. My friends all call me Kate, however."

"And your enemies?"

Whit leaned forward in the chair. "What's that supposed to mean, lieutenant?"

"The word *Kate* was found at the scene, written in the victim's blood."

Kate's stomach lurched at the thought of Nick's blood.

"I didn't see that," Whit protested.

Kate stared at him in astonishment. "You were there?"

"I found him, Kate. And your name wasn't there."

"Yes, it was, Mr. Whitney. Just under the edge of the desk. We have photographs. I'm sure, considering the amount of blood and your concern for—are you all right, Ms. Mallory?"

"I . . . Nick's blood . . . I can't stand the thought. . . ." Kate pressed her trembling hands to her head.

Whit left the office for a moment and came back with a cup full of water. He dipped his handkerchief in it and held it to Kate's forehead for a moment. "If you feel as though you're going to faint, put your head between your knees."

"I'm all right now, Whit. I'm sorry. It was just the thought of Nick. . . ." Kate leaned back in the chair, still pressing the damp handkerchief to her forehead.

Whit turned to Sattler. "You're saying Nick wrote Kate's name in his own blood while he was lying there?"

"Apparently not."

"I'm not sure I understand, lieutenant," Whit said.

"There was no blood on the victim's fingers, Mr. Whitney."

"No blood?"

"What I'd like from Ms. Mallory is a list of any enemies she might have."

Kate sat up. The handkerchief fell to her lap, forgotten. "But I don't have any enemies, lieutenant."

"Oh, yes, Ms. Mallory," Sattler said. "I'm very much afraid you do."

Sloan Whitney paced around the room, his temper visibly at a boiling point. "I don't see why you called me in the first place."

"I need your help," Kate told him. "I didn't know who else to call."

"You used your own lawyer when you divorced Nick. Call him."

"Please, Whit! I'm worried about Nick."

The agony in her voice made him pause in his pacing, but his own voice gave away nothing. "So am I, but I don't see what that has to do with you."

"Surely you don't believe I'd write my own name in blood at the scene of a crime if I were the one who shot him, do you? Someone tried to kill Nick and then frame me for the murder."

"Why?"

"I don't *know* why. Do you realize that Nick and I haven't been in the same room, or even spoken on the phone, since our divorce? I have no idea why anyone would want to murder Nick in the first place, let alone why they might try to frame me for it."

"What about his memoirs?" Whit asked her.

"What about them? I'm sure the police have them now."

"They're missing."

Kate's heart skipped a beat. "Then no one knows what was in them."

"Nick knows. And he's still alive. For now."

"None of us wanted the memoirs to appear," Kate admitted. "We had a meeting about it. We all tried to come up with some way to stop Nick from publishing them."

"And what did you decide?"

"We didn't decide anything."

"Someone did." Whit stood up abruptly. "I don't feel like playing games, Kate. Do you know what Nick said when they asked him who shot him?"

She shook her head.

"He said, 'My wife.' I happen to know he refers to all four of you that way. So I'd say the odds are good that it's one of you. That is, unless the whole witch's coven of you got together and tried to do him in."

"In which case he would have said, 'My wives.' You promised to help me, Whit. For Nick's sake. We've got to find out who did it."

Someone pounded on the door. "Kate!" Juliet called.

Whit opened the door and she swept inside, hardly glancing at him. "Oh, Kate! They've arrested Toby!"

Allison Hilliard was still waiting in the conference room. Toby Flynn was gone. "They told her she could call her lawyer when they got to the station," Allison said.

"But why Toby?" Kate asked.

"I hope you would have said the same thing if they'd carted me off," Allison said with just the trace of a sardonic smile.

"Really, Allison. What did they say?"

"They said that since she was his last wife, it was obviously her he was referring to when he said his wife shot him."

Kate wheeled around to Whit. "They're wrong. You just said so."

"How did he know they were going to arrest Toby?" Juliet asked suspiciously.

"They haven't arrested her," Allison corrected. "Not yet anyway."

"Whit just told me that Nick referred to all of us as 'his wife.' You have to tell them, Whit."

Surprisingly, it was Juliet who echoed her. Surprisingly, since Juliet had never shown any particular fondness for Toby Flynn. It was almost as though they were really sisters, all four of them, Kate thought, as Allison finally added her blandishments to Juliet's.

"I told them that at the scene," Whit pointed out.

"Tell them again," Kate begged. "Please."

Whit left finally, shaking his head but promising to talk to the authorities.

"Now what?" Juliet said when the door had closed behind him.

"How is Nick?" Kate asked.

Juliet turned away suddenly. It was Allison who answered. "No change."

Kate took a seat by the door. The lieutenant's words continued to echo in her ears. "Enemies," he had said.

Toby had been furious when she found out Kate was prying into her life. Kate tried not to think how much angrier Toby would be if she found out to what lengths Kate had gone in order to stop Nick from writing his memoirs. If Toby had been furious before, she would be beyond fury now.

Angry enough to kill Nick and put the blame on Kate?

A science fiction movie. The aliens had him.

Wires and tubes were connected to his body. He wondered if his head was shaved.

". . . awake now," someone said. The words seemed to echo and reecho in his head.

He tried to say "Aliens," but the word came out a croak. Someone lifted a cup of ice to his lips to moisten them.

"Nick? Can you hear me?"

That was Whit's voice, but the creature behind the mask didn't look like Whit. His voice came and went like a bad radio transmission from an old movie. The original version of *The Thing*. ". . . police here," Whit was saying. "Who shot you?"

"Bad . . . connection," Nick said. It was a feeble attempt at a joke.

"Did he say a Mafia connection?" someone demanded.

"Nick?" Whit pleaded. "Tell us who it was. Who tried to hurt you?" His voice broke.

"Hurt me," Nick said, surprising himself with the weak sound of his own voice. "She took everything. She hurt me."

"Who, Nick? Which one was it?"

"Toby," he said. "Toby did it."

Then he sank back into the soft darkness.

Toby was the lead story on the evening news. All channels. She didn't bother to cover her face as they led her down the halls. Everyone in America knew what she looked like.

Kate flipped off the set. She had come home long enough to change clothes. Now she was on her way back to the hospital.

When the phone rang she grabbed it, afraid it might be the hospital calling about Nick. Instead it was Leonie Denton. "I just wanted to get your thoughts on Toby Flynn's arrest."

"Look, Leonie, I don't believe—"

"What do you think her motive was? The memoirs?"

Kate's own guilt surged up, almost choking her. It was a moment before she could say, "I don't believe Toby is guilty, Leonie."

"Are you saying you think it's one of the others: Juliet, Allison? Which one?"

"Did you ask them the same thing about me?" Kate demanded angrily.

"Nick loved you, Kate. Everyone knew that."

Kate felt the sudden tears fill her eyes. "And I love him. But that doesn't mean I want to see Toby suffer unfairly. I'm certain she had nothing to do with this."

Before Leonie could say anything, Kate slammed the phone down. It rang again almost immediately, but she didn't pick it up. If it was the hospital, she couldn't get there any faster. She was leaving right now. She had something to straighten out.

· · ·

The first step was a fight with Whit. "I need to see Nick," she insisted. "Alone." She had already discovered he had been moved to a private room. And that he had said nothing else about Toby.

"I really don't think that's wise. For you or Nick."

"You just tell Nick I have to see him. I have to talk to him about Toby," Kate said desperately.

"Kate, you told me earlier you hadn't spoken to Nick since your divorce. Leave it at that."

"No." Her guilt made her strong enough to face Whit's disapproval. "Tell him what I said. Exactly what I said. He'll see me."

To Whit's amazement and irritation, she was right.

Her first sight of Nick, his face pale, almost as white as the sheet beneath him, almost undid her. She could feel tears springing to her eyes.

"So this is what it takes to get you in the same room with me," Nick said, his voice not much more than a croak.

"I would have come for less." Kate pulled a chair close to the bed, sat down, and then burst into the tears she had tried so hard to restrain. She buried her face against the mattress.

"Don't, Kate," Nick said, stroking her hair. "It's all right."

"I was so worried about you." Her voice was muffled by the sheet.

"I'm too tough to die."

"Good." Kate reached for the tissues on the stand beside his bed and daubed at her eyes. "I look awful now, don't I?" All those years and he had barely changed. If only the calendar had been as kind to her. If only what Leonie said was true. Did he still love her?

"You always look beautiful to me, Kate. I've missed you in my life."

"I don't see why, Nick. I'm an imposter. A fraud. You created this wonderful image called Kathleen Mallory that I can't live up to."

"You've done just fine," he told her. "Look at your books. That's no fraud."

She shook her head impatiently. "And it's my fault about Toby."

"Toby?"

"I know why you said what you did about her. You have to tell the police it wasn't Toby who shot you."

"Why should I do that?"

"Because it was all my fault, Nick. Everything."

He smiled weakly. " 'Everything' covers a lot of territory."

"I set you up with Catherine Wescott."

"Then I owe you some thanks, because Cat is going to be the same kind of superstar the rest of you were. She's my fifth try at the gold ring. I'll make it again. You'll see. Everyone will see."

"Oh, Nick! You just don't understand! It was because of the memoirs. None of us wanted you to publish them. You don't realize how they could hurt."

"I can see why Toby would be upset. She's got a lot to answer for, and I intend to nail her to the wall. But you, how could you be hurt, Kate? I had nothing but good to say about you. About how I turned you into a star."

"And you would tell about *me*, the real me: Kate, not Kathleen."

Nick nodded, puzzled. "Of course. The public wants to know about the real you."

"Don't you understand? I don't want *anyone* to know the real me. That's why I thought of using Cat to stop you. I didn't tell any of the others, even Toby."

"There are a couple of little things I don't understand here, Kate. Why would Toby care anything about Cat Wescott? And why would Cat have anything to do with my memoirs?"

"Because Toby is Cat's mother. And you're Cat's father."

If Nick's face had been pale before, it was positively ashen now. "Are you sure?"

"I'm positive. It took a lot of digging; Toby hid her tracks well. Apparently she tried to contact you when she found out she was pregnant, but she couldn't get through."

Nick was silent for a long moment. "I found out she was under age," he said finally. "I called the whole thing off."

"Cat Wescott looks like the rest of us, doesn't she? Like Juliet when she was a young girl? I thought so as soon as I saw her. I knew you would never be able to resist her. That was why I arranged for you to meet her, to interview her. I was sure once you saw her you would become involved with her. And then I was going to blackmail you. So you wouldn't write about us."

Nick grinned at her. She wondered if he was taking her seriously. "There are depths to you I never suspected, Kate. So what do you suppose happened?"

"I finally realized this morning that Cat was at your house that night. She was, wasn't she?" Nick nodded. "She must have read through the manuscript and figured out that she was your daughter. She was overcome with shame, and she shot you."

"I see now where you get your plots."

"I didn't intend to put you in any danger, Nick. I just needed some kind of hold over you. So you see, everything is my fault. You have to tell the police that Toby wasn't responsible."

"Only Toby was, more than I knew. You realize that not only did Toby take control of my company away from me, she got rid of my child too. She's more of a bitch than I ever thought she could be."

"Please, Nick, you know it had to be Cat who shot you. Tell the police the truth."

"Oh, it was Cat all right. We were alone in the house. But she wasn't reading the manuscript. I was working on it. I heard a noise and turned. I didn't see her, but I saw a flash of her hair, long and blond."

Kate touched her hair automatically. "But why did you say it was your wife who shot you?"

"Cat *is* my wife. We were married in Mexico the day before I was shot. That's why I had called Whit to come over. I wanted to tell him I'd been a damn fool for the fifth time."

Why did she feel as though she had been struck? She was the one who had made sure Nick would meet Cat Wescott, she thought bitterly. What a fool she had been! "But why did you tell the police it was Toby who shot you?"

Nick's pale face grew grim. "Maybe it was my way of paying her back for some of the grief she's caused me."

"Nick! You can't be that bitter."

"She stole Picard Productions from me."

"But to have her arrested on an attempted murder charge! You've got to tell the police the truth."

"Hell, no! Let Toby sit in jail until she rots. She doesn't give a damn about me, and I don't give a damn about her."

"But it wasn't Toby's fault. It was mine! I'm the one who set you up with Toby's daughter."

Nick had slumped back on the pillow, his face even paler, if that were possible. "All Toby's fault," he mumbled. "She's the guilty one. I told the police that."

A nurse entered the room. "That's enough visiting for now," she said firmly.

"I'll be back, Nick," Kate told him.

"I won't change my mind." Nick turned his face to the wall.

Kate's guilt continued to gnaw at her. She remained at the hospital, waiting for the next visiting period. As soon as she was allowed, she was back in Nick's room.

This time, he didn't rouse when she entered, didn't acknowledge her presence, and his breathing was a raw, rasping sound in the hospital room.

She leaned over the bed. "Nick?" she said softly. "Are you awake?"

"Kate?" he said weakly. "Where have you been?"

"Counting the moments until I could see you again," she said lightly.

He reached for her hand and squeezed it tightly. "Dear Kate," he said. His hand was warmer than her own. "I love you better than all the others."

Did that include Cat? she wondered. But she couldn't allow herself to be sidetracked. It was her fault Toby had been arrested. She had to set that right. "Do you remember what we were talking about before? About Toby?"

"Toby's in jail. Whit told me. I'm glad. Let her rot, the bitch. She stole Picard Productions. Didn't even change the name." He seemed to have forgotten she was there.

Kate leaned closer. "Nick, please listen to me. You have to tell—"

He grasped her forearm so hard that she winced. "I love my daughters. You know that. I would have taken care of Cat too. Just like Dani and Eden. Toby shouldn't have hidden her from me. She took the company and she took my daughter. I'll make her pay, Kate. You'll see."

"Nick, it wasn't her fault. It was mine. I'm the one who involved you with Cat." His eyes were murky, feverish-looking. "Nick! It was my fault."

For a moment his glance cleared. "I know you better
than anyone else. I should have realized how much you
value your privacy. It wasn't your fault. You were desperate. But Toby—she may not have pulled the trigger,
but if she hadn't dumped Cat none of this would have
happened."

"Nick, you've got to tell the police the truth."

He laughed, a grating sound that turned into a gasp. "Tell
them . . . I married my own daughter . . . and then she
tried to kill me? No, Kate. I don't believe I will. Let her
sweat for a change." He closed his eyes.

"Nick? Are you all right?"

"You better call the nurse, Kate. I think . . ." His voice
trailed off.

"Nick!"

She pushed the call button and in less than a minute a
nurse was there. Kate found herself out in the hall.

They moved Nick back into intensive care that afternoon. Juliet came that evening with the girls. Eden had
arrived from France only that morning. All of them sat
in the conference room, waiting for the doctor's report.
When it came, Juliet gasped and began to cry. The girls
reached for each other's hands. The doctors had delayed
taking the bullet out, concentrating first on repairing the
damage it had done to Nick's body. Now they felt that the
bullet had driven a bit of clothing into the wound, causing
an infection. Nick would face surgery again. This time he
might not make it.

Kate stared straight ahead, wondering if she had managed
to sign Toby Flynn's death warrant.

She had thought only of herself when she set the plot
in motion to introduce Cat Wescott to Nick. She hadn't
realized how deep Nick's hatred of Toby was.

It had been easy to arrange the meeting between Nick and

Cat. Money was all it had taken, money to the Wescotts' lawyer. Peter Burns felt he was doing Beth Wescott a favor by getting Cat out of her life finally.

And what about Cat? Where had she gone after shooting Nick?

Kate left the hospital at 11 P.M. When she reached home, she called Peter Burns, hoping for information about Cat. However, the lawyer told her that not only had Beth not seen Cat, she seemed to be getting over the loss of her strange daughter. "So don't send her back," he thundered and hung up.

Kate sat staring into space for a long time. Finally, she dialed Sloan Whitney's number. "Whit?" she said when he answered. "Kate here. What's the latest on Toby?"

"My God, Kate! Do you know what time it is?"

"What about Toby?"

"She's still in jail."

"Can't you do anything for her?"

"This may come as a surprise, but it's not my intention to represent all Nick's ex-wives. And I need my sleep." He hung up.

How to dress was Kate's biggest question the next morning. She would not be herself today but Kathleen. Because only Kathleen could carry out what she intended to do.

Kate spent an hour picking out the right outfit, a sedate suit, and then she packed an overnight bag, as if she were only going to a fashionable hotel for a short visit.

At 8 A.M. she called Whit's office and asked his secretary to have him come out to her house at 9 A.M. Then, almost as an afterthought, she called Leonie Denton's office at *LA Today* and left the same message.

Only then did she call the police and ask for the lieutenant who had questioned her at the hospital the day Nick was shot.

TWENTY-FIVE

"**I** WAS THE ONE WHO SHOT NICHOLAS PICARD."

Kathleen Mallory made the announcement as casually as if she had asked the three of them if they wanted another cup of tea.

Leonie Denton nearly dropped her teacup. She glanced around at the others. Sloan Whitney was gazing at Nicholas Picard's second wife in open-mouthed amazement. So much for consulting your lawyer before your confession, Leonie thought, amused.

Lieutenant Sattler of the LAPD looked anything but amused. "Look, Ms. Mallory. I'm a busy man. I don't have time for this."

Kathleen Mallory looked confused. "Don't have time? Lieutenant Sattler, I'm trying to tell you that I was the one who shot Nick, not Toby Flynn."

"What is it now, Ms. Mallory," the lieutenant asked, his voice heavy with sarcasm, "a new book? Or maybe a new movie? What I don't have time for is to give a PR boost for whatever you're selling."

Kathleen Mallory turned to her lawyer. "Whit?" she appealed.

"I thought you left the stunts up to Juliet," Sloan Whitney said angrily.

Leonie frowned at the mention of Juliet. "Tell me, Kathleen. Exactly why did you do it? Shoot Nicholas, that is?"

"To stop him."

"Stop him from what?"

"Publishing the memoirs."

The housekeeper reappeared. "A call for you, lieutenant," she told the policeman.

"Thanks for the invitation. It's been an interesting morning," Sattler told Kathleen Mallory. "For your information, Toby Flynn doesn't need your help. She's been released from custody. Now, if you'll excuse me," he said and followed the housekeeper out of the room.

"Have you gone nuts, Kate?" Sloan Whitney demanded. "What kind of idiotic reason could you possibly have to say such things?"

"I'm glad they let her go." Kathleen Mallory sat down suddenly, her face twisted by tears. "I knew Toby didn't do it," she told the lawyer. "I was the one who set Nick up with Cat Wescott."

"Kate, for God's sake! Shut up!" Sloan Whitney turned around to glare at Leonie. "Haven't you heard enough?" he demanded. "You can see she's not feeling well. Why don't you get lost?"

"Certainly." Leonie smiled at him serenely. He was an eligible male, after all. For that matter, so was the lieutenant. And while the threat of Mark Maxall's firing her had vanished with her scoop on the shooting of Nicholas Picard, her blowup with Mark in Mexico City had left Leonie definitely in need of a male, an eligible one this time. But not Sloan Whitney. Not just now, anyway. The lawyer was too involved in soothing Kathleen Mallory's feelings at the moment.

Leonie went in pursuit of Sattler. However, when she questioned the housekeeper, she found the lieutenant had already left.

That was all right. Leonie knew where to find him. She might also know something that would interest him.

Because, to answer Sloan Whitney's question, she had indeed heard enough.

Cat Wescott. Maybe she was the key.

But first Leonie called in her column for tomorrow: TOBY FLYNN OFF THE HOOK.

"A publicity stunt," the lieutenant said when Leonie dropped by his office later in the day. "You know that as well as I do. Only in LA would she have both her lawyer and a gossip columnist standing by."

"Columnists can be useful sometimes, lieutenant. Especially when it comes to the right kind of publicity for building a career." Leonie looked up at him from beneath her lashes. She had all the statistics on him. He was divorced, but then who wasn't these days? "Tell me, why didn't you believe Kathleen Mallory's confession?"

"Off the record?"

Leonie nodded.

"She had the opportunity. Hell, they all had the opportunity; all of them were in the city that night and none of them had an alibi. But I've seen plenty of murderers, and Kathleen Mallory just doesn't fit the bill."

"I understand you were considering her at first."

He gave her a sharp look. "How do you know that?"

"I have my sources," she said archly. "Why did you change your mind?"

"Someone tried to frame her." He shook his head before Leonie could ask. "No. I can't tell you how, even off the record. When Picard said it was Toby Flynn, it looked right because the Flynn woman has some kind of grudge against her. Besides," he said, "look at Mallory. Do you think she did it?"

Leonie considered for a moment. "No, but I don't think this confession was for her personal publicity. She's never been that sort. There's something else behind it. So," she went on brightly, "why did you decide Toby Flynn wasn't up for the part of attempted murderess?"

"We received some information I'm not at liberty to disclose."

"Even off the record?"

"Even off the record."

"Just the kind of information I'd like to get my hands on," Leonie observed. "If you're looking for another candidate, I do have a clue for you."

He was annoyingly unresponsive. Anyone else would have suggested talking about it over dinner. He simply said, "Give."

"Cat Wescott. I don't know who she is, but she's connected with Nicholas Picard. Recently, I would judge. After you left the room, Kathleen said she was the one who set Nicholas Picard up with Cat Wescott. Sloan Whitney almost had a hernia."

The lieutenant didn't change expressions. "Thanks for the information."

"You already knew about her, didn't you?" Leonie guessed.

His annoyed glance told her she was right.

"Who is she? What's her connection?"

"That, Ms. Denton, you'll have to find out from someone else."

As if she couldn't, Leonie thought as she left his office.

It took her five phone calls and less than an hour to find out the identity of Cat Wescott. She was the fifth Mrs. Nicholas Picard, the wife, no doubt, that Nicholas Picard had said shot him that fateful morning he was found. Letting all four of the former wives off the hook, so to speak.

Coincidentally, she was missing. On the lam, probably. And the best part, Leonie thought, was that she had found it out in time to reduce Toby's release to a single sentence in her column and fill the rest with speculation about the illusive Cat Wescott.

·   ·   ·

Nick was just finishing breakfast when Whit knocked on the open doorway of his room. "Solid food at last," Nick said by way of greeting. "You can't believe how I've waited for this day."

Whit didn't even grin in response. He walked over to the bed and stood there, staring down at Nick.

"What's wrong?" Nick asked him.

"We've got a problem. The police just found Cat Wescott."

"All right," Nick said and sighed. "Kate was after me to tell the truth about Cat. And Toby. I guess you know I married Cat."

"If the marriage is legal. You did know she was only fifteen?"

"I sure know how to pick them, don't I? First Toby, now Toby's—" He stopped suddenly.

"Toby's what?" Whit demanded.

Nick took a deep breath. "Kate claims Cat Wescott was Toby's daughter. And you'll recall that Toby and I were briefly involved when Toby was about fifteen."

"Oh, shit!"

"Not a very lawyerlike observation."

"This isn't funny, Nick. How did you manage to fuck up your life so thoroughly?"

It seemed pointless to say that Whit hadn't done too well himself. "I don't have to tell anyone that part of it. Kate won't, and I'm pretty sure Toby won't. Nobody else knows. So do the police want a statement? How much trouble am I going to be in for lying about Toby? Can we claim I was delirious? I was, you know."

"Nick—"

"I didn't realize what you were asking me the first time. And then I saw that if I just kept quiet I had a chance to get back at Toby for what she'd done to me. So that's why I didn't come clean. Actually, I can't really swear Cat meant to shoot me. Maybe she was just fooling around with the gun. Only I don't know where she got it; I don't have a gun in the house. I never really saw her, just a glimpse of her hair when—"

"Nick! She's dead."

"Who's dead?"

"Cat Wescott."

Nick stared at him. "Cat's not dead. She—she can't be."

"They found her body this morning."

"What happened to her?"

"She was murdered."

"Who would murder her? She was so beautiful."

"Nick, listen to me. This is important. There's a police lieutenant here to talk to you. Don't say anything except yes or no."

"Why shouldn't I?"

Whit had already turned away. He opened the door. "You can come in now, lieutenant. My client is ready to talk to you."

"Thank you. Hello, Mr. Picard. I'm Lieutenant Sattler, LAPD. You're feeling better, I see."

"I was until I found out Cat was murdered," Nick said bluntly. "Who did it?"

"Nick," Whit warned.

"That's what we're trying to find out, Mr. Picard. Your attorney said you had some additional information about the night you were shot."

"Toby wasn't the one who shot me. It was Cat. I don't know why. I really didn't see her. We were alone in the house. I heard a noise. I looked up just as the gun went off and saw just a glimpse of her hair."

"And why would Cat Wescott, or I should say Catherine

Wescott Picard, have shot her husband, Mr. Picard?"

"I don't think my client—"

"It's okay, Whit. I don't know, lieutenant. Maybe she went crazy. Maybe she committed suicide afterward."

"Maybe that's what you wanted us to think. You see, Mr. Picard, Cat Wescott couldn't have been the one who shot you. She died *before* you were shot."

"That's impossible," Nick blurted out.

"Not only that, the bullet in the Wescott girl matches the one we dug out of you. Maybe you killed her and tried to commit suicide. Or tried to shoot yourself to establish an alibi. Only you fouled up and shot yourself in a more vital area than you intended."

"That's crazy," Nick said. "What about the gun? Did you find a gun?"

"No," the lieutenant admitted. "But it's entirely possible someone else got rid of it. Mr. Whitney was the first on the scene."

"Am I being accused of something here?" Whit demanded.

Sattler gave him a long steady look. "Not yet."

"How do you know that Cat was killed before I was shot?" Nick demanded.

"The coroner established her time of death as before eight P.M. You called Mr. Whitney's house at twelve-thirty A.M. His telephone answering machine records the time of each call on the tape. He was kind enough to turn it over to us."

"Am I under arrest?"

"Not yet, Mr. Picard. I'll be in touch."

When the lieutenant closed the door behind him, Whit said, "I swear to God, Nick, I had no idea when I turned the tape over to them that they'd use it like this. I thought it would help."

"You think I'm guilty!"

"I didn't say that."

"Whit, if you don't believe me, who will?"

Kate opened the door herself and saw Sloan Whitney standing there. She took one look at his face and cried, "What's wrong? Is it Nick? Is he worse?"

"He's going to be charged with murder."

"Nick?" For a moment she thought she was going to faint. Everything dimmed. She started to sway.

Whit grabbed her by the arm. "Hold on, Kate. I need you. Nick needs you."

"Just let me sit down."

When she was on the sofa, Whit brought her a glass of water. "Okay now?"

She wasn't okay at all, but she nodded anyway. "Why would they think Nick would be guilty of murder? He couldn't possibly murder anyone."

"The police found out that Cat Wescott had been a prostitute. They were struck by how much she looked like you—and Juliet. It turns out that there have been at least a dozen Juliet Brittany/Kathleen Mallory look-alikes brutally beaten. Three have been murdered. Four, if you count Cat Wescott."

"But what has that got to do with Nick?"

"They think he's the pervert who has been doing the beatings and killings."

"They can't possibly."

"Hang on," Whit said. "It gets worse. Do you remember the night you had a prowler in the house? You called the security guards."

"And they thought it was some kind of publicity stunt? I certainly do. I also remember that Nick was with Juliet that night instead of being home with me." It still hurt, even now.

"Only now Juliet says Nick wasn't with her. She also says she was attacked later by a man whose face she never saw. She claims she never went to the police because after what happened to you she was afraid she wouldn't be believed."

"She can't really think it was Nick?"

"That's what the police are saying. And Allison Hilliard claims she had a near-fatal accident while she was married to Nick. She was swimming late at night, and someone, whose face she didn't see, dropped a tangle of garden hose on top of her. She says Nick brushed her off when she tried to tell him about it. She thought it was because he was involved with another woman at the time—Toby Flynn. The police think Nick might have been responsible for the accident. Only they don't think it was an accident."

"Whit, this is crazy!" She went over to the phone.

"Who are you calling?"

"Juliet." Kate stabbed in the numbers violently. "Juliet? This is Kate. What in the hell is going on?"

"Kate? What are you talking about?"

"Whit is here. He just told me your crazy story. I don't believe a word of it. You never told me anyone tried to attack you. What are you trying to accomplish?"

"Did you know he married her?"

"Yes. I found out a few days ago. Is that why you lied?"

"How do you know I lied?"

"I know you, Juliet. You'll say anything that comes into your head when you're angry."

Juliet's voice dropped. "They told me he had married her, and then they asked me about your prowler. I didn't know she had been murdered."

"You have to tell them the truth, Juliet. This isn't some silly game. Nick is going to be charged with murder."

"It could have been us. Would he have cared?"

"You know he would. Listen, Juliet, I want you to talk to Whit. Tell him the truth."

She handed the phone to Whit and sat down again,

watching the kaleidoscope of emotions on his face as he listened to Juliet. When he finally hung up, he seemed stunned.

"She just acts without thinking," Kate told him. "She still loves Nick. I"—it was an effort—"I do too. Love makes you do crazy things."

"What about Allison Hilliard? Is she lying too?"

"Allison is different. You know that any publicity about her marriage to Nick is going to be detrimental to her husband's political career. I don't think she would say anything like that if it wasn't the truth—but she didn't accuse Nick."

"No, but the police will." Whit's shoulders slumped. "At least you're off the hook now. Actually, all four of you are, as far as the police are concerned. Now I only have Nick to worry about."

"Whit! You don't think for a moment that Nick—"

"No, I don't. But the way things are stacking up, I'm going to have a hard time proving it."

"We've got to do something!"

Whit leaned over and patted her hand. "I don't think there's anything you can do."

It was Toby Flynn who showed up at Kate's door next. "Leonie Denton told me what you did," she told Kate. "You didn't believe it was me who tried to murder Nick. You even confessed. I wouldn't have done that for you. I hated you, you know."

"I know," Kate told her. "And you still should. This whole mess is my fault. If it hadn't been for my stupid idea of introducing Nick to Cat, none of this would have happened. Whit says the police are sure he murdered her. That he's the one who's been beating and murdering prostitutes who look like me and Juliet"—she glanced at Toby—"and you."

"He's not the john who was beating up on your look-alikes." Toby took a deep breath. "I know. I was a prostitute. You probably found that out when you were digging into my past."

"Toby, I'm sorry for that."

"I really admired you, Kate. Actually, it was Kathleen Mallory I admired. I never thought of you as a real person. You were just an image in advertisements and in the movies. I heard that a john was looking for a Juliet Brittany look-alike, and he was willing to pay big bucks for a little fun and games. I thought Juliet was some over-the-hill bag, but you were really hot. I was smart enough to see the resemblance between you and Juliet, and that I already looked a little bit like you, so I talked somebody into funding some plastic surgery. That's how I got this face." She grinned at Kate. "They say imitation is the sincerest form of flattery. You should feel very flattered."

"And when you got your new face?"

"I met the john and he tried his best to rearrange it."

"Who was he?"

"I don't know. But it wasn't Nick. I'll swear to that."

"They won't believe you," Kate said desperately. "Especially since I already messed everything up by trying to confess." A new thought struck her. "My God, Toby. You're lucky that john didn't kill you."

"So he got Cat instead." Toby looked pale. "I never thought of her as a real person. Or as my daughter. Her picture was in the paper today. She looked like me, didn't she? Like us."

"Nick thought so too. Oh, Toby! It's all my fault she was murdered! I wanted to stop Nick from writing the memoirs. I wanted it more than any of you."

"Not more than me," Toby said fiercely.

"More," Kate insisted. "I wanted it enough that I arranged for Nick to meet Cat. I knew that once he saw her, he wouldn't be able to resist getting involved with her. And then I was going to blackmail him. Now look what's happened. Cat's dead, and when they find out she was really his daughter—"

"But she wasn't, Kate," Toby said gently. "I was going to blackmail Nick myself, when I was pregnant with her. I was going to make him think she was his daughter. But she wasn't."

"Whose daughter then? . . ."

"His. The john that beat me up. Probably the one who killed her."

"We've got to tell someone, but who will believe us?"

"Nobody," Toby said.

"It's him," Elsa said, cupping her hand over the phone.

"Hang up," Gwen told her urgently.

"I can't just hang up."

"Then give the phone to me." She yanked the receiver out of her sister's hand. "Don't call again," she said angrily into the phone. "You'll be sorry if you do." She slammed the receiver down and began to sob.

"Gwen. Honey," Elsa said. "Don't cry."

"When I think of what he's done to our girls."

"You don't know it was him."

Gwen glared at her sister. "Yes, I do. And you do too. If I knew his name or where he lived, I'd see that he got the same thing Mack did."

"Gwen!"

It was Gwen's turn to comfort Elsa. "I'm sorry, dear. But all these years we've run such a good operation. Maybe I'm getting too old for this."

"Never," Elsa said.

She sounded so much like the old Elsa that Gwen glanced at her hopefully.

Elsa was rummaging for her purse. "Little girl's room,"

she said, and hurried down the hall. When the bathroom door closed behind her, Gwen laid her head down on the battered desk. This is my punishment, she thought. Mack didn't go to hell. I did.

Oliver Brittany sat in his bedroom, the receiver lying on his knees. After a moment, it began to make rude sounds at him. Slowly he replaced it. What was he going to do? he wondered. He knew why Gwen was so mad, but if he couldn't get a girl for tonight, he was going to go crazy.

He never meant to hit the girls, never meant to hurt them. But they were never quite right, and when they weren't right he couldn't come. That made him so angry that the only release he could find was with his fists.

Oliver whimpered, remembering the other things that had happened. He wasn't the crazy one. He wasn't the one who killed some of them.

She had done that.

Slowly, he rose and went to his closet. The locked box sat at the back of the top shelf, where a casual glance would not reveal it. He carried it back to the bed and opened it. Inside were his treasures, neatly filed. First the snapshots and studio portraits of Juliet as a child. Those he lingered the longest over. Then the worn copy of *Playboy* with the photo spread of her. He took time to leaf through the well-thumbed pages again. None of the others had been as pretty as Juliet, he thought.

Tenderly, he laid the magazine on top of the photographs of Juliet. It was, after all, only one of four.

Kathleen Mallory was next. His photographs of her had been clipped from magazines, or else they were candid shots, taken on family outings, when Eden and Dani were young, where he had carefully clipped away the other people.

Then Allison Hilliard.

Then Toby Flynn.

Then—the others.

He divided the contents of the box into five piles. The first four piles were for Juliet, Kathleen, Allison, and Toby. Busily he sorted through each one, seeking the best photograph. It angered him almost beyond bearing that the best photograph of each of the four women was one that had appeared in *Playboy*, taken by Nicholas Picard.

Finally, he turned to the fifth pile, the girls he had bought from Gwen and Elsa. Posed on the beds of cheap motels, spreading their legs to show him their treasures. He stroked himself, remembering how it had felt with each of them.

But never as good as it had been that first and only time with Juliet. That was why the rage always built up inside him.

He turned back to the four ex-wives of Nicholas Picard. He wondered how it would feel to murder one of *them*, to place his hands around her neck while he was deep inside her, while she was gasping in the throes of an orgasm. He let himself imagine what it would be like as he bucked against her and her gasping turning to panic.

Oliver Brittany looked down. His penis strained against the cloth of his trousers.

It would feel good, he decided.

The only question that remained was which one it would be.

"You look like hell," Frederick Yates said from the doorway.

"Freddie?" Nick sat up, ignoring the wince of pain that movement caused. "I didn't know you cared." He wasn't joking.

Frederick looked at him for a moment without speaking. Then he said, "Frankly, Nicholas, neither did I." He sat down beside the bed. "I understand you're much better now. I'm glad."

Nick found himself speechless. How many years had he and Freddie played this game? Now, suddenly, the rules had changed.

"Sloan Whitney told me that you might be in difficulties because of the murder of that girl. I want you to know that I will give you any assistance you might need. In spite of your opinion regarding dinosaurs, the studio is not without its resources. What of them are under my command, will be at your disposal."

Nick was absurdly touched. "Freddie." This gray-haired elderly gentleman wasn't a Freddie anymore, Nick realized. "Frederick. How can I thank you?"

"It's what Morgan would have wanted." Frederick stood up. "And what someone else wants. You know, Nick, you've had all the luck in this life. You had all of Morgan's love and all of Juliet's. In neither case was there any left over for me."

"Juliet and I haven't been together in years, Frederick."

"Do you really believe that changes anything?"

Juliet sat in front of her dressing table, brushing her hair. Long, lovely, blond, it fell past her shoulders. It was past midnight and she was alone in the house. When the man's face reflected back at her from the mirror, she almost started. She took a deep breath. "Hello, Papa." She continued to brush her hair.

Oliver Brittany put his hands on her shoulders. She could feel their warmth through the thin silk of her dressing gown. "Juliet," he murmured. His hands stroked upward, caressing her neck; then they tightened convulsively, his fingers biting into the soft satin of her skin.

"Just a moment, Papa," she said softly. "Let me make myself beautiful for you." He was staring at her image in the mirror, at her breasts, at the imprint of her nipples against the silk. "Papa?"

"Yes," he said, releasing her and stepping back.

She opened a drawer of the dressing table and reached inside. She didn't have to look at her hand. Instead she watched him, in the mirror. Their eyes fastened together. When she grasped the butt of the revolver, she stood up and turned to face him.

Oliver Brittany stared at the gun. "Where did you get that?"

"Where you hid it." Juliet reached up and pulled the wig off, letting the long blond hair drop to the floor between them.

"Juliet?" He took a single step backward.

"Pick it up," she told him.

Slowly he knelt, never taking his eyes from her face, and reached blindly for the wig.

When he straightened, Juliet said, "Put it on."

"What?"

"Put it on your head, Oliver."

"No, I—"

She motioned with the gun. "Put it on."

He pulled the wig down over his head. He looked ridiculous with the long, blond hair framing his time-ravaged features.

Juliet looked right into his face. "Good-bye, Papa," she said, and pulled the trigger.

The call from Eden came at just past midnight. The police were still there when Kate arrived. Dani was pacing up and down outside. She sprang at Kate like a lioness. "Where have you been?"

"I came as soon as Eden called. What exactly happened?"

"I'm not sure of the details." Dani was pulling her inside as they spoke. A policeman stood at the foot of the stairs. "My mother," she said brusquely. "Miss Brittany needs her." Dani took the stairs two at a time. Kate had no choice but to follow. "Juliet's father tried to kill her. She shot him. She had to." Dani stopped on the stairs and swung around to face Kate. "You understand, don't you? It was self-defense."

"For heaven's sake, Dani. You act like I'm here to attack Juliet. I came because Eden called me. Because she said Juliet needed me."

"You judge her too harshly. You always have. Just don't do it this time." Dani started to turn away.

Kate grabbed her arm. "What's that supposed to mean?"

"I know you blame Juliet because you and I aren't close, because she's been more like a mother to me than you have. But it's not her fault, it's yours. You always pushed me away. Just don't take out your personal obsession on her tonight. She needs you too badly."

This time when Dani turned away, Kate followed her meekly, trying to digest what her daughter had just said. Eden was standing at the door of Juliet's bedroom. When she saw Kate, she flew into her arms and hugged her tightly.

Kate's only rational thought for a moment was that she and Dani had not even said hello, let alone hugged each other. "How is she?" Kate asked Eden after a moment.

"The doctor is with her now. He's going to give her something to put her to sleep. Oh, Kate! It's terrible. She just stares into space. She won't talk to me or Dani. Will you stay? Will you be here when she wakes up in the morning?"

Kate could feel Dani tense behind her, waiting for her answer. "Of course I will," she told Eden. "You're both too young to remember, but she took care of me one time when something happened I couldn't cope with."

"She told us," Eden said, her voice muffled against Kate's shoulder.

A wave of anger rippled through Kate. How could Juliet have done that? The old anger about losing Dani to Juliet almost resurfaced again. Kate fought it back. "Then you know," she said calmly, for her own benefit as well as theirs, "that I'll be here when she wakes up."

So were the police. Kate sat beside Juliet, holding her hand, as Lieutenant Sattler talked to her. Juliet had slept fourteen straight hours and still appeared slightly out of it. Kate couldn't be sure if she was really taking in what was being said. She squeezed Juliet's hand. "Are you listening?"

Juliet nodded, but her brilliant blue eyes still had a dreamy not-quite-there look about them.

Sattler tried again. "What we're saying, Ms. Brittany, is that the gun is the same one that was used on Nicholas Picard and Catherine Wescott. You say it was your father's?"

She nodded again. "He had it for years. I knew where he kept it. I was so afraid of him that I . . . I. . . ."

Kate put her arm around Juliet's shoulders. "Mr. Brittany was a very strange man," she told the police lieutenant. "I was frightened of him too."

The lieutenant stood up. "The gun is registered in his name and his fingerprints were on it." Now he directed all his remarks to Kate, as though he felt Juliet would not be able to take anything else in. Perhaps he was correct in that assumption, Kate thought. Juliet still appeared to be in another world. "We figure he stole the wig from Ms. Brittany and wore it the night he murdered the Wescott girl and tried to kill Picard. That explains why Picard said he thought he saw his wife's blond hair just before he was shot."

"What's going to happen to me?" Juliet asked suddenly.

"Self-defense." The lieutenant stood up. "Don't worry about it. The case is closed."

"Are you sure?" Kate asked him.

"Look at those marks on her neck," the lieutenant said. "No judge or jury would question those."

Kate followed his glance. Oliver Brittany's hands had left a chain of bruise marks around Juliet's smooth neck—like a necklace of black pearls.

Kate stood too. "Thank you, lieutenant." She walked him downstairs.

At the door he paused. "This has been a pretty traumatic experience for Ms. Brittany. She told the policewoman last night that she was molested by her father as a girl. She'll need professional help to get over this."

"I'll see that she gets it," Kate promised.

When she got back upstairs, Juliet was still sitting exactly as she had left her. "Is he gone?" Juliet asked, her voice quiet, hushed.

Kate nodded. She sat down beside Juliet once more.

Juliet reached out and clutched Kate's arm. "Tell me it's over!" she begged, her fingers closing convulsively. "Promise me it's over, Kate!"

"I promise," Kate soothed, but Juliet's fingers continued to clutch painfully at her arm.

Lieutenant Sattler came by in person to give Allison Hilliard the news. He even brought Oliver Brittany's box of "souvenirs" to show her.

"Very interesting," she told him. "I suppose I should feel honored to have been included."

"You're taking this very lightly, Ms. Hilliard. We feel that after murdering Ms. Brittany his intention was to go after the rest of you."

"What about Nick's memoirs? Were they recovered?"

Sattler shook his head. "We don't know what happened to them."

"Have you talked to Nick? Is he still planning to write a book?"

"The subject didn't come up. I find it interesting that you seem to be more interested in your ex-husband's book than the fact you were a potential murder victim, Ms. Hilliard."

"That's because my ex-husband's memoirs have destroyed my marriage, lieutenant. My husband is divorcing me." Allison laughed harshly. "He felt that the stigma of a divorce was less damaging to his political career than being married to Nicholas Picard's ex-wife."

Sattler shifted in his chair. "Frankly, Ms. Hilliard, he sounds like a real bastard."

Allison laughed. A genuine laugh. One she hadn't thought she had in her. "Frankly, lieutenant, he is."

It was later that same afternoon that Senator MacLaren called on Allison. "I understand that the Picard murder case has been settled."

"Yes it has, senator." She gave him a steady look. "If you came by to talk to Wilson, he's no longer living here. I assume he discussed the fact that he was getting a divorce with you."

"Yes, he did," the senator said. "A sad thing when a marriage breaks up, my girl. I told him so."

"But you advised him to go ahead with it?" she guessed.

He sighed heavily. "Yes, I did. I suppose he's already put the wheels in motion?"

"Yes." It was an effort suddenly to blink back the tears. Her father had always been an avid supporter of Senator MacLaren's. It hurt that MacLaren had encouraged Wilson to dump her.

"Good!" the senator said explosively. "I was afraid he might back out at the last moment."

"Well, you've got your wish. Now what?" she said angrily. "Are you going to look for a nice new political wife for him?"

"Wilson Keating can go straight to hell!" Senator MacLaren said. "I have a new candidate."

Allison blinked. MacLaren was Wilson's strongest supporter. Without him, he couldn't win. "Who?" she asked bluntly.

"You."

"You must be joking!"

"I never joke about politics, my dear. It's much too serious a subject. When Wilson decided to divorce you, he lost his biggest asset. I'm not the only one who is aware of how heavily Wilson Keating's political success depended upon his lovely wife. The thought has been in my mind for some time that you alone would be a much stronger candidate than Wilson ever dreamed of being. That's why I encouraged him when he consulted me about the divorce. It wasn't his political career I was thinking of, it was yours."

Me? Without a man to hide behind? No more Wilson, or Nick, or Daddy? Allison decided she liked the idea. "And how far are you willing to support me, senator?"

"First we conquer California, my dear. I made Wilson governor of this state; with you I have much better material with which to work. Then—well, there's already been one actor in the White House." He grinned at her. "Why not try for two?"

Allison grinned back. "Why not?"

"There's just one thing," Senator MacLaren said slowly. She could feel his glance on her body. Her throat constricted as she waited for what he was about to say. "Don't you think you ought to try to gain a little weight?"

She stared at him in astonishment.

"I don't mean to insult you, my dear, but you look as though the first strong breeze might carry you off."

Toby opened the bottom drawer on the right-hand side of her desk and took out the gray steel box. She unlocked it with the key she wore on a gold chain around her neck. Inside the box were an envelope and a newspaper clipping. The envelope was all she had of Momma—the check that had been returned, with the word *Deceased* scribbled under Momma's address on the front of the envelope.

The clipping was an article from the *Times* about the murder of one Catherine Wescott Picard. Toby paused over the newspaper photograph of Cat, obviously a reprint of a school picture. For so many years, if Toby thought of her daughter at all, it was as a tiny baby with pink booties. How strange it was to look at the photograph of the stunning young woman and realize she was the daughter Toby had never seen.

She studied the man's photograph the *Times* had printed with the article on Cat's murder. Oliver Brittany. Juliet's father. Cat's murderer.

What if he had walked into Juliet's living room that night the ex-wives congregated there to discuss ways of stopping Nick from writing his memoirs? Toby would have recognized him as the sadistic john who beat up Juliet Brittany look-alikes, even after all these years. But what would she have done? How could she have guessed that he would kill Cat and try to kill Nick?

Toby looked at Cat's picture once more. No wonder Cat had looked like another Nicholas Picard creation, enough like Juliet to be her sister.

She was.

Toby laid Cat's obituary, clipped from the morning paper, in the box and then locked it once more and replaced it in her desk.

She turned to the papers on her desk. These, too, would go in the box once they were complete. They were the charter her lawyer had helped her draw up for the organization she planned to fund to help street kids and runaways in Los Angeles. In less than a year she planned to have a hundred-bed shelter up and running, which would get at least a few of the runaways and teen prostitutes off the streets.

While she was waiting in her jail cell, waiting for someone to connect Toby Flynn, producer, with that long-ago teenage runaway named Toby Gilmer, Toby had realized that there were a lot of other children like herself and her daughter—the discards of society.

When she was released and realized no one was going to connect her with that murder in Texas, it had seemed to Toby like a sign from above that she should do something for somebody else. She had started work on the foundation the day she was released. Money wasn't everything, she had learned in jail.

But it was still damned important, she thought, as she made a note to herself to call her accountant in the morning. She would make sure the foundation got a good healthy start, but there wasn't any reason not to see what kind of benefit she could get from it on her taxes.

"Mother?" It was Dani on the phone. "Did you know that Dad got out of the hospital yesterday? Eden and I had dinner with him last night."

"I'm glad to hear that," Kate said. "What did you talk about?"

"You."

Kate was so surprised she couldn't respond.

"Mother? Are you there?"

"I'm here. Why in the world would you talk about me?"

"He still loves you, you know. He told us so."

"I'm sure Eden wasn't too pleased to hear that."

"For heaven's sake, Mother. Can't you ever just accept anything?" She heard Dani take a deep breath. "He would like to see you. He asked me to tell you that."

Kate felt her heart leap.

"Will you see him?"

"Yes," Kate whispered. "Oh, yes!"

"When? This afternoon?"

"Are you sure?"

"I'm sure, Mother."

"This afternoon, then."

"I'll call and tell him so," Dani said.

But after Kate hung up, her jubilation faded. She walked over to the mirror and looked at herself, really looked at herself. She hadn't gone through the elaborate ritual this morning, the one that turned plain Kate into Kathleen.

"He wants you," she told her image in the mirror, "but which one of you does he want?"

She knew the answer. Reaching for her makeup case, she began the ritual.

The phone rang just as she was about to leave. She ignored it, knowing the housekeeper would pick it up.

The woman stopped her at the door. "It's Miss Brittany, ma'am. She's very upset."

"Kate!" Juliet cried when she picked up the phone. "Dani told me. You're not going to Nick's, are you?"

"Of course I am," Kate said calmly. It was such a strange feeling, knowing she had won. Juliet's hysteria only made her calmer. "I'm sorry, but I really don't have time to talk now."

"Kate! Please! Don't go!"

The words were still pouring out when Kate laid the receiver back in the cradle. "If she calls back," Kate told the housekeeper, "tell her I've already left."

You can't stop me now, Juliet, she thought as she got into her car. Her heart surged painfully in her chest.

No one can stop me now.

"Nick? I have to talk to you!"

The voice on the phone jolted Nick into the past. How many times had he answered Juliet's call? He felt the tug. He would always feel the tug.

That one lousy line of dialogue.

No more, he decided. Facing death made a man examine his life. "Not this time, Juliet. You're a big girl now. It's time you made it on your own. I have my own life to live and so do you."

"Please, Nick." She was sobbing into the phone. "You don't understand. You have to listen."

"I'm sorry, Juliet." Gently, he replaced the receiver.

The phone rang again almost immediately.

He ignored it.

It rang again. And again.

He reached over and unplugged it.

Kate was coming. Dani had called earlier to tell him so. Nick dozed in the sunlight, waiting for his life to begin again.

Nick heard the click of a woman's heels on the flagstones. When he opened his eyes, he saw perfection coming toward him. From the billowing dress, whipping around her calves, to the huge straw purse clutched in her hands, Kate was a vision in white.

I created you, Kathleen Mallory. The thought made his heart sing. Of all his goddesses, she was the most significant creation. With Kate, he'd had less to work with, and yet the results had been more spectacular than with any of the others. Toby had teased him about playing Pygmalion. With Kate, he had done exactly that.

Nick got slowly to his feet, clutching the back of his lounger for support. When she neared, he held out his arms and she came to him. He buried his face in her hair. "Oh, Kate," he murmured. "You don't know how I've missed you all these years."

And then he heard it: the click of another woman's heels across the flagstones.

"Juliet?"

She looked awful. Her hair was a tangled mess, her face was pale and without makeup, but worst of all were her eyes. The wild expression in those vivid blue eyes made him hug Kate closer.

"Step away from her, Nick," Juliet said, and he saw the gun in her hand.

Without conscious thought, he maneuvered his body between Juliet and Kate. "Put the gun down," he told her. "You don't want to do something you'll be sorry for."

"You should have listened when I called you, Nick." Tears were running down Juliet's face. "You shouldn't have hung up on me. I didn't want this to happen." In spite of the tears, the gun was steady in her hands, pointed straight at Kate. "I didn't think I could ever kill anyone, not until I shot Papa. Don't make me do it again. Step away from her. I don't want you to get hurt."

"I can't, Juliet. If you're going to murder her, you'll have to shoot me first."

"I'm not going to murder anyone, you fool!" Juliet shrieked at him. "Step away from her."

That was when Nick felt it, a hard finger of steel pressed against his armpit.

"Kate?" He looked down and saw a statue with a stranger's face. The white straw bag lay on the ground at her feet. She had a .38 revolver pressed against his body.

"She's not Kate," Juliet said. "She's Kathleen now."

"Kate!" he said urgently.

The gun in the statue's hand never wavered. It remained pressed against Nick's ribs. Now he could see that Juliet's gun was trained not on him but on Kate.

"You created her in my image. With me—I think you really tried to help me find my true self. But not Kate. You made Kate into something she wasn't. She was just plain Kate in private, but in public she had to be Kathleen Mallory. 'The most beautiful woman in the world.' And she felt like an imposter. You should have seen her when you left her for Allison. She was a complete basket case. Maybe that was when it started. I don't really know. But even then it might have been all right if Jonah Rome hadn't died."

"Jonah," the statue echoed, and a shudder ran through her body.

"I think Jonah's death was what made her personality split. She became two different people. It was Kathleen who did all the evil things. And when she became Kathleen, I'm sure her conscious self didn't know what she was doing."

"How do you know all this?" Nick asked her.

"I guessed some of it. But I didn't know all of it until after you were shot. I found Papa's diaries. I burned them. But first I read them. He . . . had a thing about young girls who looked like me. He would hire prostitutes and then beat them up afterward. I don't know when she got involved with him. I think it was when she came back to Los Angeles after Jonah Rome was murdered. She stayed with me for several weeks while her rental house was being repainted and redecorated. That's when she and Papa must have . . . What he wrote was so garbled and sick I couldn't really tell. But she looked so much like me that Papa would have done anything she asked. She was the one who murdered Cat Wescott, but Papa was with her. She made him help her take Cat's body away. They tried to hide it in a canyon. Then she came back here alone and tried to murder you."

"But why?"

"Maybe because you married Cat. Or maybe because you were going to turn Cat into another one of your creations, another Juliet Brittany. Another fake. I had hoped it would end with Papa's death, but—"

"Cat," the statue said. "She was evil. Another fake. Oliver promised he would help me punish all the fakes."

Nicholas suddenly realized that she was staring at him with a strange intensity.

"You," she said. "Nick. Nicholas Picard is the one who makes the fakes, isn't he?" And then she answered herself in a voice that made Nick's skin crawl. "Not anymore." She jabbed the barrel of the revolver into his ribs.

"Kathleen," Juliet said with a desperate urgency in her voice. "I'm a fake."

"No!" Nick cried. "Don't say that! She'll—"

"A fake!" Juliet screamed. "Why don't you kill me?"

Nick felt the gun leave his side and saw the statue swing the barrel toward Juliet.

He was still weak on his feet. When he lunged at her, she shoved him away with one hand. He fell to the flagstones heavily. "Kate!" he shouted.

The gun didn't waver.

"Kathleen!"

Her finger began to squeeze the trigger.

Desperately, he cried, "Who is the biggest fake of all?"

The statue paused at his question and then swung the barrel around to point at her own head.

Nick lashed out with his feet just as she pulled the trigger.

EPILOGUE

1991

THE WOMAN WOKE WITH A START AT 4 A.M., HER heart racing with panic. Nothing to worry about, she soothed herself as she lay staring at the ceiling. Nothing at all. But she worried, nonetheless, because today would be another test.

At 5 A.M., unable to lie there any longer, she rose and paced around the room, pausing now and again to look out the barred window through the predawn darkness to the parking lot.

At 6 A.M., one of the nurses unlocked the door and came in to help her dress. The nurse brought the makeup kit and stood by, ready to lend a hand, as she applied the cosmetics. Once a new nurse had asked her why she didn't look in the mirror and had turned her to face her own reflection before she was complete. She had been comatose for three weeks after that.

This morning the nurse said, "Are we ready to look in the mirror now?"

She nodded.

Still, she tensed as the nurse turned her toward the mirror. At the sight of her face in the cool silver surface, she released the breath she had been holding painfully in her lungs. It was all right. It was more than that, it was perfection.

At 7 A.M. she heard the rattle of the breakfast trays in the hall. When her own door was unlocked, she felt a momentary twinge of hunger. It vanished as soon as she remembered this was the day of the test. The scrambled eggs dried to hard yellow marbles on her plate while she drank the coffee and waited for the knock on her door.

The knock came finally at just past 10 A.M., followed by the sound of the lock.

The head nurse entered. With the head nurse—as she had known it would be from the date circled in red on her calendar—was the ghostly reflection of herself.

The test had begun. She was ready.

The flint-sharp eyes of the head nurse surveyed the room, accounting for the spoon on the tray beside the breakfast plate, the comb on top of the dresser. Once, six months ago, the head nurse stepped outside the room, leaving her alone with the ghost.

The ghost wore a tiny white scar on its left arm from that visit.

"Good morning, Kate," the ghost said. "How have you been this month?"

She sat, staring straight ahead.

"How lovely your room looks," the ghost said.

"She arranged the flowers herself," the head nurse said. "She saw the roses when she went for her walk yesterday and decided they would make a nice bouquet."

"You have such exquisite taste, Kate." The ghost's voice was calm, but she could see that the ghost was beginning to lose its nerve. "Did I tell you the girls send their love? The wedding went off without a hitch. Dani and Ray are now somewhere in the Caribbean. I told her you would expect photographs of the wedding *and* the honeymoon."

She sat, staring straight ahead.

The head nurse and the ghost exchanged glances.

"Miss Mallory?" the head nurse said. "Would you give me your autograph?"

She stirred then and took the glossy eight-by-ten photograph the head nurse handed her. When she saw her own face, panic fluttered in her stomach for a moment, until she glanced at the mirror and saw the same face reflected back. Relieved, she took the pen and scrawled her name across the bottom of the photograph, adding *To one of my dearest fans.*

"She loves it when we do this," the head nurse said, handing the photograph to the ghost. "Dr. MacPherson suggested we keep a supply of these photographs on hand."

The ghost looked down at the photograph and then across at her. The ghost's lips began to quiver.

"Kate!" the ghost said suddenly, dropping to its knees in front of her. "Kate, please talk to me! Please say something!"

She sat, staring straight ahead.

"Kate, please! Please, please talk to me!"

The head nurse hurried forward and took the ghost by the shoulders, assisted the ghost to its feet, and eased it out of the room. When the door closed behind them, she heard the click of the lock.

She sat staring straight ahead.

But her heart danced with elation. The test was finished, and she had passed.

Even as late as last month, a faint quiver of recognition had responded deep inside of her when the ghost spoke that hated name.

Not today.

So many times in her life she had been hurt and humiliated, and it had all been Kate Mallory's fault. No more. Finally, the bitch was dead.

"For heaven's sake!" Juliet exploded when they were in the hall. "Can't you do anything about her hair?"

"Now, Juliet," the head nurse soothed, "you know what Dr. MacPherson told you. She doesn't like it when anyone else touches her face or her hair. You don't want her going comatose again. Remember how awful that was?"

"But she looks like an old woman!" Juliet cried out and then burst into tears.

The head nurse put an arm around her shoulder and guided her down the hall, away from the room.

"I'm sorry, Amanda," Juliet said after a moment. She and the head nurse had become friends over the past year.

"I know, dear. But she's getting the best of care. Perhaps it would be better if you didn't come as often—better for you."

"I have to come. I can't leave her here all alone."

"Well," Amanda said with determined cheerfulness, "your lovely husband is still waiting patiently. Why don't you just stop in my office and freshen your makeup? I'll give you a quick cup of coffee, and you'll be as good as new."

"Thank you. You're a lifesaver."

As Juliet followed Amanda down the hall, she glanced again at the photograph Amanda had handed her. Hard to believe the ghastly woman in that locked room, her lank gray hair tumbled about her shoulders, her sallow, haunted face blotched and streaked with the kind of awkward makeup attempts that would shame a five-year-old, was the same person.

Kathleen Mallory, Kate had scrawled across the bottom of the picture.

The most beautiful woman in the world.

The photograph blurred as Juliet's tears began again.

Amanda glanced over her shoulder. She came back and put her arm around Juliet. "I know," she said. "I know."

Outside Amanda's office, Juliet glanced in her compact once more and then hurried down the hall. In spite of Amanda's comment about patience, her husband was no longer in the waiting room. As she pushed through the big front door of the clinic, she saw him strolling across the grounds, his hands jammed in his pockets, his head down, as though he were studying the texture of the grass.

"Nick!" When he looked up, she waved.

He came toward her, smiling. "How did it go?" he asked her. "How does she look?" The doctors decided it was best for Kate if she didn't see Nick, so only Juliet visited her room.

Juliet extended the photograph. "Just the same."

It was a lie she felt she owed Kate.

Side by side, they strolled toward the parking lot. "What were you writing while you were pacing around?" she asked, with just the tiniest tremor of apprehension.

Nick chuckled. "You know my habits well. I was working on the new screenplay."

Relieved, Juliet slipped her hand into his. It had taken months, but she finally found Nick's memoirs where Papa had hidden them. She made a point of giving the manuscript back to Nick before their wedding. She hadn't asked him not to publish his memoirs. Nor had she told Allison or Toby what she had done. As far as they knew, the memoirs had vanished. They would have thought her action extremely foolish. They would have been wrong. When Nick asked her to marry him again, Juliet knew she no longer had anything to fear. She linked her arm through his. "I love you, Mr. Picard."

"I love you, too, Mrs. Picard."

From her window, high above the parking lot, she watched Nick take the ghost in his arms, and she laughed aloud, delighted by the vividness of the fantasy.

It wasn't real. Only she was real.

She turned to the mirror and stood there savoring her reflection.

Kathleen Mallory.

The most beautiful woman in the world.

DONA VAUGHN is the author of three published books. She lives in the greater Houston, Texas, area with her husband and their two children.

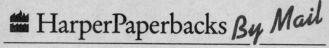